M000087621

The Sword of the Maiden

Kathleen C. Perrin

Also By Kathleen C. Perrin

History

Seasons of Faith and Courage

Fiction

In *The Watchmen Saga*:

The Keys of the Watchmen, Book 1

This book is a work of fiction. Any references to historical events, real people, or real locales are used fictitiously. Other names, characters, places, and events are the product of the author's imagination. Any resemblance to actual events, locales, or persons, living or dead, is entirely coincidental.

Summary: After being abruptly separated from Nicolas, Katelyn is anxious to be reunited with him, even if it means being whisked back in time again to the turmoil of medieval France during the Hundred Years' War. But before they can consider the future of their relationship, they must carry out their perilous commission to assist the most iconic figure in French History, while being pursued by their old nemesis, Abdon, who threatens their mission.

1. Historical Romance—Fiction. 2. Joan of Arc—Fiction. 3. Time Travel—Fiction.
4. Historical Mystery—Fiction. 5. Mont Saint Michel—Fiction.
6. France—Fiction. 7. Medieval History—Fiction.

To see photos of Mont Saint Michel and Joan of Arc sites, visit the author's website at:
www.kathleencperrin.com

LANGON
HOUSE

Copyright © 2015 Kathleen C. Perrin
All rights reserved.

The Sword of the Maiden / Kathleen C. Perrin. — 1st Ed.
Watchmen Saga: Volume 2

Library of Congress Control Number: 2015919135
Published by Langon House, Salt Lake City, Utah

ISBN-13: 978-0692576922
ISBN-10: 0692576924

Printed in the United States of America by CreateSpace

To my mother, the most faithful and quietly
courageous woman I have ever known.

Acknowledgements

Once again, I would like to thank my Breton husband, Yves, who has given me incredible support, sound advice, and technical assistance while writing this book. Better yet, near the end of the project, as I sat at the computer for many long hours each day, he came home from his full-time job and fixed dinner because I was working under a deadline.

Best of all, however, are the wonderful adventures he has taken me on while doing research for this book. Together, we retraced La Pucelle's footsteps in France. If you would like to do the same, don't miss our recommendations at the end of this book of the must-see places to visit, as well as my historical notes separating fact from fiction. Also, be sure to see photos of some of these incredible places by visiting my website at: **www.kathleencperrin.com**.

A very special thanks goes to my daughter Christine Vance. Her opinion, suggestions, and support have been invaluable to me in telling this story, and I am particularly grateful for her incredible cover design. Without the countless hours she has spent working on my behalf, *The Watchmen Saga* would never have come to fruition.

I am grateful to Kalie Chamberlain and Stephanie Curtis Perrin for their great recommendations and editing, as well as to Paul Perrin, who assisted with the Kindle version. I must likewise express appreciation for my advance readers, Teresa Bell, Becky Clayton, Anne Crain, and Chris Tueller for their suggestions and careful proofreading. It's amazing what several sets of eyes can spot!

And of course, I have to give credit where credit is due. This story could not have been told were it not for the amazing faith and courage of a simple French farm girl named Jehanne.

Prologue

THE SMOKE ROSE IN A GENTLE SWIRL, like a prayer rising to heaven. But the time for praying was past, and the heavens did not answer the prayer.

Soon, the smoke thickened, and the blue sky transformed into a sickly, gray haze. Several hundred English soldiers—not only the regular garrison protecting the castle, but also a considerable number assembled for an attack on Louviers—looked on, exuberant about the fruits of war. After months of inflicting humiliating defeats on the French in smaller battles, it appeared that ultimate victory would finally be theirs.

A single bird flying from the French holdings in the south was engulfed by the smoke, as if it too had been conquered by English supremacy. Surely a sign of divine approval.

As the flames gained in intensity, so did the output of heat, and the soldiers stretched out their arms and moved backwards, attempting to counter-balance the crush of the crowd. The crackling of the fire and the clamor of the masses were not enough to block out the final cries of the foe, which were not cries of submission but pleas to a higher being.

Several of those soldiers most devoted to the English cause—who just moments before had hailed the calculated offensive move as brilliant—stood still as statues, transfixed as if in a stupor.

Beads of sweat trickled down the face of one particularly brutal combatant, one who had personally sworn to bring down the enemy with his bare hands. It was as if the worn soles of his boots had fused to the ground, making it impossible for him to escape the aftermath of the unprecedented assault.

As the soldier looked around him, he saw several of his comrades-in-arms with drops of moisture running down their faces as well, but they were not beads of sweat. They were tears.

Part One

But God hath chosen the foolish things of the world to confound the wise;
and God hath chosen the weak things of the world to confound
the things which are mighty.

1 Corinthians 1:27

Prenez chascun une houe
Pour mieulx les desraciner,
S'ils ne s'en veullent aller,
Au moins faictez leur la moue
Ne craignez point à les battre,
Ces godons, panches à pois,
Car ung de nous en vault quatre,
Au moins en vault-il bien troys.

All of you join in and take up your hoes
To uproot our enemy, vanquish our foes.
And if they're not willing to vacate our lands,
Make faces at them, and then strike with your hands.
Fear not to attack them, for we are not pawns!
Drive them away, all those pudgy Godons.
One of us Frenchmen's worth four of their men,
Or certainly three—now, attack them again!

Old French Song from the Hundred Years' War Era

Chapter 1

MY LITTLE BROTHER JACKSON IS REALLY getting on my nerves. Ever since we got back from France, he has been bugging me about what really happened to me at Mont Saint Michel.

"Look, Katie," he keeps saying, "I *way* know there's something you're not telling me."

"No way," I say, just to egg him on.

"Yes way," he replies. "Your little act might fool Mom and Dad, but it doesn't fool me. Now are you gonna tell me what happened, or am I going to have to torture it out of you? Don't you trust me? I won't tell anyone."

Yeah, right. Like I'm so sure he won't tell anyone.

But he keeps pestering me. "So I have to figure it out like Sherlock Holmes, huh?" he says. "Okay, then, just so you know, I'm not going to leave you alone until I *do* figure it out. And I will, you know. Besides, you're not that good at keeping secrets."

Great. Now I have to add "detective" to Jackson's list of accomplishments. Renaissance Man *and* teenage sleuth all rolled into one.

But I mean, really. Do you think I could actually tell him the truth? Could I just casually say to him, "Jackson, I would love to tell you about what really happened to me. Michael the Archangel visited me. He chose me to be one of his Watchmen called to protect Mont Saint Michel because I, Katelyn Michaels, am so very special."

That wouldn't fly, because the truth of the matter is that everyone knows Jackson is the 'special' child. *He's* the one who is smart and gifted. He's the one who knows everything about everything. He's the one who has the encyclopedia memorized, so he'd never believe I was 'chosen' for anything.

Then I would give him the details. "You remember that guy we saw dressed in the monk robe when we first got to Mont Saint Michel? Well, his name is Nicolas le Breton, and he is a Watchman as well. He traveled forward in time to bring me a time key so that I could go back with him to 1424 and save Mont Saint Michel and its villagers from the invading English armies during the Hundred Years' War.

"And remember Gothman who knocked me down on the West Terrace of the abbey and stole my enseigne? You know, the guy who split your chin open with his chain and left you that manly scar? Well, Jackson, his name is Abdon, and he is one of Lucifer's fallen angels. He's been waiting nearly six hundred years in a variety of human hosts for me to show up at Mont Saint Michel so he could stop me from going back to save the Mount. You see, Abdon is bent on discovering the secret of Mont Saint Michel. And if he can't discover the secret, he'd just as soon take the Mount apart stone by stone while he's at it."

I can just see his look of dazed confusion now. And then I'd have to jump right in before he made any snide comment about my sanity. "About that secret, Jackson. Well, actually, that's the part I really *can't* remember. I didn't even know there was a secret. I guess Nicolas didn't trust me with it at first, but then he finally told me about it when I was in a semi-conscious state, so unfortunately, I don't recall what the secret of the Mount is. I'm still working on that one."

I have to admit, the secret business is really bothering me. Neither Jean nor Nicolas ever said anything to me about there being a secret. They just convinced me that if the English conquered Mont Saint Michel, it would set into motion a whole sequence of events that would change the future, including the existence of America as we know it today. But I was pretty cranky when I first arrived in 1424, so I guess they felt they couldn't trust me with the secret.

But the biggest puzzle for Jackson, and all my family members for that matter, is my injuries. They are the only physical evidence that something really bizarre happened to me at Mont Saint Michel. I mean, one minute I'm with Jackson in the abbey's refectory, and the next time he sees me, just a couple of hours later, I'm almost dead from a raging infection. If I didn't have the injuries, there wouldn't be any questions. But how could I tell any of them I got the cuts escaping from a Godon ship (Godons are what the French called the English back then), or that my shattered and infected ankle occurred when an English guard dog attacked me? That's why Nicolas had to send me back home while I was unconscious: to save my life with twenty-first century medical intervention.

Here's the kicker, though. It would be great to see Jackson's face when I told him one other tiny little detail: the fact that as my cover story, I was introduced to the Montois as the wife of Nicolas le Breton. Unfortunately for Nicolas and me, the villagers insisted on holding an actual marriage ceremony to provide a bit of merriment to their otherwise bleak existence. So, technically, I'm a married woman.

How could Jackson or anyone believe any of that? So instead I just tell them all, "Honestly, I don't remember anything. I have no idea how I got these horrific injuries." Don't get me wrong. I sincerely appreciate everyone's concern. I guess it takes facing death to realize how blessed I am. I have even forgiven Dad and Adèle. I'm still sad at what Dad's betrayal did to Mom, but I've figured out that harboring bitterness isn't going to solve anything. It will just make me a miserable person. The best thing I can do now is to help Mom move on with her life and find some happiness of her own. And right now, I'm not doing a very good job of that, so I better buck up and stop thinking about the Big Secret. And about Jean le Vieux dying at the hands of Abdon to protect my identity. And about Nicolas. I'm having a heck of a time not thinking about Nicolas.

As a sharp pain from my right ankle ripples up my leg and wracks my entire body, another type of pain hits me. It's just as sharp, but it is a pain I can't medicate. A pain my doctor will never hear about, a pain my mother will never be able to kiss away. It is a pain I can't really find the words to describe, like a wrenching of my soul and an implosion of my heart.

Do I honestly believe I can just go on with my life as if the events at Mont Saint Michel hadn't occurred? I am Katelyn Michaels, a Watchman. My job is not done. I know I must return to Mont Saint Michel. And, I must return to Nicolas. I am *compelled* to find him. I don't know how and I don't know when, but I must go back. And I know all that without even hearing the voice of the Archangel.

And there's another issue constantly on my mind, one that is causing me increased anxiety every single day. Nicolas warned me. Abdon. He's out there in some unknown host body, and he will stop at nothing to prevent me from returning to Mont Saint Michel. And Abdon is about the scariest being I've ever had the displeasure of meeting.

I know Abdon will try to stop me.

Chapter 2

THE FRENCH FARM GIRL HAD NEVER BEEN considered particularly bright or particularly brave. She knew what others thought of her, but it did not trouble her. It was more important to be kind than to be brave. She was an obedient child and a hard worker, and she tried her best to be loving and thoughtful to her family and neighbors. The fourth of five children, she spent most of her time helping her older brothers with the farm chores, tending the cows, learning to spin and sew at her mother's knee, and caring for her younger sister, Catherine.

Although she wasn't bright or brave, she *was* god-fearing. She went to church gladly and regularly, and she was committed to the service of God. The villagers were often the beneficiaries of her ministrations, and although her family was not wealthy, she always sought ways to attend to the ill and give alms to the poor. She did it not for the praise of others, but because she truly loved those around her. She loved both God and man.

Life was not easy on the farm, but she nonetheless considered her existence idyllic. She had loving parents, happy siblings, and there was always enough to eat on the family table.

But as she grew older, the girl felt a shadow beginning to hang over her. It gnawed in the darkest recesses of her mind, like the rats that gnawed through the grain bags in the root cellar. The rats were never caught, but everyone knew they were there because of the evidence they left behind. Like the un-trapped rats, the girl couldn't catch the elusive shadow, and it continued to plague her.

Her father Jacques scolded her for always finding a way to listen in on his conversations with the village men. As she brought refreshment for his visitors, or tidied up the room, or wiped away the crumbs from the hand-hewn plank table, Jacques would scowl at her and say, "These are not concerns for females. Begone with you, child." But his scoldings were only half-hearted, and the girl thought he was secretly proud of having a daughter who seemed interested in current events.

She knew the English had captured important cities in western France and that all of Normandy had been swallowed up by the hated *Godons*. She listened as the men described the tide of war that had plunged portions of the French countryside into a miserable state, with farms reverting to overgrown scrub brush as they were abandoned by the fleeing populace. She thanked God that her little hamlet far to the east had not been touched, and although burdened by excessive taxes levied to support the war, her father assured her that all he was concerned about was his fifty-acre plot of ground producing enough food to feed seven mouths.

But in her heart, the girl knew better. She knew it was only a matter of time. Her only peace came from focusing on the spiritual aspects of existence, and she soon found herself seeking refuge nearly every day in the parish chapel next to her home.

It was then she finally identified the shadow that plagued her. It was the shadow of impending doom. It was the shadow of war.

Chapter 3

BY THE END OF AUGUST AS I'M GETTING ready to start my senior year, my emotional well-being is still in question, but physically, I'm doing better. I can actually walk without crutches. However, I'm finding my last visit with my orthopedist before the school year starts to be no different than medieval torture.

"It's amazing how her body has healed," Dr. Daily says to my mother, as if I'm not sitting right here on the exam table listening to him. "You see how she has nearly gotten back her full range of motion?"

I grit my teeth as he wrenches my foot from side to side like a farmer cranking the steering wheel on his rusty tractor.

"Oh yes, to be young again," he adds as he twists my ankle with so much force I feel like kicking him.

"Can she swim?" my mother asks frantically. Mom knows I can't wait to get back in the pool. Swimming will be the perfect therapy for my injured arm and leg, and swimming competitively will force me to push through the pain that continues to plague me. Swimming might even help get my mind off of all that happened at Mont Saint Michel. Mindless, repetitive strokes, concentrating on breathing and kicking and how my body feels as it knifes through the water. Saltless water.

Water without deathly-cold, grasping suction trying to pull me under, or perilous tides, or blinding sand, or uncouth Godon kidnappers . . . or miraculous seals. Regular warm, un-salty, chlorinated water. Swimming pool water.

But what my mother doesn't know is that being on the Swim Team is no longer the most important thing in my life. It *might* have been six months ago when we actually last spoke together about swimming, but it doesn't even rate up there with the top twenty-five most important things anymore. Granted, my swimming abilities served me well while escaping from the English ship in Mont Saint Michel Bay after I'd been kidnapped, but I will always be a strong swimmer. Now, it's time to start figuring out what other skills I might need when I get back to Mont Saint Michel and about just how I'm going to get there. As good of a swimmer as I am, I don't think swimming is going to do the trick. It's a long swim to France.

"Well, now, I'm not sure about swimming," Dr. Daily says with a laugh, bringing me back to the present. "Could she swim before she broke her ankle? Ha ha, just a little bit of my 'Daily' dose of humor. But the real answer is yes," he affirms. " I think swimming would be about the best thing she could do. It's great cardiovascular exercise without unduly straining her ankle. Yes, Mrs. Michaels," he addresses my anxious mother instead of me, "your daughter is cleared for swimming."

But later that afternoon, it becomes clear to me that I'm not going to be swimming after all. When I sit down to finalize my fall schedule on-line, I press the button to confirm the class schedule I had already chosen at the end of my junior year—the period I like to call BC (before Collins)—and a message appears on the screen. "Not authorized for swimming."

"What do you mean I'm not authorized for swimming?" I say out loud. "I certainly am authorized! Just ask Coach Jensen."

11

And then, the screen goes blank for a second, and a new class schedule appears. A class schedule that does not include my morning Trig class or my afternoon Swim class that leads right into Swim Team practice after school. Instead, I've been scheduled for A.P. French IV (which is pretty surprising since I've never taken French I, II or III), and A.P. Medieval European History II (which is also surprising, since I haven't taken A.P. Medieval European History I).

At first, I think this is some ridiculous computer malfunction, and I keep trying to pull up my original schedule. Nothing works. It's as if that new schedule is fixed in stone. And it's especially odd that I have apparently received authorization for the Advanced Placement classes when I haven't taken the necessary pre-reqs. That's when the hairs on the back of my neck stand up. I actually turn around to see if there's someone in my bedroom. And no, I don't hear the Archangel's voice, but it's pretty clear who changed my class schedule. It is both extremely spooky and extremely reassuring. Isn't that what my English teacher Mrs. Hunter calls a dichotomy?

But it *is* reassuring. No, I didn't imagine everything that happened on the Mount, as much as that answer would be the most logical one. Yes, the Archangel Michael *did* speak to me that day before I entered the abbey church. Yes, I, Katelyn Michaels, *did* go back in time. Yes, I *am* a Watchman.

It hits me pretty quickly that the Archangel still needs me and some inexplicable skills I have to offer. And that means I will be returning to Mont Saint Michel. And—I hope beyond hope—to Nicolas.

As soon as I realize this, I stop bursting into uncontrollable crying fits in public. Oh, I still cry plenty in private—about not having been able to prevent Jean's death and about having lost Nicolas—but now I have a renewed sense of purpose and direction. I also have two new classes that the Archangel wants me to take, and history is one of them. I need to learn everything I can about

Medieval European History II, (which I learn covers the period from 1000 to 1500 CE).

When school finally starts, I get a message to go to the office on the very first day.

"We'll have to have your mother's signature, dear, in order to confirm that a parent has approved your schedule changes."

Jeez, I can hardly wait until I'm eighteen. That will be in exactly three months. But there's nothing I can do about it. I'm going to have to tell Mom about my new schedule today. It's bad enough I have to tell her I've decided to take French so I can converse with Adèle, but how am I going to explain to her that I've dropped swimming and added an A.P. European History class that's being offered that same hour? Like she's going to buy *that* without some digging.

Though they try not to be completely obnoxious about it, it's always the same thing. "How are you feeling today, Katelyn? Did you have any nightmares that might give us a clue as to what happened to you, Katelyn? Or have you remembered anything, Katelyn? Have you figured out how you got those cuts? Or those bruises? Or the dog tooth marks on your foot? Or that mangled ankle? Or who stitched you up with sewing thread? Or why are you always crying?" Or . . . or . . . or.

When I approach Mom about the schedule change after school—after I had actually gone to the Medieval European Class and after I'd told Coach Jensen that my ankle just hadn't healed enough for me to be competitive on the Swim Team this year—Mom goes ballistic.

"Katelyn," she cries. "You're not yourself. What's the matter, honey? Why don't you tell me the truth? Swimming has always been so important to you. I just don't understand."

"Mom, I love swimming," I say, and use the same logic I used with Coach Jensen, "but I just can't face not being in top form. I haven't done any conditioning all summer. I haven't even been in a pool. Can you imagine how embarrassing and painful it would be for me to not match my times from last year? Don't you get it, Mom? I can't *not* be at my best. I can't be a liability to my team when someone else should be there in my place. And I know Coach Jensen. She's loyal to me, and she wouldn't cut me. It's not fair to her, and it's not fair to someone else who deserves the spot I'd be taking. So it's just better all around for me not to swim this year. And fortunately, Mr. Bailey, one of my favorite teachers, has a European History class that same hour."

I think my argument is pretty darn good. I almost convinced *myself* that's the reason I don't want to be on the Swim Team. Surely, it will convince her. I can't tell her the truth because that's even harder to explain. I'm not the one who chose not to swim. I'm not the one who chose to take French. I'm not the one who chose to take the history class.

Finally, my mother calms down, and the next few days pass without any major altercations. I think she feels I'm too fragile to cross. But I'm getting stronger both emotionally and physically, and I'm learning to listen to my impressions.

I don't even balk when on Saturday, I drive past a climbing gym and decide I need to learn how to rock climb. I feel compelled to know how to free climb a vertical wall, and rappel down with a rope. And so I stop, and I take my first climbing lesson. Trust me, climbing hurts my ankle a lot more than swimming.

And now, a few Saturday sessions later, I feel pretty secure about climbing that wall, even though they never let me try it without the safety harness. I have no idea why I need to be able to climb, but I'm just going with the flow.

I'm also still crazy about all things electronic, and the idea that I might have to use my twenty-first century techno-skills again somewhere back in time just gives me more fodder for my addiction.

Dad gave me quite a nice sum of money when I left France. "It's to replace the devices that were stolen from you at Mont Saint Michel," he said. But I saw it for what it really was: his way of trying to make amends for having sent me and Jackson off to Mont Saint Michel with Adèle . . . and without him. Or maybe it was just for abandoning us in the first place. Whatever motivated him was not important to me at that point, and I certainly wasn't going to let him down by not accepting it, was I? No. So I've been scouring the internet for the newest gadgets and gizmos that might come in handy . . . somewhere and somehow. I don't feel special inspiration about anything specific, but I've just been going with my gut and ordering some interesting items on-line. And as an added benefit, it has been another way to keep my mind busy.

But there's more—more than just the change in my class schedule, more than climbing lessons, and more than ordering the latest gadgets. Way more, because last night I finally got some answers. Last night, I had a dream.

No, I didn't hear or see the Archangel Michael in my dream. Nicolas wasn't in it either. But I *did* see Jean—dear precious, beloved Jean le Vieux who had given his life to protect me. In my dream, I was sitting in Jean's cottage, by the fireplace in the hand-carved chair he had made for his cherished Marie. Jean was sitting on the bench by the table. I felt the warmth of the blazing fire (we never had a blazing fire when I was there during the siege because we didn't have enough wood to burn), and I felt safe. Completely and totally safe and peaceful. In fact, it was the most comforting dream I have ever had in my life. I had felt so much guilt over Jean's death, and in the dream, he reassured me over and over again that it was the plan. It was his destiny to give his life to protect me. It was what he wanted. He had waited so long to be reunited with his wife and son, and that blessing had finally been accorded him.

And then, as the shadows created by the fire cavorted across his gentle face, Jean said to me, "But your mission is not over, Katelyn. There is more for you to do. More that only you, Katelyn Michaels, can do to protect Mont Saint Michel."

I could feel the caring emanating from him. I had known Jean for such a short time, and yet his love was all-encompassing. It gave me an instant understanding of the love God feels for all of his children. That love filled the crevices of hurt that had opened up in my heart. It filled the spaces of doubt and discouragement that had been drilled into my mind, and it soothed the constant pain of my knitting bones and healing skin.

"Katelyn, you are a Watchman," Jean said. "You will be called upon soon to return to your duties. You will know when the time is right."

In my dream, I rose to go to him. I longed to feel the comfort of his embrace, but he motioned for me to sit again.

"I haven't learned everything I need to learn from you, Jean," I cried. "Can't I come back to you, to your time. Before . . . ?" I wanted to say, "Before Collins killed you," but I couldn't bring even my 'dream-self' to pronounce those words.

"No, my dear. You *have* learned all you needed to learn from me. You have been called because of other attributes and skills that are yours alone. You will know what to do when the time comes."

I've heard those words before, and look where they got me.

At that point, I saw Jean's image start to fade from my vision. I jumped from the chair to reach out for him, but there was nothing to grab. He was gone. I started to cry and begged him to return.

"Please, Jean. Don't leave me," I sobbed. "I need you. I don't know what to do. How do I get back to Nicolas? Is he waiting for me? Please, Jean. Please, tell me! Will I see him again? Will I see you again?"

By this time, I'd fallen to the floor of Jean's cottage in uncontrollable sobs. Tears streamed down my face. They were both tears of relief at his reassurance that I had no reason to feel guilty, that he was happy and that he had finished his mortal mission, but they were also like acid, burning tears over the loss of both him and Nicolas. The loss of two men I had truly and completely loved.

In my dream, the fire went out, and it was freezing. I was cold and disoriented and alone. How could I go on without my mentor, or without Nicolas, the man I had married? The man I had loved and lost before I could even tell him of my feelings? I *couldn't* do this on my own. I wasn't as strong as Jean. I couldn't have survived all those years alone, like he did, without someone to help me. I wouldn't know what to do without Jean or Nicolas. I was incapable of doing it on my own.

It seemed in my dream that I remained like that forever—frozen to the floor, feeling totally abandoned. Then I felt Jean's hand upon my head. I didn't see it and I didn't touch it, but I knew it was Jean's hand. His gentle touch ignited a rush of heat and reassurance that coursed through my entire body. I felt surrounded by love and comfort once again. And then, he pronounced his final words.

"Learn of the Maiden, Katelyn, and take her the sword."

Chapter 4

AS THE FRENCH FARM GIRL GREW OLDER, the rumors of increasing conflict began to flood her peaceful valley. In an irony of the times, with mounting taxes creating an increased burden on the family, her father supplemented his income by taking a position as a village tax collector. He also headed up the village watch, and consequently, his home was often the place where the locals congregated to discuss their growing concerns.

Not wishing to be noticed by her father or his friends, the girl made herself invisible as she listened to their frank debates about the mad French king, Charles VI, whose delusional periods made him unable to effectively govern or rally his troops. During those periods, she learned, the country was ruled by sparring members of the Royal Family, who themselves became embroiled in their own internal battles for power. This created even more chaos in what was quickly becoming a fractured France.

One autumn evening in her tenth year, the girl's godfather, Jean Moreau, from the nearby village of Greux, stopped by while the girl was helping her mother clean up after supper.

"Jacques, Jacques, have you heard the news?" Moreau called out as he tethered his old mare to a fence post outside the cottage door.

"Jean, come in and warm yourself by the fire," Jacques invited. "Now just what news do you bring? Good, I hope."

"'Tis the King. The King is dead," Jean cried. "The mad King Charles is dead."

The girl turned to her father to gauge his reaction. She was not certain what this news would mean for her family.

"Aye, and so soon after the English king's demise," muttered Jacques. "Is it Divine Providence or God's wrath being poured out upon us? I am not certain. With both Edward of England and Charles dead, 'twill surely bring about an increased struggle for power."

"Since the English king's successor is yet a babe, his uncle, John of Lancaster, the Duke of Bedford, shall serve as regent. He is a formidable enemy, Jacques. He has already rallied the English troops, and with Paris in the hands of the traitorous Burgundians, I fear the news is bleak. Paris will fall to the English. It is an outrage."

The girl knew that the Duke of Burgundy's allegiance to the French crown was tenuous at best. If all of Burgundy were to fall to the English, France could be lost. She stopped her sweeping and caught her father's eyes for the fraction of an instant.

"Bedford will soon be drinking Burgundian wine to toast his victory," Jacques said with a hiss. "'Tis a vile thought. But what of the Crown Prince, the Dauphin? Perhaps Charles' son will rise to the occasion. Perhaps he will strengthen the French army."

"Jacques, you are many things, my friend," said Moreau, "but a fool is not one of them. The Dauphin may not be mad like his father, but he's a spineless twit. 'Tis said he cares more for his wardrobe than he does for France. Besides, with Reims in the hands of the Burgundians, 'twill be impossible for the Dauphin to claim the crown that is rightfully his."

Although the girl didn't know much of politics, there was one thing she did know: to be considered the legitimate ruler of France, the king's coronation had to take place in the Cathedral of Reims. The girl had heard of, but never seen, the majesty of that monumental cathedral in Northeastern France. She knew that the coronation of French kings in Reims dated back nearly a thousand years. Long before the towering stone walls of the cathedral had even been built, Remigius—the Bishop of Reims—baptized, and then with holy oil, consecrated the legendary Clovis as King of the Franks. That unction had been sealed by God himself. It was performed with oil from the Sacred Phial, brought from heaven by a dove, and thus King Clovis had been granted the Divine Right to rule.

The subsequent archbishops of Reims had been given the Divine Right to consecrate all of France's kings. Once Charles received that heavenly unction, the girl was certain that the 'spineless twit' would be blessed from on high. He would be endowed with power from the Almighty. With God as his protector, Charles VII would be victorious. If Charles could only get to Reims, France would be saved. Over the next weeks and months, this became the girl's prayer. She prayed to Saint Catherine, to Saint Margaret, and even to the Archangel himself, Saint Michael. Her words were always the same: "Help the Dauphin Charles get to Reims."

But over that same period of time, more bad news continued to filter in. The English regent, Duke John of Bedford, was successful in cementing alliances with not only the Duke of Burgundy, but with the Duke of Brittany as well. It seemed that France would be lost as much due to French infighting and betrayal as to the power of the enemy armies. And now, like ravenous wolves, the Godons were clawing their way towards the peaceful village of Domrémy. With that cloying shadow hanging over her both day and night, the dutiful daughter insisted on helping as Farmer Jacques began to fortify his holdings.

As she worked alongside her brothers and father digging ditches for a defensive wall, she sang with them the words of the song from

Normandy that had spread like wildfire throughout the valley. The haunting melody bemoaned the plight of the Norman farmers who, without the support of the French military or king, were attempting to drive out the English army by taking up their poor imitations of weapons: "All of you join in and take up your hoes, to uproot our enemy, vanquish our foes!" It now seemed a dire possibility that the girl and her family would have to defend themselves like the Normans.

And indeed, over the next two years, the villagers of Domrémy found themselves forced to live up to those words. While their little patch of isolated territory remained loyal to the French crown, they were surrounded by Burgundian-held lands, and the enemy often sent bands of marauders into the village and its surrounding countryside. The raids created more fear than actual damage, and the girl found herself more and more on edge. She was grateful to have her father and her able-bodied older brothers there to defend the females of the family. Her fear seemed poised to overtake her. She fought the demons of dread on a daily basis.

Then a tiny beacon of hope arrived in 1424, when her godfather Jean Moreau visited again. Just as two years earlier he had arrived with news of the King's death, Moreau appeared one evening after supper shouting that he had news.

"Jacques," Jean called out. "I bear tidings."

"And what might they be, my friend?" asked the farmer, inviting Jean to come in and enjoy a glass of ale.

"A messenger crossed through enemy lines to spread the word," Jean explained, as he sat and accepted the pewter mug offered by his goddaughter.

"Mont Saint Michel has held firm," he sputtered after taking a swig. "The English have given up their blockade and have abandoned hopes of conquering the island. Surely it is a miracle. A sign! Surely Saint Michael himself has saved his island. France will now prevail!"

The girl listened carefully as her godfather spoke of the ramifications of this victory. If the tiny island of Mont Saint Michel, located just off the coast of Normandy, could withstand years of English attacks and then a total blockade, surely this would motivate the rest of France to hold firm.

"But how can we possibly be victorious without a leader? We still have no king to unite us," Jacques countered, as he lifted his legs so his daughter could sweep underneath his feet with her handmade twig broom. She felt his eyes boring into her, and she deftly turned her head to avoid making eye contact.

"But don't you see? This victory will give the Dauphin the courage to unite his forces and get to Reims for his coronation. France will be victorious in driving the Godons from our lands. With Saint Michael on our side, how can we fail?"

"The Dauphin will certainly need Saint Michael on his side to muster the courage he needs to lead. He cannot do it on his own, so I hope you are right, Jean," Jacques said. "I hope you are right."

The young girl noticed how her father rubbed his calloused hands together over and over, as if by focusing his nervous energy, he could somehow make the conflict disappear. The cracked skin of his fingers was embedded with soil from years of heavy labor. No amount of washing would ever cleanse them. Her eyes fixed on those battered but powerful hands. Hands that had fed her, hands that had tenderly caressed her cheek, hands that had thus far protected her family from the Godons.

I bet the Dauphin's hands don't look like Father's, she thought as her mother signaled her to fetch a refill of the fermented ale made from apples grown in their small fruit orchard. *He really* is *a spineless twit, but I hope Godfather Jean is correct. I hope this victory of Saint Michael will inspire Charles to get to Reims.*

That night, as the young girl climbed into bed, she worried about her homeland. She worried that the English would invade her village and harm her family. She had heard about the atrocities of war and she knew that women were particularly vulnerable to the depravities of invading armies. She shuddered as she thought of herself and of her pure and innocent sister Catherine being abused by those filthy English scavengers. To allay her mounting anxiety, she concentrated on her godfather's words about Saint Michael. She had seen his effigy on a small medallion proudly worn by the Widow Bertrand in the village. Madame Bertrand had actually made a pilgrimage to the Mount as a child and proudly wore her enseigne around her wrinkled neck. Michael was the Dragon Slayer. He had fought valiantly against Satan and his unseen armies of evil spirits. Surely France would not fail with the Archangel Michael's support. For the first time in many months, a feeling of warmth and security enveloped the girl and lulled her into a deep and uneventful sleep.

The next morning, as she was gathering eggs in the chicken coop, she heard someone calling her name.

"Jehanne," the deep voice said.

She turned, but saw no one. She went outside and called to see if her father was seeking her, but she failed to see a single soul. She knew her father and brothers were in the fields thinning carrots.

I must have been daydreaming.

As she recommenced her egg gathering, she heard the voice again. This time, it was accompanied by a flash of bright light. She blinked, shook her head, and once again looked all around her. But there was no one about.

When the voice came to her the third time, it was as clear as a bell, and she knew she was not imagining it. It was a man's voice, deep and resonant. The sudden awareness came to her that this was the voice of an angel. It filled the empty spaces between her ribs and lungs and caused her fingertips to tingle in joyful abandon. The voice cut through the apprehension she had felt the day before and buoyed up her spirits like the ringing of the church bells for *Complines*. And then a vision opened up to her, and before her eyes, she saw the angel in his full glory and splendor. It was Saint Michael, the slayer of that evil dragon and the victor of the siege against his Mount. And he was accompanied by many angels from Heaven.

"Jehanne," said the Dragon Slayer, "I have been waiting for you for a very long time. Everything depends upon you. You will know what to do when the time comes."

Chapter 5

FOUR LONG YEARS. NICOLAS HAD BEEN alone for four long years. Completely alone. No voices, no inspiration. No Archangel. No Jean le Vieux, and most of all, no Katelyn. He had prayed to God for help, he had begged for the Archangel to enlighten him, but all to no avail. Surely, the Archangel did not mean for Nicolas to live his existence in this manner. Surely, Michael would not leave him comfortless. Even Jean had been blessed to have his Marie—for a time.

The only redeeming factors for Nicolas were that Abdon had not given any indication of his evil and threatening presence, and that even though the Godons continued to control all of Normandy, they had been relatively quiet. There had been no new attacks on the Mount. In general, the English had left the Montois in peace. The blockade that had nearly resulted in the starvation of every man, woman, and child living on the Mount had been lifted by Katelyn's brilliant Operation Dark Moon. Now, the Montois were allowed to come and go to the Mount as they pleased, without hindrance or interference from the Godons. The English had even allowed certain pilgrims, those fortunate enough to have the means to buy safe passage, to visit the Mount.

Other thoughts came to Nicolas. *Perhaps the Archangel only speaks to his Watchmen when the threat from Abdon is grave. Perhaps Jean lived through periods like this, periods of feeling abandoned by Michael.*

His tutor had never told Nicolas of such times. True, Jean had spoken of the loneliness before Marie had come. He had spoken of the despair after she had left (and after losing Katelyn, Nicolas finally understood Jean's agony at losing his beloved Marie), but he had never mentioned being completely abandoned by the Archangel.

Nicolas had not had the opportunity to ask his mentor such pointed questions. His tutelage had been all too brief. When Katelyn Michaels had come from the twenty-first century, time had raced by for all three of the Watchmen. If his time with Jean had been brief, his time with Katelyn had been even shorter. It was just a blur. And yet, not even forty-eight months, not even fourteen hundred and sixty days, not even thirty-five thousand hours without her had done anything to dim the feelings Nicolas felt for Katelyn, or the excruciating emptiness he felt without her.

In his final hours with Katelyn, he had promised he would go to her again. He begged God to allow him to keep that promise. And because of that promise, Nicolas had even attempted something Jean had warned him not to do. His tutor had repeatedly instructed Nicolas that his key could be used only at the Archangel's instruction. And yet, one day, Nicolas had gone to the Guest Hall, located on the middle level of the abbey's *La Merveille*, had inserted his key into his jobber's mark keyhole, and had asked to be taken forward to Katelyn's time. He didn't know how he would contact her, but he was ready to try anything. But nothing had happened.

Then he had beseeched the Archangel to take him back in time to confer with Jean le Vieux. If he could just have another hour, another day with his mentor, time to ask all of the unanswered questions that plagued him, perhaps he would be given the strength to go on. But again, when he attempted to turn his key, there was no response. The key was ineffective. The heavens and the stones were silent.

After that, Nicolas had even abandoned his visits to the sacred chapel, Notre-Dame-Sous-Terre.

His despair about being left to his own devices as a Watchman caused additional agony. Guilt and inadequacy threatened to destroy him.

I am not worthy of being a Watchman, he chastised himself. *Jean survived an eternity alone, before I came to give him reprieve from his solitary task. I am an unprofitable servant. I am unworthy to follow in his footsteps. I have even defied his charge to only use the key when instructed. That must be why I have been abandoned.*

He implored God to forgive him for his disobedience. He begged for enlightenment. But the silence continued.

Only his craft kept Nicolas going. He had completed his stonemason's apprenticeship with Jean before Katelyn had arrived, and even at his young age, he had risen through the ranks from apprentice, to journeyman, and now to master mason. This level of skill allowed him to freely travel as he wished and work for any patron anywhere he wanted, but of course his only patron was Saint Michael, and his only job site was the abbey church.

The English siege of Mont Saint Michel had made it impossible for work to continue on the reconstruction of the church choir, which had collapsed in 1421. During the siege, there had been no food, no funds, and no direction. All of the workers but Jean and Nicolas had left the Mount. Now, Nicolas continued Jean's work alone.

Although he could not single-handedly rebuild the abbey choir, he continued to place its new foundation, stone by stone, following the plans left behind by the chief architect. The newly-built church apse was to be in the same beautiful Norman style as the abbey's principal building, the three-storied monastery that had come to be called *La Merveille*. Even without the jobber's marks visible, Nicolas could identify which stones had been carved by Jean in that structure because he had been trained by the master stonecutter himself. Jean's work permeated the entire edifice, and Nicolas drew comfort from it.

Five days a week, Nicolas reported to the construction site, but there was no chief architect. There were no master craftsmen, there were no stonemasons, and there was no Jean. Nicolas was the chief architect, the master craftsman, and the stonemason.

There was no one at the abbey who could pay him wages for his continued labor, for the reprehensible Abbot Jolivet, who held the abbey's funds, had betrayed the monks by siding with the English invaders. The abbot had left the Mount in 1420 and moved to Rouen where the Duke of Bedford had established his headquarters. Jolivet's allegiance and loyalty to the monarchy of France were as invincible as a rose petal in a hailstorm, as firm as a dab of Norman butter in the noonday sun.

After Nicolas's effective and impressive application of Katelyn's battle plan, the monks were even more indebted to the young stonecutter. So, in an attempt to repay the debt and as a token of their desire to remunerate his continued work, the monks offered the only thing they could offer him: simple sustenance. And so twice a day, Nicolas took his meals with the monks, and although their vows of silence did not allow him any meal-time conversation, it was still better than eating alone in Jean's cottage, without Jean and without . . . Katelyn. As the monotone chanting from the rule of Saint Benedict that accompanied each meal infused his brain, the chanting constituted two times a day when his thoughts were drowned out. Besides, he had no other goods to barter for food.

At low tide on the sixth day of each week, Nicolas made his way to the little unfinished chapel on the stony beach on the far northwest side of the Mount to fulfill the final promise he had made to Jean le Vieux.

He remembered that horrible night four years earlier with crystal-clear clarity. The final, horrific hours of Operation Dark Moon. Jean had taken Katelyn to the abbey to send her back to her time for medical care. He had realized she would not survive the ravages caused by the poisons that had entered her body from her shattered foot, suffered while trying to save Nicolas from being pulled into the perilous sands of the bay.

"Nicolas, get her home," Jean had pleaded. "She will not survive if you don't get her home immediately. And Nicolas," the old man had paused and looked up to the heavens, "will you finish Michel's chapel for me?"

Collins had held a knife at Jean's throat, threatening to kill him if he didn't reveal Katelyn Michaels' identity.

"Papa, you know I will," Nicolas had said through his sobs.

And then a cry had rung out over the terrace: "Stop. Stop! I'll tell you."

Katelyn had regained consciousness and had crawled out onto the terrace from behind the guardhouse. "Let him go, and I will tell you who I am."

"No, Katelyn," both Watchmen had cried simultaneously.

"Katelyn, don't say a word," Nicolas had besought her, after helping her to a standing position. "If you don't say anything, Abdon will never . . ."

"Now this is an interesting development," Collins had said in English. "I didn't count on you coming back to life, my little vixen. I feared you were too far gone. I know you are not Kallan Mikkeldatter, the Duke of Bedford's niece, but I do know you are the one responsible for this fine little display tonight. Yes, you are the one who ruined what should now be my victory celebration! So pray tell, who are you and how is it that you have such remarkable powers?"

"Release Jean and I will tell you," Katelyn had begged, as Nicolas pressed her body to his chest, trying to quiet her.

"You cannot let him die, Nicolas," she had whispered to him.

"We must, Katelyn. It is the only way to keep you safe."

But it hadn't kept her safe, and it hadn't saved Jean, for just as Jean threw himself and Collins over the edge of the Western Terrace, the impetuous lass in her fevered state had blurted out her identity. It would be of no import to Richard Collins, who was soon dead as well, but the wretched soul of the fallen angel Abdon, who had taken refuge in Collins' body, would never die. And it was of import to him.

So in the end, Jean's death had not protected Katelyn's identity. But Jean's actions *had* protected the secret of the Mount, just as they had when his own son, Michel, had been sacrificed to prevent Abdon from learning the secret.

And so, to fulfill his courageous and faithful mentor's dying wish, Nicolas labored to complete the chapel Jean had commenced years earlier as the final resting spot for his beloved son. His only child. The chapel would be dedicated to Aubert, but Jean knew, and Nicolas knew, that it was built over the very spot where Michel's broken body had landed after having been thrown from the West Terrace by Abdon. It was the child's final resting place, and after four years, Nicolas had nearly completed the work.

In his lonely despair, Nicolas wondered if, at the completion of Michel's sanctuary, his own work would be finished as well.

Chapter 6

SINCE I DREAMED OF JEAN, I HAVEN'T received any other instructions. At least not through dreams or voices. And no more mysterious computer glitches. But I do know I need to learn as much about medieval French history as I possibly can. Whoever could have imagined that I, Katelyn Michaels, would sacrifice Swim Team to take a history class? Jackson Michaels, yes, but no, not Katelyn. I am definitely a changed person.

Although I've had no dreams, I have received some rather odd impressions, and I am learning to pay attention to them. Impressions were how the Archangel helped me escape from the Godons and develop a plan to save the Mount. So now, I try not to discount thoughts that come to my mind. Unfortunately, I've had a really hard time following these impressions because I can't explain them to my mother. To be honest, I'm not exactly thrilled about them either.

The minute I heard that one of the new student teachers was organizing a fencing club after school, I was all in—despite my ankle. I convinced Mom that fencing would be the perfect therapy, although that was a ridiculous argument, because I can assure you, fencing, like climbing, hurts my ankle a whole lot more than swimming! Anyway, I told her that since I no longer have Swim

Team practice after school, it made perfect sense. Well, actually it really made no sense to me, but I'm going with my impressions. If I'm going to figure out this sword thing I'm supposed to be taking to the Maiden, I guess I ought to know a bit about sword fighting. So that impression wasn't completely out in left field, although I now know that the fencing foils, sabers, and épées have little in common with heavy medieval swords. But, it's a start.

Mom has had a harder time trying to figure out why all of the sudden I also want to learn how to ride. Horses, that is. That was my second impression. And I happen to know first-hand that there are no horses on Mont Saint Michel, so that one has me really puzzled. Unlike the fencing lessons, which are free, it costs a lot of money to take riding lessons. Money that Mom doesn't have. She put a kibosh on riding lessons and immediately called her sister.

I can just hear her now, speaking to Aunt Lizzie, who has replaced my father as her confidante. "Ever since that horrible experience in France, Katelyn just hasn't been herself. I think she may have brain damage, because now she wants to fence and ride horses! You know her, Lizzie. That isn't our Katelyn. And just how are fencing and riding going to help her get a scholarship? Does she think I'm made of money? I was counting on her getting a swimming scholarship, and now that's obviously not going to happen. It would have been such a great story, too. You know, teen swimmer recovers from life threatening injuries to break state swimming records."

I feel sad that I'm ruining my mother's dream for me, but it is *her* dream, not *my* dream. I have more consequential things to worry about now, like how to save the world from Abdon, or how Nicolas, who promised he would always come for me, will find me here in America. Unfortunately, those are not things I can explain to Mom.

Then I can hear Aunt Lizzie saying, "Well, you'll just have to make sure her father hears about this and let him know that you expect him to pay for every dime of her college education. After all, it's all *his* fault."

I'm proud of Mom for finally breaking the 'blame your father for everything' cycle, but Aunt Lizzie isn't quite there yet. I can't fault her for that. I felt that way up until my time travel escapade. Nothing like barely surviving death to knock some sense into me.

I've also had a hard time explaining to Mom why I've pretty much lost interest in my usual routine and friends since France. Oh, I've tried to get back in the swing of things with them, but talking about who asked whom to the Homecoming dance just doesn't do it for me anymore, and I really couldn't care less about which shade of pink looks best with Nicole's complexion.

Don't get me wrong. It's not that I don't care about my friends anymore; it's just that my priorities have changed drastically. I'm anxious to learn all I need to learn in order to be prepared to return to Mont Saint Michel. I'm surprisingly passionate about the fencing lessons, and my instructor says he has never seen a student take to it with such natural ability.

Although my social life has suffered, my relationship with Jackson has only gotten better since France. Not that it was *that* bad to begin with. I still tease him incessantly, but I'm also always pumping information from him (which he finds pretty unusual), and I'm actually starting to learn some stuff *he* doesn't know. That's because of my Medieval European History class. I have an added incentive to really master what I'm learning in that class. Who knows? Lives may depend upon it!

I've learned all about the 1066 Battle of Hastings when William, the Duke of Normandy, invaded England to claim its throne after his cousin Edward died without any direct heirs. It seems that's what all the bickering between France and England has been about for centuries. The royal families of France and England had intermarried so often that their battles were all about relatives fighting over who had the most legitimate claim to the throne of each country.

Now we're learning about the Plantagenets,[1] the royal family of England who descended from William and originated in France. To make matters worse in France, the Plantagenets kept intermarrying with the French royal line, the Valois family, like Eleanor of Aquitaine who first married the King of France, then divorced him and married the Duke of Normandy who became Henry II of England. So Eleanor was first Queen of France, and then Queen of England. See what I mean? Crazy! I'm starting to figure out why the Hundred Years' War began! Such a tangled web.

I'm actually enjoying my History class, and I'm doing pretty well in French too, even though my teacher tells me my vocabulary is strangely archaic. How do I explain that one? But while I'm applying myself in school, my social life is getting worse.

Little by little, my friends have stopped calling, and I find myself becoming more and more isolated. I know it is happening, but I don't care enough to change it. I just want to get through school, learn as much of the stuff I can that might be of help to me in my 'other' life, and somehow get back to Nicolas. I know it will happen. It has to happen.

But that type of thinking has also presented me with a terrible dilemma. If I somehow make it back to Nicolas's time in the fifteenth century, it means giving up my family. But if I stay with my family in the twenty-first century, it means giving up Nicolas. Neither choice makes me happy. I don't know what to do, and I find myself falling deeper and deeper into a black hole.

Mom sees it happening as well, and she is beside herself. If I had a dollar for every time she says something like, "Why don't you call

---

[1] For more information about the Plantagenets, read *Katelyn's Historical Commentary* at the end of the book.

Nicole this weekend, dear, and go do something with your friends," I would have enough money to buy a plane ticket to France. And it isn't just thoughts of Nicolas and Jean that consume me. I am paranoid about Abdon. I see him in every unfamiliar face that walks past me, in every store clerk, and even in my male teachers at school. And now, I'm starting to see him in familiar faces as well.

I know my behavior is destructive. I know my obsessing over Abdon is counter-productive, but I can't stop it. I am starting to feel anxious all of the time, and I don't like leaving the house except to go to school. Mom finally insists that I get some counseling. She keeps reading all kinds of articles about Post-Traumatic Stress Disorder. And so I finally make a deal with my mother. I will start going out with my friends again if she agrees to let me take riding lessons once a week. I'd heard somewhere about how horse therapy helps children with autism and other psychological or physical problems, so I convinced her it would be like getting professional therapy for PTSD, but a lot cheaper.

So I'm making an effort to feign interest in my friends' so-called struggles to appease my mother, but when I think about the real struggles the Montois faced during the siege of 1424, it doesn't make it very easy for me to feel sorry for Lindsay when she didn't get the lead in the school musical, or for Jake, who missed the PAT that could have won the football game last Friday night. After all, I've watched people starving to death. But, I have to try. And this afternoon is my first riding lesson. Maybe a horse will bring me some clarity.

Chapter 7

NIGHTS WERE THE WORST. DURING THE DAY, Nicolas could at least focus on the angle at which he held his chisel and the amount of thrust he applied to his hammer. He could drown himself in the physical effort it required to move block after block of stone on a system of pulleys and logs with no help from anyone. From the West Terrace, he could watch the bay for any signs of storms or dream of what was happening in his homeland. From his vantage point, he saw Brittany's coastline daily. He wondered about his parents, and his little sister, who would be quite grown up by now. She might even have married, and he wasn't there to celebrate with her.

In the cloister, he could contemplate the imagery of the Garden of Eden, or he could look up to the open skies above the garden for any signs of divine approbation, and although he could not converse with the monks, except on special occasions when conversation was required, he could at least be in their presence, rather than being alone.

Even the Widow Mercier—who had been so kind and concerned about him after the loss of Jean and Katelyn—had abandoned him. After long months of depravation during the siege, her frail body had given up the ghost some few months earlier. At least he did not have to answer any more of her questions about Katelyn's fate. Not knowing when or if Katelyn would ever return, Nicolas had been obliged to concoct some story about her injuries requiring her to be evacuated in the middle of the night of the famous battle to receive care from a nunnery in Brittany that specialized in cases such as hers. Then he expressed his continued hope that she would one day recover and be able to return to her broken-hearted husband.

The rest of the Montois knew not to even ask him about Katelyn. Nicolas's facial expressions said it all. He was distraught and shattered by the loss of both Katelyn and Jean, and although they did not ask, Nicolas knew they wondered why he had not left the Mount to return to his wife in Brittany. After all, in their manner of thinking, what was there now to keep him on the Mount? They did not know his presence there was not up for negotiation. They did not know that his lot in life had been predestined. They did not know that he was Jean's replacement. They did not know he was a Watchman.

There was no sign of Abdon, so it was even harder to fight the fight when one could not identify the enemy. Nicolas found his heart beating faster when he crossed paths with anyone unfamiliar who came to the Mount . . . and he searched the faces to find Abdon. Then, he started looking for him in the familiar faces as well. It was the not knowing where Abdon was that he found hardest of all.

And so the days passed in a mixture of anxiety, sadness, and drudgery for Nicolas. The days of his pleadings with God were replaced with mindless days of monotony and physical exertion carried out in a semi-conscious state.

Then one day, after Nicolas had given up imploring the heavens, Brother Thibault arrived.

Chapter 8

I'VE HAD ANOTHER DREAM. IT'S A FLEETING dream, and in it, I'm holding my time key in my hand, rubbing the raised portion of the jobber's mark on the back of the enseigne with my thumb. Then from my top dresser drawer, I pull out the other enseigne, the one Jean sent back with me from 1424. *His* key. His final gift to me that he placed in the zippered pocket of my backpack. The key he will never be using again because of me. No, that's not right. Jean won't be using his key because of Abdon. *I* am not responsible for Jean's death. *Abdon* is responsible. I have to keep reminding myself of that. Anyway, in my dream, I place the two keys side by side with the jobber's marks facing up. My symbol is a squished square, and his is a squiggly X.

ם א

That's it. That's all I remember. When I wake up, I pull both of the enseignes from my drawer and place them side by side, as I did in my dream. And then the impression comes. I need to figure out the meaning of the symbols on the keys. They have something to do with the secret. I don't know where to start, but since the symbols are from the Middle Ages, I wonder if my history teacher will have some insights, so I draw them out on a piece of paper.

Later after class that day, I ask him if he knows what they represent.

"Hmmm," he says. "I think the X is a Hebrew letter, but I don't know about the first symbol. Why don't you ask Mr. Dreyer, the German teacher? I think he speaks a little Hebrew. He might know. Why? Where are these symbols from?"

I'm not prepared for that question, and I kind of fumble around before going with an answer that's close to the truth.

"Oh . . . well . . . my brother and I saw these marks carved in the stones of the Mont Saint Michel Abbey in Normandy when we were in France this past summer. I think they're called jobber's marks."

"Yes, jobber's marks. Well then, they're probably just random shapes the stonecutters chose as their marks to identify their own stones. They probably don't have any special meaning. But you know there is a tradition that the stonemasons who built Solomon's Temple in Ancient Jerusalem passed on their craft through subsequent generations of stonemasons. Have you heard of the Freemasons?"

"Yeah," I say. "It's some kind of secret organization. Weren't a lot of the Founding Fathers Freemasons?"

"Well the Freemasons don't like us to use the word 'secret.' They call themselves a fraternal organization, and although their membership has dwindled in recent decades, they were once very influential throughout Great Britain and America. And you're right. Many of the Founding Fathers *were* members. Anyway, they claim their special knowledge and rites go back to the stonemasons of Solomon's Temple, which were carried down through the local stonemason guilds in medieval Western Europe. I've never heard of it specifically, but maybe some of the Hebrew letters from King Solomon's time were disseminated as jobber's marks throughout the guilds."

I don't know anything about Freemasonry, and I don't think it has anything to do with my jobber's marks, or the secret of the Mount, but the idea that the Hebrew letters may have been passed down through the ages from stonemason to stonemason makes some sense. Still, I want to know for certain if they *are* Hebrew letters, so after fencing club, I stop by Mr. Dreyer's office.

"*Guten Tag, Herr* Dreyer," I say, quite proud of myself for learning from one of my friends enrolled in German how to say hello. "You don't know me. My name is Katelyn Michaels and I was told you might know some Hebrew."

"Yes," he says, "I've studied Hebrew. How can I help you?"

This time, I'm prepared with a better storyline. "I don't mean to take your time, but I have a friend who is into cryptology, and he sent me this message. I just wondered if you could tell me anything about these symbols. Here," I say as I hand him the paper on which I've drawn the symbols. "I think the squiggly X is a Hebrew letter, but I don't know what the squished square is."

"You're right, Ms. Michaels. This X-like symbol is the Hebrew letter called *aleph*. And the other symbol is also a Hebrew letter called *mem*. It's usually notated with a top swirl like this," he says as he draws the letter. It looks kind of like a house with a chimney.

"But when the *mem* is the final consonant in a word, it's notated like this with a tiny swirl," he draws the letter on my paper, "*or* the way you have it. What did you call it? A squished square? It's actually more of a rectangle, but you get the picture. Either is correct." He draws the two different forms of the letter *mem* when it is the final letter in a Hebrew word.

"Do these letters, *aleph* and *mem* have any special meaning?" I ask. "You know, like Alpha and Omega in Greek mean 'the beginning and the end,' or something like that?" I'm having a hard time trying to figure out how to phrase my question.

"No, not in and of themselves they don't. They are phonetic letters, like in our alphabet. The *mem* makes an 'em' sound just like our letter M, but the *aleph* is a silent letter, unless it has a vowel attached to it. The problem with Hebrew is that the vowels, which are added to the letters by a series of lines and dots, aren't notated in modern Hebrew, and there's no vowel sound notated with this *aleph*."

"I don't understand what you mean." I'm completely lost. It's Greek to me! No, actually it's Hebrew.

"Well, in Hebrew, the vowels are implied and are not required. It's kind of like shorthand. If I wrote the English word 'ltr,' could you read it?" he asks.

"Ah . . . I guess that's supposed to be the word 'letter.' "

"Yes, that's it. You were able to figure out the word just by using the consonants, but it also could have been 'later,' so you see, you can't always be sure with Hebrew. If the vowels aren't notated, you have to determine the meaning from the context. Sorry, that's more information than you probably wanted."

"So do the *mem* and *aleph* spell out a word?" I ask as I point to my page. "I guess you'd have to change the order if the final consonant *mem* is supposed to be the last letter."

מ א

"No. Actually, Ms. Michaels, Hebrew is read from right to left, the opposite of English. So this is correct."

Jackson would know that. He'd know that Hebrew is read from right to left, but *I* didn't know it. I mean how many seventeen-year-old non-Jewish American girls know anything about Hebrew?

"So is it a word?"

"My vocabulary in Hebrew isn't very extensive, but it could be at least two words that I know." He writes out the two words as he explains. "With one dot below the *aleph*, it would be the word 'if,' or it would be the word 'mother' with two dots below, like this:"

$$\text{אִם} = \text{if} \qquad\qquad \text{אֵם} = \text{mother}$$

"If? Mother? That's it?" I say in dismay. *This is my big clue?* "That doesn't make any sense."

"If that doesn't mean anything to you, maybe that isn't the entire message. Maybe your friend is sending you clues word by word."

"Maybe," I say, and then thank him for his time. I have so many questions. What on earth are Hebrew letters doing on our time keys? And do they really have something to do with the secret of the Mount that Jean and Nicolas had conveniently failed to tell me about? Having the *mem* on my key could simply be a phonetic representation of my last name, Michaels, but why in Hebrew? And the silent *aleph* doesn't make any sense phonetically for Jean's name. Of course, I don't know if he had a family name. Maybe that's it— just the first sound in our last names. But, that doesn't sit right with me.

Then I have another thought come to me. In order to make sense of these letters, I need another letter, not another word as Mr. Dreyer suggested. Another enseigne. It has to be Nicolas's enseigne. *His* time key is the key to this puzzle. I never paid attention to what the symbol was on his key. Actually, I don't think I ever *saw* his key. Now, I regret not having asked him about it. Well, too late for that. About six hundred years too late!

Chapter 9

THE YEARS PASSED BUT THE VOICES REMAINED, and so did the war. Jehanne grew to be a serious girl, and the other young people in the village often accused her of being too pious. While the girls her age were singing and dancing, Jehanne went to church and prayed. She never swore, and she confessed her sins gladly and as often as she could. Although she was generally thought to be mild-mannered and the champion of the underprivileged, she had also become known for her temper, which erupted whenever she heard someone blaspheme God's name or commit other wrongdoings she found offensive.

When she was younger she had helped look after her father's cows, but as she grew to the age of reason, she avoided going too far abroad for fear of the soldiers, whom she knew were capable of unspeakable acts.

One morning, Jehanne's brother, Jacquemin, came running into the house without even bothering to remove his dirty wooden sabots, caked with mud from the fields.

"Venez," he called. *"Dépêchez-vous!* Hurry! We must leave without delay. The Burgundians are coming. They are going to attack! Papa is readying the wagon."

Most of the people in Jehanne's village of Domrémy supported the French cause, even though they were surrounded by Burgundian-held lands. The villagers in nearby Maxey, just a stone's throw to the east along the Meuse River, were supporters of the Burgundians, who supported the English claim to the throne.

It wasn't uncommon for the children from the two villages of Domrémy and Maxey to fight with each other and return to their respective homes both bloodied and well-wounded at night, but Jehanne could tell from her brother's demeanor that this was more than a little skirmish between neighbors. She assisted her mother in quickly gathering all of the valuables they could collect, extra clothing, and bedding, as well as a basket of foodstuffs. Then she helped her little sister Catherine don her cape and sabots.

As they exited the stone home, Isabeau, Jehanne's mother, closed the wooden shutters tightly, while reciting the *Pater noster*. Her father Jacques opened the gate to the field where the cows huddled together under a wooden shelter and shooed them out. While Jacquemin was harnessing the horse to the wagon, her other brothers, Pierre and Jean, efficiently loaded their belongings. They were among the lucky ones of the small village. They had both a horse *and* a wagon.

"Papa, where are we going?" asked Jehanne. She knew that six leagues to the north of Domrémy, in Vaucouleurs, was a fortress manned by French soldiers led by the garrison captain, Robert de Baudricourt, who was an ardent supporter of the Armagnacs and the Dauphin Charles. Baudricourt had valiantly held off the Burgundians for eight long years in this hostile territory. But taking the road to the north meant passing through Champagne, with more potential enemies, and the journey would take nearly twice as long as heading south to Neufchâteau. If her father could get their old farm horse, aptly named Clovis, to do more than saunter, they could reach Neufchâteau in under two hours.

"We must head south. I have been told that Vaucouleurs is under siege and that Baudricourt has sent soldiers to protect Neufchâteau."

Although she said nothing to her father, Jehanne prayed in her heart that Baudricourt might also himself have traveled south to Neufchâteau, for it was imperative that she speak to him. Her voices had instructed her to go to Robert de Baudricourt. Succeeding in having him—an important commander of the King's troops—listen to her—a simple, illiterate farm girl—was the first step in the arduous journey she knew lay ahead of her.

A single shiver overtook Jehanne's slender frame, which turned into a constant trembling as a fine mist of rain began falling. It then developed into uncontrollable shaking as their intrepid Clovis, unaware of the danger that stalked his passengers but anxious to please his master, gave his all to pull his hooves out of the vise of the thickening mud that paved the road to Neufchâteau. Tears welled up in the young woman's eyes, and then tumbled over her lower eyelids to run their course down her wind-reddened cheeks. Her mother, with Catherine on her lap, grabbed a woolen bedcover with one arm and clumsily spread it over her and her daughters' heads. Then with that same arm—an arm which had always provided strength, support, and unfailing faith to Jehanne—she pulled her eldest daughter in close to share her body warmth.

"Fear not, dear child," Isabeau whispered into her ear. "I know you are frightened. But God is good, and we have been so abundantly blessed. Our house is sturdy and strong. It is of stone, and is mercifully free of exposed timbers that might catch fire easily, like many of our neighbors' dwellings. You will see. Our home will stand strong and survive the attack of the approaching marauders. And Papa released the cows. They are smart cows, Jehanne. They are French cows. They will not stand silently by, waiting to be slaughtered by the malicious puppets of the English. They will never allow themselves to be taken by the Burgundians! We will be able to gather them back to the cowshed when we return home."

Jehanne was discomfited by her lack of self-control, but her mother had no way of knowing that Jehanne was not shivering over scattered cows, or even about the possible loss of her cherished house, the only home she had ever known. She could not tell her mother that her trembling was out of fear that she would not be strong enough or brave enough to leave her home and family forever, or that her shuddering was for a much greater cause . . . for the cause of France. Her tears were not even for her beloved townsfolk, many of whom she had cared for and served during her childhood years.

No, her tears were tears of utter terror that she would not be wise enough with her words or courageous enough with her actions to convince Robert de Baudricourt that she, Jehanne of Domrémy, Jehanne La Pucelle, the simple, illiterate daughter of the farmer Jacques d'Arc, had been called by the Archangel Michael to save all of France.

Chapter 10

OF COURSE. IT IS SO OBVIOUS. THE MAIDEN is Joan. Joan of Arc. In French, she is called Jeanne d'Arc, but I learned that her real name from her era was Jehanne. She has been called many things over the centuries, but she called herself Jehanne La Pucelle. Joan the Maiden. Her role in the Hundred Years' War is legendary, and although *I* didn't know the details about her and the Hundred Years' War, I'm learning, and I'm making it my mission to learn even more.

Everyone knows the basic story about how Joan of Arc helped the Dauphin (that means crown prince) claim the throne of France, but what I didn't know until I started studying about her is that as a young girl of thirteen, she claimed the Archangel Michael visited her in a vision of light. Imagine that! Well, I, Katelyn Michaels, *can* imagine that. I didn't see any light, but I certainly heard his voice, and I still feel his inspiration. So, yes, I believe it. Joan also had other heavenly visitors—she identified them as Margaret and Catherine, women venerated in the Catholic Church as saints. She called them 'her voices,' and they instructed her to save France from English domination by helping the son of the mad French King Charles VI, the Dauphin Charles, to claim what was rightfully his: the throne of France.

There was one small problem, however. In order for Charles to be considered the legitimate king, his coronation had to take place in the city of Reims, in the cathedral of Notre-Dame de Reims, and the city of Reims was in northern France, and northern France was under English control. Do you think the English were even the least bit interested in allowing Charles safe passage to Reims? No. Not on your life.

So why, you ask, did Charles have to have his coronation in Notre-Dame de Reims? It all stems back to Clovis, the first ruler to unite all of the Frankish tribes into one kingdom back in the fifth and sixth centuries.[2] That's where he was not only baptized as a Christian, but was anointed with some miraculous oil to be King of France. From there on out, any man who had visions of claiming the throne of France had to receive that holy unction by the archbishop of Reims. I guess it *was* a pretty big deal for the Dauphin Charles to make it to Reims.

That's what Joan's voices told her to do to save France, to get the Dauphin to Reims, which was no simple task. It meant liberating several cities from the English along the way. It meant leading the French army against the English, a pretty remarkable accomplishment for a young, illiterate girl from Eastern France. And she did it! She got the Dauphin to Reims. But then the newly crowned king, Charles VII, turned his back on her and allowed her to be captured by the English and their Burgundian supporters. He did nothing to stop her from being tried for heresy and burned at the stake.

---

[2] For more information about Clovis and his 'holy unction,' read *Katelyn's Historical Commentary* at the end of the book.

So with my newly found passion for all things Joan, when my Medieval European History teacher, Mr. Bailey, told us that half of our term grade would come from a term paper, I elected to do my paper on Joan of Arc. When I turned in my chosen subject to Mr. Bailey, he cautioned me.

"I'm not sure that's a very good choice, Katelyn. So much has been written about her, and I don't want to see a simple regurgitation of historical facts. You better have some original thoughts or I can assure you, you won't get a very good grade."

Frankly, I'm not motivated by a good grade. I am motivated by trying to keep myself and possibly others alive somewhere back in time. I don't yet know what I will be called upon to do as a Watchman, but I'm pretty sure it has to do with Joan of Arc . . . and with her sword, or actually, with the sword I am supposed to take to her. Really? Me? Helping Joan of Arc, arguably the most famous female in medieval history? Maybe the most famous French woman in all of history? The idea that I can in any possible way help Joan of Arc save France is pretty original thinking, but I can't exactly write about that in the paper. But I *am* going to learn every single thing I can about Joan and about her sword, and so that is the theme of my term paper: "The Sword of the Maiden."

I've studied every single primary source and read as much about her sword as I can, and I've learned that there's very little written about Joan's sword except in the transcripts of her trial, where she told her accusers that her voices told her where to find the sword. I have, however, learned a lot about the folklore surrounding swords in the Middle Ages, and I've come to understand they had very special meaning back then. In fact, there was an almost cult-like adoration of swords in medieval times. Swords even had names, both in fiction and in actual history. King Arthur had *Excalibur*, Beowulf had *Nrunting*, Roland had *Durendal*, Charlemagne had *Joyeuse*, and El Cid had *Tizona* and *Colada*, just to name a few of the famous fictional and historical swords.

And what about Joan's sword? Well, I have some pretty interesting ideas about it. I don't think Mr. Bailey can accuse me of not having any original thinking after he reads what I've been writing. My paper is coming along nicely, and even Jackson is impressed at my new-found passion: writing a term paper about a sword.

"Honestly, Katie," he says to me, after I've spent nearly all day today, which happens to be a Saturday, doing internet research on the family computer. "I don't even recognize you anymore."

We have two display screens for the desktop in the den, and it is so much easier to write and do research there than on my laptop. Jackson whines. "Whoever thought I'd be fighting over the computer with you on a Saturday. Saturday? Really? What's the deal?"

"I just want a good grade in history," I reply. "That's the deal." I try to sound convincing, but I don't think he's convinced. He looks at me with the strangest expression on his face, and then he shakes his head and leaves the room.

"Mom," I hear him screaming. "Will you please tell Katie it's my turn for the computer?"

"Katelyn," Mom hollers back. "It's Jackson's turn to use the computer. Why don't you call Nicole and go do something fun? Isn't there a dance at the school tonight?"

Whoever thought my own mother would be forcing me to go to a high school dance with my friends? All I want to do is learn about Joan of Arc and her sword and get back to Nicolas. Well, aside from brandishing a sword myself at my fencing opponents—not a sword, actually it's called a foil—and aside from pushing my favorite stallion, Midnight, to gallop at a breakneck pace. But other than my fencing club and Midnight (my new best friend), my social life is pretty bleak. No dances for Katelyn. Besides, Katelyn is a married woman.

"Well," I make my counter-offer, "how about I go riding? That will get me out in the fresh air doing something physical after being cooped up all day. Does that meet with your approval? I'll pay for the ride with my allowance."

"Dear, I think it's great that you've found some new interests, and I think it's quite amazing that both your fencing teacher and your riding instructor say you're a natural at both of these new pursuits, but don't you think you should cultivate relationships with actual people, instead of with a sword and a horse?"

"It's not a sword, Mom, it's a foil," I reply. I just can't resist. I know what she's getting at, and I'm trying to get her to change the subject—by getting mad at me.

"Katelyn, you know exactly what I mean. Don't get sarcastic with me, young lady."

"I'm *not* being sarcastic. I'm just informing you that my fencing weapon is called a foil. Actually, there are three weapons in fencing: foil, saber, and épée. I guess technically, the épée *is* a sword, but we only use foils in our fencing club. You know, we're kind of a low-budget fencing operation."

"Katelyn Michaels. Enough. You *are* being sarcastic, and I don't appreciate it. Go ahead and go riding, but remember, I don't think you should go. I wish you'd go to the dance with your friends, so don't blame anyone but yourself when you don't get asked to the Senior Ball."

Although I don't care one whit about the Senior Ball, I really *should* have listened to my mother about not going riding.

Chapter 11

AFTER THE IMMEDIATE THREAT FROM THE siege of
Vaucouleurs had abated, Jehanne's family returned to their village
from Neufchâteau, and as her mother had promised, their home was
still standing. However, the same could not be said for all the
villagers of Domrémy, and there were still plenty of repairs to be
done on Jacques d'Arc's property. The cows and other livestock had
to be gathered back in, fences had to be repaired, and the barns
needed rebuilding after having been torched by the marauders.
Jacques and his sons worked from dawn until dusk, while Jehanne,
her mother, and young Catherine attended to their needs, spun wool,
sewed linen fabrics into clothing, and also assisted the impoverished
inhabitants of the village. Jehanne's renowned flat cakes were
particularly appreciated by her less-fortunate neighbors.

As the month of May dawned in the year fourteen hundred
twenty eight, Jehanne was happy to see the weather improve. But the
news from the West was inauspicious. The English had launched an
attack on Montargis, a fortified city to the northeast of Orléans, and
had also seized other crucial positions north of the Loire River.

By mid-month, Jehanne became increasingly anxious. As word
of the English offensives filtered into her little valley, she understood

that the Godons were gaining control of more and more territory. Soon, the Dauphin—who ruled from the city of Bourges far to the south of Paris—would have nothing left of France to rule. Jehanne's voices had been urging her to go to Robert de Baudricourt. They assured her that the garrison commander would provide her with traveling companions to accompany her into French-held lands to reach the Dauphin. She realized she could no longer ignore her voices.

Jehanne had already turned sixteen and was well into her seventeenth year, an age where it was natural for her parents to be concerned about finding the right husband for her. She shared her birthday with the sacred Feast of the Epiphany, the sixth day of January, the date which celebrated the arrival of the Three Magi to visit the baby Jesus. Jehanne's parents liked to tell her the story of how all the roosters of the village crowed as she was born, which was unusual, because her birth came several hours before dawn.

"'Twas as if they were heralding your birth," they told her. "As if they were proclaiming a new dawn."

Perhaps remembering the events of my birth will help them understand that I have a mission other than what they have planned for me, she thought.

Although she had been careful about protecting her parents from the entire truth about her voices, she was insistent with them that her lot in life was not to be the wife of a farmer, regardless of how prosperous he might be.

"I have made a pledge to God," she explained to her parents. "I will remain pure and chaste for as long as it is pleasing to Him."

She knew her parents assumed that by such a declaration she meant to take the vows of a nun. She also knew they would have been pleased to give a child to God, but Jehanne hoped they would understand that *her* way of serving God had been dictated to her from on high. The Archangel Michael himself had told her to believe what her voices said, for it was by the order of God Himself. No, she would not be a nun, but it was with extreme trepidation that she wondered how she, a poor, uneducated girl who knew neither how to ride nor how to lead an army, could possibly do as the voices commanded.

The opening finally came for Jehanne to go to Vaucouleurs when a kinsman, Durand Laxart, visited the home of Jacques and Isabeau. Durand lived in Burey-le-Petit, not far from Vaucouleurs, and he knew Robert de Baudricourt personally. When she spoke to her uncle about returning with him to Burey-le-Petit for a visit with her aunt, Durand replied that he was amenable to the idea as long as she had her father's permission.

"Father," she suggested tentatively, "I should like to visit Aunt and Uncle Laxart. The road to Vaucouleurs is safe once again, and I think it would do my soul good to have a change of scenery. Could you and Mother spare me for a week to make such a visit?"

"Jehanne," he replied, "although the English and Burgundians may have halted their raids in our little valley for a season, the *écorcheurs* are still running rampant throughout the countryside, and I fear it is not an opportune time for travel." Jehanne knew that the *écorcheurs* were a band of vicious brigands who pillaged for neither the English nor the French cause, but to fill their own pockets.

"But Father," she insisted, "I have complete confidence in Uncle to protect me, and besides, we will be traveling during the daylight hours and will arrive well before dusk. And Uncle has agreed to accompany me back home to you and Mother in a week or so."

Jehanne's mother, perhaps because she had witnessed firsthand the anxiety that recent events had caused her daughter, convinced her husband that it was not a foolhardy notion. "She is such a good lass, Jacques, and rarely asks for anything. Can we not allow her this one small pleasure?"

And so it was, that on the thirteenth day of May, Jehanne set off with her uncle to journey to Vaucouleurs via Burey-le-Petit. Her entreaties for her uncle to take her to meet Robert de Baudricourt began immediately upon her arrival at his home, barely after she had greeted her aunt.

"Uncle," she insisted. "I have a message of great import for the captain of the king's garrison."

"How can you, a mere girl, have a message of great import for Robert de Baudricourt?" Durand asked with pronounced consternation.

Jehanne, no longer reluctant to hide her true mission, decided that it was in her best interest at this point to tell her uncle and aunt the truth. The time had come for her to be forthcoming. She could no longer deny her heavenly tutoring.

"I have received instruction from on high to go to Chinon to the Dauphin. I am to assist him in making the journey to Reims to be crowned as King of France."

She was prepared for her uncle to be incredulous, but she was not prepared for him to laugh. After all, she had been commanded by God Himself through His holy emissaries to perform this sacred mission. Would he laugh at God?

"Jehanne," he replied while trying to recover his composure after his laughing fit, "whatever has your poor mother been feeding you to entertain such fanciful notions?"

"I assure you, Uncle, it is not because of any personal desire that I attest to these words, but because I have been commanded of God to do so. I have received the visitation of the Archangel Michael himself instructing me that I shall be the instrument to save France."

"You, the daughter of Jacques d'Arc and Isabeau Romée, have received a visitation from the Archangel Michael?"

"Yes, and that is not all," she explained, hopeful that her uncle would believe her words. She was not entirely naïve. If she had not heard the voices herself, she would have been incredulous as well. "I have received directives from Sainte Margaret and Sainte Catherine as well. Their voices come to me and they have urged me to go to Robert de Baudricourt. This is the first step in my mission."

"You converse with angels and saints? You honestly expect me to believe that, child? And you genuinely believe that you, a simple farm girl, are equipped to save all of France?" This time his guffaw was offensive.

Jehanne could no longer hold in the tears that threatened to destroy her composure. How did the Archangel expect her to perform her mission if no one believed her? She wiped her tears with the back of her hand and gathered her thoughts before replying.

"Have you not heard the prophecy that France would be ruined by a woman, and afterwards restored by a maiden who comes from the borders of Lorraine? Uncle, *I* am that maiden. *I* am La Pucelle of which the prophecies speak."

"Jehanne, my dear girl," Durand shook his head as he addressed her, gently taking her by the shoulders. "Yes, I have heard the prophecy, which some say issues from Marie d'Avignon. In fact, I have heard many versions of the prophecy: that the maid would come forth from an oak wood and work miracles, and that she would be a virgin bearing a sword. Although I can certainly concur that you are indeed a virginal maiden, and a lovely one at that, and that you hail from Lorraine, and although you may even have a plethora of oak trees in your village, I have not seen any of your miracles, nor are you bearing a sword. I cannot begin to comprehend how these unsettling times must have impacted the delicate balance of a gentle soul like yours. I choose to withdraw my judgment and instead exercise compassion for you, but we shall not speak of these things again."

But speak of them they did. After an entire week of such non-stop petitions, Jehanne finally succeeded in getting her uncle to give in to her request. Although she did not know if it was because she had finally convinced him that her voices were genuine, or if he simply could no longer put up with the incessant supplications, it was of no importance. Durand Laxart agreed to take Jehanne to meet the captain on the morrow, and further promised that he would not interfere in her undertaking.

The next day dawned bright and clear. Jehanne took it as a sign of good fortune. Today was the day she would commence her holy quest. To give more credence to her position as a future leader of armies, Jehanne asked her uncle to allow her to borrow his cloak, which hid her female apparel. When the duo arrived in Vaucouleurs, they were greeted by a pair of soldiers manning the fortified gate leading into the city.

True to his promise, Durand did nothing to undermine Jehanne's quest. When asked by the guards to state his business, Durand simply replied, "We have come to speak with Robert de Baudricourt. I am Durand Laxart from Burey-le-Petit, and we have a message for him about the Burgundian offensive." It was enough for the gates to be promptly opened.

Immediately upon entering the city, Jehanne recognized Robert de Baudricourt, who was standing amongst a small group of men-at-arms in front of the fortress. Although she had never seen him before, she knew immediately who he was.

Unfortunately, his reception of Jehanne's message was even less amenable than her uncle's. When she stated her case and then virtually commanded him to assist her in being taken to the place where her lord, the Dauphin, abode, he didn't laugh at her like her uncle had. Instead, he became extremely vexed.

"Laxart, what is the meaning of this affront? Why would you squander my time with such frivolity? Is this girl related to you?"

Jehanne could see her uncle shrink at Baudricourt's words, and he was certainly quick to distance himself from her. "I bade the lass not to bother you, Sire, but alas, I could not convince her of the folly of her ways. She is a relative of my wife and hails from Domrémy where her father has property holdings of some fifty acres."

"Then return her immediately to her father and please instruct him to give her a lashing. How dare she make such arrogant claims? And how dare she waste my time when I have such urgent matters to which I must attend?"

Durand grabbed Jehanne by the right hand and withdrew her immediately. As they left the city confines, she removed his cloak and returned it to him. Tears of disappointment poured down her cheeks, and although her uncle tried to half-heartedly console her, her humiliation was complete.

She was returned the next day to her father, who was told of the entire incident, but who did not heed the captain's words to inflict a lashing. In fact, he embraced his tender-hearted daughter. That evening, as her family gathered to sup, Jehanne recounted the events of the past few years of her life. She told them everything. She told them of having heard the voices and having seen the Archangel. It was time they knew the truth. They questioned her pointedly and tried to suggest that she had been mistaken, but the truth was the truth, and she could not and would not deny it.

Having had her message so completely and resoundingly rejected by her uncle and by Baudricourt, Jehanne retreated into herself. She had neither the fortitude nor the disposition to attempt a second visit to Robert de Baudricourt. Her parents and siblings said nothing of her claims, but she inwardly prayed that they would come to believe her remarkable narrative.

Two months later, in July of fourteen hundred and twenty-eight, the Anglo-Burgundians initiated their most relentless campaign against Vaucouleurs to date. Lord Antoine de Vergy himself, the Burgundian governor of Champagne, led an army of several hundred men-at-arms through the Meuse River valley, terrorizing everyone and everything in their wake. Incensed that Vaucouleurs remained the only fortified city in the region still loyal to the Armagnacs and the Dauphin, Vergy had no mercy for the villages along the river that supported Robert de Baudricourt.

When the church bells of Domrémy sounded the alarm, Jehanne and her family and the other villagers once again sought refuge in Neufchâteau.

Vaucouleurs was besieged yet again, but this time with disastrous results. Baudricourt was forced to sign an agreement with the Burgundians effectively tying his hands. He would no longer encroach on their forces. At the same time, word spread that hundreds of English reinforcements had landed in France and were massing for the campaign to take Orléans. The future of all of France seemed doomed.

When Jehanne returned to her village, the signs of destruction were even more widespread. The interior of her home and of her beloved Church of Saint Rémy had been desecrated and damaged by fire. Every wooden structure in the village had been burned, and every single field planted with life-giving grain, corn, and vegetables had been razed, destroying the crops that would keep the villagers alive during the coming winter.

Upon seeing the total devastation, Jehanne retired to the burned-out church and fell to the ground.

"I cannot do this alone," she cried out to her voices and to her God. "No one will listen to the words of a simple maiden. I have neither the facility of speech nor the skills of warfare to convince any man of my sacred mission. Please, Michael, please send me assistance. Please, God, give me the tools to carry out Thy great work. Please, open the way for me to accomplish the task that has been given me. Please, place someone along my path who will believe in me!"

But the heavens were silent.

Chapter 12

WHEN I GET TO THE DIXON RIDING STABLES on Saturday afternoon, I have a vague sense of uneasiness, but I shake it off. A good ride will clear my head.

As Jonah Dixon, the fifteen-year-old son of the stable owner, greets me, he says, "Katelyn, I know you always like to ride Midnight, but he seems a bit jittery today. I think we'll have you try Milly, the bay mare."

"Oh, come on, Jonah. You know I can handle Midnight. I need a good hard ride today, and Milly just isn't going to fit the bill."

"Your riding skills have definitely improved faster than any student I've ever seen, Katelyn. You're a natural in the saddle, but Midnight just seems off. If you don't want Milly, I can let you ride Sally, or if you insist on a stallion, I'll even let you ride my horse, Thunder."

"Isn't that just typical of you men," I say, inwardly chuckling at how he seems to puff up with pride at being called a man. "First, you tell me I'm not capable of riding Midnight because he's too high-spirited, and then you suggest I ride your mares? And honestly. You name the stallions Midnight and Thunder, but the mares Milly and Sally? Really? Don't you think that's a little bit misogynistic?"

"Katelyn," he admits. "I don't even know what that word means."

"You know, being prejudiced against females."

I guess the combination of an almost eighteen-year-old female calling Jonah a man and then the threat of a sex discrimination claim quiets him right down. I'm in a no-nonsense mood. I refuse to be intimidated.

"Okay, if you insist," he says reluctantly. "But don't say I didn't warn you if Midnight throws you! It'll be your own fault. If you're sure you want Midnight, I'll saddle him up. But, just to be on the cautious side, I insist on coming with you today."

"Okay," I agree halfheartedly. I want to be alone for the ride, but since Midnight isn't my horse, and these aren't my stables, I really don't have much say in the matter, despite my bravado. "At least let me help you saddle up the horses. It's time I learn how to do it myself."

"Sure," says Jonah. "I'll let you have a go at Midnight, then. He has always responded well to your touch, so maybe you can get him to calm down."

Jonah opens the tack room, and I help him gather up the equipment and lug it to Midnight's stall. The sleek black stallion *is* jittery, but he relaxes immediately when I reach up to pat his neck. I always bring an apple for my mounts, and he knows it. He leans over to sniff my jacket pocket.

"Yes, Midnight. You remember, don't you? I do have a treat for you, so munch on this while I get your saddle on." Jonah and I both enter Midnight's stall as I extend my hand. I don't even flinch when Midnight takes the apple into his mouth and leaves me with horse slobber in exchange. Jonah watches patiently as I drape the saddle blanket up high over Midnight's back, sliding it back down from the withers so the horse's hair will not be pushed down into an unnatural position, just as Jonah has taught me. He allows me to heft the heavy saddle over the stallion's back by myself. I buckle the cinch straps under Midnight's belly, tighten them gradually and look at Jonah for approval. He readjusts one strap slightly, and then pronounces the job perfectly done.

"Okay, now the bridle," Jonah says as he hands it to me. I allow Midnight to finish his apple and then pat his neck as I slowly raise my arm to place the reins over his head. I insert the bit far back into his mouth and gently slip the headpiece of the bridle over his ears and buckle the throat latch after measuring four fingers between Midnight's throat and the strap, as I have seen Jonah do. I reassure the wary animal with calm words, and although he doesn't move, as our eyes meet, his penetrating glare bores into my soul, as if he's trying to communicate something to me.

"What is it, buddy?" I say as I buckle the chinstrap and lead him from the stall. "What seems to be the trouble with you today?" He nudges me away with his nose as if he doesn't want me near, and then neighs as if in distress. I pull in the reins to bring Midnight closer to me for more reassurance. By this time, Jonah is saddling up Thunder. I don't want Jonah to see Midnight's uneasiness . . . or my own, but I briefly wonder if I haven't been too hasty in insisting that I ride the stallion. I've become paranoid about everything in my life, and at that moment, I make a decision I hope I won't regret. I grab the pommel and hoist my body up onto Midnight, trying to ignore his skittish movements.

Jonah has no idea that I'm tugging as hard as I can on Midnight's reins to keep the horse under control as he approaches on Thunder, but it's too late for me to back out and admit that he was right, so I let the horse do his thing. Midnight takes off like a bolt of lightning, and once he senses I'm no longer fighting against him, I can almost feel his tense muscles relax. He heads straight for the riding trail that circumnavigates the little lake on the property. We fly across the wooded trail with Jonah and Thunder in pursuit.

The fall air is cool, but the sun is shining and warms my skin. The syncopated pounding of Midnight's hooves on the hard-packed dirt of the riding path lulls me into a state of complete relaxation, which is why I am completely unprepared for the violent jolt that occurs just as Midnight slows near the turn in the path that abuts the lake. I am utterly disoriented as I feel myself sailing off of his back and into the water.

As I pull myself up from the muddy lake bottom that has serendipitously cushioned my landing, it takes me a few seconds to register the fact that Midnight has either balked or reared up to throw me. It's my own fault. Jonah warned me that the stallion was in a bad mood. But that doesn't jive with the concussive blow I felt right before I went flying through the air. Either Midnight hit something, or something hit us. I see Jonah frantically trying to rein in Thunder who is headed straight into the water towards me, but the massive animal bucks and twists like a contortionist, throwing Jonah off his back like a rag doll. Thunder's nostrils flare and the look in his eyes is one of pure hatred—and that hatred is directed at me. Almost as if Jonah's mount—not my mount—is trying to kill me!

I dive into the now murky water perpendicular to his line of attack and swim underwater as far as I can go, which isn't very far given the fact that I'm in heavy riding clothes and boots. When I surface, I'm stunned to see that Midnight has lunged into the water to block off Thunder's access to me. It suddenly dawns on me. Midnight is trying to protect me! It must have been Thunder who hit us, causing me to fly through the air. The lake water reaches the haunches of the two horses, but they still manage to rear up and assault one another with their front legs in a display of pure brutality, the likes of which I have never before witnessed. Jonah, who is limping and bleeding from his nose, moves towards the two beasts as quickly as he can, while hollering at them in utter panic to stop. It's like a scene out of a horror film. Animals gone wild!

I drag myself out of the water and yell at Jonah to do likewise. And then suddenly, it's over. Thunder completely collapses and Midnight backs out of the water, approaches me, and nuzzles me. There's blood on his chest and neck, but after a cursory examination, I can see they're just superficial wounds.

Jonah approaches Thunder, who has also exited the lake. His head is down, and he looks as contrite as a little boy caught raiding the cookie jar. The look of pure evil is gone from his eyes.

"What in the heck was that?" Jonah looks at me with a totally dazed look. "I've never seen anything like it! Katelyn, are you okay?" He grabs Thunder's reins, and the now docile horse starts nibbling on some shoots of grass by the shore.

"I look a heck of a lot better than you do, Jonah," I say as Jonah wipes the blood from his chin with his calloused palm. "Even though I'm a muddy mess, I'm not limping or bleeding! I should be asking *you* that question."

"No, it's just a bloody nose," he says, "and a bit of a twisted ankle, but I think we're both pretty lucky to come out of that one alive! Honestly, it's like Thunder attacked you! What on earth?"

Unfortunately, I know that it *isn't* something on earth. I had never even considered the possibility that my adversary might inhabit the corporeal form of an animal, but I know that is exactly what has just happened. Abdon has just tried to kill me. My enemy has not only crossed the Atlantic to attack me in America, but he has crossed the line between human and animal hosts. It is terrifying.

Later, after sneaking into the house so Mom can't see my disastrous condition, I shower and retreat into my bedroom. I've made a decision. I can't continue this way. I have to get back to Mont Saint Michel. I decide to send an email to my father begging him to insist that Jackson and I go to France over the Christmas holidays. After the horrible events of the past summer, Dad agreed not to rock the boat about shared holidays, but I decide to tell him the truth.

Well, at least part of the truth. I'm suffering from PTSD, and I feel pretty strongly that going back to the Mount and facing my demons head-on is the only way to start dealing with it. Besides, with my eighteenth birthday coming up on December 8, I will officially be an adult and can make my own decisions if push comes to shove. However, I have no intention of making my mother mad, and maybe it will be in everyone's best interest to have Jackson stay home with her so she won't be alone for the holidays. Hopefully that will be a good compromise.

And so trying to block the terror of seeing Thunder's eyes fixed on me, and realizing that Abdon is still intent on killing me in any way he can, I turn on my laptop and open my email. That's when I get the shock of my life.

Chapter 13

THE PRAYERS OF THE YOUNG WATCHMAN had been heard after all. Brother Thibault arrived one bitterly cold October evening of fourteen hundred and twenty-eight. Nicolas had been alone for over four years.

At first when the monk knocked on Jean's door (Nicolas still could not view the cottage as his), the young Breton was wary. The monks rarely left the abbey and never knocked on his door. And since they were dedicated to the Rule of Saint Benedict, they certainly did not converse with the Montois, except when absolutely necessary. Besides, this was a monk Nicolas had never seen before, and he was mistrustful of anyone he did not recognize. He looked for Abdon in every face and listened for him in every voice.

"*Nozvezh vat,*" the jovial-looking fellow greeted Nicolas in Breton, his native tongue, and then introduced himself: "*Thibault eo va anv.* My name is Thibault." Nicolas looked at him in stunned silence.

"Well, are you going to invite me in, lad? I understand that you have been waiting for me." The man's voice was rich and booming.

"I . . . I . . ." Nicolas could not get a single sentence out of his mouth as he looked at the stout man. His head was tonsured in the manner of the Benedictines, but with his round belly, he looked like none of the monks at Mont Saint Michel, who in spite of the fact that the siege was over, still did not have enough to eat their fill.

"I have been sent to you by Jean le Vieux. I have had a long journey, and would sorely like to rest my poor tired feet! Will you invite me in or not?" These statements were even more astonishing, but Nicolas opened the door and gestured for the monk to enter. However, he did not invite him to sit.

"You seem surprised, Nicolas. Have you not been praying for me to come? I am here to assist you in your duties."

"You have been sent by Jean to assist me in my duties?" Nicolas repeated the monk's own words.

"Aye, that is correct. Jean warned me that you might be suspicious. I assure you, lad, I am not Abdon, and yes, I know all about our adversary, although I have not yet met him face to face." He stopped and chuckled, and added, "Or should I say, spirit to spirit, for I know his corporeal form changes often."

"Jean sent you?" Nicolas repeated. "How is that possible? Jean died four years ago."

"Have you forgotten the power of the keys?"

"What do you mean?" Although Nicolas could understand the words this man of the cloth was speaking, he could make no sense of them.

"The time keys. Before he died, Jean traveled forward in time to the present. He just spent several weeks with me tutoring me in all that it means to be a Watchman, and then he returned to your time."

"But how did *you* get here? With a time key?"

"Alas, no. I have no time key as you have. I came by foot, clear from Finistère, which is why I am so weary . . . and hungry," he said as he patted his belly. Finistère was the nethermost region of Brittany, the heart of Breton culture, which is where Nicolas also called home.

"I still do not understand. Why did Jean not tell me of such a journey he took to find you? He would not have left me comfortless. Before he died, he would have told me that you would be coming. He would have prepared me."

"That I cannot answer, but perhaps he did not have the opportunity to tell you."

"What do you mean?"

"He explained to me that the Archangel had given him specific instructions to seek me out and tutor me on the very morning you and all the Montois were preparing to defend the Mount from Abdon's invasion in the year fourteen hundred twenty-four. What did he call it? Operation Dark Moon? And I had been waiting for him to come because I had been prepared. I had heard the Archangel's voice. Jean told me it had been made known to him that his life would end the very night he returned, and I suppose that is what happened. Am I right?"

"Yes, you are right. He died the night of Operation Dark Moon," replied Nicolas, without giving any of the tragic details.

"Well, then, I assume he never had the opportunity of speaking with you that day because of the frantic preparations. Or perhaps he simply did not dare tell you what his fate would be. If you had known he would die, you would have made choices to protect him, which might have resulted in a different outcome of Operation Dark Moon."

"Yes," Nicolas admitted. "If you are who you say you are, and if what you say is correct, I don't think I would have been able to properly do my part that night. I was already preoccupied with Katelyn's well-being. Adding worry about Jean might have been too much. It makes sense now . . . but this is all difficult to understand."

"He agonized over you, Nicolas. He explained to me in detail all that had occurred with the young girl from the future, Katelyn Michaels, including your personal feelings for her, and he was hopeful that her plan to rebuff Abdon's attack on the Mount would be successful. In any case, he explained that because of her raging illness, the girl would have to be returned to her time, and he fretted for your well-being. He worried that without him and without Katelyn, you would be despondent. And so, that is why I am here. You see? Jean did *not* leave you comfortless. He sent me! I have been called to take his place as a Watchman."

Nicolas stood staring at the monk with his mouth wide open. In spite of all the information that Brother Thibault had given him, the young man was still wary. Richard Collins, and consequently Abdon, would have known every single detail that Thibault had given. And besides, there were still some things that did not make sense.

"I fear you remain dubious of my identity," Brother Thibault said, looking around for a place to sit.

"Can you blame me?" Nicolas said, still not ready to offer the man a chair in the home of his beloved mentor. "Jean never told me anything about you, and neither did the Archangel, yet here you are claiming to be a Watchman. You have no key, and no key was left with me to prepare for you. What would you have me think?"

"I think you are just as Jean described: extremely cautious about sharing any of the mysteries of this hallowed place. That is our calling, to protect the great secret of this Mount. In fact, Jean told me that you did not even trust Katelyn Michaels with that information, so you concocted an elaborate story to convince her that if she didn't help you save Mont Saint Michel, her country, America, would not exist as it is in her future time." At this statement, Nicolas felt the blood rush to his face. It was true. He had not even trusted Katelyn, the only woman he had ever loved.

"And as for the key," the portly fellow continued, "Jean explained to me that only a handful of the Watchmen have ever been given time keys. Their power to change the course of human events, to interfere with man's God-given right to make choices for himself, is far too great for them to be distributed arbitrarily. They have not been necessary to protect the secret of the Mount except for in these turbulent times. To my knowledge, and from what Jean explained to me, you, Jean, and Katelyn are the only three Watchmen who have received that privilege. But just to assure you that I am indeed who I say I am, I will tell *you* the secret of the Mount. If I were Abdon or one of his emissaries, or even Lucifer himself, and knew what I am about to tell you, I would certainly not be revealing myself to you. I would not need to, for *I* would control the power of the stones."

And so, Brother Thibault recounted in the exact phrasing Jean had used to explain the great secret of Mont Saint Michel to Nicolas, a secret which had been protected for generations. It was a secret that had to be kept not just from other humans, but especially from those fallen angels, those followers of Lucifer, who had been cast out of heaven before the beginning of time, for if they knew the secret, they would have power over all mankind.

"Now, have I established that I am not Abdon? May I sit and rest my weary feet?"

"Yes," said Nicolas as he embraced Thibault and then pulled out the stoutest chair from the table that he could offer him. "May I apologize for my less than warm welcome," Nicolas said. "Indeed, I have learned to be mistrustful of everyone. I am so grateful to have you here, and you are right. I *have* been praying for someone to come. I had all but given up praying for guidance, so I am overjoyed. I do not know how much longer I could have gone on all alone. But I fear my elation does not squelch the many questions I still have of you."

"Have you a cup of cider and perhaps a scrap of bread to offer your humble servant?" Thibault said as he sat on the chair that had been proffered him. Its timbers creaked in agony under his weight. "I fear my chair is as unwelcoming as you, my boy," he chuckled.

"Well, kind sir, Jean may have told you of our penury of past years. I dare say that the wood of that chair has not been called upon to bear up a visitor of your . . ." Nicolas hesitated, in an attempt not to offend.

"Oh, just say it, lad. Fear not to hurt my feelings, for I have heard all of the words, and it is not as if I am blind! Stoutness? Girth? Breadth? Size? Mass? Encumbrance? Heftiness? Yes, I know them all. And they are well-deserved descriptions, and I come by them honestly, I fear, for I am a lover of food. Pure and simple."

"Well, it is a good thing you didn't come five years earlier, then," said Nicolas. "Yes, my dear new friend. You would not have fared well on Mont Saint Michel back then."

"Quite true, my boy. 'Twould not have been a pleasant thing for anyone around me to see. Brother Thibault deprived of food. All I can say is that I am certainly grateful that the Archangel did not require my assistance during the years of the siege, of which Jean did inform me, for I fear that Thibault without food is worse than no Thibault at all!" he said with a gleam in his eye. Nicolas laughed out loud. It was a marvelous feeling and a marvelous sound.

"And now, about that bread and cider? And as I eat, I shall answer all of your questions."

A scrap of bread and a cup of cider were about all that Nicolas had to offer, for since he took his meals at the abbey, his cupboards were all but bare. However, he managed to scrounge up a suitable repast for his new companion. When Brother Thibault had settled in, Nicolas peppered him with a litany of questions.

"I still don't understand when or how Jean could have left Katelyn's side on that day? He was with her in the house and he would have had to go to the abbey to use the time key."

"Oh, it wasn't that difficult. While the Widow Mercier was tending to your delirious Katelyn, he took a brief leave of absence from her side—just the time it required for him to walk to and from the abbey. Although he spent several weeks with me, he returned to the exact time he left, so it would have only been a matter of fifteen or twenty minutes that he was absent."

"But it still doesn't make sense," Nicolas continued. "The time keys only work in the proper keyholes, the jobber's marks, and those are in the abbey. My keyhole is in the Guest Hall, Jean's is in Saint Martin's Crypt, and Katelyn's is in Notre-Dame-Sous-Terre. So if Jean traveled forward in time to tutor you in the present, then he would have come forward to Saint Martin's Crypt. And if that is the case, he could have come to see me here on the Mount! And how would he have been able to travel in his weakened condition all the way to and from Brittany to visit you?"

"Well, lad, there are a few things he told me that he obviously had not told you. Again, perhaps because he worried that if you knew what would happen in the future, you might make different decisions. He could not have that happen. The fact is that many, many years ago, when he was living alone on the Mount, he was instructed to travel to several different locations in this vast land of ours. One of those trips was to Brittany, specifically to the Landévennec Abbey in Finistère, where I have been a cloistered monk for the past twenty years. His first trip there was long before my time. While there, he carved his keyhole in the stone of the abbey chapel for his use at some future time. I do not know that he knew when he would be using it, only that he was doing as the Archangel instructed."

"So you mean, his time key took him directly to your abbey? Directly to you . . . just a few weeks ago?"

"That is correct, lad. Although he left from the abbey here on the Mount, his time key took him to Landévennec. And then when he returned to Mont Saint Michel, he left from Landévennec and ended up here. I do not know how it works, but I do know that it is the Archangel who controls the time and place to which you are taken when you use your key. You still have to have a keyhole to go to any place other than here, but you do not have the power to just go flitting about as you wish."

Nicolas knew about that. He had tried to use his key to go forward in time to find Katelyn, and nothing had happened.

"And I must say," Thibault continued, "Jean's arrival was well-timed for me because like the abbey here on the Mount, Landévennec is a Benedictine monastery, and I was getting mighty tired of living the Rule of Saint Benedict. That was my dear mother's idea. That I become a monk, I mean. She thought I would learn the discipline she was never able to teach me. 'Tis not as if I have anything against Saint Benedict, mind you, but twenty years of living his rule has let me know that *my* best way of serving God is not through deprivation. Can you just imagine the trouble I got myself into there?" he asked as he patted his substantial girth. "As I have indicated, I am not good at curbing my appetite, and I am even worse at curbing my tongue! The rule of silence was almost impossible for me to bear. The only thing that kept me going was my visitations from Saint Michael who assured me that he had need of my special talents and skills, and that I would know what to do when the time came."

Nicolas knew all about that kind of message.

"And just as I was giving up hope," he continued. "Jean came and took me out of the monastery. I was not one of the abbot's favorites, that is for certain. He was rather pleased when I announced that I was leaving the order. These past few weeks constitute the most fun I have experienced in my entire life! Even the miserable journey to get here was exciting." He laughed in such a merry-hearted manner that Nicolas was soon unguardedly laughing along with him in spite of the hint of sacrilege the merry monk's words engendered.

"So, I am not quite sure what your presence here means," said Nicolas as his guest pushed his chair back from the table and waddled into the larder where Nicolas had retrieved the small meal.

Thibault lifted dishes and peered around pots, obviously trying to see if there wasn't some other morsel of food he could enjoy. "Are you going to join the monks in the abbey or are you going to stay here with me?"

"Heaven forbid, my boy. No. I am now a *retired* Benedictine monk, if there has ever been such a thing. The good Lord knows me for who I am and mercifully will now allow me to serve Him in a different fashion. I am simply n t cut out to go without keeping my belly full . . . or my thoughts reined in." His boisterous laugh nearly caused the house to shake, and Nicolas felt his heart dance with happiness. Laughter. It was such a simple thing, and yet one that Nicolas hadn't experienced in a very long time. It was healing and cathartic and life-affirming, all rolled into one simple gesture. After so many long years of sadness and loneliness, this beautiful, wonderful, delightful soul had been sent to relieve the young Breton's distress. Surely Michael *was* aware of his aching heart after all. Nicolas offered a silent prayer of gratitude to the heavens, and to Saint Michael specifically.

"And I already have some ideas about how I will be able to fill these empty cupboards for us. You see, before my mother convinced me that my lot in life was to be a Benedictine, I already had a trade. I am a skilled blacksmith. 'Tis true that my skills were appreciated at the monastery, but here, I shall use them to provide us with income. And," he added, "I am an expert cook. I will put some meat on those skinny bones of yours, lad. In addition, I am here to assist you, Nicolas. I shall be watching the Mount, while *you* now embark upon a journey of your own."

Nicolas tried to interrupt to ask what on earth Thibault meant by that statement, but the jovial fellow didn't even take a breath before continuing his sentence. "I have had my fill of traveling, I can assure you of that. And the brigands that are out and about throughout our beloved Brittany? Why, 'tis a disgrace, it is! 'Tis a wonder I arrived here in one piece. The English have done nothing to improve life for the poor Breton and Norman peasants, and it is time for us to take back our lands."

"I am to take a journey, you said?" Nicolas rushed in with his question.

"Why yes, of course. That is why I am here, lad. Remember when I said that Jean had traveled to several places to make keyholes?"

"Yes, I was about to ask you about that, but you didn't give me the . . ."

Thibault jumped in before Nicolas finished his sentence. "And it involves your beloved Katelyn, Nicolas. Yes indeed, laddie. I bring you good tidings of great joy, just like the heavenly hosts who announced the good Lord's birth. Oh, now, do not think I am being irreverent, although that is one of the many accusations my dear abbot had against me. No, I am certainly not comparing myself to God's glorious angels, but I think you will be happy with the news I bear. It will not be long before you see your cherished wife. That is, if she is willing to see you again!"

Nicolas sat with his mouth wide open again. This man . . . this wonderful, glorious man . . . was simply full of delightful surprises.

Chapter 14

THERE IT IS ON MY IPAD. A NOTIFICATION from Facebook that 'Le Breton' has messaged me. There's no picture with the profile, but I know no Breton other than Nicolas. I feel the blood drain from my face and I get lightheaded. I recognize the symptoms of shock, so I quickly lower my head between my knees.

No, this isn't possible. Just stop the wishful thinking and get yourself under control!

Then it dawns on me: it cannot possibly be from Nicolas. This is Abdon's doing. The monster who has already tried to kill me earlier today via horse trampling is now moving on to emotional torture. I'm not certain which is worse.

The blood starts rushing again and my racing heart threatens to explode, but I force myself to raise my head up and take some deep breaths. My brain tries to instruct my index finger to tap on the message, but my finger won't respond. It takes me several attempts before I'm finally able to open the message. That's when I really go into shock.

My darling Katelyn, I read. *I know you will be shaken when you receive this message in such an unconventional fifteenth-century manner, but I assure you, it is genuine. Just to confirm that I am who I say I am, cast your mind back to the day I retrieved you from the beach after you had been kidnapped by the Godons. When I got you back to the house and into your bed, I told you I had been wrong about you, that you were the bravest woman I had ever known. You asked me to look at your wounds, and you instructed me how to sew them up with that unique filament you had brought from your time. Or remember the night of our nuptials. We were left alone in the house. I went back to my bedchamber, and then you called me into your own chamber to help you remove your wedding garments. I touched your neck, and . . . then Jean came up the stairs. Or how about when Gaspard and I got you back to the farmhouse after Collins' dog had bitten your foot as we were escaping from the Ardevon bastille? You asked me if the skin was broken on your foot, and I bandaged it with strips of fabric from my shirt. Then we shared what you called a 'sandwich' made from the foodstuffs we had taken from Collins. I could go on, but I think you will realize that no one but the two of us would know those facts. Remember what Jean taught you? The evil ones cannot see our actions unless they are in our presence, and they cannot read our thoughts. Nor can they travel back and forth in time. Remember, to get to your time to try to stop you from coming back to save Mont Saint Michel, Abdon had to change mortal hosts for six hundred years!*

Yes! This *is* my Nicolas. He's right. No one could know those facts but the two of us. A feeling of intense warmth washes over me. It dissipates the emptiness that has been left inside me by the loss of both Nicolas and Jean, and it calms the pure terror from the incident at the stables earlier today. A sense of intense love surrounds me, and for the first time since I returned from 1424, I don't feel alone. But how is this possible that Nicolas . . . got on Facebook? I read on.

I hope you are well. Oh, how I have missed you and longed for you, Katelyn. For you, it has been but a few short months since we parted, but for me, it has been over four years. More than four years alone, without Jean . . . and without you.

I gasp as I process this fact. Nicolas has been all by himself for more than four years. It is hard to fathom. I wouldn't have been that strong. I wouldn't have survived alone for that long.

Katelyn, the Archangel has need of you once again. I hope he has prepared you, for I have no understanding of what our mission together is. I can only tell you that in spite of the great success of Operation Dark Moon, I once again fear for the safety of the Mount. France is without a legitimate king, and the English are poised to take over the whole of France. If this happens, I fear our enemies shall once again threaten to seize and destroy Mont Saint Michel. But the worst part is that I have no idea of where Abdon is. It is much better to know who your enemy is than to see him in every familiar and unfamiliar face. I have been on guard every single moment, and I fear he is cultivating a host who will have even greater power than Richard Collins. For these long years, I have prayed that he has not found you or harmed you.

I understand what Nicolas means. It's exactly what I've been doing. But unlike him, I *have* unfortunately crossed paths with Abdon, and I wonder if I will be able to keep it together until I can once again be with someone who understands my paranoia. I continue reading.

We have need of you here, Katelyn. We have need of you to save France and to return our occupied lands back to the throne of France. We have need of you to strengthen our weak Dauphin. I do not comprehend how you are to do this. I know only that you and I will be called upon to take a long journey.

And so you must get to Mont Saint Michel. I know the Archangel will open up a way for you to convince your family that you need to come here again. I know it will not be an easy task, especially after the condition in which they found you when I sent you back to them. But you are smart, Katelyn, and you are resourceful—the most resourceful person I have ever known. You will find a way to come, and I will be here waiting for you. I beg you to reply to this missive, even if you do not yet have the answers as to when you will come. The Archangel has allowed me to travel back and forth in time to send and receive these messages.

His confidence in me is moving. After all, I certainly wasn't very smart or resourceful when I first got to 1424, and back then, Nicolas wasn't reluctant to let me know how he felt about my lack of resourcefulness! But I *had* redeemed myself. I *had* found a way to save

Mont Saint Michel. However, a sparsely populated tidal island is not all of France. Nicolas is speaking of saving ALL OF FRANCE. It is an entirely new proposition. I am somehow supposed to help Joan of Arc save France. I mean, honestly! Doesn't the Archangel have someone a tad more qualified than I am?

Then a verse in Corinthians comes to my mind as soon as I express self-doubt: *But God hath chosen the foolish things of the world to confound the wise; and God hath chosen the weak things of the world to confound the things which are mighty.* Well, if God wants foolish and weak, He has come to the right place! I continue reading Nicolas's message, savoring every single word.

You may wonder how I conceived of this unconventional manner of contacting you. You taught me well in your twenty-first century ways, Katelyn. I remembered that you had spoken of a way that people all over the world communicated with each other using the magic boxes. And so, when I came forward to your time, I began casually asking people if they could think of how I could contact an American tourist girl I had met. It took some time for me to understand, and it is still incomprehensible and miraculous to me, but a kind employee at the inn where I am lodging allowed me to use his magic box, which is connected to what you call the 'internet.' That very patient gentleman helped me set up what he called an 'email account' and then a 'Facebook profile.' Then he taught me how to get on what he called the world-wide web, connect to Facebook, and do a search for you. Can you imagine my joy when I saw your image appear before me? You were alive and well! It was pure joy! It has taken much time for me to find the correct letters on the tapping box to create this message, but time is something of which I have plenty. For me, this whole manner of communication is incomprehensible, but I am told that in your time, most people know how to do these things. Your century is amazing. So full of miraculous inventions. Now, my friend here has told me I can check his box every day to see if you have responded.

I actually laugh out loud as I try to picture Nicolas typing on a keyboard. Joy! Imagining that in my mind is a moment of pure, unadulterated joy, something I haven't felt for so long. Just like the joy he felt at seeing my picture on Facebook.

Now I best warn you, Katelyn, for I am not blind to the reality that you enjoy a certain level of comfort. I can't help but giggle at his words. I think about how furious Nicolas was with me when I first went back in time and complained about everything: the food, the clothing, the lack of hygiene, the lack of bathroom facilities. He thought I was a spoiled brat, and actually, from his perspective, he was right. I acted like a spoiled brat.

We are in the late months of the year 1428, and it is winter here, so bring warm attire and footgear. But it must not appear too strange or call attention to us, for we will not want to be conspicuous. You will be required to ride a horse for our journey, and it is best that you come with apparel to disguise you as a male. You know, like Kallan Mikkeldatter? I can give no other counsel except that I trust you will think of other items that might be of assistance in our task. Perhaps you are already aware of what we are to do, and you can enlighten me. *I hope that is the case.*

My mind is already reeling with thoughts of everything I need to take that would fit within the constraints of time travel and within the space of a large backpack! I will have to be a shrewd packer.

And Katelyn, I bear some good tidings. We have another Watchman. Another comrade has arrived to assist us in the cause. He is a jovial fellow, a former Benedictine monk from my region of Brittany. He has done much to brighten my life, and he will stay vigilant at the Mount while you and I make our journey somewhere to the east, to lands of which I know nothing.

It makes me happy that another Watchman—one who seems to have a great sense of humor, at that—has been called to join our little band of brothers, particularly after considering what it must have been like for Nicolas to be all alone. I am happy. Nicolas is happy. It feels so, so good to feel completely happy again. Yes, I know there will be problems. Yes, I remember what it's like living without the comforts of the twenty-first century, but I have all of those comforts now, and they haven't brought me happiness. True happiness doesn't come from stuff. It doesn't even come from having a toilet and a hot shower. No, happiness comes from others. It comes from positive relationships, from having a sense of purpose, and from serving others. Maybe I'm becoming an adult in more ways than just my chronological age. And then I smile as I read the final line.

I am awaiting your reply with great anxiety and anticipation, wondering if you are safe, and if your heart is still with me and with the Mount. N.B.

After finishing the final lines of the message, I sit there and try to figure out how I'm going to tell my mother that my heart *is* with Nicolas le Breton on Mont Saint Michel.

Part Two

…the watchman see the sword come…
Ezekiel 33:6

…she is delivered to the sword.
Ezekiel 32:20

Priant à Dieu, qu'avant qu'aye vieillesse
Le temps de paix partout puist avenir
Comme de Cueur j'en ay la desirance
Et que voye tous tes maulx brief finir
Tres crestian, franc royaume de France!
Tres crestian, franc royaume de France!

My pleadings to God are that before I grow old
Tales of peace everywhere shall one day be told.
'Tis the wish of my heart, 'tis my fondest desire
To witness the end of the enemy's fire
On this noble kingdom, most Christian of lands,
To see France, roy'l kingdom, return to French hands.

Poem written by Duke Charles of Orléans
during the Hundred Years' War Era

83

Chapter 15

THE DECEMBER WIND IS BITING AND HEAVY with moisture as I walk across the drawbridge to enter the village street of Mont Saint Michel. My hair is piled up under a red velvet cap, and I pull the cap down low over my ears and forehead. It is exactly six o'clock in the evening. I had been forced to do a bit of finagling to arrive at this exact time—like pretending I had a leg cramp so that we missed the earlier shuttle to the Mount. The tourist rush is winding down. Far more people are headed back down the street to leave the Mount than are entering the courtyard. As I look up at the portcullis above me, I feel two completely conflicting emotions: joy and fear.

First of all, I am overjoyed that I was able to obtain a blessing from both of my parents to make this trip. Soon, I will be with Nicolas again, and the thought makes my heart sing with joy. Getting here was no easy task. I had no choice but to put my persuasive skills to the test, especially with Mom. I *had* to come. Nicolas had sent for me, and that meant the Archangel had sent for me, so I had to find a way. When I first suggested the possibility, Mom went crazy.

"You've got to be insane," she said to me. "After everything that happened to you last summer in that ghastly country? You want to go back? Katelyn, if you want to see your father, then he will just have to come here. And you can quote me on that. I don't give a fig about what the courts say. Besides, how could you even think of abandoning your poor mother at Christmastime?" She looked at me in that accusing way she had, which always made me feel guilty even if I hadn't done anything wrong. It must be a 'mom' thing. I don't know, but she's got it down to a fine science.

But I wouldn't be deterred. I told my mother that it wasn't about being with Dad for Christmas but that it was all about my emotional health. I convinced her that the only way for me to get over my Post Traumatic Stress Disorder was to go back to the source. You know, like getting back on a bike after you've fallen off. I informed her I didn't think I could move on with my life until I had faced my demons. And of course, that's where the fear I'm feeling right now comes in, because little does she know that a simple little catch phrase like 'facing my demons' has a whole new meaning for me, because I'm pretty sure I'm going to have to face my demon all right. And it's a genuine demon in every sense of the term—Abdon.

As for my dad, he was thrilled to have me come for Christmas. The only way my mother would agree to it, however, was if Jackson stayed with her. She simply could not face being all alone for Christmas, and I certainly don't blame her for that. And of course, another of her stipulations was that Dad pay all of my expenses, which he was more than happy to do. I still think he carries a lot of guilt about breaking up our family.

To sweeten the deal, I also convinced my mother that I didn't want a single thing for either my birthday or for Christmas other than her permission and her blessing to spend the Christmas holidays with Dad in France. The fact is that I am now an adult. I am eighteen years old. I tried not to make an issue of that and acted like I still required her permission, but legally, I can make my own decisions now. She knew that, but I had no intention of hurting her, and so I didn't play the 'adult' card—just the PTSD card.

In addition, I assured her that I would come home and finish my senior year of high school minus the drama of the first semester. That might be hard. I know that whatever happens during my mission with Nicolas, I have given my word. I must and will return to my mother, and with a new attitude. For at least another five months. Then after I graduate, who knows? I don't know what my future holds. Or would it be better to say that I don't know what the past holds for my future? But I do know that this calling or vocation as a Watchman is not something that's just going to disappear. And that kind of thinking makes my brain and my heart hurt, so for now, I will just try to deal with the immediate future (or past).

Mom's final stipulation is going to be a bit of a challenge. She told Dad that he had to accompany me to Mont Saint Michel and not let me out of his sight. I don't know how literally she meant that, but somehow Nicolas and I are going to have to find a way to meet without my dad and Adèle making it a foursome.

When all of the arrangements were made for me to fly to Paris, I begged Dad to let me come to Mont Saint Michel at the beginning of my visit and then to drive back to Paris to celebrate Christmas in their apartment. He wasn't too thrilled about the idea of picking me up at the airport in the late morning of December 20th and then driving straight to Mont Saint Michel, but I insisted. I told him that the only way for me to enjoy Christmas was to get the demon business out of the way first.

So he arranged to take a week off of work, and here we are. I'm exhausted after a ten hour flight to Paris and a three and a half hour drive from the airport to Normandy, but I can't complain. After all, this is what I asked for. And, I was not only civil to both Dad and Adèle in the car, in spite of being tired, but I actually enjoyed Adèle's company. I can see why Dad fell in love with her, and that's saying a lot. She is charming and cosmopolitan, but still down to earth. She's trying very hard to have an authentic relationship with me. When I think back about how grumpy I was the first time she brought me here, I have to admit, I'm embarrassed.

During our drive, I express a genuine desire for Adèle to share with me every bit of information she knew about Mont Saint Michel. I've tried to read everything I could get my hands on about the Mount, but who knows? Maybe something she tells me in the car today will come in handy. Like what she told me the last time I was driving here with her that really did come in handy: the business about the fat pig being thrown over the walls of the embattled Carcassonne. I'll have to ask Nicolas if that pig ploy worked, because although I got a general report of my Operation Dark Moon from the recording Nicolas left on my iPhone, I didn't get many of the specifics. I'm anxious to hear more details about my battle plan.

As I walk along the village street, pulling my suitcase towards the Du Guesclin Hotel, the pain in my right ankle shoots up my leg like a fire-tipped arrow. It is a constant reminder of my last trip to Mont Saint Michel, and also a reminder that there are evil forces that do not want me here. I stumble slightly on the uneven cobblestones but then force myself to concentrate on walking without a limp.

My breathing starts to speed up, and I feel my heart hammering so hard against my ribcage that I feel like it's going to bolt out of my chest and run for cover. Dad must sense that I'm nervous, because he places his hand on my shoulder and squeezes it lightly. I'm looking at every face and listening to every noise. It gives me an idea of how the Secret Service must feel when they're protecting the President of the United States. I scan the crowds around me for a monk's robe, although I'm pretty sure that Nicolas has figured out how to dress for the twenty-first century by now. I also find myself looking for the Goth crowd, although I'm also pretty sure that if Abdon is still using his Goth host of last summer, he would have considered changing his appearance. I see no Woolrobe or Gothman.

The questions dash through my mind like a herd of deer darting away from oncoming traffic. Can Abdon leave his human host at a whim to enter a stallion in faraway America? Can he jump back and forth between hosts and continents? Are there other fallen angels with him? Does he know I'm here? I feel that horrific flood of fear inside my chest. It's the rush of adrenaline starting to build up in my body, ready to spill out into a full-fledged panic attack. I know what it is, and I *have* to control it. I am Katelyn Michaels. I am a Watchman. I am weak, but I have been chosen to confound the wise and mighty. The Archangel has placed his trust in me and so has Nicolas. I can do this. I must do this, and I must do it to pay homage to Jean le Vieux, who gave his life to protect me.

I force myself to breathe more slowly. Dad is looking at me with a quizzical look in his eyes.

"Katelyn, are you all right?"

"This is hard for me, Dad," I admit honestly. "It's tough to come back here, but I know I have to do it. I'll be okay. Thanks for being here with me."

"Katelyn, I don't know what answers you think you'll find here, but I want you to know that I'm here for you. I'll do whatever you want me to do."

"Well, for now, let's just get to our hotel, have a good meal, and get some sleep. I'm tired after my long trip. We'll see what tomorrow brings." I have to spit the sentences out of my completely dry mouth. I don't know if I can actually eat anything, and I'm certain I'm not going to be getting much sleep, but what else can I say? "Well, actually Dad, I'm waiting for my beloved husband who was born in the early 1400s, and I'm also a bit nervous about the fallen angel who wants to kill me." No, I can't exactly go with that explanation, so I just put my arm around Dad's waist and give him a hug.

When I replied to the message I received form Nicolas, I explained to him that I wouldn't be able to get to Mont Saint Michel until December, but I couldn't give him the exact date until a few weeks later. I also expressed my amazement at his resourcefulness in finding a way to contact me using twenty-first century technology. This was his reply:

Katelyn, I wish for you to know that in these past four years, I have done everything in my power to make contact with you, but it was not the will of the Archangel for me to use my key to travel to your time until I was so instructed. Having now been allowed to come forward in time, you should know that it was your tutoring in the use of your magic boxes that allowed me to find you. You were an inspired teacher, and nothing, including my ignorance of such twenty-first century wonders as this world-wide spider web, would have prevented me from finding the means to communicate with you.

Oh, how I have hungered these long years to learn if your medical practitioners were able to heal you of such unyielding injuries. You shall never comprehend the joy I experienced upon receiving your reply and learning that you are well. Surely, 'twas the most magnificent missive ever to have graced my days. And now, as thoughts of being with you once again begin to flit through my mind, I can barely contain my emotions. I have waited these long years, and to delay our meeting for a few insignificant moments is but a brief inconvenience. Do not fear for the day or the hour of your coming. I will be here regardless of when you arrive, but Katelyn, when you come, cover your hair with a cap of the color and fabric of your wedding dress. I will find you. I will come for you. I will always come for you."

I never had the occasion to tell Nicolas about my all-time favorite movie, *The Princess Bride*. I mean how do you really explain a movie to someone from the fifteenth century? Well, since I *made* a movie in the fifteenth century, I guess I could explain it, after all, but *The Princess Bride* will be for a future conversation. And I intend to have that conversation, because I actually downloaded the movie onto my laptop. I hope Nicolas and I will have the time to watch the movie together. In spite of the fact that Nicolas is not familiar with the film, he unfailingly leaves me with Westley's promise to

Buttercup. He 'will always come' for me. No other words could tug at my heartstrings so completely.

Yet as I read his instructions about the cap written in such couched terms, it also confirmed to me that Abdon was present on the mount. Nicolas wanted me to disguise myself from Abdon. Then, even though I sent Nicolas several other emails, I didn't hear back from him. That made me panic. Had Abdon done something to prevent Nicolas from contacting me again or intercepted our messages? I can't let my mind go there. I have faith in Nicolas *and* in the Archangel. When I finally had my travel plans finalized, I was understandably leery about writing down the exact date and time I would be arriving, so I followed his example and figured out a way to encode the information in my final email.

And so now, here I am. Waiting for Nicolas. Wearing a red velvet cap reminiscent of that magnificent gown Madame Mercier lent me for my wedding—the gown belonging to her deceased daughter. Just touching the velvet fabric brings back memories of that night . . . the night I became Nicolas's bride. But a bride in name only. I remember the feel of his finger grazing my neck as he undid the ribbons of that red velvet dress, which I could not undo myself because of my injuries. The night I may have *become* his actual wife, had that moment not been interrupted by Jean.

As I think about those moments that are seared into my brain for eternity, I wonder if my meeting with Nicolas will be awkward. Will our relationship pick up where it left off? Or will there be distance? It has only been a matter of months for me since I last saw Nicolas, but for him, it has evidently been over four years! His words indicate that his feelings haven't changed. But I'm nervous. Why am I nervous about seeing Nicolas again?

I offer a silent prayer that Nicolas will find me soon, and I pray even harder that Abdon will not try to prevent us from meeting, because I know he is here. And then I realize, I am *not* nervous about seeing Nicolas. I am anxious, elated, even euphoric about seeing Nicolas. No, my nerves are not about Nicolas. It is Abdon I'm worried about. And I'm not just nervous. I am scared to death.

Chapter 16

NICOLAS STOOD ON THE LOWER RAMPARTS that looked directly out over the walkway from the bridge where the horseless wagon—which he had learned was called a shuttle—dropped off and picked up the visitors to Mont Saint Michel. From this vantage point, he could see every individual coming or going. He was wearing a navy blue wool sweater, a matching knit scarf he had wrapped around his chin, and a blue and white knit cap, which the sales clerk had told him was typically Breton. He didn't know if Katelyn would grasp the cap's significance, but it didn't matter. It covered his blond curls, and the cap, coupled with what he now knew were called sunglasses, completed his disguise.

On his first journey to the future, Nicolas had not seen Abdon and had been unhampered in his quest to communicate with Katelyn, with the help of many willing villagers and visitors. However, on the second trip—before Nicolas had altered his appearance—as he was preparing to leave the restaurant with the internet, Nicolas had spotted Abdon in what Katelyn had called his 'Goth' persona. He was looking into the restaurant window, and when their eyes met, Nicolas bolted out of the establishment through a back entrance.

Once he realized that Abdon was still frequenting the Mount, Nicolas had done everything he could to change his own appearance on each of his visits forward in time. He had exchanged some fifteenth-century coins for twenty-first-century currency and had made several purchases at the village store. On each occasion he visited the future, he rotated his purchased garments so that he looked different each time. Abdon, however, had responded in kind by altering his appearance as well. And so it was a constant game of cat and mouse.

From that point on, Nicolas not only disguised himself but refrained from sending any more messages to Katelyn, concerned that Abdon would be able to intercept them. The Breton didn't understand all the nuances of how this unusual means of communication functioned, so he didn't want to take any risks. However, he had nonetheless visited his kind friend to retrieve Katelyn's messages—which he immediately deleted—sent to his new email account and he was pleased she had grasped the need for caution, for she had found an ingenious way of letting him know the exact time and date on which she would be arriving. She had written in her final communication: *Nicolas, I am coming. We will be staying in your countryman's hotel. I told you the month in my first email. For the hour, think of the number of stitches you gave me in my arm, and double it. For the date, it is the exact number of stitches in my thigh. I'm hoping that after four years, you will remember, but we talked of it several times. Remember how I told you that you did as good a job as any twenty-first century doctor would have done?*

Her allusion had been brilliant, and of course he remembered. In fact, he would never forget. It was one of the hardest things he had ever had to do—insert a needle and that strange thread into the flesh of his brave, amazing Katelyn. Oh yes, he remembered. Nine stitches in her arm and twenty in her leg. Abdon would never have known that fact. And so he had known that Katelyn would be coming on the twentieth day of December at the eighteenth hour of the day, which was six o'clock in the evening. She and her parents would be staying at the Hotel Du Guesclin. Du Guesclin was a famous Breton knight who had been successful in fighting the English during the early years of the Hundred Years' War, and there was no other inn on the Mount that fit her description.

Nicolas had carefully perused the village today for signs of Abdon but had seen neither hide nor hair of their adversary. Nonetheless, the fact that Abdon was unseen did not mean he was absent. Abdon was there . . . somewhere, and it was unsettling not to know what to look for. The fact that it was winter, which meant that it was not unusual for several layers of clothing to enrobe the visitors, worked both as an advantage and a disadvantage. Anyone, *including* Abdon, could hide under a plethora of garments.

When Nicolas spotted the young woman in a red velvet cap descend from the shuttle on the bridge, he immediately knew it was Katelyn, even though her features were completely enveloped by her cap and scarf. He would know her anywhere . . . under any circumstances. He knew how she carried her body and how she moved her arms. He knew that tilt of her head and how she turned to look around her. The strangest sensation of heat filled his chest and then spread throughout his entire body until he felt like shedding the woolen clothing protecting him from the cold winter gusts. Just the sight of her had an astonishing physical impact on him. It had been four years since he had felt such reactions, and he had all but forgotten Katelyn's effect on him. If he had been unconstrained by fears of her safety, he would have rushed to her and embraced her on the spot. But that, he knew, was out of the question.

She was in the company of an older gentlemen and a very pretty woman, obviously her father and her French stepmother. This was the woman Katelyn had told him about. The woman for whom she had harbored such ill-will and outright hatred. As he watched, he saw Katelyn help the woman lift her valise from the shuttle, and his heart skipped a beat. From the way Katelyn was interacting with the woman, he could tell there was no animosity between the two of them. In fact, he saw signs of actual affection. Katelyn had found a way to transform her destructive feelings, and this was gratifying to Nicolas. Her hot-headed temper had abated. She had learned to forgive and had unmistakably mellowed. But then when he saw her slap away her father's hand as he attempted to pull her valise, which appeared to be outfitted with a set of wheels—oh, weren't the inventions of the twenty-first century marvelous?—Nicolas was also reassured that she hadn't lost her combative or independent nature. She was still the same Katelyn, just a wiser and more mature Katelyn.

He watched closely as she strapped a smaller bag on top of her rather bulky valise, which had an extendable handle. It seemed like a hefty burden, but Katelyn managed to maneuver the load without too much difficulty. And then his heart dropped as he discerned a hesitation in her gait. She stopped, readjusted her valise to pull it with her left hand, and then continued walking—with a slight syncopation in her stride. Although she tried to compensate for the slight limp, it was evident to his knowing eyes. She bore irrefutable reminders of her last visit to Mont Saint Michel. Nonetheless, just the fact that she could walk after the horrific injuries she had sustained was a cause for rejoicing, and he pronounced a prayer of gratitude for the miraculous twenty-first century curative proficiencies.

As Katelyn and her parents entered the outer courtyard, Nicolas moved up the ramparts where his body was blocked by the stone walls, but he could still peer down over the village to observe their progress. He could tell Katelyn was unsettled, because she continually looked around her, but he himself was unsettled. He scanned the entire area, even looking into windows of the buildings lining the street for signs of Abdon. Where was he? Because of Nicolas's concerns for their adversary, and also because of Katelyn's parents, Nicolas had no intention of approaching her in public, and so when he saw the trio enter the lobby of the Du Guesclin Hotel, he relaxed for a moment.

As soon as Nicolas had received the information about where Katelyn would be staying, he had done his reconnaissance. He knew the layout of the small hotel. There was an access door from the ramparts directly into the hotel's restaurant. The big picture windows of the restaurant offered an unimpeded view out over the bay, and consequently, a view from the ramparts into the hotel.

Nicolas stood there for several minutes, debating about whether or not to enter when he saw a hotel employee leading the trio through the restaurant. They were headed straight towards him. Nicolas turned immediately to face the sea as they exited and stopped at the first door to the right of the restaurant entrance. This was clearly one of the hotel annexes, accessed from a tiny accordion door that opened directly onto the ramparts. A narrow set of stairs led to rooms one level up. Nicolas couldn't believe it. He could not have planned it better if he had tried. Clearly, this was one of the Archangel's tender mercies.

The hotel employee was explaining to Katelyn's stepmother that there were two keys for their rooms: one to open the door to the stairs, and the other to open their individual rooms on the landing at the top of the staircase. He then offered to take her hand luggage and invited her to follow him up the staircase.

"Dad," said Katelyn, "that staircase is so narrow. No room for two-way traffic, so why don't you carry up Adèle's bag, and then you can come back for your luggage after the clerk comes back down. I'll stay here with the bags." Nicolas pulled the scarf up around his face to leave only his eyes showing, removed his sunglasses, and then dared to look to both the left and the right to see if there was anyone approaching on the ramparts from either side. No one was in sight.

"You're right, Katie. There's not much wiggle room. I'll just be a jiff!" Nicolas could hear Katelyn's father wrangling with the bag to fit it through the narrow space left between the wall and the opened accordion door.

"Take your time. I'm not going anywhere!" she replied.

Brilliant! Thank you, Katelyn, thank you, thought Nicolas as he slowly turned to look at her. Four long years and here she was, just a body's length away from him. It took every jot of self-control he had not to rush to her and enfold her in his arms. She turned at just that instant, and in spite of the fact that only his eyes were visible, the look of elation in her own eyes was easy to read. She recognized him.

Nicolas put his finger to his mouth, and pointed up the stairs. He knew it wouldn't take long until Katelyn's father and the hotel clerk returned.

"*Ma chérie,*" he whispered. "when you are certain that your parents are settled in their room, quietly slip back down the stairs and open the door for me." He turned back around and moved further away from the door.

At just that moment, the hotel clerk and Katelyn's father returned.

"Mademoiselle," said the employee, "you go up first, and I will carry your bag for you."

"*Merci,*" said Katelyn, and Nicolas could hear the three of them navigating back up the staircase. He turned again and scanned the area for signs of Abdon. He saw a young family with a babe in arms and a toddler approaching him from the upper ramparts, but there was no one else in sight. Again, he scanned all of the building windows visible from his vantage point, but didn't see anyone looking out at him. He hoped he would not have to wait long. He felt vulnerable out here all alone, right in front of the door that led to Katelyn's room, the person on this entire Mount who needed the *most* protection. He did not wish to call attention to himself, and especially not to her.

He was grateful when he heard the clerk skip back down the stairs, pull the accordion door shut, relock it, and enter back into the main building through the restaurant entrance. Hopefully, Katelyn would be able to come back down the stairs swiftly and open the door without her parents hearing anything.

The waiters and waitresses inside the restaurant were commencing their preparations for the evening meal, and Nicolas kept his back to them, trying to appear like a typical tourist admiring the view and interacting with a gregarious seagull sitting atop the rampart wall. However, it was getting dark, and he knew he could not linger much longer. Finally, after what seemed like time without end for him, he heard the sound of the accordion door's bolt being manipulated. He casually sauntered away from his seagull comrade, as if he had lost interest, and moved to the inside of the rampart pathway, so that he could slip inside the stairwell unseen as soon as Katelyn maneuvered the door open.

Without a word to her, he crept past her up the staircase as silently as he could, avoiding the centers of the steps, which he had already learned by listening, made a creaking sound. He didn't say a word to Katelyn, nor did he wait for her to relock the door and follow him back up the stairs, knowing that she could provide an excuse for her presence there, but there was no amount of explanation he could give to justify his own presence to anyone who confronted him. He prayed she had left her door cracked open, as he did not know which of the rooms on the landing was hers. She had.

He pushed the door open slowly and slithered through the narrow space just as Katelyn's father opened the door to his room.

"Katelyn," he called out. "Is that you?"

"Yes, Dad. I thought I might have left my camera on the ledge down here. I pulled it out to snap a photo, but I guess I slipped it back into my bag," she called up to him, with what to Nicolas sounded like a voice as calm as a windless day. She was amazing, this

Katelyn of his. "I obviously didn't look in my carry-on very well. I'll look again," she added as she reached the landing.

"Let's go look for it now," he said as he stepped out of his room and onto the landing. "There was a young man loitering out on the ramparts while we were coming up to the rooms, and he could have snatched it." Nicolas could hear Katelyn cough and clear her throat.

He hurtled into the washroom, and actually leapt behind a curtain that enclosed the bathtub just as Katelyn and her father entered her room. She made quite a bit of noise as she rummaged through her affairs and talked out loud to herself. Nicolas knew she was making as much noise as she possibly could to cover any sounds she feared Nicolas might make.

"Now, where could I have put that darn thing?" she chuckled. "Dad, I think I'm losing my mind! For heaven's sake, I just had it in my hands, but I can't think what I did with it. Oh, here it is," she finally said. "Hallelujah. It wasn't stolen."

"Good, Katie. I know how important your camera is to you. That would have been a rotten way to start out your vacation. What time would you like to go down to dinner? I bet you're starving."

"Dad, I think I've changed my mind about eating. I am so exhausted, and we did have a big lunch. I think I'll just have a hot shower and go to bed."

"But dear, you've got to eat something," her father countered.

"You know what?" she said, and Nicolas could hear a crinkling sound. "I've got a couple of granola bars. I think I'll just munch on these and call it good. You go and have a nice dinner with Adèle. Just the two of you. By the way, thanks for not making me share a room with you and Adèle. That would have felt just too weird for me. Anyway, the truth is, right now, I'd rather sleep than eat. I bet I could sleep for fifteen hours straight. I didn't get a wink of sleep on the plane, and I don't think I could sit through a two-hour French dinner. Besides, I heard the clerk tell Adèle that they don't start dinner service until 7:30. By then, I'll be sound asleep."

"You're sure, Katie?"

"I'm sure. I just want to sleep. Let's plan on meeting in the morning for breakfast. I'll set my alarm and knock on your door at 9:30. Is that too late for you two?"

"Well, it is vacation. Adèle might be able to sleep in, but I can't think of the last time I got up that late."

"You should go have an early morning walk and explore the Mount before all the tourists arrive. After all, this is your first time here, Dad, and that's the time to explore—before the hundreds of tourists arrive. But I know my body. I need to make up for all that sleep I lost. Trust me, I will be a much happier camper if I get my sleep." Nicolas had no idea what she meant by being a happy camper, but he was certainly impressed by how she was handling the conversation.

"Okay, if that's what you really want. Are you sure you'll be okay here? All by yourself? You seemed nervous when we first got here."

"You're right. I was nervous, but I feel totally safe here. After all, not only will I lock my room behind you, but the door to the stairs is locked as well. Be sure and lock that door when you go to eat. That will make me feel doubly secure. And please, Dad, don't be the typical father and try and check on me when you come back up from dinner. I'm not a kid. I'm an adult. I'm not going to let anyone in my room, and there's no way anyone could break in."

"Okay, Katie, I won't."

"And will you guys try to be quiet when you come and go tonight? I've got my earplugs, but those stairs are kind of creaky."

"I've got it. You don't want anyone to wake you up. I promise. We'll be quiet. I love you, dear," he added, and Nicolas heard him kiss his daughter on the cheek. "I'm so happy you wanted to spend the holidays with us, and I'm proud of you, Katie. You have been so kind to Adèle. It means a lot to me . . . and to her. You've grown up, and I just want you to know how grateful I am to have you as a daughter."

"Thanks, Dad. I'm glad I came, and I appreciate everything you've done to make this trip possible for me. I hope you know that I don't take it for granted, either. I know how much all this costs, and I'm grateful for you. And I love you too, Dad. Now, you go and have a great night with your beautiful wife, and I'll see you in the morning."

As Nicolas heard Katelyn's father close the door and then heard her turn the key in the lock, he prayed that Katelyn would be able to keep her promise. He hoped she *would* be seeing her father in the morning.

Chapter 17

I CAN HARDLY CATCH MY BREATH. THIS IS the moment I have been anticipating for nearly six months. After locking my room door, I walk into the bathroom. I open the shower curtain and for what feels like forever, we stand there looking at each other . . . without moving a muscle. Nicolas had told me in his message that for him, our separation has been for over four years, but he doesn't look a day older. Except no monk robe this time around. He's dressed in twenty-first century clothing, which seems odd, but he is my same Nicolas. I look into his eyes . . . those eyes that had first attracted me to him the very first day I met him. His earnest eyes. The most expressive brown eyes I have ever seen. Now, they are baring his soul to me. Nicolas still loves me.

He removes his hat and scarf and allows them to fall to the surface of the tub. I reach my hand towards him, and our fingers touch. It's more than electrical energy that passes between us; it's like an unbreakable connection. He grabs my hand, steps out of the bathtub, and then takes me in his arms. His sweater feels like wool spun on heavenly looms. I breathe in the smell of Nicolas and it's more powerful than the most perfect scent ever created. He smells of happiness and joy, of completion and infinity. I weave my fingers into his hair, and time stands still as his golden curls wrap around my fingers, tying me to him for eternity.

"Katelyn," he whispers. "My darling, beautiful Katelyn."

"Nicolas," is the only word I'm capable of pronouncing.

He lifts my chin and his lips press into mine for just an instant, and then he touches them lightly to my forehead, my cheeks, my chin, and then buries them in my hair. Although our lips meet for only the briefest of moments, it's everything I've dreamed of, everything I'd hoped for. Actually, that's wrong. It's more than I dreamed of, beyond anything I could've imagined. It's magic and wonder and safety. It's comfort and love in a form I've never before experienced. It's like coming home after being lost, like drinking in the water of life after nearly dying of thirst. It's the purest form of total devotion I've ever experienced.

He takes me by the hand and leads me out of the bathroom. With my head still spinning from his kiss, I stumble and bump my shoulder into the wall, then quickly sit down on the edge of the bed so I don't fall to the ground. Nicolas kneels on the floor next to the bed, and takes my hand in his once again.

"Katelyn," he whispers to me, "words cannot express the joy I feel at seeing you again. I did not know if I could go on without knowing you were safe and well. And now that I see you and feel you in my arms, I know that all I have dreamed of, all I have imagined, is indeed my truth. You complete me and heal me in ways you will never know. You are my beacon in the darkness and my one true song of redemption."

I bring his hand to my lips and kiss each of his fingers.

"Oh, that you and I could simply bask in the emotions of this moment," he continues, "but I cannot allow myself to follow my natural inclinations. There will be a season sometime in the future when we will have both the time and the freedom to consider the ramifications of our relationship, but unfortunately, now is not the time, and this is not the place. As intoxicating as it would be for us to be together here, alone and uninterrupted, the reality is that your father and stepmother are next door, Abdon is hovering about somewhere ready and prepared to hinder our mission, and we have a commission to carry out. 'Tis one which requires our undivided attention."

So it's true. Abdon is here. I'd felt that presence of evil as I entered the village walls. It was like walking in pitch-blackness. I had felt certain someone was following me but couldn't see anything around me in the obscurity. It had almost been as if I could feel his vile breath on my skin. Even my dad had sensed my discomfort. Nicolas has confirmed my worst fears. Abdon is still here, and he's still trying to stop me. The warmth in my soul is replaced by a chill that changes everything. Nicolas is right. This is neither the time nor place to indulge our personal longings.

"Katelyn, we must leave immediately and go to the abbey before it closes so that we can return to my time. The Archangel has been merciful. A special holiday sound and light display opens tonight, and the abbey is open two hours later than usual. Otherwise, we would have been forced to wait until the morrow, and I fear what havoc Abdon might have waged. We must depart just after your father and stepmother go down for dinner, so they will not hear us leave. Pack what you will take with you. Also, I advise you to change your appearance, as will I, so that we look different from when we arrived here."

And so, in spite of my complete and total exhaustion, and in spite of my complete and total desire to rest in Nicolas's arms, I force myself to get up off the bed. He silently helps me as I lift my opened bags onto the bed. I have so many questions, but I understand that questions will have to wait.

From my wheeled suitcase, I quietly remove two backpacks, a large one for my clothing, sundries, a wide assortment of nonperishable food items (I haven't forgotten what it is like to be hungry in the fifteenth century), and some dollar store items that will make a long journey in less than suitable conditions more palatable. The smaller backpack is just for my electronic gear. I hand the large one to Nicolas and then efficiently sort through my belongings, handing him the items to pack. I already know exactly what I'll take, because I planned it out, knowing we'll be traveling in wintertime. I cautiously place my electronics into the smaller backpack, which will be covered by a long, brown cloak that'll fit right in with fifteenth-century fashion trends. I know. I've done my research.

Then I pull out a pair of brown leather riding boots from my suitcase. I'm going to miss my sneakers, but I don't think I'll be able to swing wearing them in fifteenth-century France like I did last time, and Nicolas warned me to bring male clothing to make me less conspicuous. With that in mind, before I left the States, I purchased the most comfortable and warmest pair of boots I could find that still look like they could pass for medieval footwear. I remove my shoes, place them back into my large suitcase, and prepare to pull on my boots, but Nicolas stops me. He pulls my hand away from my right foot, and removes my sock. When he sees the scars on my ankle, he closes his eyes and lowers his head. I see him quickly wipe his eyes, and then he pulls my sock back up and helps me pull the boot over my foot.

"I am devastated about your foot, Katelyn," he whispers. "I know the worst part of that injury came from your trying to save my life after the attack by the Godon soldiers out on the sands of the bay. I shall never forget your bravery."

"It's no more than you would have done for me," I counter, as I pull on my other boot. "Nicolas, I have no regrets about what I did, and I know that you, like Jean, would do anything to protect me."

"I hope you truly believe that, because it is the truth. I just pray that we will not be obliged to test that assertion," he replies. "The only thing that assuages my guilt about your injuries is that I was successful in getting you back to your time so that your doctors were not only able to save your life, but to make it possible for you to walk again. I wish to hear the entire story about your return to your time, but . . ."

"Yeah, I know. Not now. There's no time. Frankly, there's not that much to tell. I didn't regain consciousness for a couple of days, and I guess it took a while for anyone to find me. Notre-Dame-Sous-Terre isn't on the main tour circuit, you know. I'm pretty lucky I didn't die," I explain as I stuff my hair into a slouchy brown cap, reminiscent of my Kallan Mikkeldatter's cap, but this one is actually stylish in my world . . . and clean!

"'Tis not luck, but divine intervention," Nicolas concludes, as he finishes fitting all of my items into the backpack. "After all, for centuries, pilgrims have come here to petition Saint Michael for his healing blessings, and there is no one more important to him than you, Katelyn, for your work is not done. 'Tis Michael himself who kept you alive until you were able to obtain assistance. When I sent you back, I feared initially that you would die from the fever and poisons that had entered your body from your wound, and then I worried that if you did survive, your foot would have to be amputated. And I know you, Katelyn. You would detest being less than able-bodied."

"That's for sure," I admit as I check to make certain I haven't forgotten anything. "I would not have been a happy camper about that." He looks at me quizzically, and I add, "That means I would've been pretty grumpy, and you've seen what I'm like when I'm grumpy. It wouldn't be pretty."

He laughs softly and then says, "Well, then we are doubly blessed that you are able to walk. 'Tis a veritable miracle. Is it painful for you?"

"I wish I could say that it doesn't bother me," I reply as quietly as I can, "but the truth is that it pretty much hurts all the time. But, little by little, the pain gets less, and there are times now when I don't even think about it. And I agree, I think it's a miracle too. I'm alive, and I can walk. Later, I'll show you my lovely scars from your handiwork. I don't think any twenty-first century doc could have stitched me up any better than you did! I think you need to go into medicine, Nicolas," I say as I lift the smaller backpack up onto the bed and verify that all the zippers are closed. It's small, but it's still heavy. I hope I've thought of everything I might need. Since I had no idea of exactly what we'd have to do on this expedition back in time, I tried to think outside the box, and I've got some pretty great stuff. Then I check to confirm that I have the chain around my neck with my enseigne, along with two other important souvenirs from the fifteenth century.

"Ah, I shall look forward to seeing my, what do you call it? Handiwork? But now, it would seem, is perhaps not the best time."

"One day, we'll have to *make* time for us, Nicolas. This is torture," I say as I touch his cheek. "Have I ever told you that I love you? I do, you know. I love you, Nicolas."

"Those words are like healing balm to my heart, *ma chérie*," he whispers as he clasps my hand for a brief instant, and then lets it go. He pulls off his sweater, and stuffs it into my backpack. He is wearing a brown sweatshirt underneath. "And they are words I hope to explore at a later time. Now, we must prepare to leave. I hear your father and stepmother opening the door now." He motions for me to be quiet.

After we hear them open and then relock the door at the bottom of the stairs, Nicolas suggests I use the bathroom before we leave, and when I'm through, I come out with his hat and scarf and suggest he use the facilities as well. He has obviously learned how to use a modern bathroom, because I hear the toilet flush and then the water running in the sink. Boy, am I ever going to miss toilets. Unfortunately, I know that from sad experience.

"Nicolas, I have so many questions," I say when he comes back out.

"And I wish I could answer them all, but alas, I fear there is no time."

"No time," I say, "when we can *travel* back and forth in time. It's so ironic. I guess 'no time' will be our new mantra.

"Mantra?" he asks.

"A mantra is like a word or phrase you use that sums up the situation." Nicolas still looks unsure, so I add, "Like how I say 'okay' all the time, so we used it as one of our code words at Ardevon?"

"Okay," he says, smiling as he draws out each syllable of 'okay.' "It makes my heart sing to hear that word again, Katelyn. I haven't heard it pronounced in four years. And now, we have a new . . . mantra? Is that the word? 'No time.' That will be our code then. Now, do you have everything?" he asks, as he stuffs my bed pillows under my covers to make it look like I'm asleep in the bed. He's been watching way too much TV.

"Well, I wish I could fit the toilet in my backpack, but I don't think it'd work, even if I could take it," I say with a smile. But I'm not kidding!

"You have not lost your strange sense of humor. I can see that you are still my same Katelyn," he says as he wraps his navy scarf around my neck. "As I recall, you were not impressed by our arrangements for your private needs, and I'm afraid that hasn't changed. What has changed, however, is that at least we are not starving on the Mount. That does not mean you will have access to the same foodstuffs as in your time, but I think you will be pleasantly surprised with our new Watchman, Brother Thibault. I suppose we should not call him Brother, as he is no longer a monk, but that is how I address him, and he does not object. He has a talent for the preparation of food," Nicolas says as he pulls a black beanie out of his pants pocket and pulls it down over his hair, being careful to tuck up all of his blond curls.

"We actually have a chef?" I say. "A cook? No way!"

"After your last experience, this will be like heaven for you, Katelyn. And not only does Brother Thibault cook, but he has been able to provide food for us by exchanging his skills as a blacksmith. In fact, he has established a workshop in the garden behind the cottage, and the villagers and monks come to contract his services."

"Ahhh," I say. "*Of course* he's a blacksmith. I just happen to need a blacksmith, and so, *voilà!* We have a blacksmith," I add but don't elaborate. Another blessing from the Archangel.

"You need a blacksmith?"

"Yeah, I'll tell you about that when we get back to the cottage. But, Nicolas, it's going to be really hard for me to go to Jean's house and not have him be there."

"I understand 'twill be difficult for you, Katelyn. I have had four years to get used to his absence. But we must be grateful for the blessings that have been extended to us, particularly that we are together again," he says as he picks up my suitcase, zips it closed, and places it on the luggage rack. He has left the room neat and clean. I just hope I will be back in this room at 9:30 in the morning to meet my dad and Adèle.

"You're right. That is the greatest blessing of all: to be with you, Nicolas, and I'm anxious to meet Brother Thibault," I say as he lifts the large backpack and slings it over one shoulder. "Nope, like this." I readjust it for him and guide his other arm through the strap. I know it is way too heavy, but hey, I'm going to take as much as I possibly can. After all, as I've said before, there's no Walmart in fifteenth-century France!

"Another amazing invention from your time," he says about the backpack as he adjusts its straps. "Like your valise on wheels. One day, I hope to be able to spend more time with you in this century to discover all of your wonders. Once again, we never have enough time." Then he tries to take the small backpack from me as well.

"No, I've got it," I say and slip my arms through the straps. I ask him to help me place the cloak over the backpack. I want my electronic gear as protected and hidden as possible.

"Okay, let's roll," I say and turn off the lights.

I lock the room door and we silently creep down the stairs, avoiding the creaky center of the steps. When we get to the bottom and get the door opened, I motion for Nicolas to stay close to the building wall and to start moving towards the upper ramparts. Since the staircase door is so close to the restaurant door and picture windows, I know we can't afford to stray even an inch in the opposite direction, or we could be spotted from inside the restaurant. I have no idea where my father and Adèle are sitting, but it is critical for us to slip away unseen.

I reclose the door and lock it as quietly as possible, and then follow Nicolas, who is walking slowly so that I can catch up with him. I smell the tangy air of the sea and actually relish the brisk air that whips around my face. It momentarily re-energizes me, and for just an instant, it distracts me from the fear of what lies ahead. When I reach Nicolas, I ask him to stop briefly so that I can put the room key into one of the zippered pockets in the backpack he is carrying. I don't want to risk losing it since I will need it when I get back.

The walkway on top of the ramparts is three to four feet wide, and I walk on the seaside next to the battlement wall that serves to prevent falls into the abyss below, while Nicolas stays on the village side. We hit the first set of stairs that leads to the upper ramparts. We can get all the way to the abbey by taking the ramparts, but there will be dozens of steps to climb. That's when I begin to feel the fatigue set in, and my ankle is aching. It's not surprising, seeing as how I haven't had any sleep in about forty-eight hours.

"I know you are exhausted," Nicolas says, as he looks around us, "but we have no choice but to hurry." It's dark, although we have a little bit of light from the nearly full moon above, and so far, we haven't crossed paths with another soul. The Christmas tourists are either all at dinner, or they are at the abbey seeing the sound and light extravaganza.

"Yes, I know," I say. "There's no time." I wasn't kidding when I said that was our new mantra.

"Please, let me take your bag," Nicolas pleads.

"No, I can do it. Let me just take your arm." I grasp his arm with my left hand, my good hand, and we begin the long trek up the steps. The steps are the bad news, but the good news is that the ramparts follow the contour of the island, and we have curved around so that we are no longer visible from the entrance to the hotel dining room. If Dad and Adèle happen to come out of the restaurant, they won't see us.

After yet another set of steps, we've nearly reached the point above the village where the ramparts form a semi-circular watchtower. This spot served as a tactical defensive position for Operation Dark Moon, but now serves as a viewpoint for tourists to watch the incoming tide. As we climb the final step, it's as if we are hit by a wrecking ball, which sends us both flying across the stone pavers. I feel the rough surface of the stones rip across my cheek like coarse sandpaper, and then when my head crashes into the rampart wall, for the second time for me on the stones of Mont Saint Michel, everything goes black.

Chapter 18

FORTUNATELY FOR NICOLAS, BUT unfortunately for Katelyn, she prevented him from being injured. As the impact sent her crashing into the rampart wall, he collided into her and was cushioned by her body. Nicolas heard the thud as Katelyn's head hit the stone parapet, and that sound ignited a super-human fury in him that took his foe by surprise. Nicolas slipped his arms out of the straps of Katelyn's pack, grabbed the attacker who had head-butted the couple, and flung him as far away from Katelyn as he could, as if he were but an insubstantial bit of flotsam.

By the light of the nearly full moon, Nicolas could see that although Abdon's hair was still jet black, he had it slicked back and was no longer sporting the black eye or nail paint of his Gothman persona. But Nicolas had no trouble recognizing him. His pernicious breath infected Nicolas's lungs, and his malevolent eyes seared into his own like the very flames of hell themselves. Nicolas didn't hesitate for a second. He lunged at Abdon as the stunned assailant attempted to get to his feet. He grabbed him by the shoulders, and pressed his back into the bulwark. But just when Nicolas thought he had control of the situation, Abdon lashed out with his right hand, making contact with Nicolas's upper left arm and slicing through his flesh. Nicolas hadn't seen a knife, and yet the searing pain was enough to confirm to him that Abdon had some type of concealed weapon.

Nicolas jumped back from Abdon, tripping over Katelyn's motionless legs and falling backwards, hitting the chain link fence that surrounded a deep well in the center of the fortified tower. Abdon charged him and just before making contact with Nicolas, Katelyn—who had not moved a muscle since the initial attack—raised her left leg and tripped Abdon, slowing his movement and changing his trajectory. That slight effort on her part shifted the momentum once again, and Nicolas was able to roll out of the direct line of impact and leap to his feet. For his part, Abdon fell nearly on top of Katelyn.

Before Nicolas had the chance to attack again, Abdon jabbed his arm towards Nicolas, displaying the most wicked-looking weapon Nicolas had ever seen. The moonlight glinted off a polished silver blade that extended out at a right angle from Abdon's fist. At first it appeared to grow right out of his hand, but then Nicolas could see that it was attached to some type of metal apparatus that fit over Abdon's knuckles. With his left hand, Abdon simultaneously grabbed Katelyn's right ankle and twisted it viciously, causing her to scream out in pain. Nicolas knew it was her bad ankle, and his fury intensified.

"Back off. You come any closer, Breton, and I'll slice her to pieces," Abdon snarled as he focused his wrath on Nicolas, all the while twisting Katelyn's ankle as she writhed in pure agony. He was like a rabid dog going in for the kill, and Nicolas did as he was told. He was unarmed and unwilling to take any risk with Katelyn being in such a vulnerable position. But while Nicolas drew all of Abdon's attention, he could see from the corner of his eye that in spite of the brutal hold Abdon had of her ankle, Katelyn was fully aware of their precarious situation. Nicolas watched as this astonishing woman, this valiant Watchman who had just been knocked senseless, made the split-second decision that probably saved both of their lives. She bent her left leg—her good leg—and kicked Abdon in the groin with all of the force she could muster.

As Abdon pulled in both his arms and legs and doubled over in pain, the weapon that had been gripped in his right hand clattered across the stone pavers. It landed right at Nicolas's feet and he kicked it out of Abdon's reach. For her part, Katelyn pulled her legs to her chest, grabbed the backpack that Nicolas had been carrying, and scooted to the opposite side of the fence surrounding the well, leaving the battlefield free for Nicolas's counterattack. Fortunately, there were no other people in sight to interfere with what he was about to do. He threw himself onto Abdon's body and pinned the writhing man to the ground.

"Although I have given you a wide berth up until now because I hesitate to harm your human host," Nicolas snarled at his adversary, "you have just made it impossible for me to allow you to continue to inhabit his body."

"You might win this battle," Abdon hissed in return, "but *I* will win the war. I will always be there, and you will never know who I am, or where I am. And I will watch the expression on your face with ecstasy as I kill your beloved Katelyn before your very eyes. Yes, I will take great pleasure in doing that."

At that menacing provocation, Nicolas began punching Abdon over and over in the stomach. He didn't feel the pain in his upper arm, or notice the blood that was dripping from it. In spite of the ferocity of Abdon's attempts to defend himself, Nicolas was more determined, fueled by his rage and the confirmation he felt in his heart that there was no other choice. He knew this was the will of the Archangel. Katelyn had a mission to perform, and Nicolas refused to let this vile monster interfere yet again.

Nicolas punched Abdon in the chest with all of his strength, knocking the wind out of his adversary and weakening his resistance.

It was all Nicolas needed. While the revolting creature gasped for breath, Nicolas succeeded in pushing Abdon's body up against the bayside rampart wall. Abdon once again caught his breath and renewed his efforts to get free, but Nicolas finally managed to get Abdon to the top of the wall. Abdon clawed with all of his might to hold onto the rough stones to prevent Nicolas from pushing him over. Then, with an irrevocable action, Abdon kicked Nicolas hard in the chest, causing Nicolas to fall backwards, but the effort also caused Abdon to lose his balance. With not another sound, not a scream, nor a cry, Abdon himself flipped backwards over the wall.

As Nicolas rushed to the parapet and peered over into the void, he saw it was full tide, and instead of landing on the stony beach below, Abdon's body hit the water. The light of the moon lit the bay, but Nicolas did not stop to see whether Abdon surfaced and was still alive, because he heard Katelyn sobbing behind him. Whether dead or alive, Abdon would not be able to stop him from getting Katelyn into the abbey tonight and down to Notre-Dame-Sous-Terre.

Nicolas rushed to Katelyn and knelt at her side. With tears streaming down her face, she was rubbing her ankle.

"Nicolas," she wept quietly. "Is he dead?"

"I cannot be certain. He fell into the water. Even if he is alive, he will not be able to stop us from getting to the abbey. We must go before anyone comes." He picked up her pack and slung it over his right shoulder. "I hope nothing is broken," he added.

"We'll have to wait and see about my electronic stuff," she said as she shifted her backpack under her cloak. "I think your scarf and my cloak protected it. Besides, my head and shoulder took the brunt of the fall. They sure feel like it, anyway. Good thing I had my hair stuffed into my cap. That probably kept my scalp from splitting open. Just what I *don't* need—more stitches!"

"I am so sorry this had to happen, Katelyn. I have been apprehensive about Abdon and have been on constant alert for him, but I fear he outwitted me tonight. I failed you miserably."

"You certainly did not fail me, Nicolas. You saved my life!" she said as she wiped her eyes and attempted to stand.

"No, Katelyn. Abdon would have gotten the better of us had you not administered that well-placed kick just when you did. *You* are the one who is amazing. Particularly after your terrible fall and then Abdon's torturous twisting of your foot. Where did you learn to defend yourself like that?" he asked as he bent to help her to her feet.

"It's just a little something my dad taught me. He told me it was the best way to protect myself from unwanted male aggression," Katelyn said through her tears. She inadvertently grabbed his upper left arm for support, and he finally felt the full impact of his wound. He winced and groaned.

"You're bleeding," she cried as she examined the blood on her hand illuminated by the moonlight, "and you're bleeding a lot! If that blade sliced all the way through your clothing, it must be pretty bad. We're gonna have to get that looked at immediately before you lose too much blood. Just when I thought we had been spared from more stitches." The sight of his blood seemed to stem Katelyn's tears.

"I hope you packed your magic twine," he said as she shifted her hand to his right elbow. He tried to remain as calm as he could in an attempt to help Katelyn regain her composure.

"My magic twine?" she asked.

"Yes, you know, the one I used to sew your wounds?"

"Oh, my nylon thread. As a matter of fact, I've got something even better," she said. "I've got the real supplies that doctors use. I actually ordered a suture kit on-line, you know through the internet that we used to communicate with each other. You can order products that are then delivered to your home. I ordered all the first aid supplies I could afford." Nicolas wasn't sure what she meant by 'first aid,' but he assumed she meant items to be used for medical purposes. Her last little jaunt in time had given her plenty of incentive to come prepared. "However, it would be foolish for us not to have you looked at by a real doctor. Let's get some help for you, and then we can leave tomorrow."

"Katelyn, I do not trust that Abdon's host is dead. He has uncanny abilities, and you heard him. He will stop at nothing to prevent you from going back with me. Once again, whatever our mission is in 1429, *you* are the key to its success. We must leave tonight, and we have got to get to the abbey within the next fifteen minutes if we want to do that. If I could stitch you up with absolutely no knowledge of how it is supposed to be done except for your own instructions, then you will be able to stitch me up. And to do that, we shall just have to wait until we get back to Jean's cottage . . . our cottage," he amended. "Brother Thibault will assist you. But we cannot take care of it here. We must make haste."

"Yeah, I know," she said, "no time. But seriously, Nicolas, you could bleed to death before we get there. Besides, do you think anyone's going to let us into the abbey with you bleeding all over everything like that? I admit, it's dark out, but you're leaving a trail. Look," she said as she pointed to the drops of blood that covered the stone walkway. "We've got to apply some direct pressure to the wound and get that bleeding stopped. And we've got to do it now. I'll use your scarf. Sit down on the steps and take off your sweatshirt," she ordered as she unwound his scarf from her neck, "and put your head between your knees. Now that you've seen the blood and felt the wound, you're going to get lightheaded and I don't want you to pass out."

"No, I will be fine, Katelyn," he insisted as he sat on the top step, removed the backpack and wriggled his bleeding arm out of the heavy fabric of the garment she had called a sweatshirt. Then, he obeyed her directive and lowered his head between his knees.

"Besides, I am in your very capable hands. Just hurry and do what you need to do."

Nicolas was almost grateful for his injury, for Katelyn's take charge attitude was a radical shift from her earlier tears . . . tears that were justified. After all, her life had just been threatened yet again, and she had sustained not only a blow to the head, but what was probably unbearable distress as Abdon cruelly twisted her damaged ankle. It was another reminder of her courage and ability to adjust to extraordinary conditions, even when in pain. When he remembered the many unkind thoughts he had voiced to Jean about her when she first accompanied him back in time, he felt instant regret. Oh, she had her petulant personality, and that had not changed, but he had never known a female who had as much strength of character or resourcefulness as Katelyn Michaels.

Katelyn unzipped a pocket on the side of the large backpack and pulled out a small square of patterned fabric. "Last time I brought a bandana," she said in a soothing tone of voice, "I used it for the sliced chin Abdon gave my little brother with his chain. Totally déjà vu. I'm going to just put this directly over your shirt for now," she said. "I'll get a better look at the wound later when we get to the cottage." She pressed the fabric directly over the injury and then lifted up Nicolas's other hand and instructed him to hold the makeshift bandage in place while she wound the wool scarf firmly around his upper arm. She tucked the two ends in under the wrapped portion so that there was no knot protruding. "Now, do you think you can get your arm back into your sleeve?" she asked as she pulled out an odd rectangle that made a crinkling sound. She helped lift up his sweatshirt and assisted him in getting his arm back into the sleeve. "Now, let's clean you up a bit with some wipes," Katelyn said as she extracted some small moist sheets from the package, which she used to wipe first his hands, and then her own hands. "Okay, that ought to hold for a while. Please hold your arm close to your body, and try not to move it. We can't afford to have that bandaging job come undone. We'd better get going. Are you okay? Can you stand up? Do you feel like you're going to vomit?"

"No, I think I will be okay," he insisted. "You are the one with the head injury. And you can hardly walk."

"Yeah, I've got a goose egg the size of Rhode Island on my head," she agreed as she rubbed the top of her head. "I could have a concussion and be the one vomiting here very shortly!" He had no idea what a goose egg, Rhode Island, or a concussion were, but he assumed it meant she had a lump on her head. "We're a pretty pathetic duo," she continued as she assisted him to a standing position, while shifting her position so as not to put any weight on her right foot. "Talk about the blind leading the blind!"

"It's dark, but we're not blind," Nicolas said as he hefted up the pack again onto his right shoulder and then hurried over to where Abdon had disappeared over the wall.

"Just an expression," Katelyn explained as she joined him, looking over the rampart, "meaning that neither one of us is in good condition, thanks to Abdon. As much as I hate that evil being, I still can't get it through my head that the Goth might be Abdon's second host who has died from a fall. I'm just glad he fell and you didn't have to push him, though. Do you see him, Nicolas?"

"No, but that doesn't mean he did not survive the fall. The water may have prevented his host's death. Regardless, we know that Abdon will always be around, trying to kill us and preventing us from performing our mission. And if I have to kill his host to protect you, Katelyn, I will. And I shall have no qualms about it. Either we kill his host and make him find another, or he will kill us. But this time, he did not succeed." Nicolas left the wall and strode over to where he had kicked Abdon's weapon. "And it could have been much worse for us tonight," he said as he picked it up. "*Regarde!* Look at this!"

Katelyn took the weapon from Nicolas and examined it as they made their way around the fenced well and started up yet another set of stairs heading towards the abbey. It was made of a smooth silver metal and looked like four finger rings hooked together, with spiked barbs on the top of each of the rings. In addition, jutting out from the side was a small but deadly-looking blade.

"Wow! No kidding," Katelyn whispered as she slipped the weapon over her fingers and then closed her hand into a fist. "This is a nasty little reminder of Abdon's intentions. They're called brass knuckles, by the way, but I've never seen anything like this, with the knife jutting out of the side." As she punched her hand forward, she revealed exactly how deadly the sharp barbs could be if aimed at a foe, and then she jabbed her hand to the side, demonstrating the potency of the short blade. "This is what cut through your clothes and skin. Jeez, we could both be dead," she said as she threw the weapon over the ramparts into the sea. "Sorry, Nicolas. Brass knuckles might come in handy in medieval France, but I could never use any weapon belonging to Abdon."

"I understand," Nicolas said, and then taking a cue from Katelyn's description of their possible physical woes resulting from their confrontation with Abdon, but also from her sense of humor, he added, "Now, let us make a dash for the abbey before we both lose consciousness, vomit, or bleed to death. This is going to be close."

Chapter 19

THIBAULT WASN'T QUITE SURE WHAT TO expect when Nicolas returned one chilly December night with the much-admired Katelyn Michaels, but it certainly was not the sorry-looking couple he saw before him as he opened the door to a frantic knock. By the light of the oil lantern Thibault held to illuminate the scene, he could see that Nicolas had his head down, and his arm draped over Katelyn, who was trying to hold him up. In addition to trying to support his weight, she also had a very large pack hanging from her left arm. She looked like she was on the verge of collapse. Rarely had he seen such a bedraggled duo.

"Hurry, hurry," said the young woman from the twenty-first century, who appeared to have streaks of dried blood on her face, "I'm just about ready to collapse." He had judged her condition aptly! She transferred Nicolas's dead weight to Thibault, who lifted his friend into the cottage. As the girl followed him inside, he noted from the corner of his eye that she was limping severely as she dragged her pack in behind her and pushed the heavy door shut. Either supporting Nicolas had been beyond her physical abilities after suffering the wounds during her last visit to the fifteenth century, or she had sustained a new injury during what had evidently been a turbulent journey to get here this time.

Thibault gently positioned Nicolas in the only chair in the room that had a supportive back and arms, besides the one he knew had been hand-hewn by his predecessor, Jean, for his wife, Marie. Thibault had always found Nicolas's relationship with Marie's chair somewhat odd. He would often find the young man stroking the chair, readjusting its position near the hearth, or even speaking to it, and the lad was adamant that no one ever sit in it. Thibault knew that Nicolas had never known Jean's wife, so he assumed that it was the young man's way of honoring his fallen mentor. It was a piece that had issued from Jean's own hands and heart. The choice of where to place Nicolas was an easy one, for the former monk respected his young companion's views. Besides, he could not judge the young man's behavior, for he himself had a relationship with an inanimate object as well.

Thibault glanced at his cherished mechanical clock sitting on the mantel above the fireplace and noted that it was just past the ninth hour in the evening. Yes, Thibault loved this clock. The impressive timepiece was the only item Thibault had brought with him from Landévennec. It was a gift from Brother Guillaume, his truest friend at the monastery, who was a skilled clockmaker.

The highly regimented schedule of the monks divided between daily work and strictly regulated prayers required accurate timekeepers, and most monasteries had someone who could either build or maintain timepieces, and that someone at Landévennec had been Brother Guillaume. Furthermore, Brother Guillaume had developed his skills into a commerce that benefitted the entire monastery because his timepieces were not only accurate, but they were also exquisitely crafted. His magnificent timekeeping devices were sold to wealthy connoisseurs and brought in a substantial income, which in turn allowed the abbot to provide costlier materials for Guillaume to employ in his trade. Thibault's own skills as a blacksmith had also supplemented the abbey's coffers, but in no way compared to Guillaume's coveted abilities.

When Brother Guillaume had learned of Thibault's departure, he had silently approached his dear friend and from beneath his robes, he had revealed a bundle wrapped in burlap and twine, indicating that it was for Thibault. The monks had learned to express themselves efficiently through a series of hand signals and signs as they lived the Rule of Saint Benedict, which required them to refrain from speaking for much of the day. Then, with his finger to his lips, Guillaume made it clear that Thibault should make no mention of the parcel to anyone, least of all to the abbot.

Thibault had successfully transferred the parcel from Guillaume and concealed it beneath his own robes as he left the abbey. It was not until much later, as he sat for a brief meal along the journey to Mont Saint Michel, that he had dared to unwrap the offering from his friend. When he had discovered the dazzling timepiece, he had felt ready to burst with tears of regret at leaving the Rule of Saint Benedict behind, but he could not weep. He had never been able to weep, even when he wanted to. He just felt his emotions welling up tightly in his chest, making him feel as if his heart would burst. It was much worse than tears.

The clock had survived unscathed from all of the vicissitudes of his difficult journey. Now, he devotedly wound the clock twice a day to ensure its continued accuracy, and twice a day, he thought of his friend Guillaume, wishing him both health and happiness, something Thibault himself had found difficult to feel at Landévennec. So Nicolas had Marie's chair, and Thibault had Guillaume's clock. They were not so different after all.

Thibault's reveries were interrupted by Katelyn's further pleas for assistance. "Can you please get some water boiling? And I need some type of basin or bowl, because I think I'm going to hurl." Then realizing he might not have understood her outburst in her native tongue, she repeated her requests in a strange-sounding, rapidly-fired French.

As she flung her cloak to the ground and removed another smaller pack, Thibault's initial impression was that she was not only bedraggled, but that she didn't much look like a girl either. Dressed in male clothing, she was tall and thin, had hardly any meat on her bones, and didn't have the obvious feminine curves that would normally allow him to identify her as being of the female gender. If not for her high-pitched voice, Thibault would have mistaken her for a waif-like boy. However, when she removed her cap and her silken locks tumbled down well below her shoulders, he caught a glimpse of what must have attracted Nicolas to her. Nicolas, for his part, looked even worse than Katelyn. His eyes were fluttering, his face was as pale as a ghost, and his clothing was covered in blood.

Because of his girth, Thibault wasn't the hurrying type, but he responded with as much alacrity as he could muster. Obviously, Nicolas's journey into the future had not been without incident, as the young man had hoped it would be. The infamous Abdon, whom Thibault had not yet had the displeasure of meeting, had clearly made an appearance ... or the girl's parents had somehow discovered her plans to abandon her family in favor of a jaunt back in time with the charming Nicolas. But judging by the severity of their wounds, at least one of which looked to be caused by a knife of some sort, Thibault felt fairly convinced that his first assumption was the correct one.

He handed a pewter bowl to Mademoiselle Katelyn, who was rummaging through her pack, and then she immediately leaned over the bowl and began emptying the contents of her stomach in the most unladylike fashion possible. It was positively disturbing to Brother Thibault, who was not only unaccustomed to the presence of females, but also preferred to ignore any type of negative connotations associated with the intake of food. It gave his own stomach quite a turn. What a first impression! Then, however, his refined upbringing by his mother set in, and he reverted to his most hospitable self. He turned to block the disturbing display from his eyes and set about to place a pot of water on the fire to boil.

"*Je suis désolée.* I'm so sorry," announced the girl from the future when her stomach-churning exhibit had ceased. She opened the door and placed the recipient of her stomach's contents outside on the street, then came back in and looked up at Thibault with the warmest blue eyes he had ever seen. He immediately melted and forgave her for her unceremonious entrance.

"Do you speak English?" she asked. "I don't know if I have the clarity of mind to find the French words right now. My French is quite a bit better than when I first came to France, but I'm feeling pretty stressed right now, and I'll be a lot more comfortable in my native language."

Thibault had an exceptional grasp of the guttural language because of the English soldiers who marauded throughout his beloved Brittany. The Breton monks had been advised not to take sides in the decades-long conflict between France and England, but instead to do all they could to be cordial to their "guests," so because he was so starved for conversation, he soon became the resident English language expert. But this girl's strange English was nearly incomprehensible.

"Yes," he confirmed, "but I am afraid that I do not understand much of the English you speak. If you will speak slowly and attempt to restrict your vocabulary, I think we shall come to understand each other."

"I apologize for . . . all of this. I think I have a concussion." She hesitated, obviously comprehending that her words meant nothing to Thibault, and tried to explain. "I've had no sleep in fifty hours, and that, on top of a head injury and an ankle-wrenching, all thanks to Abdon, has left me feeling pretty crummy . . . unwell. Then add to that the fact that Nicolas has been seriously injured, and I've had to get him here without either of us losing consciousness, and it's a bit more than I can handle. I'm Katelyn, as I guess you know, and you're Brother Thibault. I'm happy to meet you, but we'll have to save the formal introductions for later. Right now, I desperately need your help."

"What can I do, mademoiselle? Have you need of sustenance?" It was the first thing that popped into his mind. Before the arrival of the two young Watchmen, Thibault had just finished clearing the table from his evening meal, and the sweet aroma of lamb and basil filled the room. In a gesture that had become an unconscious display of his appreciation for all things alimentary, Thibault rubbed his belly, happy from the copious repast he had just consumed. And there was still plenty with which he could put together a pleasant meal for the two, but somehow he didn't think food was on the minds of his young companions.

"No, not now. Maybe later. Now we have more urgent matters to worry about. Can you lift Nicolas on top of the table for me? I've got a pair of scissors, and we're going to cut off his clothes." Thibault understood the first part of her instructions, but wasn't certain what the second part meant. He hefted the young man easily onto the long wooden table while Katelyn continued to search through the large pack she had dragged into the room. Nicolas moaned as Thibault moved him, but then closed his eyes and remained still.

"I need as much light as possible," Katelyn instructed as she laid out a series of objects on a crisp white towel she had unrolled on the table next to Nicolas's body. "Bring me all the lamps or candles you have. And a cup of water, please, to rinse out my mouth," she added.

She placed an odd apparatus around her head, and Thibault gasped when he saw her flip a tiny lever and light appeared. "My Petzl headlamp," she explained, but her explanation meant absolutely nothing to Thibault. Nicolas had tried to prepare him for the marvelous inventions of the twenty-first century that improved the comfort of people in the future. If this was a sampling, then Thibault was surely in for more astonishment.

He brought her the requested cup of water, and then began gathering the oil-burning lamps and candles, placing them where she indicated while she rinsed out her mouth. He watched as she then picked up an instrument, which she indicated was called 'scissors,' and placed her thumb and first three fingers through two handles on a set of opposing blades and commenced cutting through the thick outer garment Nicolas was wearing. Thibault was familiar with a similar cutting instrument with two parallel blades attached by a hinge on top, but Katelyn's 'scissors' were particularly fast and efficient.

By adjusting her head position and the strap around the light apparatus protruding from her forehead, Katelyn was able to direct the beam of light where she wished. She now focused that light on Nicolas's upper left arm. As she cut through his sleeve, Thibault could see a thick band of dark blue wool wrapped around his limb. It was completely saturated with blood. Katelyn carefully unwound it while at the same time moving her fingers in and out of the layers so that she could apply direct pressure to the wound. When she had succeeded in removing the wool band, Thibault saw another piece of fabric underneath. It was saturated to the point that the original color of the fabric was not discernable.

"How much longer is it going to be before that water is ready?" Katelyn asked as she continued to press down on the wound. Her face looked pale, and Thibault prayed that there would be no more incidents of stomach emptying.

"It should not take more than a few minutes."

"Can you take over for me here?" she asked as she indicated his need to press firmly down on the saturated fabric. "Keep the pressure steady. I need to sterilize . . . to wash my hands and my instruments."

Brother Thibault continued to hold the fabric firmly onto Nicolas's wound, but he watched Katelyn as she aligned several small paper squares on the table. Then she picked up some metal instruments and placed them directly into the pot of water, which was beginning to bubble.

"Now, I need you to carefully watch what I do," she instructed, "because you are going to have to do the exact same thing when I tell you to."

He watched her carefully as she went to a basin of water that sat on the sideboard and thoroughly washed her hands up to her elbows using a soapy liquid she pressed out from a small bottle. However, she didn't touch the cloth set there for wiping her wet hands. After that, she opened another bottle of a clear liquid and with a small piece of gauzy fabric she had removed from one of the paper coverings, she applied the liquid to every inch of her hands. She left the two bottles and another piece of the gauze sitting on its paper wrapper on the sideboard.

"I certainly didn't know I'd be using this stuff so darn soon," she mumbled to herself as she went about her ritual. "You're going to have to assist me, and this will not be easy for you. I hope you have a strong constitution. It won't be easy for me either, because I already feel sick to my stomach and because I've never done this, but I *have* read the instructions and watched the procedure on YouTube. Forget about that, I'll explain that to you later. Anyway, Abdon sliced Nicolas's upper arm with a knife. I haven't looked at the wound yet, but it's going to require me to sew the flesh closed, just as if I were sewing a piece of fabric. I have special instruments to help me," she explained, "but it's critical for you to do everything I say. Do you understand?" she asked more a question as to whether he understood her English, rather than as a command.

"Yes, I understand. I will do what is required of me." This *was* one astonishing young woman after all, thought Thibault as he contemplated her ability to handle this trying situation. Except for midwives who assisted the village women in bringing their children into the world, he had never known of a woman attempting to do any type of medical procedure, and this is one he had never heard of. Stitching up flesh?

"Good. I'm really going to need you to be strong. You're going to have to just trust me on this, but one of the important things we know in the future is that only completely sterile items—that means items that have been boiled or washed with a special cleaner—can touch the wound or Nicolas could get very, very ill. That includes our fingers," she explained as she pulled on a set of thin, flexible gloves. Thibault had never seen anything like them. She bent her arms at the elbows and held her hands straight up into the air.

"Now," she continued, "when I tell you to remove the pressure, I want you to cut away his sleeve with the scissors there to leave his arm completely uncovered. Then I want you to quickly carry over the pot of boiling water without touching any of the items inside and set it on the bench next to me. After that, you need to get some clean water and you are going to scrub your hands with the products I used, just as you saw me do." With a nod of her head, she indicated the two bottles on the sideboard.

"Once you do that, you can't touch anything, and you're going to put these flexible gloves on without allowing them to touch anything either. I'm going to put your set of gloves, here on this paper." Thibault also noticed a package she had opened that contained a small curved needle with black thread already attached to it.

"Don't let your gloves touch anything else," she reminded him. "Not the table or any part of your body. While you're doing that, I'll clean the wound with special medicine, and then when your hands are clean and your gloves are on, I'll ask you to dab away the blood with this gauze while I do the stitching. Any questions?"

"*Eh bien*, I think I understand. But do not hesitate to tell me exactly what I need to do."

"Okay," she said, and then added, "Oh yeah, you don't know that word. Good," she amended, "I'll tell you exactly what I need you to do. Are you ready?"

"*Oui*," he confirmed.

"All right. You may now remove the bandage and cut away his sleeve."

Thibault did as she requested, rapidly ascertaining how to employ her strange scissors. As he pulled away the saturated bandage and sleeve, he felt Nicolas flinch as his arm moved. Thibault was amazingly undaunted at the sight of the thick blood gushing out of the wound, which appeared to be about as long as his middle finger. He wrapped the blood-soaked bandage into the sleeve and threw the bundle into the corner of the fireplace, well away from the platform on which the boiling pot sat.

"Good," said Katelyn, "now turn his arm so that the wound faces straight up." This time Nicolas didn't shift, and Thibault checked to make certain he was still breathing. He was. It was probably a good thing he was unconscious, for Thibault couldn't imagine what it would feel like to have a needle enter one's own flesh. The good news was that the blood was not gushing now, but just oozing.

"Now bring me the boiled water and go wash your hands."

Thibault used the towel on the sideboard to protect his hands as he carried the hot vessel to the bench. As he proceeded to scrub his hands the way he had seen Katelyn do, he watched as she poured a liquid from a little bottle into the wound, and used the gauze to clean away the blood. Her face turned even paler than it had been, but she clenched her teeth tightly and continued to flush out the cut. When her patient's wound had been cleaned enough so that the two edges were clearly visible, she unfolded a large white sheet of what looked to be some type of paper. In the middle of the paper, a hole had been cut out, and she placed this hole strategically over the wound. Once the paper was in place, she used a pair of pincers to retrieve two sets of what looked like her scissors, but which were entirely made of metal and were much smaller. She placed these two instruments onto the paper that extended over Nicolas's arm onto the hard surface of the table, and then picked up one of the instruments, which Thibault, who was now pulling on his gloves, could see had blunt, rather than sharp ends. She clamped the two ends of the instrument around the curved needle.

"Ready?" she looked up at him and asked.

"I am ready," he confirmed.

"Please pick up some of the gauze and dab the blood away so that I can see the edges, particularly in the middle." After he had done so, with her left hand, Katelyn brought the edges of the wound together. "Can you hold it just like this for me," she asked. "Don't squeeze too hard. Just hold it lightly so that the edges of the skin touch."

Thibault felt his stomach lurch as he looked at the raw flesh, but if Katelyn could do this with her injuries and no sleep, he could do it too. She aimed her lamp directly at the wound and then used her scissor clamp to insert the needle into the center of the gash, going through both sides of the skin. Then she tied a knot in the black thread, and cut the thread with the other instrument, which was indeed a pair of scissors.

"Why don't you just do a continual looped stitch," he asked, as she dabbed away the blood to inspect her first stitch.

"Well, that would be a lot easier, but it isn't as secure. With each stitch tied off individually, it eliminates the worry of having all the stitching come out if the final knot doesn't hold."

Her hand was surprisingly steady as she continued to put in individual stitches, working from the middle out to each end. After the first few stitches were in, she told Thibault he could release the skin and he instinctively knew how to dab away the blood so that she could see exactly what she was doing. They made a good team, and Thibault felt a sense of pride in the fact that together, they had been able to perform this act of service for Nicolas. A wound like this could maim someone for life, or even result in death. Nicolas had been fortunate that Katelyn had known how to curb his blood loss.

The entire procedure took some time, but when they were finished, Katelyn had put in twelve individual stitches. Although it was cold in the cottage, Thibault could see that she was sweating and clammy, and all of the color had gone out of her face. She sat down on the bench, put her head between her legs, and then actually stretched out onto the narrow bench, so that she was lying on her back.

"You're going to have to finish the bandaging, Brother Thibault, because I don't think I can do anymore. And you need to make him swallow one of these capsules, and make sure he takes one every twelve hours." She touched an odd brown tube on the table laid out by her other supplies. "Oh yeah, I'd better open it for you, child-lock and all," she said as from her supine position she lifted the tube and used both hands to remove its white lid.

"Just tell me what to do, and I shall do my best to follow your exact directions," he promised.

Her voice was getting weaker and weaker, but her instructions were clear. "There is a little bottle that says Betadine on it. Squirt it all over the wound, and then tear open the large square of paper. Inside is a gauze pad . . . a bandage."

She waited for him to locate the bottle and bandage, nodded as he held them up. She waited while he applied the liquid, and then continued. "Fold the bandage in half, but don't touch the side that will go on the wound. Then wrap the wide roll of gauze over the bandage and all around his arm several times until it is secure. You can cut the gauze with the scissors. There is a little green spool of tape . . ." she paused, knowing he didn't understand that word. "The green spool has a narrow band of fabric which will stick to the gauze. Wrap it all the way around his arm on the top and bottom of the gauze, and overlap it. It will stick together and hold the bandage in place. But first, please bring me another basin, because I'm going to throw up again, and then I think I might lose consciousness."

And she was right. She did both.

Chapter 20

WHEN I WAKE UP, I INITIALLY HAVE NO IDEA where I am. The last thing I remember is walking through the outer courtyard of Mont Saint Michel with my father and Adèle. I recall touching the English cannon in the courtyard, the one that dates back to the siege of Mont Saint Michel during the Hundred Years' War. The Montois had brought it inside the city walls after the English attack on the mount had failed. I remember that surge of electrical energy that coursed through me when I touched it, realizing that it was there because of me. Because of Operation Dark Moon. And that's all I can find in my brain.

Then I recognize the heavy velvet curtains attached to a frame suspended from the ceiling beams above. They are Madame Mercier's bed curtains. And the lumpy straw pallet beneath me is familiar as well. Yes, I recognize this place. I am in the bedroom of Jean le Vieux's cottage, except there is more furniture in the room than last time I was here, which was about six months ago for me. I remember that for Nicolas, it was over four years ago.

I am fully dressed—except for my boots—and I'm lying with a heavy wool blanket over me on the bed I slept in when I was last here six months ago. I reach out and touch the bed curtains, thinking of the Widow Mercier with great fondness. I hope she's still alive. I have such tender memories of her remarkable kindness to me, and I shudder when I remember how unkind I was about her deceased daughter's clothing she'd offered me. Fortunately, Nicolas had been wise enough to cover for my heartless behavior. But that was before I had come to grips with being yanked out of my life and pulled back into fifteenth-century France at war. Before I had fallen in love with Nicolas le Breton.

My head is killing me and I have to go to the bathroom, which I unfortunately realize means using the chamber pot. I *don't* have fond memories of that, but when nature calls, it calls! However, when I try to raise my head, everything starts spinning, and I lie back down quickly. I touch the top of my head, and discover that the entire top of my scalp is tender to the touch, and there is a giant lump. My right ankle is also throbbing, and my ears are ringing.

I reach into the recesses of my foggy brain and strain to remember how I got here. It's as if each little detail starts as a tiny spiral of color that spins in my mind until it becomes a giant spiral. Color after color spinning until a kaleidoscope of colors come together to create an entire rainbow spectrum of pinwheel memories. And there it is. The point of black in the center of those memories: Abdon. Everything comes flooding back about the fight with Abdon on the ramparts. I must have plowed head-on into that rampart wall when Abdon head-butted us, and sure enough that goose egg is still there. I remember telling Nicolas it was the size of Rhode Island, but now it feels like it's the size of Texas. No doubt I've been suffering from a concussion. Then I remember the horrific agony I'd suffered when Abdon twisted my ankle. That torturous pain had almost been intolerable at the time of the attack, but I'd tried my best to block it out as soon as I'd realized that Nicolas was bleeding from a knife wound.

I remember sitting on the steps as I did my best to bandage Nicolas's arm, and our rush to get to the abbey before it closed. The ticket taker looked at us dubiously, but we both made an effort to put on our happy faces, and obviously the lighting had been too dim for her to catch the fact that Nicolas was bleeding! Then, by the time Nicolas made it to the top of the Grand Degré staircase, he was going into shock. As we reached the West Terrace, I felt the sleeve of his sweatshirt and realized it was saturated. Climbing the many stairs had probably caused his heart to beat faster, and that in turn had pumped more blood out unhindered by my feeble bandaging attempts. I knew he'd lost a lot of blood, and I didn't have a clue how I could possibly get him back to the fifteenth century.

"Katelyn," he instructed in a voice that was barely a whisper, "you must help me get to the Guest Hall. I do not believe I can endure much more. Then you must make your way to Notre-Dame-Sous-Terre by yourself. There, turn your key in your keyhole, the indented jobber's mark, like you did the first time you traveled back in time."

"But how do I control what day and time I go back to?" I asked as we headed down into the lower levels of the abbey, completely oblivious of the artful lighting and resonant Gregorian chants that were being piped throughout the abbey for the sound and light show. I hope I have another occasion to experience that mystical experience of being in the abbey at dark with medieval music and moody lighting. It must have been quite a show for the holiday revelers. But then I realize I don't need a reproduction of the medieval atmosphere, because I'm right smack in the middle of it! And right now it isn't feeling all that mystical because I still desperately want a flush toilet and running water. Then my thoughts return to that discussion with Nicolas about how the time keys work.

"The Archangel controls the day and hour, Katelyn," Nicolas explained to me as his breathing became shallower and shallower. "He will take us back to a time when we will not risk being discovered in the abbey, and I assure you that we shall both arrive at virtually the same time. But you will have to find your way back to the Guest Hall to help me get to the cottage. Can you do that?"

At that time, in spite of the fact that I felt physically incapable of helping anyone, I knew I was in better condition than Nicolas, and so I assured him that I would come for him.

Nicolas had dropped my backpack and I was supporting his weight and dragging both him and the heavy pack behind me. I don't know how I did it, but I did. The small groups of tourists scattered throughout the abbey had given us some odd looks, but no one stopped us to question us or to offer help. That's just as well. How could I have explained that I was trying to get a bleeding man to a time portal so that he could return to the fifteenth century?

Anyway, I managed to get him to his keyhole, which was fortunately located on the floor in the corner of the Guest Hall next to the massive set of fireplaces. On the other side of the hall, a small group of visitors was inspecting an artfully illuminated monk's robe dramatically suspended from the ceiling. I helped Nicolas sit on the cold stone and placed his enseigne in the grooves so he could reach it. I wanted to examine his enseigne to look at his symbol and see if it was a Hebrew letter like mine and Jean's, but now wasn't the time. He told me to leave him there because he couldn't use the time key until the hall was completely empty of other people, and he instructed me to do the same.

After a few wrong turns, I finally found the wide staircase that led down to Notre-Dame-Sous-Terre. I had only been here in person once before (well, once when I was conscious), and I would not have found it from my memories of it, but I had studied everything I could get my hands on about the abbey after I'd returned home. I knew from studying photographs that the doorway into the chapel was not visible from the bottom or top of the staircase because it was set so deeply into the side wall of the staircase. I also knew that since it was not on the regular tourist itinerary, the door was kept locked, but I had to trust the Archangel on this one.

As I reached the heavy Romanesque barrel arch, I was greeted by the sight of two solid wooden doors meeting in the middle of the arch, and they were firmly shut. In fact, they looked as if they hadn't been opened in centuries. I eyed the keyhole in one of the doors and my heart sank. As I lifted the round, rusted ring that opened the right door, it slid open silently. Thank heavens. No one was inside, but a dim light on the right side of the double-naved chapel illuminated what I knew from my studies to be what archeologists believed to be the original stones of Saint Aubert's oratory, which in modern times had been opened up some time in the 1960s. My keyhole was located on the stone wall in an arched alcove located on the right side as one faced the opening. It was close enough to the altar that I could reach out and touch it.

And then that transcendent vortex of light and motion whisked me back to Nicolas's world. But I didn't have time to focus on that inexplicable, miraculous experience because I was frantic about Nicolas. By the time I made my way back to the Guest Hall, Nicolas was lying there, unconscious, and I felt like joining his party. The only way I managed to get him back to the cottage was because of a surge of pure adrenaline, and of course, with the aid of the Archangel. I fully realize that I could never have done that on my own. And so I am grateful.

Then I remember stitching him up. I can't believe I actually did that. I was feeling so sick by the time we made it to the cottage, that I didn't think I could do anything but collapse into the stout arms of Brother Thibault. I'm sure it was a combination of factors, but mostly the effects of my head trauma on the ramparts. I was pretty sure I had a concussion, but I had no choice but to force myself to stay alert and do what I had to do . . . with a few vomit-pauses added in. After all, Nicolas had done it for me after I'd been sliced up while escaping from the English sailors without even having a clue what he was doing, except my rather incoherent instructions. At least *I* had watched some rather gory YouTube videos about stitching up wounds. Another tender mercy from the Archangel, who gave me the impression to bring a suture kit and study the surgical art that every eighteen-year-old girl from the twenty-first century should have mastered. I mean, really. Who knows that kind of stuff? None of my friends, that's for sure. But I am now not only a Watchman, but I guess I'm also the surgeon-in-residence for Mont Saint Michel.

I think I finished stitching him up, but that part's kind of fuzzy right now. Anyway, now I'm desperate to find out how he's doing. I have no idea how long I've slept, but it's light outside, so it must have been all night. I instinctively look at my watch, but realize it doesn't mean anything. After all, I've just traveled back, let's see . . . nearly six hundred years. Yeah, my watch isn't going to be too accurate with that kind of time shift.

I have to battle with the vertigo that's threatening to send me back to my comfortable horizontal position on the bed pallet, but I finally figure out that if I keep my head down and get on my hands and knees, I can keep it under control. So, like a humiliated puppy, I force myself to crawl across the wooden floor to reach the dreaded chamber pot. Because Nicolas told me in his email, I know it is the end of the year 1428, but the room actually feels much warmer than it was when I was here before—in the month of October of 1424. That's because there is a cheerful fire burning in the fireplace, which was boarded up when I was here before. There is also a plain table with two chairs, on which a pitcher of water and a wash basin have been set. My backpacks are placed on a simple wooden chest at the foot of the bed, which I recognize from my last visit, but there is also a heavy armoire with ornately sculpted wooden doors reflecting the Gothic architecture of the abbey church. Things have obviously improved since last I was here. To me it is a witness of the success of

Operation Dark Moon. The Mount is no longer under siege, and firewood is obviously more readily available. No more burning furniture and doors. It's a comforting realization.

After extracting my toothbrush, toothpaste, and some tissue from my backpack, I empty my overfull bladder, and breathe a blessed sigh of relief. Then I manage to sit at the table where I brush my teeth, with my head lowered over the basin to keep the dizziness under control. Getting rid of that horrific acidy taste of vomit feels glorious. I also wash my hands and face. Then, once again, I get back on my hands and knees and continue my crawling trek to the door and raise myself up on my knees to open it.

"Yoo-hoo," I call out. "Brother Thibault, can you come help me?" I smell the most marvelous aroma wafting up the stairs from the kitchen. It's a far cry from the congealed corned beef stew Jean had made me swallow my first night in 1424. When I smell the aroma, I realize I'm starving. No, I mean really, really starving like during the siege, which is odd. I shouldn't be *that* hungry. Of course it's true that I didn't have dinner last night, but I'd stuffed myself with the famous Breton galettes and crêpes at a little crêperie in Caen with Dad and Adèle yesterday afternoon. Regardless, whatever it is that Thibault is cooking smells divine, and I want some right now.

"Mademoiselle, mademoiselle," he calls out to me as he starts up the stairs. "You have finally wakened. Let me assist you." I soon learn that although Thibault is plus-sized, he is also very strong. He sweeps me up into his arms, carries me effortlessly down the stairs and sets me in Marie's chair, the chair, which according to Nicolas, I had treated with disrespect that first night in 1424. Now, I guess it is officially *my* chair.

"What about Nicolas?" I ask the minute I'm seated. I still need to lower my head to keep the dizziness from overcoming me. "Is he okay? I mean, is he well?" Wow, just like before, I realize how often I use that word 'okay.' I've got to hurry and teach it to Brother Thibault so we can continue with this communication business.

"Not only is he well, mademoiselle, but he's gone to fetch you more water from the spring. He informed me that you don't care for our cider. But I guarantee that if you have a swig of Brother Thibault's cider, you will not be disappointed," he says as he laughs and pats his belly. "Ah yes, the apples of Normandy have lived up to my every expectation. Yes indeed."

"Seriously? You mean Nicolas is up and about?" I ask as I try to draw him away from the subject of apples to the subject of Nicolas.

"If you mean is he conscious and functioning, then the answer is yes. And my dear, I have not seen him this happy since I arrived here. You have worked some magic in more ways than one." He grins at me from ear to ear, and once again offers up a great belly laugh. I am beginning to like this jolly fellow. With a white wig and beard, he'd make the best mall Santa Claus ever! Or a radio or TV commentator because of his deep and resonant voice. Too bad he was born in the wrong century.

"Wow, so our little surgery session worked," I say.

"Mademoiselle Katelyn, your skills were amazing, and I dare say that you saved his life," he confirms, "or at least prevented him from losing the use of his limb. And after you had, um . . ." he hems and haws and then finally comes out with it, ". . . emptied the remainder of your stomach and lost consciousness, I finished bandaging him. Then, I cleaned you both up and carried both of you to your respective bedchambers. Ah, and rest assured, I have been certain to administer his medicine as you instructed: one of your strange lozenges every twelve hours. It seems to have been efficacious. After a good night's sleep, he was as good as new. But, we have both been concerned about you. How are you feeling, my dear?" He looks at me with genuine concern and care. He is like a giant teddy bear, and I have the urge to just jump right up and cuddle him. But I resist the temptation, knowing how that twenty-first century impulse will appear to a fifteenth-century former monk.

"I'm still a bit dizzy, and my head and ankle hurt, but I think the worst is over," I answer as I find myself smiling at him. "But I'm so relieved about Nicolas," I say, inwardly thanking the Archangel for inspiring me to bring antibiotics. I'd convinced Dr. Daily that I was nervous about going back to France where an infection had nearly done me in, and so to humor me (which was exactly what I had intended), he had given me a generous prescription for penicillin. Just in case. And the 'in case' had arrived much sooner than I could have possibly imagined!

"So you've already given him his medicine this morning?" I ask. "What time is it anyway?" For the first time, I notice an intricate clock sitting on the mantel. It's made entirely of a dark coppery-looking metal and is open-sided so that I can see the gears and whatever other mechanisms make a fifteenth-century clock work. The face has beautifully hand-painted Roman numerals. It is exquisite. I didn't even know they had clocks in the fifteenth century, let alone fancy clocks. The one thing I *do* know is that it wasn't here in 1424.

"Ah, I see you are admiring my clock," says Brother Thibault "'Twas a gift from a dear friend of mine, my only friend at the monastery, to be precise, and I carried it carefully during my long journey here. As you can see, it is approaching the noon hour, and yes, Nicolas has already received his lozenge this morning, and yesterday morning and evening as well."

"What?" I blurt out. "How long have I been asleep?"

"Oh, my dear girl, you have been dead to the world for many hours," he informs me with a chuckle. "Yes, indeed. But let me see, just how long was it? It was about ten o'clock at night when you finished sewing up Nicolas's arm. You arrived just after I had finished my evening meal. These lovely salt marsh sheep make the most delightful dishes . . ." he adds, and then I try to bring him back to the subject at hand.

"So, how long did I sleep?" I ask again.

"*Eh bien*, you slept all through that night, and then you missed the morning repast and then some lovely omelets and a chicken dish I whipped up for us yesterday. Yes, and then you slept through all of last night, missing breakfast again this morning. So, it has been about thirty-eight hours." Obviously his way of counting time was counting the number of meals served in a twelve-hour period. Oh, yes, I was going to like this man.

"I slept for thirty-eight hours?" I cry out, stunned.

"Yes, my dear. I assure you, we continued to verify that you were still breathing normally," he says, "but we came to the conclusion that the best remedy was to allow you to sleep for as long as you needed, although I cannot fathom myself going that long without nourishment. But from what Nicolas told me, you had not only gone many hours without sleep when he came to fetch you, but that you received an injury to your head thereafter. Sleep was the best medicine for you. But now you must be ravenous, mademoiselle, and you have wakened just in time to have a bowl of my mutton stew."

No wonder I am so hungry. I've been asleep for nearly two days! "Yes," I reply. "I'm starving, and your stew sounds wonderful." I'm finally able to stand without the dizziness sending me flat to the floor, and I tenderly test out my foot and walk to the table. My ankle still hurts, but I don't think there is any permanent damage. I can walk just fine.

So here I sit waiting for Nicolas, sharing a meal prepared by a former Benedictine monk, who makes certain I pause while he offers a word of thanks over the food before sitting down. I think mutton is lamb, and I haven't had a lot of experience eating lamb, but Nicolas was right. Brother Thibault's culinary skills are top-notch. He would be a colorful candidate for the cooking competition *Top Chef* back home. I'm not usually a stew person, but this meat is as tender and savory as any I've ever tasted, and the rich, dark broth is seasoned with some unidentifiable herbs that give it a unique flavor. Small chunks of carrots and potatoes, and some other vegetable (turnips, maybe?) are cooked to perfection. Perhaps the stew tastes so good because I'm so hungry, but I don't think so. After all, I still remember Jean's horrible corned beef and cabbage concoction, and I was hungry then. No, this is really good. It's a pleasant surprise to know I will not only have food while I'm here, but I'll have *great* food.

"Thank you so much for the meal. This stew is delicious," I say and Brother Thibault breaks out into a smile as wide as the Cheshire Cat's.

"I am so pleased you find my meager skills acceptable," he says with his merry grin exposing surprisingly white teeth. "Nicolas told me you would approve of my culinary attempts."

"Are you kidding?" I say as I slurp the remaining broth from the bottom of the bowl. "Is there enough for me to have another serving?" I ask, surprised at my gluttony.

"Certainly. Nicolas should be here shortly, and we shall both sit and dine with you," he said as he refills my bowl and sets it before me.

"This is the best fifteenth-century food I've ever eaten. But I'm afraid that's not saying much since I hardly ate anything last time I was here. You know, with the siege and all. But, honestly, this is as good as any twenty-first century food I've eaten." *Well, maybe not cheesecake,* I think, *or molten lava cake, or homemade mac and cheese, or fish tacos, or . . .*

Just then Nicolas enters, and his eyes light up as he sees me. "Katelyn," he cries out as he empties a large bucket of water into a pewter pitcher on the sideboard and then fills one of the pewter mugs with water for me.

"I am glad you are awake," he continues. "Are you . . . okay?"

"Yes," I say as I attempt to rise to greet him, but I lose my balance as the vertigo hits with a vengeance. If my darn head weren't spinning out of control, I think I would have jumped into his arms right then and there and kissed him.

He presses his hand on my shoulder to gently push me back down and hands me the water. Thank heavens! Fresh, clean spring water, and I can drink as much as I want. I was always dehydrated during the siege because water was rationed.

"Just sit and regain your strength, Katelyn. I believe your head injury has left after-effects. What about your foot? Are you able to walk?"

"It's painful, but fortunately, I don't think Abdon did anything more than just aggravate the old injury. It'll be better in a few days. But Nicolas, I'm so glad to see you. How is your arm? I'm anxious to see the wound. Has Thibault changed the bandage?"

"Calm yourself. Sit and let us eat together, and I shall attempt to respond to all of your questions. I am feeling amazingly well, Katelyn. According to Brother Thibault, you did a masterful job of caring for my wound. I guess we can now exchange arm examinations. You show me your scar where I stitched you up, and I shall show you mine! But for now, let us enjoy this marvelous repast."

And what a 'repast' it is. Actual food that tastes good. I can hardly wait to see what Thibault comes up with for dinner. Even though I'm perfectly full, I can't help but imagine what treat he has in store for tonight.

After our meal, I change Nicolas's bandage. I'm amazed at how good his wound looks. There are no signs of infection, and the skin is already starting to heal. Then I show him his own work on *my* arm (but not my thigh). It's equally impressive. I also explain how the twenty-first century doctors opened up my ankle injury, which I suffered while trying to save Nicolas on the sands of the bay. With a metal plate and eight screws they reattached my foot to my leg, cleaned up the infection, and sewed me back up. Now we both carry scars from our encounters with Abdon, as if we needed any more incentive to detest him. After the pleasantries of sharing our battle wounds, it's time for the three of us to get down to business. Watchman business. Even with my spinning head, I am completely at ease taking control of the conversation, just as I had with the planning of Operation Dark Moon. I surprise myself!

Who is this amazingly confident woman? I can't help but wonder.

The first thing I do is ask Brother Thibault about how he came to join us. After I learn about his calling to come to Nicolas on the mount and his tutoring sessions from Jean le Vieux, I can't stop from getting emotional, remembering the man I will always cherish. Then he explains that Jean used his time key to travel directly to Landévennec Abbey from the abbey here on the mount. That is something I never knew was possible, and I'm particularly surprised to learn that it was just a short time ago that Brother Thibault was in his presence. It's hard to grasp.

"It hardly seems fair that he was allowed to visit with you in the future, but not with us," I reply.

"That is precisely what I told him," replies Nicolas as Brother Thibault rises to clear the table. "But Brother Thibault has assured me that Jean was exultant to leave this existence and move on to a better place. He knew he would die during that final encounter with Abdon, and he had no regrets. He had completed his work, Katelyn. We must be happy for him and live with the conviction that he has been reunited with his adored Marie."

It's at that point that I wipe my tears and pull out the neck chain from under my sweater and show them the emblems I carry near my heart.

"Nicolas, I hope you understand why I couldn't wear this ring on my finger in my world, as you may have wanted me to," I say, "but it's always close to my heart. It's not only a reminder of Jean, since it belonged to Marie, but it's a constant reminder of you . . ." I hesitate. Do I really want to mention that Nicolas gave it to me as a wedding ring? It's not as if we can talk about this right here in front of Brother Thibault. But I had to finish what I'd started. ". . . because you gave it to me as a symbol of your . . . undying devotion, and it means more to me than you will ever know." Our eyes connect, and I can feel myself blushing. Nicolas reaches over the table and touches my hand tenderly, and then draws his hand away. Boy, do I ever want to kiss him, but I hurry and change the subject. We will have to work through this when we get a moment. *If* we get a moment!

"And this is Jean's enseigne, which you must have sent back with me, Nicolas." I had found it among my belongings in my backpack when I was in the hospital in Rennes, but I'd never learned why it had been given to me.

"No, 'twas not I who gave it to you," he reveals. "For four long years, I have wondered where it was. Jean himself must have placed it in your knapsack, Katelyn. It was his acknowledgement to you that he cared about you and that he trusted you. He had already packed all of your possessions when I went to retrieve your knapsack before sending you back, except for the few magic boxes I put in at the end. There was no time for me to go through your things, because I was desperate to get you sent back. I am relieved to know that you have it. When we recovered Jean's body after his fall, the time key was not with him, and I feared it had been stolen."

"Well, it has been a comfort to me, but also a bit of a puzzle," I say as I think about the Hebrew enigma, "but I'll explain that to you later. We have much more important things to discuss first. Remember? No time!" I move on to the second item of business: I want Nicolas to tell me everything he knows about our mission.

"First of all, can you tell me what the date is?" I start the conversation.

Nicolas turns to Thibault. "I know we are in December, but I'm not certain of the exact date. Do you know, Brother Thibault?"

"Yes," he replied. "It is the eighteenth day of December in 1428."

"Okay, good," I say. "That helps. I'll tell you more about why I need to know the date later. But first, you told me that we'd be traveling. So do you know where we're going and what we're supposed to do when we get there?" I have some ideas of my own, but I want to hear what Nicolas and Thibault have to say first before I share my thoughts with them.

"I was hoping you would be able to enlighten me about that," he replies. "Most of what I know comes from Brother Thibault. Please, tell her what you told me, Thibault."

"Well, my dear," he begins, "it seems that neither you nor Nicolas knew that the time keys could not only take you through time, but they can also take you to different locations, like when Jean came to visit me in Landévennec. However, that type of travel requires the keyhole to already have been carved in the place to which you travel. Jean explained it to me when he came to visit me in Landévennec. He had visited my abbey many years ago at the direction of the Archangel and had placed the keyhole there, not knowing when he would use it."

"So do you think that has something to do with us?"

"Yes," he replies. "It does, in fact. Jean told me that in addition to traveling west to Brittany to cut the keyhole at Landévennec, he had also been instructed to travel east to cut other keyholes. It must have been many years ago, before the war threatened the safety of the mount. Anyway, he informed me that those keyholes were to be used by you two to carry out an important mission while I stayed on watch duty here. Whatever your mission is, it ultimately has to do with protecting the Mount, because that is what we have been called to do."

"Did he happen to tell you where those keyholes are?" I ask. There is only a portion of our mission that I feel fairly confident about, and the rest is just a foggy haze. I'm hoping Brother Thibault can give me the specifics I don't know.

"No," he replies as he rises to refill my mug with water. "Just that they were to the east. I assumed they were someplace in France, but I do not know that as a certainty. Besides, with the English controlling so many of the French lands right now, there is not much of France left. Here my dear, you need to drink. After all, you have been without food or water for a long time."

"Thank you," I reply. "You are so kind. I hope you realize how grateful I am for your hospitality. That meal totally improved my mood and helped me focus."

"Mademoiselle," he replies. "I am your humble servant, and this is your home as much as mine."

"Yes," confirms Nicolas, who reaches across the table to touch my hand again. This time he leaves it there. "This is your home, Katelyn, for as long as you are willing to stay. I hope you know that."

Then he squeezes my hand and entwines his fingers with mine. I hope it doesn't embarrass our Benedictine friend, but I'm just great with it, as long as Nicolas is. His squeeze gives me the fortitude to press on.

"So Brother Thibault, and please call me Katelyn, by the way," I instruct. "Mademoiselle is way too formal for me." Besides, I'm not really a mademoiselle anymore. In case they've forgotten. I'm a married woman. I'm legally Nicolas's wife in this era.

"While Jean was tutoring you, did he explain anything about our mission?" I want to know every word Jean said to him.

Thibault lowers his head, and his jovial countenance darkens. Then he looks at Nicolas, who nods his head to continue. "He explained to me that the fate of France, and thus the fate of Mont Saint Michel, hangs in the balance, that if you do not succeed in whatever it is you are called upon to do, France will be lost, and the English will finally have their way with this sacred place. He said that if that happens, the first thing they will do is destroy the abbey and the entire Mount, because this island has become a symbol of open rebellion against the English. It is a repudiation of their claim to these lands."

At this unwelcome news, Thibault stands and walks to the fireplace and puts another log on the fire. Even though the temperature is warm and cozy, a definite chill has entered our souls, and unfortunately, I don't think firewood is going to help.

"And mademoi.... Katelyn. There is more," he says as he returns from stoking the fire. He seems reluctant to actually say the words. "I have already told this to Nicolas. Now I will share it with you, my dear, though I fear 'twill not be an easy message to deliver. But 'tis the most important part of what Jean told me. He instructed me to convey this message to you both, without alteration. He said that if the Mount is taken by our enemies, Abdon will ultimately discover the secret we have been called upon to protect, and the world as we know it will finally and entirely be in Satan's control. There will be little we can do to stop him. And then he said, 'Tell Katelyn that Nicolas will be there to give her support, but that it all depends upon her. It all depends upon Katelyn.' 'Tis what he said."

Suddenly the impact of our mission hits me like a ton . . . no, two gazillion tons of brick. I've been sitting here thinking about kissing Nicolas and wondering what Brother Thibault is going to make for dinner, and then he springs this on me. I have the fate of the world in my hands! Not just my fate, or the fate of Nicolas or Thibault, or the fate of my family. Not just the fate of the abbey or the village of Mont Saint Michel. Not just the fate of France, or even the United States. Thibault has just told me that I am carrying the fate of the world on my shoulders. Apparently, *I* am the only one who can prevent Satan from taking over the world! If I hadn't already seen everything I had seen here on the Mount, I would just cast it away as a big joke. But I know it isn't. I know Jean would not say such a thing if it weren't true. It's why he sent his enseigne back to me. To let me know that he had faith in me. That he believed I could do whatever it is I have to do. But, it is simply too much to bear. After all, I really am just an average eighteen-year-old American teenager. For heaven's sake, I've never even lived on my own! And now I'm supposed to save the world from Satan? Seriously? Even Nicolas has lost every smidgen of color in his face. I do the only thing I can do. I start to cry.

Nicolas stands immediately and moves to my side of the table. He sits down on the bench next to me, places his arms around me and pulls my head onto his shoulder. I cry like a baby.

"I was afraid to tell you," Nicolas admits as he strokes my hair. "I was afraid you might not come. 'Tis a heavy burden to place on your shoulders. Especially after all you have been through."

"Did you honestly think I wouldn't come with you?" I ask through my tears. "Did you think I'd just abandon you?"

"I hoped you wouldn't," he admitted. "But with you back in your time, in your comfortable world, I wasn't sure. I'm sorry," he said. "I should have had more faith in you."

"Don't apologize, Nicolas. I hardly have any faith in myself," I say as a flood of total fatigue and darkness comes over me. "And I think it's about time you tell me the entire secret business, but I don't think I can process any more right now."

Gone is the amazingly confident woman. She existed before I had the fate of the entire world resting on my shoulders. That woman was the know-it-all who thought she had it all figured out. One: take a little jaunt to deliver a sword; two: figure out my relationship with Nicolas, and three: return to my home and finish high school. One, two, three. I hadn't figured on four, five, six . . . ad infinitum.

"Actually," I say as a violent wave of nausea and vertigo hits. The room is spinning out of control. "I think I need to lie down and rest. Can we continue this conversation this afternoon? And maybe I'm going to have to ask you, Brother Thibault, to carry me back up to my bed . . . or you might have to clean up after me."

With an alacrity that surprises even my spinning self, Brother Thibault jumps to his feet and takes me in his arms.

I've figured out that Thibault doesn't take too kindly to my rather disgusting habit of hurling. I don't exactly like it myself. Fortunately, Nicolas grabs a bowl and places it in just the right spot.

Chapter 21

EVEN THOUGH KATELYN HAD WARNED Nicolas about the symptoms of concussion, he was still worried. He sat by her bed all afternoon. Finally, at about four o'clock in the afternoon, she stirred, first moving her head from side to side, and then opening her eyes. Nicolas sat there holding her hand as she looked up at him.

"I'm sorry, Nicolas. The room was spinning, and I just couldn't keep my eyes open," she said, as Brother Thibault walked in the room.

"Katelyn, you have no reason to apologize," Nicolas assured her and leaned forward to press his lips gently against her forehead. "You warned me that you feared you had a serious head injury, and you were right. Are you feeling any better?"

"Way better. The spinning has finally stopped. Just in case it returns later, since you're both here now, let's continue our conversation from this morning. But I think I'll stay in bed if you don't mind."

"Katelyn, we completely understand your situation. If you need to rest, we shall wait until tomorrow and leave you to get more sleep," Brother Thibault suggested.

"No really, I want to talk. Do you mind staying in here with me?" she asked. "I know it's probably not proper in your century, but desperate times require desperate measures." They both assured her that they were not offended by the proposition. "So, if I remember correctly, neither of you knows where Nicolas and I are supposed to travel to. Is that right?"

"I fear that is correct," replied Nicolas. "We know only that it is somewhere to the east, as Brother Thibault explained to us yesterday."

"And the Archangel didn't speak to either of you or cause you to have impressions in your mind about what our mission is?" she asked.

"No," Nicolas answered. "Only what Jean told Thibault—that we would be required to travel while he stayed here to protect the Mount. Without Thibault's bringing the message to me, I of myself would have had no idea that we even had a mission to perform. Sadly, the Archangel has not seen fit to speak to me, either by word or by impression."

"Don't worry about it, Nicolas. The truth is, the Archangel didn't exactly speak to me either, but he *did* prepare me." She proceeded to explain to them how the Archangel had arranged for her to study certain subjects at her school, like the French language and the history of the period in which they were living. Then she explained how she had felt impressed to learn some new skills, including how to ride a horse and how to fight with a sword, which she called fencing. Nicolas felt his stomach drop to his feet as she mentioned the latter skill. It made him feel particularly uneasy. He didn't like hearing of such ominous-sounding preparations as far as Katelyn was concerned. As for himself, he was somewhat versed in swordplay, but he certainly did not like the thought of Katelyn being obliged to defend herself in such a manner.

"And then I had a dream," she continued as Nicolas focused again on what she was saying. "Jean came to me."

"So he *did* visit you," Nicolas replied. "Just as he visited Brother Thibault. Oh, that I had been as blessed to receive a visitation from him. I prayed for comfort for so long."

"You're right, and I'm grateful I had that dream, because in it, Jean told me what our mission is."

"He did?" asked Nicolas with excitement, his dejection forgotten. "Why did you not share that information with us this morning, Katelyn?"

"Well, I wanted to know everything the two of you knew first, because when I say Jean told me what our mission is, that's not exactly correct. He alluded to it. I had to do a lot of pondering, studying, and research to put it all together, but I think I have at least the broad outline."

"So what did he tell you?" Brother Thibault joined in the conversation from the opposite side of Katelyn's bed. "Oh, this is so thrilling! After twenty years of the same routine over and over again, this is like heaven for me. Action, excitement, adventure!"

Both Katelyn and Nicolas laughed at his enthusiasm, but then Nicolas brought them back to reality. "Yes, and danger, life-threatening injuries, and the fate of the world on our shoulders! But go on, Katelyn. Tell us what Jean told you."

"First, I have to explain to you that when I had the dream, I was in agony, thinking that I had caused Jean's death," she explained. "In the dream, I felt an overwhelming sense of love from Jean, and he assured me that he didn't blame me for his death and that he was happy. It *was* comforting, so again, Nicolas, I understand how you must feel. I received comfort, and you were left alone. It doesn't seem fair, and I'm not sure I understand why that is. But to answer your question, Brother Thibault, I remember Jean's exact words in my dream because the minute I woke up, I wrote them down. He said: 'Katelyn, you are a Watchman. You will be called upon soon to return to your duties. You will know when the time is right.' So he made it clear that my mission wasn't over, that there was more for me to do. And then he gave this clarification. He said, 'There is more that only *you*, Katelyn Michaels, can do to protect Mont Saint Michel.' It was kind of overwhelming, but at the same time exhilarating, because I hoped it meant being with you again, Nicolas." She looked at him with such clarity of sentiment, Nicolas felt his heart start to beat faster.

"Is that all he said?" Nicolas asked, breaking off the eye contact with her, but once again taking her hand in his. "That is not sufficient for us to know what we are being called upon to do."

"You're right," she said. "There was one final phrase. And it is the essence of our mission. He said 'Learn of the Maiden, Katelyn, and take her the sword.' And then I woke up."

"Learn of the Maiden, and take her the sword?" asked Brother Thibault with a look of total confusion on his face. "That is all?"

"Yeah, that's the extent of it. But I think I have it figured out. It's actually pretty simple. Nicolas," she continued, "inside my small backpack is a black folder . . . let's see, maybe you would call it a portfolio? . . . Oh, I don't know. It's like the hard covers of a book with a bunch of loose papers inside. Can you find it and bring it over? I want to show both of you some documents I brought with me. Brother Thibault, move your chair over here by Nicolas so you both can see."

Nicolas found the portfolio and brought it to the bed and handed it to Katelyn while Thibault moved his chair. Katelyn opened the folder, removed two pages from inside. Then she placed one of the pages on top of the blanket covering her legs, turning it so that the two men could view it from the correct angle.

"I don't know if you've ever seen a map before, but this is a drawing that represents the country of France," she explained as she moved her finger around the page. "This is what it looks like in my time, in the twenty-first century. It includes everything inside the black line." Then next to that, she placed another document. "This is a map of what the same territory looks like right now—in your time. The portion colored in green represents the lands that the kingdom of France controls during these wars with the English, what we call in the future, the Hundred Years' War. You are living in the last decades of that war. France is just this small portion in green. Everything else in purple is under the control of England or of the Burgundians, who are the allies of the English. You can see that the English control at least half of what is traditionally considered to be France, and of course that includes all of Brittany and Normandy along the northern coastline, where we are right now."

Then she pointed to the territory on the right side of the map. "To the east," she continued, "everything in yellow is the territory currently controlled by the Holy Roman Empire. It includes what, in my time, we call Germany, and a large portion of what in my time is part of eastern France, the territories of Alsace and Lorraine."

"It is a sobering image," Nicolas acknowledged. "There is barely anything left of France as compared to the map from your time. If the French armies can't turn the tide, we have no hope of protecting the mount from the English."

"Yeah, that's it exactly," she replied. "And that's where this maiden that Jean spoke of comes in, and I can assure you, it isn't me. I am *not* the maiden, in case you thought that. No, she is a genuine person from your time. Since that dream, I've done as much studying and research as I could about her. She even called herself 'The Maiden,' or in French, 'La Pucelle.' That was the name she gave herself, so I was pretty certain she was the one Jean was referring to, but she will be called by many names in the years to come. Her name in this century is Jehanne, but in addition to La Pucelle, she is or will be known as the Maid of Orléans, the Maid of Lorraine, Jeanne d'Arc in French, and in English, Joan of Arc. But I think we should just get in the habit of calling her Jehanne, since that's her current name. Her father is a man called Jacques d'Arc, and her mother is known as Isabeau Romée. Her father is a farmer living in the Meuse River Valley in Lorraine in what, in my time, is in Eastern France, but which is now in these lands currently occupied by the English," she said as she pointed to the fifteenth-century rendering of France.

"You see this little village called Domrémy right here in the English-controlled lands, close to the border of the Holy Roman Empire?" They both nodded as she pointed it out. There were very few cities shown on the map, but obviously because of the importance of this small village, it was among them.

"Well, this is where Jehanne was born just a few short years ago, in 1412, and it's where she has lived her entire life up until now. In my time, everyone knows the story of the young girl from Lorraine— even in America, we know her story. In fact, she is probably the most famous Frenchwoman who has ever lived. She's definitely the most important historical figure from the Hundred Years' War. She received the commission from heavenly visitors, including the Archangel Michael, to save all of France by taking command of the Dauphin's army and defeating the English invaders."

"Wait," interjected Brother Thibault. "You say that this girl is from Lorraine and that she was given the commission to save France? That she calls herself La Pucelle . . . the virgin?"

"Yes, that's exactly what I said. And she does. Save France, I mean," Katelyn replied. "Why, Brother Thibault? Have you heard of her?"

"I have an acquaintance," Thibault explained. "Actually, he's a former monastic colleague of mine named Brother Girard. He was with me in Landévennec, and then several years ago, before Abbot Jolivet turned his back on France and threw his lot in with the English regent, the Duke of Bedford, Jolivet heard about Girard's particular talents in reading and copying old manuscripts. Even though Landévennec has a fine library, it is not as fine as that of Mont Saint Michel. Jolivet requested that Brother Girard be transferred to the monastery here to work in the scriptorium. A few weeks ago, I happened upon Brother Girard in the village. He was trying to procure some supplies for the scriptorium from the mainland, and I struck up a conversation with him. That would never happen inside the abbey, mind you, but he seemed anxious to talk about the project he was working on. It concerned a group of prophecies in Latin which appear in several chronicles in the abbey's library. He told me that the prophecies concerned a virgin who would come from the borders of Lorraine and who would save all of France. He was compiling the prophecies, and he seemed anxious about them. He tried to tell me that her coming was imminent. At the time, I wasn't particularly interested, but now it seems rather fortuitous, doesn't it?"

"Yes," said Katelyn. "That is absolutely her! I've read all the prophecies about her. They're mostly attributed to Saint Elizabeth, Saint Bede, and a fourteenth-century French mystic named Marie d'Avignon. Some people even claim they come from Merlyn of King Arthur lore, but that can't be true because he was a legendary figure. Anyway, Thibault, I think you should speak to your friend again and learn if there's anything else that would add to what I already know about Jehanne."

"I will find a pretext to cross paths with him again. In the meantime, please continue with what our role is in Jehanne's story."

"Well, I think our role is to take her a sword, which I believe will give her the confidence and the credibility to carry out her formidable task. Her sword will become a symbol of her divine commission."

Nicolas could hardly grasp what she was saying. A sword was going to turn the tide of the war with the English? It sounded too simplistic, but he was willing to listen to Katelyn's further explanation.

Katelyn turned to Brother Thibault and said, "The sword is also one of the reasons why you are with us right now, Brother Thibault, in addition to protecting the Mount in our absence. And, no, it isn't just to prepare us delicious meals, although I for one am pretty stoked about that. But the reality is that it's not just a coincidence you happen to be a blacksmith. No, that was by design . . . the Archangel's design."

She pulled out another document from her portfolio and handed it to him. "You are going to duplicate the weapon in this photo— oops, sorry, you don't know what a photo is, but just trust me on this—you're going to make a sword just like this for Jehanne La Pucelle, the young woman who is destined to save France, and Nicolas and I are going to deliver it to her!"

"I do not fully comprehend," exclaimed Brother Thibault as he examined the page. "Where did you get this image, and how do you know this is to be her sword?" The image on the page showed a very plain steel blade, with five simple crosses etched vertically into the steel at the top of the blade itself, right below the curved, cross-guard. The grip was wrapped in what looked to be dark brown leather, and the pommel of the hilt looked like a thick stack of coins, round in front and back, with a circular edge.

Nicolas understood these remarkable images—called photographs—from the future and assumed that this sword, Jehanne's sword, had somehow survived for six hundred years and that a magic box, like the one Katelyn had used during Operation Dark Moon, had engraved the image of it for her to bring back in time. "Is this a photograph of her actual sword?" he asked.

"No, Nicolas. Actually, no one knows what became of her sword," Katelyn answered, "and no one really knows for sure what it looked like. This is only a reproduction of what it might have looked like, based on Jehanne's own words. Her only documented description of it stated that 'there were upon it five crosses.' No, this isn't a photo of her sword, but Thibault is going to forge one that looks just like this, and it is going to *become* her sword. Nicolas and I somehow have to transport it to Jehanne, and it has to be at a certain time and place."

"And why is it so important for her to have this particular sword and to have it delivered in a specific time and place?" asked Brother Thibault.

"First of all, because that is what history has dictated, so we can't change that, but the real answer to your question is that this particular sword was said to have certain mystical powers which enhanced her claim of being commissioned by God to save France. Let me explain. First of all, tradition states that Jehanne's sword was the very sword used by the great Frankish ruler, Charles Martel, who was the ruler of France from 718 until 741. Normally, I wouldn't know anything about him, but I've been doing a lot of studying since I received Jean's message."

Katelyn pulled out another page from her portfolio, this one the image of a statue of Charles Martel. "Have you heard of him?" she asked.

"I have," replied Brother Thibault. "I know what I have been taught by the clerics. He is revered by the Church because he prevented the powerful Moorish armies of the Islamic Caliphate from conquering France."

"Yeah, that's exactly right. He was a great military leader known as the Prince of the Franks. He spent his life consolidating his power in France in a series of military victories, first against the Germanic tribes in the east, and then he did exactly what you said, Brother Thibault. At the Battle of Tours in 732, he defeated the Moorish army that had taken control of much of southern France. In fact, that battle gave rise to his name, 'Martel,' which as you know in French means 'hammer,' because it is said he hammered away at his enemies. Even in English, his nickname reflects that. My history teacher likes to call him Chuck the Hammer. In my time, historians believe that had he not prevailed, Islam would have taken over France and perhaps the remainder of Western Europe, and even England. The clergy and Christians *do* revere Charles Martel, as you said, Brother Thibault, because they believe his victory not only halted the Arab conquest, but that he also rescued Christendom from Islam. In addition to that, Martel was the grandfather of the great Emperor Charlemagne, King of the Franks, who united most of Western Europe and laid the foundations for modern France and Germany. So do you get why having his sword would be considered a big deal?"

"A big deal?" asked Brother Thibault.

"Yeah, I mean something significant," she clarified.

"*Oui, je vois.* Such a sword would be revered by the French monarchy, the French military, and the Church as well," replied Brother Thibault, "as it represents the power that led to the creation of the Kingdom of France. And by logic, Jehanne finding it so many centuries later will strengthen her claim to have the right to lead the armies of France and restore the kingdom . . . if it were truly Martel's sword. But it isn't."

"Well, that doesn't really matter. What matters is perception. Jehanne has to believe it's Martel's sword, and others have to believe it as well. There's no way of proving one way or another if it *is* Martel's sword. Belief is spread by word of mouth. That's how legends are created. Besides, the manner in which she finds the sword *is* miraculous, regardless of whether it's Charles Martel's or not. I mean, think about it. Is it any less miraculous that a couple of time travelers take the sword for her to find? It is still a miracle performed by the Archangel."

"You have a valid argument, there, Katelyn," piped in Nicolas. "But won't the fact that the sword will look brand new serve to dispute the claim that it is centuries old?"

"That's the part that's perfect about the legend, because Jehanne herself said that when the sword was removed from the ground, it was covered in rust, but the minute the priests rubbed it with a damp cloth, the rust miraculously fell away from it, and it looked like new. We just have to make it look rusty, and I've brought some perfect acrylic paint to do that. Then when the priests rub it with some wet rags, the paint will come off, and it will look like new . . . which it will be!"

"So now tell us about the way she finds the sword," asked Brother Thibault. "You said that was also important."

"Yes, because it strengthens her claim that she truly *did* hear voices from heaven, which in this case instructed her where to find the sword. That reinforces the idea that her calling to save France *was* a divine calling. She stated that her voices told her she was to obtain a sword from the little church in Sainte-Catherine-de-Fierbois, which is a small village close to Chinon." Katelyn pointed to the town of Chinon on the map. "This is where the Dauphin is currently residing. Jehanne herself said that she sent an armorer from Tours to look for it, a man she had never before seen, with the instructions that it would be buried in the earth behind the church's altar. He conveyed with him a letter for the priests of the church instructing them to send the sword to Jehanne after he found it. And he did find it, just where she said he would!"

"So you mean she doesn't find the sword herself?" asked Nicolas. "Doesn't that make it less miraculous?"

"I wondered about that myself, and then when I thought about it, I think it actually makes the miracle more credible," Katelyn said. "The fact that she herself doesn't go to find it only strengthens the idea that it is a miracle, because the sword was found exactly where she said it would be found, and by a third party who didn't know her, and evidently with the priests of the church as witnesses. That only helped spread the legend about her find. Although she stopped in Sainte-Catherine-de-Fierbois for mass on her way to Chinon, she was constantly in the company of others and had no opportunity alone to plant the sword. By the way, the picture of the sword I showed you," she said, as she lifted up that page again, "is a photo from an actual sword that currently hangs on the wall of the little church in Sainte-Catherine-de-Fierbois in my time. The church is still there—well, it has probably been built and rebuilt many times since 1429—but the sword, along with a leather scabbard, like the one Jehanne says she had made for her sword, hang on the wall to honor her. Evidently, the entire church is full of artistic representations of Jehanne. After this is all over, I'd like to actually go see the church in *my* time."

Nicolas wrinkled his brow and looked at her with consternation, wondering exactly what her last comment meant. They had so much to discuss . . . about their relationship, about their future. Did she intend to leave him and return to her life after their mission was over? But he knew this was not the time to discuss those issues. Now they had a commission to carry out, and their personal feelings could not interfere. He thought of the many sacrifices his mentor, Jean le Vieux, had made to fulfill his calling as a Watchman, and Nicolas didn't know if he had the strength to do it without Katelyn. But he had to focus on the matter at hand, and so he cleansed his mind of all personal desires and refocused it on the subject of the sword.

"And so when is this miraculous sword found?" he asked, trying to disguise his dejection.

"In early March of 1429. We will need to get to the church and bury the sword that Brother Thibault makes before Jehanne and her entourage arrive in Chinon."

"She has an entourage?" asked Nicolas.

"Well, she has to travel from Domrémy, or actually from Vaucouleurs, where she finally convinces the garrison commander of the French army there, a certain Robert de Baudricourt, to send her to Chinon to meet with the Dauphin. Since that entire journey will be made through enemy territory, he arranges to have some men accompany her to protect her. And, if I've got my dates correct," she said as she looked through some pages in her portfolio with notes on them, "she's going to leave her home in Domrémy some time in January of 1429 to convince this Robert de Baudricourt to send her to Chinon. Then, she'll leave Vaucouleurs on February 23, 1429. That's in less than two months. It will take her party about eleven days to get to Chinon, and she'll send for the sword from there."

"So within just a few weeks that sword needs to be buried. And you think that our time keys are going to take us to Sainte-Catherine-de-Fierbois near the end of February 1429?" Nicolas asked.

"Well, that's why I've been asking you so many questions about our destination," Katelyn explained. "I guess until we turn our keys and arrive at wherever it is the Archangel takes us, we won't know the place or the date."

"Katelyn, it sounds too simple to me," Nicolas said. "After all, Jean told you that there was a commission that only *you* could perform. That only *you* had the unique qualities to do. Just delivering a sword doesn't sound like that is all it entails. Anyone could do that."

"Well, I had to find a photo of what the sword looks like in the future, and bring it back, didn't I?" she asked.

"Anyone could have done that," he persisted. "The Archangel could have instructed me to go to the future and retrieve that photograph. No, there is more to it than simply delivering the sword. Besides, if our time keys take us straight to Sainte-Catherine-de-Fierbois and back, that would not entail traveling, or riding horses, a skill which you yourself admit to having been inspired to learn."

"Well, maybe we won't arrive right at the village. Maybe we'll be sent to Tours or Chinon or someplace else and have to ride horses to get to the church," Katelyn suggested.

"No, it still doesn't answer the question as to why it has to be you and you alone. There has to be more involved. Tell us more about Jehanne, Katelyn. She must have some very special qualities to be able to command the armies of France and defeat the English," said Nicolas.

"Well, that's the thing," Katelyn admitted. "She really doesn't, except for her conviction that she is inspired by God. In fact, she's really just a farm girl—a nobody. And when I say she's a nobody, I don't mean that in a disrespectful way, but I'm not kidding. She's even more of a nobody than we are! She has absolutely no education, particularly in matters of warfare. She doesn't even know how to read or write. She is functionally illiterate, and she's only seventeen years old. Well, right now, she's not even seventeen. She'll turn seventeen in January. In a few weeks. And she succeeded, or I mean, she will succeed. She will save France!"

"So she's only seventeen years old?"

"Yeah, that's what I mean. She's just a girl of seventeen with absolutely no training in leading an army."

"Hmmm," mused Nicolas, rubbing his chin in thought. Then he lifted his head and looked at Katelyn straight in the eyes. "So she's the same age as you were when you saved Mont Saint Michel?"

"Yeah, well . . . I guess that's right," Katelyn admitted. "But for heaven's sake, that was just a small island, and it certainly wasn't easy for me, and I know how to read and write, and I had some twenty-first century technology to help. I couldn't have done it without that."

"Maybe you will be helping her with some of your marvelous boxes," Nicolas suggested.

"Well, I did bring a whole bunch of stuff, even some new gadgets . . . what you call magic boxes . . . not knowing what I might need," Katelyn admitted. "But, I wasn't exactly thinking about how it could help Jehanne. It was more in case *we* needed some added help, Nicolas."

"Nicolas has told me about your gadgets, and I agree with him. I believe you are somehow going to provide Jehanne assistance with your magical wares from the future. Can you explain to us how she manages to save France?" asked Brother Thibault.

"Well, for you, it hasn't happened. But in the future, this is her story in a nutshell—I mean a shortened version of it—because it's pretty complex. Basically, she felt that if she could get the Dauphin Charles to Reims, which is here in the English-controlled lands," she pointed to the city of Reims on the map, "so that his coronation could take place in the cathedral there, where all the kings of France have traditionally been crowned, it would give Charles the confidence to reconquer all of the lands in the Kingdom of France. So she proposed to lead his army to take back the cities on the way to Reims, beginning with Orléans," she pointed out that city. "Orléans is under siege right now. Are you aware of that?"

"Because of our isolation and the Abbot Jolivet's wretched betrayal," explained Nicolas, "we only hear bits and pieces of what is happening in the outside world. But we have heard rumblings of problems in Orléans since October."

"Yes, that's right," confirmed Katelyn. "Les Tourelles were taken by the Earl of Salisbury. It's a crucial bridge with towers on it that stretches over the Loire River only about 65 miles north of Bourges. Oh jeez, I can't remember how many miles there are in a league." She looked through her papers again, and found what she was looking for. "There are about 3.45 miles in a league," she said as she removed the timepiece from her wrist and punched at its face.

"So that's about 18.5 leagues from Bourges. That's why the Dauphin had to move his court to the fortress on the hill above Chinon."

"And is she successful in lifting the siege of Orléans?" asked Brother Thibault.

"Yes. She leads the Dauphin's armies against the English and is victorious. That's why she's called The Maid of Orléans—it's her first successful battle."

"But if she is such an uneducated girl, and especially untrained in the art of warfare, how does she convince the Dauphin to let her take over his troops?" asked Nicolas.

"Well, I have some ideas about that. I believe she shares some private information with him that no one else knows, and so she's able to convince him that she really has been sent by God to help him defeat the English. I might be the one to help her figure out what that private information is. And the story of how she obtained her sword will spread throughout the land and will be shared with the Dauphin before she arrives there, so he will have heard something of her miracles before he meets her. But honestly, I'm not sure how she does it. I mean, a seventeen-year old girl leading an army? It really is miraculous. She could only do it with the help of the Archangel."

"You mean like you did, Katelyn?" Nicolas said. "After all, the Archangel inspired you, and with no experience in warfare, you developed an entire battle strategy for our little army of Montois, monks, and soldiers here on the mount. And we managed to defeat an enemy that was much stronger, much more numerous, and much better equipped than were we. An English army, just like Jehanne faces. Katelyn, it seems to me that you have already done exactly what Jehanne is supposed to do."

"It's not exactly the same thing as leading the entire French army and saving all of France," she countered. "But I hadn't really thought of it."

"But it is so clear! You are probably the only female her age in the entire world who has faced a similar circumstance, Katelyn, and done it successfully. Think about it. At age seventeen, you, a young woman with no experience in warfare, but having a commission from the Archangel Michael, managed to come up with a strategy to fight off the invading English armies. Don't you see? You are the *only* person qualified to help her. It is exactly as Jean said. He told you that there was something that only *you* could do to protect Mont Saint Michel, and he told Brother Thibault, that all of France, and indeed all of the world, depended on you. That is why you are here, and it isn't just to deliver her a sword. Oh, that's part of it, but it is so much more than that. I could have delivered the sword to her without your help. But *you*, Katelyn, you can inspire her. You can give her the confidence she needs. You are going to be her tutor, and her example, and who knows? You may even give her some of your mechanisms to assist her. I cannot do it, and neither can Brother Thibault. But you, Katelyn Michaels, you are going to help La Pucelle save France, and by so doing, you are going to protect Mont Saint Michel from destruction and save its secret from falling into the hands of the adversary. Jehanne may save France, but Katelyn, *you* are going to save the world from the master of evil himself, just as Jean told Brother Thibault you would do."

Once again, the blood drained from Katelyn's face.

"You really think we have to do more than just deliver the sword?" she finally asked.

"Yes, Katelyn, I do. It seems like Jehanne is going to need much more than her sword to conquer the entire English army. She is going to need your personal help."

"I had never considered that," she admitted. "I really thought it would be a quick trip in and out, and then . . ."

"And then what?" Nicolas asked, finally brave enough to voice his fears. "Then you go back to your life in the twenty-first century and leave me back here without you?"

"I don't know, Nicolas. I don't know what I thought," she said in a whisper. "I just wanted to get here to be with you and deliver her sword. I haven't thought beyond that. I haven't even considered that we might need to do more. I haven't considered that I would need to spend more than a few weeks here. Besides, it isn't a pleasant idea to have to stick around with Jehanne for very long. There's a lot about her story that I haven't told you, and I'm afraid it's not a happy ending."

"What do you mean?" asked Brother Thibault. "Does she betray her commission? Does she betray the Archangel?"

"Oh no, it isn't that at all," she said as tears started to well up in her eyes. "No, Jehanne stays faithful to her commission. She is valiant . . . to the end. Although her enemies try to force her to deny the source of her inspiration, she . . . oh, I can't talk about it." By this time, Katelyn's tears were falling freely.

"What happens to her, Katelyn?" Nicolas coaxed. "Tell us why you are so emotional."

"I don't think I should tell you." She managed to get the words out as her chest heaved up and down. "I don't know what to do. I'm afraid it may impact the decisions you make, Nicolas, and it can't. I know we can't change anything. We can't change her destiny."

"Katelyn, I apologize," said Nicolas. "I did not mean to upset you. It is . . . okay. You do not need to tell us any more. You shall tell us about it later, but not now. Now you need to sleep, so we can get you well as quickly as possible. You said it yourself. We do not have much time to spare." He picked up the papers she had spread out on the blanket to show them, and then reached over to put them back into the portfolio from which she had taken them. As he opened it, several other pages fell from it. One landed face up on the bed, and it was impossible to ignore. Both men looked at the scene portrayed on the page in shock.

"Is this her?" Nicolas asked. He picked up the horrific image to look at it more closely. It was a photograph of a painting showing a young woman bound to a stake by rope, in the center of a large crowd of onlookers. The spectacle was clearly taking place in the town square of a city of some consequence, because there were buildings surrounding the square and the twin towers of a large church could be seen in the background. Bundles of sticks were set all around the maiden's feet. A priest was in the forefront of the painting holding up a cross on a long pole so that it was at her eye level, and she focused on the cross as soldiers set fire to the bundles of wood. "Is this what happens to her?" he said in a hushed voice. "This is what happens to the girl who saves France? Who does this to her, Katelyn?"

Even Brother Thibault's usually jovial expression disappeared and the color drained from his face as he inspected the image.

"I didn't want you to know, but it's a heavy burden to carry all alone," she said, "and it's why I don't want to stay to see it happen. I don't want to become friends with her, knowing what indignities await her. I can't do it! I don't think I can be around to watch any of it. I know I can't change what happens to her, and I just don't think I can watch her go through it. But she *has* to. She *has* to become a martyr for the cause of France. It is her destiny, and it becomes the rallying cry for the French to forever prevent the English from controlling any French lands ever again!"

"I understand, Katelyn," Nicolas said. "Perhaps we will only be involved at the beginning of her journey, to get her started down her path. I can see why you do not wish to stay. I thought it was because you did not want to stay with me, but I was wrong. Your heart is good, Katelyn. You cannot abide unfairness and you certainly cannot imagine developing a relationship with someone and not preventing such horrific consequences. But you must be strong. This is the most important thing you have ever been called upon to do, and the Archangel has placed his trust in you, Katelyn." By this time, she was sobbing, and he held her in his arms, stroking her hair and allowing her to cry freely. It was not his place to tell her to stop crying. It would be like telling a stream to stop running downhill or the rain to stop falling from the sky. He held her and consoled her until she was ready to speak.

"It is terrible and horrifying. I don't even know her yet, but I feel like I do know her. I guess it's déjà vu. I know so much about her, and I feel a connection to her that I can't even explain. I know her heart, and I can't bear it. What they do to her is barbaric. And all in the name of religion!"

"Katelyn, now that we have seen this, you cannot keep this for yourself," Nicolas said as he placed the image back into her portfolio. "I believe it will be liberating to share it with us, and then we shall allow you to sleep. I will sit with you tonight to make certain that your slumber is not troubled. I will not leave your side, Katelyn."

"Thank you, Nicolas. Thank you. I have been carrying this knowledge around for months, and I couldn't talk to anyone about it. It has been eating me alive. You're right. It will be cathartic for me to tell you. After all of her remarkable accomplishments, after leading the French soldiers in liberating city after city, Jehanne succeeds in getting the Dauphin to Reims where he is crowned King Charles VII of France. But *he* is the one who does the betraying. That horrible coward turns his back on her! She makes him King of France, and then he turns around and allows her to be arrested by the Burgundians at the direction of their English allies. And he does nothing to save her. Nothing!" Katelyn's face was flushed and Nicolas immediately regretted encouraging her to describe the event. He could see the throbbing of a vein on her forehead, which indicated that her heart was racing, and he knew that in her current condition, it was not a good sign.

"And so they put her to death?" Brother Thibault asked quietly. "The English execute her?"

"Oh, executing her would be compassionate, actually kind compared to what they do to her," Katelyn said with pure hatred, as between her words, she tried to catch her breath. She succeeded in drawing in only short, shallow breaths. "No, the Burgundians and the English have to discredit her and all that she has done. They do everything they can to make it seem like she was sent by Satan himself. The last thing they want is to create a martyr, so they paint her out to be a devil in disguise. Can you imagine?" she cried. "Nicolas, you and I have in reality come face to face with Satan's emissary, and yet these fools take this brave, innocent girl and call her evil."

Katelyn was becoming more and more distressed, and Nicolas didn't know what to do to calm her mounting anxiety. "Katelyn, I am sorry I pressed you on this matter. You are not well and it is unwise for you to become so distraught. We shall speak of this again tomorrow. You must get some sleep now."

"Sleep? How can I sleep when I see this," she said lifting up the image. "They accuse her of lying about her voices. It would be like the three of us being put to death because we admit we've heard the Archangel. They claim her voices were not from God, and so they put her on trial for heresy, and then to cross all their 't's, they accuse her of cross-dressing, as if that could be considered a crime punishable by death, and they trump up an entire assortment of false charges! But even worse, they humiliate her and degrade her for months, throwing her into a filthy cell with lewd male guards. And then . . . you saw it," she cried hysterically. "They burn her. They burn her alive! Jehanne La Pucelle has only a little over two years to live. On the thirtieth day of May in 1431, at the age of only nineteen,

Joan of Arc will die. And many believe that it is her martyrdom, not just her victories, that inspires and ultimately saves France. And Nicolas, we have to help her achieve those victories, so she *can* be burned alive!"

With those words, Katelyn's head fell back against her pillow. Her breathing was ragged and shallow, and although her face had been flushed with emotion and anger, a sallowness set in that was even more frightening.

"I cannot bear it. I simply can't bear it," she whispered, "and I just pray that I will not have to witness it firsthand."

Chapter 22

OKAY. I'M FINALLY STARTING TO FEEL like a real person again. The top of my head is no longer quite so tender to the touch, and I can keep my eyes open. I guess I've spent a couple of days mostly in and out of sleep, but I'm awake now and the fuzzy rot in my brain has been replaced by a surprising mental clarity. And that mental clarity is focused on three things: the Fate of the World, the Secret of the Mount, and Abdon.

With the fog gone, I remember my conversations with Brother Thibault and Nicolas. My dear mentor, Jean le Vieux, told Brother Thibault, "It all depends upon Katelyn." The fate of the world depends upon me! I might be a year older, but I certainly don't feel a year wiser. I mean, really? The fate of the world?

But I can't look at the entire ball of wax, or I'll go crazy. I need to focus on this mission and this mission alone. I have to help Joan of Arc fulfill her destiny, and I think if I succeed in that, then the fate business will fall into place. I think Mont Saint Michel will be protected from an English army bent on destroying this symbol of French nationalism. So that's my first order of business. Focus on Jehanne and not the bigger picture.

Number two. The secret of the Mount. Honestly, isn't it about time Nicolas tells me what this whole business is about? It's why I've been called to be a Watchman. It's why Abdon is after me, and evidently, if it comes out, the world will be in Satan's power. Jeez, I can't even imagine what kind of a secret could have that kind of power. So, it's time for Nicolas to come clean on that.

Thirdly, where is Abdon? And how can we protect ourselves from him? Frankly, in spite of how horrific the English constable Richard Collins was as Abdon's host, it was much easier knowing who and what we were fighting. The not knowing is way worse. I mean, *way* worse. It makes me suspicious of everyone, even though I haven't actually seen anyone yet in 1428 except Nicolas and Brother Thibault. Abdon could be Brother Thibault for all I know. I'm going to have to ask Nicolas about that in private. See? Isn't that horrifying that I can't even trust my gut about one of the kindest men I've ever met? I mean, I have to come back here with Jean le Vieux gone, and the Archangel (I hope) has called a new Watchman who is just as remarkable. But I can't be sure if he's for real! That's what this ghastly not knowing does to me.

So, I finally get up and go to the window. I can hear a pounding coming from outside that I can't identify, like metal clashing against metal. As soon as I open the window, it dawns on me. It is Brother Thibault working in his—let's see what do they call it? A smithy? Yeah, I think that's it. He's working in his makeshift smithy below, which is mostly in the open air, and it looks like he's making a sword. Great! My first item of business is being handled. I call down to him, and he looks up and calls out happily to me in French.

"*Bonjour* Katelyn. *Je suis si heureux de te voir.* I am so happy to see you. I hope you were able to enjoy some much needed slumber."

"*Oui*," I reply. I have to remember not to speak English in public. The Montois still believe that I'm Bretonne, and that's why my French is a bit odd, because my native tongue is Breton, a Celtic language. "*Je me sens bien mieux.* I am feeling much better, thank you."

Brother Thibault places the sword on his workbench as he calls up to me, "*Je viens tout de suite pour te faire à manger.* I'm coming right in to make you something to eat." His booming voice echoes through the chilly air.

He doesn't give me a chance to protest but turns immediately and enters the cottage from the back door. He is so kind, and yet something just doesn't sit right with me. He's too kind! As I contemplate my situation, I take the time to look out from my window and assess my surroundings. I know from my earlier stay in this room, that I'm looking east towards the town of Avranches. It's a cold but sunny day outside, and judging by the position of the shadows of the buildings on the sands of the bay below, it seems to be morning.

I use the water in the basin that Brother Thibault has kindly left me (or is it really poison from Abdon?) to wash up as much as I can. I brush my teeth, change my underwear, and pull on some clean clothes: leggings and a tunic that look like they can pass for male clothing in 1429. After all, if I'm going to help Joan of Arc, I'd better follow her example, and try to pass as a man. Then I walk downstairs to ask some questions.

"Katelyn," says Brother Thibault with the biggest grin I've ever seen in the fifteenth century. This time he addresses me in English. "I am so pleased to see you up and walking, my dear. And wearing such fetching attire, as well. I trust that your condition has improved. Come. Sit, and I will make an omelet for you."

How could I possibly suspect this man of being Abdon's new fifteenth-century host? But I do, even though I see nothing of Abdon in Brother Thibault's eyes. He seems just too darn good to be true. Especially after my last jaunt into fifteenth-century France when I could never get enough to eat.

"Is Nicolas here?" I ask, somewhat reluctant to eat anything until I've spoken to Nicolas privately. "Before I eat, I need to speak with him."

"He has gone to fetch water from the spring," Brother Thibault explains. "You should go out to meet him. He will be so pleased to see you, and it will do you good to get some fresh air. But do not forget your cloak," he says as he brings me the brown wool cloak I'd been wearing when I arrived. "It is a lovely day, but it is chilly."

"Thank you," I say as he covers me with the cloak. "Have the Montois been prepared for my reappearance after four years?"

"Yes, when Nicolas left to go to your time, he explained that he was going to hopefully bring home his bride, and the villagers are looking forward to greeting you and thanking you for your remarkable exploits to relieve the siege last time you were here. They believe that you have been recovering from your life-threatening illness at a nunnery in Brittany."

"Thanks for the heads-up," I say and then amend it to "I mean the explanation. Is Madame Mercier still living next door?"

"*Eh bien*, I regret to inform you that she passed away a few years ago," Brother Thibault announces. "I never made her acquaintance, but Nicolas told me about her and of her kindness towards you. I believe that the years of penury she suffered were too severe for her constitution to recover."

"That makes me so sad," I say truthfully. "What about the rest of the villagers? Are most of them still here?"

"Oh, yes, my dear. Most of the Montois you would have known are still here, and because of your actions, you will be pleased to learn that life is much improved for them. Pilgrims have finally been allowed to return to the Mount, although the Godons demand that a bribe be paid to cross the sand   Of course, they call it a travel tax, but it is essentially a bribe. But fortunately, that has not stopped the pilgrims. And they have brought income back to the Montois with the renewed production of enseignes and other tokens the pilgrims seek as remembrances of their trek, along with an increased need for guides, innkeepers, and eating establishments. In fact, a rather large group of pilgrims arrived just last night to attend the three masses that will be celebrated on Christmas Day through Twelfth Night."

That's right. It's nearly Christmas! I hope I'm not going to miss Christmas with my Dad and Adèle, but I can't worry about that right now. I also know that in medieval Europe, the twelve days of Christmas are not the twelve days we Americans tend to celebrate leading up to Christmas. No, here they extend from Christmas Day to Epiphany, celebrated on the sixth day of January, which also happens to be Joan of Arc's seventeenth birthday. Nicolas and I don't have much time left to prepare.

"And I have other news that is of the utmost interest, my dear. As you suggested, I found a pretext to call upon Brother Girard, and he was quite excited to tell me that he had just found another prophecy in an obscure chronicle about La Pucelle. The reason he was so excited is because it concerned Mont Saint Michel. He found a passage prophesying that La Pucelle would be assisted in her mission by the Maiden Warrior who had rescued Mont Saint Michel. It also included a set of numerals, which he deciphered as meaning that the Warrior would be setting off on her journey to help La Pucelle this very month, and it included an allusion to a fleur-de-lis that would flower once again when these two maidens joined forces to drive the wild beast from Orléans. Pretty amazing, *n'est-ce pas?*"

"Are you kidding me?" I reply. "So now I'm supposed to be the Maiden Warrior? Is that it?"

"*Eh bien*, it is obvious that this prophecy refers to you, Katelyn. You are the maiden warrior who saved Mont Saint Michel."

Even though I'm technically a "madame" because in the eyes of the Church I'm married to Nicolas, I'm certainly a maiden in the true sense of the word. But a prophecy about me in ancient writings?

Really? This is too much to take in. In all of my studying about Joan of Arc, I've never come across a prophecy about a 'maiden' from Mont Saint Michel.

Because of my current doubts about Brother Thibault, I don't know what to make of this bit of news. In addition, now I'm worried about this Brother Girard guy as well. This just seems too convenient to find a prophesy about 'me' leaving the Mount to help Joan of Arc. Could he possibly be Abdon's new host? I need to think about it, and so I repeat my urgent need to speak to Nicolas before I eat the breakfast Brother Thibault seems so eager to make for me.

For the first time since my arrival, I leave Jean's cottage. See? I still call it Jean's cottage. Can't help it. And I'm nervous to leave the confines of its safe walls. I feel anxious about the explanations I might need to make to the Montois, but I'm also relieved that Nicolas and Brother Thibault have done the preparatory work. I'm also nervous because I don't want Brother Thibault to have any idea that I have questions about him. It seems like a betrayal. So I pull the hood of my cloak up over my head and start up the village street towards the north side of the mount, where a set of stairs leads down from the abbey grounds to Saint Aubert's Spring. I'm really not in the mood to meet anyone I know except Nicolas.

There are clusters of people out and about, but no one pays any particular attention to me. Actually, most of them look like I do, covered by heavy cloaks, and most of them are carrying hefty walking sticks. Some are also wearing wide-brimmed hats and carry large scallop shells on cords around their necks or on their hats. And then it hits me. Oh my goodness. I am seeing history in the making! I remember studying in my history class about the most important religious pilgrimages in medieval times. There is Jerusalem (which very few people could ever complete, let alone begin), then Rome, and finally, Santiago de Compostela in Northern Spain, where tradition has it that the remains of Christ's apostle James are buried in the great cathedral of that city. Faithful Catholics were inspired to make these pilgrimages in the hopes of receiving what is called a 'plenary indulgence,' which they believed could free them from paying penance for their sins.

For the French, Santiago de Compostela was the most achievable of these once-in-a-lifetime journeys, and the French traveled along several Church-approved routes, called the Chemin de Saint Jacques de Compostelle in French, or in English, the Way of Saint James. There were dozens of important stops along that *chemin*, and Mont Saint Michel was one of them.

This is so exciting! During my first visit to the fifteenth century, my exposure to actual history was limited to the starving Montois, the Godon ship, and the English camp at Ardevon. Besides, during that time excursion, I didn't know anything about French history, and honestly, I didn't care. Now, I do know something about French history and I do care. I'm pretty excited.

Another thing that thrills me is that I hear chatter. Actual chatter coming from non-starving individuals. I've never seen so much action on the Mount in the fifteenth century. It's awe-inspiring, and I can't help but feel just a little bit proud of the changes I see. There are a few metal merchant signs hanging from some of the buildings, nothing like in the twenty-first century, but hey, it's a start. Katelyn Michael's free enterprise emporium in action!

Then, a thought enters my mind. Oh no! Pilgrims *are* coming to the Mount freely now! That means just one more way for Abdon to infiltrate our nice little Watchman fortress. All he has to do is try to inhabit the body of one of the pilgrims and voilà! He can be here on the mountain. He can learn that we have a new Watchman (if, in fact, Brother Thibault is really a Watchman), and what will stop him from killing all three of us? My mind starts spinning with the ramifications of this new thought.

As I reach the lower grounds of the abbey, I come face to face with Nicolas, carrying two large buckets of water, one looped over each end of a long pole resting on his shoulders. He looks at me and stops. I think it takes him a second to recognize me with the hood of my cloak pulled up over my head. Then those dazzling brown eyes light up, and I see pure joy reflected in them. Oh, my gosh. He is gorgeous! In spite of the chill in the air, his face is glistening with sweat from the effort he has just made to carry the water up a gazillion steps from Saint Aubert's Spring, which I know sits just above the beach on the north side of the island. His blond curls cling to his forehead, and I've never seen anything as appealing. He carefully sets down the water and beckons me forward. It's not as if he can come and embrace me. We are in a public place, and furthermore, I'm wearing men's clothing.

"Nicolas," I blurt out in English before he can say anything. "I've got to talk to you. Now. Before we get back to the cottage." My breathing starts to accelerate, and I feel as if I can't get the words out fast enough. A group of the pilgrims pause and look at us as they continue to wend their way up towards the stairs to the abbey entrance. Now, I'm not so excited about them being at Mont Saint Michel, so I'm anxious to move out of their sight.

"Katelyn," he whispers, as he takes my arm and guides me out of the path of the pilgrims and around to the north side of the abbey, which offers total privacy, "I am so pleased to see you up and walking, but you must calm down. Come, sit here by me on the wall. Now tell me, what has caused you to be so excited?"

"It's Abdon. Well, it's that I don't know who Abdon is, and you see, well, I just wondered if you're . . . I mean, did you have any questions about Brother Thibault when he arrived? I know it sounds ludicrous, but you weren't the one on that Godon ship hearing about what Richard Collins was about to do to me. That experience alone makes me suspicious of everyone. If Abdon wanted to fool us, what better way than to come in the disguise of a friend. I mean, how can you really know if Thibault's claims are for real? Do you really believe he was sent by the Archangel?"

"Slow down, Katelyn. Slow down. Are you asking me if Brother Thibault could be Abdon? Is that what you are asking?"

"Yeah, that's exactly what I'm asking," I admit, and I feel tears welling up in my eyes. "And so you see why I had to come out and meet you. I mean, the guy's a saint. Thibault, I mean, not Abdon, and I wouldn't want to hurt his feelings with such ridiculous accusations to his face if it's not true, but that's what Abdon has done to me. He's made me suspicious of everyone. I can't stand the not knowing, because I know Abdon's out there. I know he's trying to kill me, and it's making me crazy. I'd rather know who our enemy is than have these horrible feelings of suspicion towards everybody. I mean, how can we really know? I know that Jean said he could recognize Abdon in his different personages, but I don't know if I can . . . or if you can. Can you? I mean, can you tell?" By this time, the tears have spilled over my eyelids, and I'm so embarrassed to be so emotional. But having a shape-shifting demon try to kill you is not exactly a picnic!

"Katelyn," he replies calmly as he touches my hand. "I have to admit that I had my doubts about him when he first showed up as well, so I can understand your suspicions, but I can assure you that Brother Thibault is not Abdon. He is exactly who he says he is: a Watchman who was sent to us by the Archangel."

"But how do you know that?" I ask. "How do you know he's telling the truth?"

"It's simple, Katelyn. He told me the secret of the Mount. If Brother Thibault were Abdon, he wouldn't know the secret. That is why Abdon continues to harass us: to learn the secret. If Thibault were a physical incarnation of Abdon, neither you nor I would be here. We would be dead, and the Mount would be ripped apart by

Abdon and Satan's other unhallowed spirits. Our mission would be over."

"But, but . . ." I fumble, not knowing exactly how to put my thoughts into words. "Wasn't it Jean le Vieux who told Thibault the secret? I mean, it wasn't the Archangel who told him. And maybe Jean made a terrible error, and Thibault is just biding his time . . . waiting for me to arrive, so he can kill both of us in one fell swoop."

"No, Katelyn," Nicolas assures me, "Jean le Vieux would never have made that mistake. He would *never* have told Thibault the secret unless he had been instructed to do so by the Archangel himself. It is not possible. I assure you that Thibault is one of us. He is a Watchman, and he is here to help us in our mission."

I breathe a sigh of relief. "Oh, thank goodness," I say out loud. "I was so panicked, because I think Thibault is one of the greatest men I've ever met. I mean the guy's just almost too good to be true, and so that's why I just couldn't get those suspicions out of my mind. And then Thibault just told me about his most recent visit with Brother Girard, and that makes me mighty suspicious."

"Yes, he told me about it as well. Congratulations on your new title, Katelyn: The Maiden Warrior, although I would certainly like to change that 'maiden' bit! Hopefully one day . . ."

I must be blushing a thousand shades of red, because he quickly adds, "So why does that make you suspicious?"

"Well, could Brother Girard really be Abdon fishing around for information about Jehanne?"

"Katelyn, you have got to calm your mind. You are seeing Abdon everywhere. Although I am not personally acquainted with Brother Girard, I do know who he is. He has been here for years— long before I came to Mont Saint Michel. And Jean knew all of the monks. He would have known if Brother Girard was suspect."

"Well, I know he wasn't Abdon's host when I was here last, but maybe Abdon's been working on him since Collins died, and he's the new host, so Jean would not have known about him," I say.

"Katelyn, stop. You cannot go around accusing everyone on the Mount of being Abdon. Brother Girard is a good man. He has a good heart. And besides, I have seen him recently. I think I would know if he were Abdon."

"Are you sure?"

"I am quite certain."

"Well, okay, but there's another thing I'm worried about as well," I continue with what I can feel is escalating panic. "What about all these pilgrims coming to the island? Abdon could easily come to the mount with one of them as his host. And we're just sitting ducks here."

"I don't know what a sitting duck is," Nicolas says, "but I have to admit, that is a more logical possibility. But remember what Jean told you about Abdon? It is not a simple task for him to be successful in taking a human host. It takes years to cultivate a willing human host. I would think that pilgrims with pure hearts, like monks, would be particularly difficult to inhabit."

"Yeah, but he could inhabit the body of an evil man and then join a bunch of pilgrims coming here," I insist. "After all, it's been over four years since you last saw him here, Nicolas. He's had four whole years to cultivate a new host." By this time, I feel the tears starting to build up again, and I fight them back with everything I've got. Why can't I control my tears? After all, I am Katelyn Michaels, the Maiden Warrior who saved Mont Saint Michel. I'm no longer just a naïve little teenager. I should be stronger than this, but I just can't help myself.

"That is true. We must be on our guard. But Katelyn, I think we will be able to recognize him, just as Jean was always able to recognize him. His voice, his eyes, his demeanor. His evil shows through. And, we must trust in the Archangel to assist us, to warn us."

"The Archangel didn't exactly warn us about that last attack—on the rampart walls in my time—now did he?" I ask. "And that brings me to the other thing I need to talk to you about. It's that secret business. You may have told me about it before you sent me back to my time, Nicolas, but I don't remember anything you said. It has been the question that's been on my mind constantly for six months. I know it's the reason Abdon has tried to kill me, let's see . . . six times now, including as a stallion tying to trample me in America. It's because of this big secret, and I want to know what it is. I deserve to know what it is and I won't take no for an answer. Don't you think it's about time you told me what the secret of Mont Saint Michel is?"

Nicolas looks at me with such intensity that I can tell something is wrong. "Katelyn," he begins, "I know you are not going to be pleased about this. You are correct. I did tell you about the secret of the Mount when you were ill and before I sent you back to your time after you saved the Mount. I felt you had proven your worth. You had proven that you were truly a Watchman, and you *did* deserve to know the secret. But I have to inform you that the situation has now changed."

"What do you mean?" I challenge. "What has changed? Have I or have I not proven my worth? Are you trying to tell me that I don't deserve to know the secret? Am I a second-class Watchman or something? Is it because I'm a woman?"

"No, Katelyn. That isn't it at all. It has nothing to do with your gender." He stops and then he takes my hand in his after looking around to make certain that no one is in sight.

"It has everything to do with the fact that I have communed with the Archangel since you arrived. While you were ill. He has made it clear to me that the only way to keep you safe from Abdon is to keep the secret from you."

"Are you stinkin' kidding me?" I rip my hand out of his and jump to my feet. "Are you kidding me? I've risked my life, I've been ripped from my century and away from my family and loved ones to come and protect this Mount and its blasted secret and yet you're telling me now that I don't even deserve to know what that secret is?"

"Katelyn, calm down. I knew you would not take this well. I am so sorry. But this cannot be changed . . . at least for the time being. There will come a time—and I do not know when that will be—when the Archangel will share the secret with you. This is not my will. It is the will of the Archangel. I cannot change it. It is the only way to keep you safe."

"Oh, you think I'm safe, do you? Well, let me tell you something, Nicolas. I haven't exactly been safe lately, have I? So why all of the sudden does the Archangel think that my not knowing the secret is going to keep me safe? Huh?" I am simply furious, and yet I have to admit, I feel just a teeny-weeny bit nervous about criticizing the Archangel. After all, I know he's the one who has brought me here. Who am I to question an angel? But I just can't help myself. I'm just so dang mad.

"Katelyn, I have no answers to give you, but he has assured me that certain events will make it clear why this directive has been given. He has given his assurance to me that by refraining to tell you the secret, I will be guaranteeing your safety. You will be safe."

"Just what does that mean? Safe? Safe from being raped or injured? Safe from being tortured or maimed? Or just safe from being dead?"

"Again, unfortunately, I cannot give you the answers you need. I do not wish for us to argue about this point, for I cannot change it, even if I wanted to. I would be disobeying God's will. However, I suggest you go to the chapel to seek enlightenment. To Notre-Dame-Sous-Terre. Learn for yourself that this is the Archangel's will. You must commune with him, Katelyn. You have heard his voice before. It is time for you to hear his voice again. You must learn for yourself why this is so."

And so, his water-bearing duties forgotten for the moment, Nicolas takes me kicking and screaming—well, metaphorically kicking and screaming—to Notre-Dame-Sous-Terre. And he tells me not to come back to the cottage until I have received the answers I seek.

Chapter 23

"OU EST KATELYN? **WHERE IS KATELYN,** Nicolas?"
Brother Thibault asked. "I sent her out to meet you. You must not
have crossed her path. I am ready to make her an omelet. Did you
see her?" Thinking of food made the retired monk unconsciously tug
on the sash of his long brown robe. Even though he was no longer a
monk, he had no desire to abandon the Benedictine attire. After all, it
was so much more comfortable than donning the tight trousers that
Nicolas and the other Montois wore. No, he would be just fine in
this apparel for the rest of his life.

"Oui," Nicolas replied as he carried in the buckets of water he
had gone to fetch. He placed the water-bearing pole next to the
chimney. "I did cross paths with her. We had some very important
things to discuss. Brother Thibault, I have heard the Archangel's
voice," he continued his explanation, "while I was gathering water at
Saint Aubert's Spring. It is the first time in so long. It was so
reassuring. I am both gratified but also disappointed."

"What do you mean?" Brother Thibault questioned. "You are
happy but sad?"

"Yes. I feel reassured and gratified that I have not been
abandoned, that I am still on the correct path serving him, that I am

indeed a Watchman. But I am disappointed because of what he told me."

"Which was?" Brother Thibault encouraged Nicolas without being overbearing. He did not want to push Nicolas. The lad's conflicting emotions were apparent and Thibault wanted to be there to offer support. Not to dictate. He had been specifically charged by Jean le Vieux with taking care of the younger Watchman, but he did not want Nicolas to feel that he was trying to imply seniority. Even though Thibault was older, Nicolas had been a Watchman for much longer than Thibault. Although there had never been a sense of resentment emanating from the younger man, Thibault never wanted Nicolas to feel that he considered himself to be the tutor. No, if anything, Thibault always tried to act more like a servant to Nicolas rather than as a leader or mentor.

"Just as I was prepared to discuss with Katelyn why we have been called as Watchmen, to tell her of the sacred confidence with which we have been entrusted—which she has proven she deserves to know, by the way—the Archangel's voice spoke to me. He told me that I could not divulge the secret to her. After all she has done, after all she has sacrificed, including nearly losing her own life, she is not to be told the reason for it all. As you can imagine, she is very distraught. I took her to the chapel—to Notre-Dame-Sous-Terre—to plead for her own confirmation from the Archangel. That is where her keyhole is, Brother Thibault, and I hope the Archangel will see fit to commune with her there. It seems fitting for her to go there. Are you not in agreement?"

Thibault had been told on many occasions that he had a gift for discerning others' feelings and at that moment, he knew there was something more that concerned his young friend.

"Nicolas," he began, not giving a direct answer to Nicolas's rhetorical question, "I can see that this is very troubling to you. Did the Archangel tell you why you are not allowed to share the secret with Katelyn?"

"Yes, and it is troubling. 'Tis troubling, indeed."

Thibault looked at Nicolas with tremendous compassion and waited. He didn't want to insist. It would be better if the young Watchman told him of the message voluntarily. Finally, Nicolas spoke again.

"As I was drawing the water from Saint Aubert's Spring, the voice of the Archangel came to me as clearly as if I were speaking to him face to face. I did not see a vision, but I heard his voice, as if he were standing next to me. It was not a delusion. It was his voice, the voice I have waited to hear for over four years." Thibault could see the emotions welling up in his young charge's face, and he placed a comforting arm around the lad.

"He told me that Katelyn's life depended upon her *not* knowing the secret." The young man took Brother Thibault's arm and led him to the bench at the table. "Sit down," he said. "His message was for both of us. These are his exact words: 'Nicolas, I know the desires of your heart. It is only normal for you to wish to share the sacred trust that has been revealed to you and Thibault. Her loyalty warrants your desire to do so for she has proven to be a true and faithful Watchman. However, the success of your mission depends upon her being ignorant of that knowledge. Should she know it, her life, and others' lives will be in danger. You and Thibault must protect her at all costs, and the only way to do that is to refrain from divulging the sacred information.' And then he was gone. His voice was silent. I pled for further enlightenment, but that is all he said."

"Yes," Thibault tried to reassure him, "I can now better comprehend why you are troubled. The lass has strong character, and she will not take this news happily. Hopefully, I can cheer her up with a tasty dish."

"That is for certain," Nicolas confirmed. "She certainly did not accept the message happily. But 'tis not the aspect of his message that I find troubling, Thibault. 'Tis rather the content of the message that distresses me. It means that Katelyn's life will be threatened yet again, and the only thing we can do to protect her is to refrain from doing the very thing she so desires. In fact, the success of our mission depends upon it. I have ruminated upon it in my mind, over and over again, and I cannot solve the puzzle. But I do know that it must mean that the threat to her will come directly from Abdon. Have you any thoughts on what the Archangel's words mean, Brother Thibault?"

"Alas, my dear boy, I fear I am not the one who can enlighten you, but I do agree with you. I fear the message means that Abdon is near. It means that as long as Katelyn remains ignorant of the sacred power of the Mount, he will not kill her. But why? If she doesn't know the secret, then he would have no reason to keep her alive," he mused, "particularly in light of her recent exploits. She saved the Mount from Abdon's evil intentions. It would seem only natural that the evil one would wish to prevent her from further assisting us in this cause, that he would want to be rid of her once and for all. You are correct. 'Tis indeed a perplexing puzzle."

"Yes. Now, you comprehend what I mean," Nicolas replied. "If he cannot glean any information from her, and knowing the success she had during her last mission for the Archangel, why wouldn't Abdon simply kill her openly, to prevent her from performing this next mission?"

Thibault sat silent for a moment, contemplating the mystery in his own mind. "Nicolas," he finally said, "I can come to only one conclusion. I fear, lad, that he intends to use her life as leverage to force us into divulging the sacred trust, just as he did with the young son of Jean le Vieux. It is unspeakable, for you know what that means, do you not?"

"Yes. It means that Abdon is going to capture Katelyn and use her as bait. It is truly unspeakable. And we cannot tell her, Thibault. We cannot inform her of our thoughts about this, for she will lose all hope of success." At this spoken admission, a single tear worked its way down the cheek of the young man who after four long years, had finally been reunited with the one he loved above all else . . . except God. Thibault's own heart, which had never known such love, felt like breaking, out of pure compassion for Nicolas. And then, a thought came to his mind.

"Yes, my boy. That is the only logical conclusion. But we must take heart! Courage, Nicolas. There is a beacon of hope, for unlike Jean's son, who was killed unmercifully the minute his father held firm, Katelyn will *not* be sacrificed. As long as we do not give in, as long as we do *not* reveal the secret, Abdon will be forced to keep her alive, for she is the only leverage he has to get us to reveal the information. Don't you see? He might torture us, and he might even torture her, but as long as we do not reveal the secret, Katelyn's life will be spared. All in all, I think it is glorious news, lad. We hold the key to keeping her safe, and Abdon does not know that we understand his evil intents. The Archangel has truly blessed us with this knowledge!"

Thibault could see the thought processes churning in Nicolas's mind. "Yes, you may be right, Brother Thibault. In a perverted sort of way, this is good news. But it also implies that all three of us might be subject to the sadistic actions of a maniacal demon. And it does not ensure that either you or I shall not be killed."

"You are correct in your thinking, Nicolas, but knowing how you feel about Katelyn, I realize that you would rather give up your own life if it meant keeping her alive. And as for myself? I have experienced more joy and happiness in these past few months with you that I cannot regret anything. If I am to die, then I am to die, and it will be God's own will. I promise you that I will hold firm should I be Abdon's target."

"Thank you, my dear brother. And so will I," Nicolas said. "But we absolutely cannot let Katelyn know of the ramifications of this message. We cannot allow her to believe that either of our lives might be endangered, for it would hinder her ability to carry out her mission if she were to be overly concerned for us. How can we justify the Archangel's message about not telling her the secret so that she will not be overly preoccupied about why?"

But Nicolas's question remained unanswered, for at just that very moment, the cottage door was opened abruptly, and Katelyn Michaels flew in. Brother Thibault didn't need any of his perceptive intuition to know that the lass was in a rage.

Chapter 24

"OKAY, YOU GUYS WIN, AND I'M ABSOLUTELY furious,"
Katelyn said to her two companions as she slammed the cottage door
behind her.

"Katelyn, I know this must be hard," Nicolas said as he helped
her remove her heavy cloak. "Come, sit here in your chair by the fire
and explain yourself. What have we won?"

"The argument, Nicolas. The stinking argument. I know you
never wanted to tell me the secret from the beginning, and now
you've got your way!"

"Katelyn," he said with a hint of sharpness, "I have not won
anything. I *wanted* to tell you the secret. I was *prepared* to tell you. In
fact, I already *did* tell you. 'Tis the Archangel who does not want you
to know. 'Tis he who removed the memories of what I told you
during your last journey here. So, I have not won anything. I am just
as disappointed as you are. But I hope you have heard his voice. Did
he speak to you? Did you hear him, Katelyn?"

She huffed as she sat down, and then she leaned over her knees
and rubbed her eyes with her fingers. Nicolas knew she was trying to
hide the tears that must have gathered during her emotional storm.
Her thick braid slid over her shoulder and thumped her on the cheek,

195

as if to further annoy her. Thibault was still sitting on the bench at the table, and Nicolas pulled up a chair next to Katelyn.

"Tell us what happened, Katelyn," he said, this time forcing his voice to be gentle. "I cannot pretend to claim that I understand exactly how you must be feeling, but I do know this must be a huge disappointment."

"I'm sorry I snapped at both of you. I know it isn't your fault, but you're right. I am *so* disappointed. I feel like I've proven myself, and I don't understand why I'm not allowed to know the secret."

"Did you hear his voice, Katelyn? What did he say to you?"

"Yes," she finally admitted. "He spoke to me. You were right about taking me to Notre-Dame-Sous-Terre, Nicolas. But it was a risky move, you know. I could have just used my key and gone back to my time, and I was tempted to do it. But . . . no, that's not really true. I would never have abandoned either one of you, even if I was furious. So I just sat there by the altar, on the stone bench where you carved my keyhole, Nicolas. I sat there and fumed, and I rubbed my fingers in the keyhole, and then little by little, I calmed down, and I started to wonder why I couldn't know the secret. And you know what? I finally understood. You told me it was to protect *my* life. The truth is, it's to safeguard *all* of our lives *and* our mission."

"Did he tell you that?" Nicolas asked, hoping beyond hope that Michael had found a way of sharing his message with Katelyn. "Did the Archangel tell you that you couldn't know the secret or our mission would fail? Did you hear his voice?" Nicolas didn't know much about the workings of the human mind, but he was starting to understand that the Archangel was very wise indeed. Michael had personalized the message he had given to both Nicolas and Katelyn.

"Yes," replied Katelyn to Nicolas's question. "As I sat there, I started feeling all warm inside. It was actually a really peaceful feeling, not a scary feeling, and then the words came to my mind, but they came as a voice. It was the same voice I heard the first time I entered the abbey church when I was here last summer with my brother. Then, I didn't know what in the heck was happening to me. I thought I was going crazy, but this time, I knew it was the voice of Michael, the Archangel."

"Do you remember his exact words, Katelyn?" Nicolas prodded.

"Yes. I do. He said, 'Katelyn, you have proven yourself worthy in every way to be my Watchman. Nevertheless, there are evil forces at work, which threaten to destroy a sacred agreement I made with God himself. This agreement must be protected at all costs, and that is why I have relied on emissaries on earth to assist me in protecting it. I cannot divulge it to you now because should I do so, your mission and your lives will be in jeopardy. You must be patient. The time will come when all will be revealed to you, but that time is not now. Be patient and carry out your mission to assist the Maiden in her quest. And this you must begin immediately.' Those are his exact words. I remember every word, because he spoke them to me three times. I guess I'm slow to learn . . . like Bishop Aubert was slow to learn. Actually, I guess I should just be glad the Archangel didn't poke a hole in my skull with his finger of light."

At this, Nicolas actually laughed. Katelyn still had her sense of humor.

"That's probably just a legend, you know, Katelyn. I mean, that Michael poked a hole in Aubert's skull."

"I'm not so sure," she replied as she pressed her hands to her skull and moved them all around as if she were actually feeling for a hole. "I mean I know what it's like to be stubborn, and maybe Aubert was even more stubborn than me. Nope, nothing there!" She smiled at Nicolas as she removed her hands, and Nicolas melted at seeing her face light up. Everything was going to be all right. But he was surprised that the Archangel had spoken of the sacred agreement, for it was an expression Nicolas himself had never used publicly to describe the secret. However, it only further validated the fact that Katelyn had heard the Archangel's voice.

"So if it's to safeguard our mission and lives, I have no choice. I'm not happy about not knowing, but I won't fight it," Katelyn said. "The secret is about a sacred agreement?"

"No," replied Nicolas. "We will not speak of it. We shall say nothing more about it. Now, it seems, we need to be focusing all of our energy on beginning our mission. Brother Thibault, how soon can you finish the sword?"

"I'll be through in just a few days. But Katelyn, you told us that the Maiden would not be leaving her home in Domrémy until January. It is still December. Did you get the impression that you should leave as soon as possible?"

"Yes," she replied. "That's the feeling I got. The Archangel will take us to the correct time and place, even if it means going forward a bit in time. Or maybe we have some prep work to do before Jehanne gets to Sainte-Catherine-de-Fierbois. My gut instinct tells me that one of the reasons we need to leave as soon as possible has more to do with not exposing my presence here on the Mount. It has more to do with Abdon. I think I should stay indoors and not let anyone know I'm here," she said. "As much as I'd like to get out and explore the Mount, as much as I'd like to visit with my Montois friends, I'm worried that one of the pilgrims coming to the mountain could be Abdon's new host. If that's the case, I certainly don't want him to know I'm here."

"That makes sense," replied Nicolas.

"As Jean told me last time, we have an advantage over Abdon, and we've got to do everything we can to maintain that advantage," she continued. "As you reminded me, Abdon doesn't have the ability to know or read our thoughts, and since he can't travel back and forth in time, like us with our keys, right now in 1428, he knows nothing about who this maiden is or what she's going to accomplish.

He will live through the events of these next few years, and obviously he will come to understand the significance of Jehanne's mission, and how it ultimately protects Mont Saint Michel. But Nicolas, you and I will succeed in our mission to help Jehanne, and at some point, Abdon will realize what we are doing, because once again, in the future his host will try to keep me from coming back to help her."

"Yes," Nicolas said. "He'll have to inhabit dozens of hosts until he finally gets to the twenty-first century to stop you, but right now, he is ignorant about Jehanne, and we've got to keep it that way for as long as we can."

"Exactly," Katelyn replied. "We can't let him know anything about Jehanne La Pucelle. We can't let him know where we're going or what our mission is. And another thing, he can't travel from one place to another in his human host instantly, like we evidently can with our time keys, unless he changes hosts. And I don't think that's something he likes to do. As you reminded me, Nicolas, it takes years for Abdon to cultivate a host. So for now, we know he has to travel the old-fashioned way! Right now, we have both time and distance working in our favor."

Nicolas was impressed with Katelyn's new take-charge attitude. It reminded him of when she developed and implemented the plan to save Mont Saint Michel. Clearly, the effects of her head injury were past. And her "gut instinct," as she called it, seemed logical. The three of them had to do everything they could not to let Katelyn's presence on the mount be discovered. He didn't think that any of the monks had seen them arrive through their time portals when both had been severely injured. Several of the monks *had* seen Nicolas escort Katelyn to the sacred chapel that morning, but Katelyn had been wearing her long cloak with her hood pulled over her head. It would have been impossible for anyone to determine who she was, let alone whether she was male or female. And the monks never questioned Nicolas's presence at the abbey. He had been given free rein to come and go in the abbey as he pleased without being stopped or questioned.

"And there's another thing that gives me hope," Katelyn continued. "Nicolas, remember I told you earlier this morning about a stallion that attacked me back home? I haven't had a chance to explain exactly what happened. It was a few weeks before I left to come to France. In fact, it happened on the very morning of the day I received your email message. I thought about it as I sat in Notre-Dame-Sous-Terre, after I received the Archangel's message, and I think we can draw some conclusions from the incident."

"What happened?" Nicolas asked.

"I told you that I've been learning to ride and to fence . . . to fight with a sword. And oh, that reminds me, Brother Thibault. I think you better make three swords. One for Jehanne, of course, but also swords for Nicolas and me. If the Archangel gave me the impression that I needed to know how to defend myself with a sword, I think I better actually have a sword—and so should Nicolas. They don't have to be fancy. I mean, they don't have to meet any specifications like Jehanne's sword."

"I will be pleased to do that," Brother Thibault assured her. "And as you say, I will not need to be quite as meticulous. I estimate that I should be able to have all three swords completed in four days or so. But I fear we will not have the time to have any scabbards made to sheath the swords."

"Then four days it is," Katelyn replied. "We'll plan on leaving four days from now, and we'll go without scabbards. Besides, Jehanne doesn't find a scabbard with her sword. She has one made by the Dauphin's armorer when she gets to Chinon. Let's see, what was I talking about?"

"The stallion, Katelyn," Nicolas replied. "You were telling us something about a stallion attacking you and what we could learn from the incident."

"Oh, yeah, so anyway, one morning I went to the riding stables. It's not like here where people own horses for transportation or for tilling the earth. In my time, people own or ride horses for leisure, for entertainment. So if you want to learn to ride, you usually go to a place where they keep horses just for that purpose."

"People ride horses just for pleasure?" asked Thibault. "I can't imagine anything pleasurable about getting my body up on a horse if I did not have to do it," he said with a chuckle. "Of course, not everyone has my stout constitution. But I digress. Sorry, Katelyn. Please continue."

"So when I got to the stables, the owner's son mentioned that the spirited stallion I usually rode seemed out of sorts, and he suggested I ride a gentle mare instead. But I wouldn't have any of it," she explained. "I didn't want some namby-pamby ride that day. I wanted to ride hard and fast."

Nicolas smiled. He didn't know what namby-pamby meant, but he did know that Katelyn would not settle for a docile mount. She would insist on riding the energetic stallion. Yes, that was Katelyn. "And the stable hand was right, and you did not heed the advice of the expert," he accused.

"Actually," she smiled back at him, "he was wrong. However, after I insisted on riding my regular mount, he insisted on accompanying me on my ride that day. And it was *his* stallion that attacked me!"

"What do you mean attacked you?" Nicolas asked.

"I mean, that horse crashed into my mount, causing me to be thrown off into a lake. Then, the stallion looked me in the eyes and tried to kill me by trampling me to death. Fortunately, my horse got between us and protected me—actually *fought* the other horse. The details aren't important, but, the point is this: it wasn't really the horse that tried to kill me. It was Abdon who possessed that horse. His spirit went into the body of that horse, and he tried to kill me.

There is absolutely no question in my mind about it. I could recognize that look and that feel. It was Abdon, all right."

"And so what are your conclusions about it?" asked Nicolas.

"Well, there are a couple of conclusions. We know that Abdon is still present at Mont Saint Michel in my time, in the twenty-first century, and that even though he looks a bit different, he's still in the same host as he was six months ago in my time. In other words, he's still got the Gothman host. And we know that because Gothman actually attacked us as we were trying to get to the abbey to come back to the fifteenth century. Are you with me so far?"

"Do you mean do we understand?" asked Nicolas.

"Yeah, do you follow my logic?"

"Yes. You are correct. It was the same host who attacked you the first time you came to France with your brother."

"Okay—and Brother Thibault, you're going to have to learn what okay means because I can't speak English without using the term. Anyway, since we also know that Abdon tried to kill me a few weeks before he attacked us on the ramparts, but thousands of miles away, across the ocean back in America, we can conclude that his spirit can travel through space. But his physical host can't. Otherwise, Gothman would have had to take an airplane—oh yeah, you don't know what that is either—anyway, I mean that Gothman would have had to travel like any human being across the ocean to America. Do you agree so far?"

"Yes," they both said.

"Your assumption seems logical," Brother Thibault added. "If Abdon had wanted to attack you in his current host as Gothman, Gothman would have had to physically travel to your home. Is that it?"

"Yeah, that's what I'm thinking. So the fact that he didn't come as Abdon meant that he didn't want to take the time to travel as a human. But, he clearly didn't have the ability to enter and cultivate another human host quickly enough to attack me and prevent me from coming to France. He must have seen you working on the computer with your friend at the hotel and known you had sent me a message to come, Nicolas, and the only thing he could do to stop me was to temporarily leave his human host. His spirit could travel through space, but it could not enter a human host and cultivate that host to kill me quickly enough. His only choice was to enter an animal."

"So what you are basically trying to tell us is that if Abdon learns where we are and wants to come after us, he will either have to leave his current human host—of whom we are unfortunately ignorant—and travel through space and enter into an animal host, or he will have to physically travel to wherever we go in his current human host. Is that it?" asked Nicolas.

"Yeah, that's my conclusion," she said. "So that's why it's so important that he doesn't learn where we're going."

"And it also means we have to watch out for large and violent animals!" added Nicolas.

"Yeah, I guess so," she added reluctantly. "Or snakes, or rabid bats. But there's also something else to learn from Abdon's attack on me as a horse."

"And that is?" asked Brother Thibault.

"To me, it means that just like when he tried to stop me from coming back in time from the future to save the Mount from the English, he has waited hundreds of years, since probably 1429, to stop me from coming back to perform this current mission. He doesn't now know why I'm here again in this century, because he doesn't know the future, but he'll learn why I came at some point during our mission. And that means that we'll be successful with the current mission, or he wouldn't have tried to stop me from coming in the future."

"Yes, that is the argument that Jean used with you, Katelyn, when you were threatening to leave the first time. You are right. It means we will be successful in assisting the Maiden to save France. It is indeed good news," Nicolas beamed.

"Yes, I think that's what it means, but it doesn't necessarily mean that things can't still go wrong. We can still mess up and change the future. I think. I don't know. I do know that we've got to be very careful. And I do know this as well: Abdon is desperate in the future. This time, he tried to stop me before I even got to France. He didn't know when I would come until he saw you on the Mount in my time, Nicolas, trying to contact me. That's when he discovered when I would be coming back, and he decided to leave his human host—which I think has got to be risky—to try to stop me. And when that didn't work, he waited until I actually showed up on the Mount. He must have been watching every single shuttle that came to the Mount in my time since you contacted me. However, what I don't know is if he knows who you are, Brother Thibault. Since we don't know who his current human host is, we've got to be really cautious. I'm afraid that if he sees you here, living with Nicolas, he's going to know that you are also a Watchman. And since Nicolas and I are going to be absent from the Mount, and hopefully he won't know where we've gone, I think things are going to be pretty hairy for you here. He will do whatever he can to learn the secret. You've learned that by now."

"*Eh bien*," said Thibault. "I'm not sure what 'pretty hairy' means, but I understand the message. I have got to be on guard for this Abdon fellow. Unfortunately, or fortunately, I have never had the displeasure of crossing paths with him, so you two are going to have to describe what I need to be watching for."

So Nicolas and Katelyn spent the next hour explaining everything they could to Brother Thibault about their sworn enemy, using the examples of the only two human hosts with whom they were familiar: Richard Collins and Gothman, and to that, Katelyn added Thunder the Stallion. They tried to describe his essence, his voice, the look in his eyes, the way he spoke in his human hosts, and the insidious way in which he was able to manipulate, humiliate, and control others.

Unfortunately for all three of them, they were so engrossed in their attempts to describe evil personified that they failed to notice the shadow that momentarily blocked the light from the cottage window. They failed to feel the chill that whipped through the room for just a single instant, and they failed to perceive the presence of malevolence, for the shadow that blocked the light was the physical embodiment of the very evil they were describing to the unwitting Brother Thibault.

Chapter 25

ONE CHILLY BUT CLEAR WINTER'S DAY IN January of the year fourteen hundred twenty-nine, Jehanne was walking home from the church when she saw her uncle Durand Laxart pull up to her house with his horse and wagon.

"Uncle," she called out to him, and then the words rushed out of her mouth unfiltered. "Welcome. I am so happy to see you. I was hoping I could visit you and Aunt again. Perhaps I can return to Burey-le-Petit with you tomorrow. You will be staying the night, won't you? Let me help you with your horse."

"Jehanne, Jehanne. Calm down. And yes, your aunt would be overjoyed to have you visit," Durand said as he and Jehanne unhitched the horse from the wagon and led him into the stable, located just a stone's throw from the house. "You would be a beacon of light in these long and dreary months, yet somehow I believe you are being disingenuous with me. Are you going to repeat your unfortunate activities of last year?" Jehanne bent down to offer the horse a generous portion of hay and then rose to face her uncle.

Just at that moment, Isabeau opened the cottage door and called out to Laxart with enthusiasm. "Come in, come in, dear Durand," she called out. "'Tis so good to see you. What of your wife? Is she well?" Jehanne was mercifully saved from answering her uncle's pointed question. Her piety would not allow her to tell an untruth, but she was not opposed to refrain from answering.

"Aye, she is well and sends her greetings to all of you," he replied.

"You have arrived just in time to sup with us," Isabeau said. "What brings you so far south on this cold winter's day?"

"I had business in Greux, and thought as it is but a short distance from Domrémy that I would come to visit. I bear news your husband will want to hear . . . and perhaps, your eldest daughter as well," he replied, searching Jehanne's face, but after her earlier outburst, Jehanne refused to allow her emotions to show.

"Please, rest here by the fire while we finish our supper preparations," Isabeau suggested. "Jacques and the boys will be here shortly. They are seeing to the cows. Catherine," Isabeau called to her younger daughter, "please fetch us a pitcher of cider. Durand, of course, you must spend the night with us."

"Thank you, Isabeau. If it isn't too much trouble, I shall," Durand replied. He moved a simple wooden chair from the table close to the fire as Isabeau and Jehanne finished their meal preparations.

After Catherine brought the pitcher back inside, which she had filled from the cider barrel in the shed, Jehanne took it from her and asked, "Uncle, may I heat you a cup of cider? 'Tis quite chilly now, but if you wait for it to heat up, 'twill thaw your cold, tired body and warm your soul."

"Jehanne, you are always so kind and thoughtful." He looked directly at her and winked. "I was hoping that perhaps your parents could spare you again for a visit to my dear wife."

Jehanne touched his shoulder briefly to let him know that she appreciated his suggestion, and then poured the cider into the three-legged pot placed over the fire, just as Jacques d'Arc and his three sons entered the house and greeted their guest.

"Durand," said Jacques after greetings had been exchanged and as the family gathered around the hand-hewn table. "I have heard so many rumors about the English advances. I hope you can enlighten us." He broke the loaf of heavy brown bread and shared a hunk with Durand.

"Yes, the news has been filtering in for weeks," confirmed Durand, "and unfortunately, it is not good. I am sorry to be the bearer of bad tidings, but it has been confirmed that in October, an army of four thousand English troops, under the command of the Earl of Salisbury, and with the assistance of a hundred and fifty Burgundian mercenaries, besieged the city of Orléans. Control of a vital bridge over the Loire River is now in the hands of the enemy, and the bridge is only twenty leagues from Bourges."

Jehanne gasped out loud. She knew that Bourges, straight south of Orléans, was the city from which the Dauphin ruled what was left of his shrinking kingdom. Because of that, his enemies laughingly called him the "King of Bourges."

"But all hope is not lost," Durand said as he looked up at his niece who was serving the men bowls filled with a hearty stew. "Orléans is fortified with walls higher than five men standing on top of each other! And 'tis said that it is being defended by twenty-four hundred Royal troops and three thousand local Armagnacs armed with seventy-one cannons. They will hold firm."

"But Uncle, what if they don't?" Jehanne replied, trying her best to keep her anxiety at bay. "If Orléans falls, there is no hope. The Godons will have free passage to Bourges, and all of France will be doomed."

"Daughter, I know how strongly you feel about the Dauphin's safety," her father said to her sharply, "but these are the affairs of men and should not concern you."

"You can rest assured, dear niece," Durand interjected, looking directly at Jehanne, "the Royal Court has been relocated from Bourges to Chinon, far to the west in the Loire River Valley. The chateau there is fortified, and the Dauphin will be safe. And there is another bit of good news. After capturing the bridge, while Lord Salisbury stood in victory on the bridge's southern *tourelle*, a cannonball was shot from the tower of *Notre Dame*. It struck Lord Salisbury directly in the face, pulverizing his cheek and eye. Our spies in the enemy camp reported that gangrene set in, and the Earl died an agonizing death eight days later."

"'Tis surely divine intervention," Jehanne replied, but her heart was troubled. Where was *her* divine intervention? Upon hearing her uncle's words about the siege of Orléans, straightway the confirmation had come to her mind that her presence was required in the beleaguered city. It was *her* destiny to lift that siege. But just as her heavenly voices offered hope and encouragement, her inner voices countered with doubt and fear. How could she possibly do anything to help the people of Orléans when she couldn't even convince Robert de Baudricourt to listen to her?

"And there is more good news," her uncle continued, this time wisely addressing his words to her father and brothers. Jehanne knew he was trying to offer her reassurance, but his words had the opposite effect on her. "'Tis said that the Duke of Bedford opposed Salisbury's plan to attack Orléans. He warned him that it was particularly unwise given the fact that the lord of Orléans, Duke Charles, was being held in captivity by the English before the attack. In spite of Bedford's evil desires to rule all of France, he nonetheless respects the age-old tenet of battle that a captive lord's lands are entitled to neutrality and should not be invaded. 'Twas immoral for Salisbury to attack Orléans in the first place, and so now, rumors are spreading that the English view Salisbury's death as a bad omen."

"And how is that good news?" asked Jacques.

"The English soldiers are unsettled and disgruntled, and they have lost their commander. Their enthusiasm for the siege has been dealt a severe blow."

"Then we must all pray that this *is* an ill-fated assault. We must have confidence that the Godons will fail in their quest to control Orléans," replied Jacques.

Finally Jehanne's heavenly voices could no longer be quieted. "Papa," she said, "I know you do not wish to hear what I have to say, but in this case, prayer will not be sufficient. Without intervention, Orléans will fall." Jehanne's brothers, who had remained reserved during the discussion, looked up at her in stunned silence. Jehanne knew their thoughts. It was not seemly for a female to intervene in a political discussion, particularly when the discussion was between two adult males.

"Jehanne, Jehanne, when will you cease this nonsense of yours?" her father replied shaking his finger at her. "You know your mother and I love you, and we do not fault your righteous desires to come to the aid of our beloved France. But we have enjoyed a measure of peace in our valley these past weeks, and I will not have you upsetting your mother and sister with talk of additional turmoil."

"But Papa, I cannot deny what my voices have told me. I must come to the aid of the Dauphin. I must convince him to travel to Reims." At this point, Catherine had started crying and was being enfolded in her mother's arms.

"Whether or not your voices have truly commanded you to go to the Dauphin, I cannot judge," her father replied sternly. "I will not refute your claims, but, my darling child, I *know* who you are." His tone lightened as he continued his diatribe, but his fervor was just as intense. "You are a wonderful, loving girl with a heart as big as all of France, but I cannot fathom how you, my daughter . . . nothing more than a simple farm girl, really . . . can assist in this armed struggle which is of a scope and breadth that is unfathomable to you. You are neither a soldier nor a leader, Jehanne. If you persist in your assertions, surely it will bring nothing but heartache to you and to us, your family who loves you."

"Be that as it may, Papa, but if I fail to persist in my quest, I shall be condemned of God, and I fear *His* wrath more than the wrath of men."

"We shall not speak of it again," her father said, and the conversation during the rest of the meal consisted of village gossip and discussions about the advisability of planting a new type of turnip that had gained popularity in the valley.

Jehanne did not say another word during supper, but before the family retired, she brought up the idea of returning with her uncle to Burey-le-Petit. "Please, Father," she said. "Uncle has come to fetch me for a visit. 'Tis a perfect time of year to go, for there is nothing to do in the fields."

She saw the thunderous look in her father's face at this request, but whether it was because of the divine intervention Jehanne sought or simply her father's reluctance to engage in any more verbal confrontation in front of their guest, Jacques d'Arc gave permission for his daughter to accompany Durand Laxart to Burey-le-Petit.

And so it was, the following morning, Jehanne took leave of her parents and siblings. She was not naïve enough to ignore the fact that they were suspicious of her motives for the journey, but she said simply, "Adieu," and then in her desire to be perfectly frank with them, she added, "I am going to Vaucouleurs." She commended them to God and then waved as her uncle pulled the wagon away from the front door. As the rest of the Domrémy villagers prepared to celebrate Epiphany, Jehanne prayed for her own epiphany about how she would get Robert de Baudricourt to heed her demands to send her to the Dauphin in Chinon.

Epiphany also marked Jehanne's birthday. She was seventeen years old, but she was oblivious to that fact as she left her family and village behind. Although she loved her family beyond words, since God had commanded her to leave, she had no choice but to obey. Even if she had had a hundred fathers and mothers, and a hundred Catherines, even if she herself had been a King's daughter, she would have nonetheless gone, for God had commanded it.

As they passed through Greux, one of her father's friends, Jean Waterin, crossed their path. She bade him adieu as well, and then added, "I am going to restore France and the Royal Family." It was more than she had been able to say to her own family. Somehow, it was easier to say this to acquaintances, than to those she dearly loved.

A tear slipped its way down Jehanne's icy cheek and fell to her cloak, as she tightened it about her to cut out the sharp barbs of winter. Silently, she prayed for strength, and she prayed that somehow, somewhere, divine assistance would be forthcoming, for she feared she would not be able to accomplish her mission without help. And this time, she knew without a doubt. This was it. This was unlike any journey she had heretofore undertaken in her short life, for her voices had confirmed it to her. This was the very last time she would see her beloved home.

Part Three

Fear not, nor be dismayed, be strong and of good courage: for thus shall the Lord do to all your enemies against whom ye fight.
Joshua 10:25

Be of good courage, and let us play the men for our people...
2 Samuel 10:12

Dieu vueille mectre bonne paix
Par toute la crestienté,
Mais que ce soit à tout jamaiz,
Si vivrons tous en loyauté.
Se crestienté fust unye
Nous menassions joyeuse vye,
Et mectrion tristesse enprison.
Ceulx par qui c'est, Dieu lez mauldie,

God desires to spread His peace
O'er all His Christian lands,
But 'twon't endure, goodwill will cease
Unless loyalty abounds.
If Christian souls would all unite,
Then joy would God disperse.
He'd banish sadness from our sight,
And wicked souls would curse.

From the Manuscript of Bayeux,
a collection of 15th Century French Songs

Chapter 26

IT IS ONE O'CLOCK IN THE MORNING ON the twenty-sixth day of December. I spent Christmas Day preparing to meet Joan of Arc, not Santa Claus. I didn't even give Christmas a second thought. Besides, I'm fully planning on being back to my century in time to celebrate Christmas with Dad and Adèle. I hope. But then, I wonder about how Nicolas fits into that equation. I can't think about that now, because I have a world to save.

Nicolas and I said goodbye to Brother Thibault with hugs and tears and lots of reminders to be careful, which he in turn repeated to us. It is time for us to commence our adventure. Yep, I've started calling it an 'adventure,' rather than a 'mission' to try and trick my mind into thinking that this little expedition has nothing to do with the fate of the world resting on my shoulders. I mean, really! Who wants to carry that kind of a burden? Certainly not me, even if I am a Watchman. No, this is just an exciting adventure, a jaunt back in history. I'll watch and perhaps assist the most famous personage of the Middle Ages, certainly the most iconic French woman who ever lived. I'm *so* lucky.

It is a waxing moon—I've learned more about lunar phases since traveling through time to Mont Saint Michel than I ever thought possible, or necessary—but there is enough light from it that I don't need to turn on the little Petzl headlamp I have strapped around my head. We are stealthily creeping across the quiet stones of Mont Saint Michel, headed towards the abbey. Well, we're trying to be stealthy, but the truth is, we're packing a lot of gear. Nicolas is loaded down with Thibault's three swords, and my large backpack filled with several changes of clothing, and the food I brought back in time with me, which consists mostly of high-calorie protein bars and snacks. I was starving once in this century, and I don't ever intend to do that again. It's not like my food supply will last forever, but at least it will keep away the hunger demons, if not the real demons. I've also filled his knapsack with a complete change of clothing and some additional warm clothing items I brought for him, some protein bars and snacks, and some camping gear and tools I think he might need.

Under my heavy woolen cloak, I'm carrying my smaller backpack with all of my electronic gear, which Nicolas calls my "bag of tricks." I've got some new techie items that I'm not sure I'll need, but hey, I went for broke, knowing how every item I brought last time was put to good use. Besides, I think I was inspired by the Archangel about what stuff to bring, including some climbing gear I taught Nicolas how to use while waiting for Brother Thibault to finish the swords. After all, one never knows if one will have to climb Mont Blanc!

I'm wearing one of Madame Mercier's daughter's simple frocks. She left all of her deceased daughter's clothing with Nicolas after my disappearance, telling him she hoped they would be useful if I ever returned. Well, here I am, Madame Mercier, and *merci* to you, even though I'd rather be in jeans. However, Nicolas doesn't think it is time for me to don my 'warrior' clothing. Since we don't know where or when we are going, he thinks I need to look like a female—at least initially. Fortunately, my hooded cloak covers me from head to toe. It will help camouflage my gender, in case being female puts me in danger upon our immediate arrival.

Nicolas knows a way that circumvents the heavy door to the abbey that closes across the Grand Degré staircase, and so I follow in his footsteps, trying not to make a sound. Nicolas chose this particular time of the night because it is late enough for the villagers to all be asleep, but early enough not to disturb the Benedictine monks who, it seems, rise at two-thirty in the morning during the winter months for prayer. I know. That sounds miserable. No wonder Brother Thibault is so happy to be a *former* Benedictine monk, because the Benedictines only eat twice a day. I mean, with only two meals a day for twenty-some odd years, who wouldn't have a food fetish? I'm not complaining. No, my stomach is happy and full right now, and I'm so grateful for that.

The past four days went by so quickly. Too quickly. I did get to hear all the details about Operation Dark Moon. I was actually pretty impressed at how well my plans worked. Hearing about their success has helped boost my confidence for Operation Maiden's Sword. However, I completely forgot to talk to Nicolas about the Hebrew letters I had discovered on Jean's and my enseigne, but now, that seems unimportant. It's not the time for me to delve into the Archangel's secrets, although I'd like to take a look at the jobber's mark on Nicolas's enseigne before we leave tonight.

Another thing I never had the opportunity to talk about with Nicolas was our relationship. For that matter, we were rarely alone. I mean, I had to stay indoors the entire time, and Brother Thibault was always nearby. But I guess it's kind of premature to talk about a relationship when we don't know if there will even be a world if we fail in our 'adventure.' Yes, we were too busy speaking of more critical issues. Like survival. We spoke of strategy. We tried to consider every circumstance in which we might find ourselves. I took advantage of Brother Thibault's commercial-quality voice to make some recordings I may or may not need, but since he's not coming with us, I've got to be prepared. Nicolas even taught me how to make a fire by striking flint and steel, and how to filter water, you know like in the reality shows *Survivor* and *Naked and Afraid* all rolled into one. I may have to survive out there in the wilds of France, but hopefully I've covered all my bases so that I won't ever have to be naked! I'm sure I'll be afraid though.

Nicolas also gave me some intense training in sword fighting. He's much better than I am, but at least I didn't make a complete idiot of myself, thanks to my fencing experience. But I have to say a three-foot-long heavy steel sword is a lot different than a fencing foil or épée, or even than a fencing saber. It's a two handed-proposition for me at best just to lift the darn thing. He gave me some excellent pointers on slashing and thrusting, but I certainly hope I won't have to use those techniques, because . . . well, you know what I mean. I refuse to think about the ramifications of slashing or thrusting with a sword. But if my life, or Jehanne's life, or Nicolas's life is on the line, I'll have to do what I have to do. Enough said.

In turn, I gave an in-depth lesson to my fellow Watchmen about the life and times of Joan of Arc, a.k.a. Jehanne La Pucelle, Jeanne d'Arc, the Maiden. I also artfully applied a combination of acrylic paints I had brought for that purpose on the maiden's new sword to make it look rusty, and then explained to Thibault and Nicolas that all it will take is a wet rag to make the sword look just like new again. Voilà, a medieval miracle! They were appropriately impressed with my faux-painting technique. Actually, I was pretty impressed as well.

And even though Nicolas and I never got to speak about the 'L' word, one evening after all three of us had spent ourselves both physically and intellectually, I did have the great pleasure of hosting the fifteenth-century premiere of *The Princess Bride* for both Nicolas and Brother Thibault. Yes, *The Princess Bride*, playing on a laptop near you. I'm not sure they really got the humor of that movie, and I think Brother Thibault was in shock that I had such a magic device. They didn't laugh once. Neither one of them. Not at: "Hello. My name is

Inigo Montoya. You killed my father. Prepare to die." Not at Vizzini's epic, "I've hired you to help me start a war. It's a prestigious line of work, with a long and glorious tradition." Now that's funny, especially to someone who's been "hired" to stop a war.

They didn't even laugh at Billy Crystal. Not once. Not even at Miracle Max the Wizard's "mostly dead" jokes or his "Don't rush me, Sonny. You rush a miracle man, you get rotten miracles." They didn't laugh at the Fire Swamp with its silly cinematographic R.O.U.S. (Rodents of Unusual Size), even after I'd compared the Fire Swamp to the sands of Mont Saint Michel Bay. Okay, well, maybe that isn't very funny.

But I think they did get the power of the love story between Westley and Buttercup. And Nicolas did smile when the ridiculous Priest said, "Mawage. Mawage is what bwings us togever today. Mawage, that blessed arrangement, that dweam within a dweam." And he's been saying "as you wish" a lot. I reminded him that the most important message of the movie was Westley's steadfast promise, "Hear this now: I will always come for you." And I told him that the feeling was mutual. I would always come for him, whether he's Westley or the Dread Pirate Roberts. Either way, I'm in.

But enough of *The Princess Bride*. I'm clearly trying to forget about the matter at hand: my own medieval adventure. So we continue to make our roundabout way up the Cliffs of Insanity to enter the abbey.

When we finally reach Notre-Dame-Sous-Terre, for which Nicolas has a key, my heart starts pounding. It sounds so loud that I'm afraid it will wake up the monks. It's pounding out my eardrums, and with every thump, I feel the level of my panic increasing. You'd think that after everything I've been through, I would be able to control my anxiety, but no. That's wishful thinking. But I'm buoyed up when I remember a quote my Dad shared with me while we were driving to Mont Saint Michel. It's from Nelson Mandela. He said, "I learned that courage was not the absence of fear, but the triumph over it. The brave man is not he who does not feel afraid, but he who conquers that fear." And so, I am doing my best to conquer my fear in spite of the thump, thump, thumping going on inside my body.

After opening the heavy door to the chapel inch by inch, so as not to make too much screeching noise, Nicolas instructs me to turn on my headlamp because it is pitch black in here. There are no windows that allow the moonlight, which illuminated our way up to now, to filter into the chapel. He leads me to the stone wall where my keyhole is located. With a contemplative look, which I can discern by the light of my headlamp, he lightly rubs his fingers over my keyhole, and then runs his hands over the stones in the opening of the adjacent wall, the stones that I know come from Saint Aubert's original oratory built in 709. Then he lowers his hand and removes my heavy backpack, which he has been carrying.

"Katelyn, take off your cloak. I want you to carry both of your backpacks. And your sword," he says as he helps me remove the cloak and my smaller backpack.

"Yeah, sure," I whisper as he helps me put my arms through the straps of the larger backpack and then hooks my electronics backpack over my right shoulder. "I know you've got your own knapsack to take, but you might as well carry all three swords since we've got them lashed together."

"Katelyn," he whispers as he pulls my sword out of the bundle of swords. Bundle of swords. A year ago, I would never have imagined using that combination of words in a sentence, but now it's my new reality. "I will take my sword, and the Maiden's sword," Nicolas continues, "but I want you to have your sword with you. I've been thinking. 'Tis not something we actually considered earlier, but I do not know if we will arrive at exactly the same time. Frankly, we cannot be assured that we will even arrive at the same place, and I want you to have all of your things."

"What do you mean?" I ask with my panic and heart-pounding escalating even further. "What are you saying?"

"We never even considered the possibility that the Archangel might send us to different destinations, but as we were coming here tonight, I could not banish that thought from my mind."

"What on earth are you talking about?" I ask, the volume of my voice increasing right along with my panic. "Did you hear his voice? Did Michael just tell you we'd be going to different places?"

"Quiet, Katelyn. Keep your voice lowered. I assure you, he did not speak to me, but I did receive that impression, so, it is a possibility we must consider. That is why I feel you need to take all of your belongings with you. Just in case."

"Nicolas," I reply in a whisper. "I can't do this without you."

"Oh, yes, you can, Katelyn. You can and you will, if that is what is required of you. I am not saying that it is what will happen, but we must be prepared for that eventuality. We must."

"But what will I do? What on earth am I supposed to do all by myself?"

"You will know what to do, Katelyn. You have already proven your ability to do that. Remember? You were all alone on the Godon ship, and you knew what to do. You devised a plan to escape. Be of good courage, Katelyn. You must not let your fear of the unknown prevent you from doing what you came here to do. You are braver than you realize. In fact, you are the bravest woman I have ever met. But we do not have the time to discuss this now. I do not know where we will be going, and I do not know if we will be together or not, but this is what you can do. If you do not arrive in a church, find out where the nearest church is to your location. Then, go there and wait for me for one hour."

He must see the look of incredulity on my face, because he amends that timeframe. "Okay, wait two hours. But if I do not come, you must assume that the Archangel has sent me elsewhere . . . to perform a different task. If I do not come, you must proceed. You can do this, Katelyn. You must take courage. Learn where you are and what the date is, and then determine what your next step will be based upon your understanding of the Maiden's timetable. I am not worried about you, for you know Jehanne's history backwards and forwards. And I do feel certain about one thing. This is your task, and your task alone. *You* are the one who will be interacting with Jehanne. *You* will be her mentor, and you will know where and how your intervention is required. You will know what to do. Find the Maiden, Katelyn. Just find Jehanne."

Now I grab onto him and I don't want to let go, and I simply can't stop the 'L' word from slipping out. Man, my timing is terrific. "I can't do this without you, Nicolas," I gasp. "I need you. I love you. Don't leave me. I just can't do this without you. I can't lose you again."

"Katelyn, do not believe for one instant that this is easy for me either," he replies as he takes me into his arms, which is not an easy thing to do since we've got a swarm of swords and packs coming between us. He backs away and takes my face into his hands and looks at me. "And I too love you, *ma chérie*, my beautiful, brave Katelyn. Oh, that I could take this burden from you, but alas, it is not to be. We must do as we have been directed. I have complete faith in you. Know this: if I am not with you in person, I will be with you in thought and spirit, but this is your task to complete. And you shall not be alone. You have God on your side, Katelyn. Do not forget that."

Then he kisses away my tears, because as much as I'm trying to channel Nelson Mandela, I simply cannot stop the tears escaping from the minimum security prison of my eyes. And then his lips stop when they meet mine . . . and the magic materializes. Nicolas kisses me in a way I have never even dreamed of being kissed. His lips speak not only of passion, but of a deep and abiding adoration and devotion which go way beyond passion. They speak of hope and patience, of perseverance and promise, and of pure and undefiled love. I can't even put into words the language of his lips, the poetry of his passion, or the compassion of his kiss, but it surpasses anything I can express. I can't refrain from claiming that this kiss even exceeded Westley and Buttercup's final kiss: the kiss that of the five most passionate kisses since the invention of the kiss left them all behind.

"And now I must leave you, Katelyn," he whispers. "I must get to my own keyhole before the monks begin to stir. I cannot say I understand what is about to happen to you or to me. I do not know what is to follow, but I will always come for you. I do not know how long it will take, but do not despair and do not forget. No matter what happens, no matter what you may believe, no matter what others may tell you, hear this now: I will always come for you."

And then he is gone.

Chapter 27

AFTER NICOLAS CLOSED THE DOOR TO Notre-Dame-Sous-Terre, he let go of the tears he had not allowed Katelyn to see. It had been gut-wrenching to leave her like that. Not only did his heart break for her, but his heart was broken for himself. But there was no time for self-pity. He wiped away the tears quickly, even though he could not wipe away his thoughts as easily.

Will we ever be together? Will I ever get to truly be Katelyn's husband? It is the only desire I have for my life. It is the only thing for which I long.

But there was no answer in the inky shadows that danced in the darkest recesses of the monastery's hallowed halls. There was no answer as he ran his fingers across the icy chill of the abbey's stones, and there was no voice that enlightened his troubled mind, full of the same shadows and the same chill. The truth was that he had a very bad feeling about what was about to transpire.

The moonlight gave a modicum of light in the passageways as he worked his way to the Guest Hall, but even without the light, he would have been able to navigate the way. He knew the monastery and the abbey church like the back of his hand. He could have navigated it blindfolded, but now he felt a different kind of blindness. It was a blindness of thought.

Something was wrong. He had been telling the truth when he told Katelyn that he had received the impression that they would not be going to the same destination. But he hadn't told her the complete truth. He had failed to tell her that he had also received the impression that he himself was in grave danger. But there was nothing he could do about it. If the Archangel had a message to give him, to help protect him, then he had better give it now, because he didn't have any more time.

As he entered the Guest Hall, he thought he heard a scurrying sound, but as he looked all around the darkened expanse, there was nothing to be seen, although the shadows in the corners of the hall could have camouflaged an interloper. However, he dismissed the sound. It must have been a rat or a bat flying up the huge chimneys that flanked the northern end of the vast hall. He had no time to worry about vermin. He could delay his departure no longer.

His keyhole was in a paving stone in the north corner of the hall next to the massive fireplaces, and with steadfast strides, he reached his destination, not afraid to tread upon an errant rat. He was, however, briefly reminded of Katelyn's inference that Abdon could possibly inhabit the corporeal form of a rabid bat, but he quickly banished that thought from his mind.

He didn't want to sit on the floor to use his keyhole as he wanted to be prepared for the unexpected upon arriving at his destination. The Archangel had always timed Nicolas's arrivals in the past so that no one was present in the Guest Hall, but with the uneasy impression Nicolas had about his safety, he didn't want to take any chances. He had no idea about where he would be arriving so he wanted to be on his feet ready to lunge at any potential aggressor. Consequently, he decided he needed to have his sword at the ready as well. That meant attaching the Maiden's sword to his knapsack, which was looped around his shoulder.

As he attempted to undo the twine that Brother Thibault had used to bind the swords together for ease of transporting, which had been loosened when he removed Katelyn's sword, his own sword slipped out and clattered to the resonant stone floor. The sound echoed through the empty chamber like a series of cannonballs making contact with a mighty fortress.

Nicolas gasped and darted to retrieve the sword, which had landed even further into the northeast corner of the hall and was not visible in the obscurity. Now he had no choice but to retrieve the sword as fast as he could and be on his way. No time to attach the other sword to his knapsack. The noise of his fumbling attempts to find and secure the fallen sword masked the footfalls that dashed across the expanse towards him, and because Nicolas faced the corner with his back to the rest of the hall, he could not see the shadowy figure that emerged from the far corner and pounced upon his back just as the Watchman leaned over, inserted his enseigne into the keyhole, and turned it.

Chapter 28

JEHANNE'S VISIT TO THE FORTRESS CHATEAU in Vaucouleurs, where the garrison commander Robert de Baudricourt had his headquarters, had been an unmitigated disaster. Her uncle had warned her not to go again, but becoming tired of the lass's unceasing pleadings, he had finally taken her from Burey-le-Petit to stay with his friend Henri le Royer in Vaucouleurs. Henri and his wife Catherine lived within the walled city near the Porte du Roy.

"But should you wish to visit the commander while you are there, you shall do so without my support," Laxart had told her the morning he accompanied her to Vaucouleurs. "I have already received a tongue-lashing from Robert de Baudricourt about you, Jehanne, and I do not wish to repeat that experience. If it is your wish to pursue your dogged desire to speak to him again, then you shall do so on your own."

After explaining to her hostess the intent of her mission, Jehanne left the home dressed in a simple red dress, hoping its color would demand Baudricourt's attention. Unfortunately, she did not realize how threadbare the garment had become. No matter. Her appearance was the least of her concerns. When she reached the outer gates of the fortress chateau which Baudricourt used as his headquarters, she recognized the gatekeeper, Jean de Metz, whom she had met briefly on her last visit to Vaucouleurs. He was one of the French soldiers stationed in Vaucouleurs, a squire in the service of Baudricourt.

"My friend," he said to her, "what are you doing here? I pray you have not come again to harass my commander. I fear it shall be in vain. After all, will not the Dauphin be expelled from the kingdom and we become English?"

Angered at his rash betrayal of her cause, Jehanne did not mince words. "Indeed, monsieur, I *have* come to this royal town to speak to Robert de Baudricourt in the hopes that he shall take me, or have me taken, to the Dauphin. But alas, he pays me and my words no mind. Nevertheless, before mid-Lent, I must speak to the Dauphin even if I wear down my feet to my knees to get there on foot, for surely there is no one in this world, neither kings, nor dukes, nor anyone else who can regain the Kingdom of France, except myself. I am the one to lead the armies of France." Although Jehanne did not feel as confident as she sounded, she was determined not to let anyone denigrate her mission. After all, it was a mission from God.

"Mademoiselle Jehanne, what gives you the authority to make such an audacious statement?"

"Indeed, though I would much prefer to spin wool by the side of my poor mother, and though, as you have made clear, leading an army is neither within the realm of my natural abilities nor my social rank, it is nonetheless necessary that I do this, for my Lord wishes it."

"And who, pray tell, is this Lord of yours who would require an ignorant girl to perform a task so beyond her reach?"

"My Lord is God. Are you wont to question His authority?"

At these words, Jehanne watched as the skeptical, weary expression left his face. He shook his head as if trying to dispel some unseen force that seemed to envelop him, and then his countenance changed to one of calm acceptance. She knew at that moment that her words had pierced his very heart. Surely, the Archangel had intervened. She was stunned when he bowed to her.

"Mademoiselle," he said with a new gentleness of tone as he reached out and patted her hand, "by this touch, I hereby give proof of my faith in you. With God as your guide, and with the permission of my commander, I volunteer to lead you before the Dauphin."

"You would do this for me?" asked Jehanne.

"I swear it so, but it must needs be with the permission of my commander. If you receive that permission, I will be the first to offer my services. And I have a comrade-in-arms, Bertrand de Poulangy, who has spoken of you in glowing terms. He is frustrated that we sit here in the east and do nothing to support the cause of France, or of her king. I am certain he would accompany us as well. When do you wish to leave?"

"Rather now than tomorrow, and rather tomorrow than later," she replied, letting him know that she would leave immediately if permission was granted.

"As we will pass through lands held by the enemy, it will be dangerous for a young maiden to be traveling, even with an escort of soldiers. Are you contemplating leaving wearing your own clothing?" He perused her red dress with an air of uneasiness.

"I understand your concerns, monsieur, and I would be willing to make the journey attired as a male if I must."

"Mademoiselle, should you receive the permission from my commander, I assure you I will procure the necessary clothing for you. Now, I bid you Godspeed in obtaining that permission."

Jean de Metz bowed and opened the gate leading into the chateau fortress.

Now confident that Baudricourt would listen to her words, Jehanne was equally stunned when she was once again rebuffed by the commander. In spite of her insistence that she was the virgin from the borders of Lorraine of whom it had been prophesied would restore France, he had actually laughed in her face and had asked her not to return to waste his precious time again. He had reminded her that his were important matters to contemplate, and not affairs for frivolous females with grandiose visions, and certainly not one dressed as poorly as she.

Jehanne was absolutely devastated. She had done all that the Archangel had asked of her. She was desirous to do God's will in all things, but she did not see how she could proceed without divine assistance. Reluctant to return to the home of her kind hosts in defeat, she instead directed her steps to the chateau chapel to pray for divine direction. In spite of the less-than-hospitable welcome she had received at the chateau, it was as if its chapel now beckoned to her. She had visited the chapel on her previous visit and had found comfort at the feet of the statue of Our Lady of the Vault.

Winter shadows stretched forth their glacial fingers to chill her to the very soul as she navigated the echoing halls of the chateau, but the minute she opened the chapel door and passed into the sacred space, she felt immediate comfort. A single candle illuminated the darkened nave, but it was sufficient to light her way. True, others might have found it less than inviting, but for Jehanne, it was like having a cloak of warmth and love envelop her.

With her head bowed in sorrow, she made her way to the statue of the Virgin, but a sound coming from behind her caught her attention. She turned to see a hooded figure sitting on the far right side of the last pew in the chapel.

At first alarmed at the presence of an interloper, her heart softened as she saw the figure remove her hood, revealing long tresses. It was a young woman. In fact, it was a young woman of about Jehanne's own age . . . and she was weeping.

"Mademoiselle," Jehanne said, displaying her typical concern for others, "I apologize if I have intruded upon your time of contemplation. I thought I would be alone here. There is clearly something troubling you. May I be of assistance?"

"Oh, you haven't interrupted anything," the lass replied in an odd and stilted accent. Jehanne had a difficult time understanding her words. "I was waiting for a friend," she continued, "but I'm afraid he's not coming." The young woman looked down at some odd contraption strapped to her wrist. Jehanne had never seen anything like it. Then the strange girl continued. "But in fact, I could use your help. May I ask you some questions?"

Jehanne approached the girl, sat down next to her, and asked, "What questions have you of me?"

"I've traveled a great distance and I . . . have been ill. I'm afraid my illness, along with the cold and a lack of food has left me confused. This may sound odd to you, but I . . . I." The young woman stopped her phrase in mid-sentence and then asked, "Would you be so kind as tell me where I am and what the date is?"

"Oh, my poor friend. You are indeed suffering. Allow me to offer you shelter and a hot meal. I myself am a stranger in this town, but I have gracious hosts who I am certain will honor my offer of hospitality."

"Thanks for your kindness. That would be great, if it's not asking too much. But I have to go back to my previous question. What town is this?"

"Why, mademoiselle, you are in Vaucouleurs, in the Meuse River Valley of Lorraine. This valley was once a part of France, but I fear that our enemy has taken control of most of these lands."

Her companion's gasp was unmistakable.

"I'm in Vaucouleurs? And the date?"

"Let me see. I am not certain of the exact date, but it must be the second week of February."

"February? And the year?"

"The year? You do not know the year?"

"No, and I'm hoping you do," replied the stranger, clutching at her knapsacks.

"Why, it is the year of our Lord fourteen hundred and twenty-nine."

Even in the darkness, it was not difficult for Jehanne to discern the look of total astonishment on the face of this strange visitor. The lass grabbed Jehanne's hand and then looked her in the eyes.

"Could you possibly be Jehanne? Jehanne the daughter of Jacques d'Arc from Domrémy?"

Now it was Jehanne's turn to be astonished. How did this stranger know who she was? It was puzzling indeed. Jehanne wondered how far word of her claims had begun to spread throughout the valley. Perhaps it was not completely unreasonable for this stranger to know who she was, after all.

"Yes, I am indeed Jehanne."

"Then both of us should be pretty darn happy, because the Archangel has been good to us. Jehanne, my name is Katelyn Michaels, and I've been sent here to assist you in your mission. The Archangel Michael has sent me to you."

Kathleen C. Perrin

Chapter 29

WHILE HIS PASSAGE THROUGH THE TIME vortex seemed particularly turbulent, Nicolas did not identify the problem until he arrived at his unknown destination and felt grasping fingers around his throat attempting to choke the life out of him. He was momentarily stunned, not understanding how the intruder had come to be clinging to him, but then the truth dawned on him. Whoever this creature attacking him was, he had jumped upon Nicolas at the very instant he had turned his key in the Guest Hall. It was a sobering thought that an interloper could be transported through the time portal with him.

The young Watchman immediately dropped his knapsack and swords, and summoning every ounce of strength he had, he jerked his elbows backward, loosening his attacker's hold. Without giving the unknown assailant any time to react, Nicolas back-kicked him in the groin, breaking his hold. Then Nicolas twisted around until he could punch the man in the face to send him backwards onto the ground.

While the assailant cursed at Nicolas and attempted to get back on his feet, Nicolas lunged for one of the swords he had dropped and brought it up waist-high in front of him in a defensive position. Even in the shadows, all it took was one look to recognize his opponent.

No, he had never before seen the dark-headed man, but it was not difficult to discern that this was the new physical incarnation of Abdon. His swarthy, pockmarked complexion and malicious countenance matched the spirit that now inhabited the mortal man's body, but it was his eyes that gave away his true identity. His eyes bore the uncontested reflection of pure evil. So, the Watchmen's sworn enemy had finally made his appearance.

"Well, well," seethed the grim-looking man with venom in his voice. He spoke perfect French. "We meet again, Nicolas le Breton."

The man looked to be in his middle years. He had probing black eyes and a furrowed brow fixed in what appeared to be a constant sneer, and a prominent but thin, crooked nose. His greasy and disheveled black hair was parted in the middle and fell on either side below his chin. In spite of the fact that his face and hands appeared free of grime and that the quality of his raiment implied a certain standing in life, there was a darkness in his appearance that hinted at his true filthy nature. He wore the long brown pilgrim's cloak and scallop shell attached to a cord around his waist typical of those who followed the Way of Saint James, but this man had none of the outward appearance of a pious believer. Indeed, it was clear there was not an ounce of piety in him. Only lust, malevolence, and vice emanated from his being. Once again, Abdon had found a receptive host.

Although it was dark, the flame from a single candle inside the structure allowed Nicolas to realize that he had been whisked through space to a small church, and he surmised that this was the church in Sainte-Catherine-de-Fierbois. Able to see the second sword in his peripheral vision, Nicolas thrust his foot backwards and was successful in sliding it far from Abdon's reach. Without a second thought, and without saying a word, Nicolas then lunged at his nemesis, lifting his sword and slashing at the prostrate man. Whether the host himself possessed lightning reflexes or whether those reflexes were enhanced by Abdon's innate abilities, it didn't matter. The results were the same. Abdon rolled with such alacrity that Nicolas missed his mark by a significant degree. Before he could even ascertain his enemy's position to strike a second time, Abdon had dashed out of the unlocked door of the church into the dark night. However, he didn't depart without leaving a final barb, which pierced the young Watchman's heart like a dagger.

"Alas, your skills in swordplay are poorly lacking, Nicolas. But because I am more interested in what you are doing here than in killing you, and because I have no weapon to force the truth out of you at this time, I have decided to let you live . . . for now at least. Yes, I believe I shall hasten my departure at this time. But never fear. We shall meet again. I shall ultimately force the truth out of you, and when I do, I promise you that Mademoiselle Michaels will be the first casualty. I cannot lie. The joy of seeing your face when I kill her in front of you is just too much to resist."

Chapter 30

SO HERE I AM IN VAUCOULEURS. AM I UPSET that Nicolas never showed up? Absolutely. But am I also relieved that after waiting the agreed-upon two hours in the chateau chapel at Vaucouleurs, where my keyhole had evidently been carved in some distant past by Jean le Vieux, the next best thing showed up? A resounding yes. And so I have to acknowledge the Archangel's hand.

For now, I just have to believe that Nicolas is in Sainte-Catherine-de-Fierbois burying the sword of Charles Martel (a.k.a. Brother Thibault) to be found in just a few weeks by Jehanne's messenger. Besides, there is nothing I can do about Nicolas now. As difficult as our parting moment was, I'm grateful he prepared me for the possibility that we wouldn't be together, because I think I really would have lost it otherwise. I was still pretty close to losing it when Jehanne walked into the chateau chapel and found me there crying. I am pulling myself together though. I can't be the one crying when I'm supposed to be here to help her!

I've got to continue with my mission, with or without Nicolas, and the first step is to find a way for Robert de Baudricourt to wise up and listen to La Pucelle. I have no idea how long I will be needed to help Jehanne, but I'm just going to have to take it one step at a time.

When Nicolas, Brother Thibault, and I discussed strategy during our four-day preparatory period, we thought it best for me not to divulge to Jehanne that I am from the future. That creates a whole new set of problems, like her insisting on knowing what is going to happen in *her* future. That is something I simply refuse to discuss with her. I can't. I can't give her any warnings. I can't reveal anything about what her destiny holds. I simply have to be there to help her reach that destiny according to how it has all been recorded in history. So instead, we decided that I should use the same cover story we used with the Montois, that I am from the furthest reaches of Brittany. That is why I have a strange name and a strange accent.

We also concluded that if in the course of my mission I need to employ any of my electronic gizmos from my little backpack of tricks, I need to pass them off with Jehanne as objects the Archangel has endowed with certain powers to assist us. That idea isn't that farfetched because I certainly *had* been inspired by the Archangel to use these gadgets from the future to help save Mont Saint Michel, and I firmly believe that one of the reasons the Archangel brought me back from the future is because I'm so good at using modern technology. Besides, relics and other sacred objects are believed to possess supernatural powers and abilities to perform miracles in this period, so I'm just going along with the times.

Now, here I am, sitting at the back of the chapel with Jehanne. Honestly! Joan of Arc. It's incredible. After I get over being star-struck, I convince her that I really have been sent by the Archangel to assist her and also to be her confidante and tutor. She puts one hand to her mouth and I see tears begin to roll down her cheeks.

"Please forgive me," she says. "Now I am the one weeping. It is because I have been pleading for divine intervention, and I cannot believe it has been so graciously and so hastily sent to me."

We embrace, and after a minute we are both calm enough to continue our conversation. It's pretty humbling to think that *I* am Joan of Arc's divine intervention.

I don't tell Jehanne that I'm from the future, or that my native language is English. I'm pretty sure she won't trust me for one second if she thinks I *am* English. So once again, I am Katelyn la Bretonne, whose French is pretty abysmal. Just to cover my tracks in case I ever break out in unexpected English, I tell her I've learned quite a bit of English while living under the English occupation. And, in complete honesty, I also tell her that I—like her—have heard the voice of the Archangel; it was he who gave me the mission to save Mont Saint Michel, just as he has given her the mission to save France. Nothing untrue about that. And that seems to have quite an impact on her—first, the fact that I have heard the Archangel's voice, and second, that as a seventeen-year-old maiden, I saved Mont Saint Michel from the English siege. I'm here to motivate and inspire, to let her know that a seventeen-year-old girl who has never had an ounce of military experience can be successful at leading an army. Well, with the help of the Archangel, that is. That's our saving grace, I mean, for me and Jehanne. We are not alone. As Nicolas reminded me, we have the Archangel, and ultimately, God, on our side.

After I tell her about my victory, she is quick to tell me that she remembers clearly when she was younger and learned that Mont Saint Michel had held firm against the English and how it had given her hope and courage. She says it gives her even more hope and courage knowing that *I* accomplished that feat when I was only seventeen—which, in her eyes, means I'm twenty-one right now. Yes, she considers me to be a full-fledged adult. Nicolas was right. Just her hearing these facts has already buoyed her confidence tremendously. She tells me that if I can do it, so can she.

Anyway, this isn't going to be easy. After all, Joan of Arc's life has been chronicled from A to Z. Consequently, Nicolas, Thibault, and I decided that since there is no mention in the historical records of any female companion linked to Jehanne, my role has to be entirely behind-the-scenes, or if I'm not behind-the-scenes, I've got to be dressed as a male soldier and pass myself off as one of the military escorts assigned by Robert de Baudricourt to accompany her to Chinon. I can't rewrite history. That means no staying with Jehanne at Henri le Royer's house, as much as I'd like to be there with her.

To remain anonymous, I warn her that she must never speak of my true identity as the woman Katelyn to anyone and that she must do everything in her power to keep our friendship a secret. Because she did so in history, she *can* speak of her voices, of her instructions from the Archangel, but she can never mention any guidance given by me. In truth, all of her guidance *is* coming from the Archangel. It's just coming indirectly through me. However, I assure her that I will remain with her disguised as a male soldier named Kaelig for as long as I am needed.

After learning that I can't accept her offer of hospitality, Jehanne tells me of a respectable inn inside the walled city where I can find safe lodging. We both agree that I will have to go there dressed in my male soldier persona, as it is extremely unseemly for a young woman to go to an inn unaccompanied by male protectors, so before we leave the chapel, she guards the door and I change into my male clothing right there and then. We make arrangements to meet tomorrow in an abandoned church outside the Porte Chaussée, one of the southern gates into the walled city of Vaucouleurs, and then, we leave separately.

When I find the inn recommended by Jehanne, I pass myself off as Kaelig, a young Breton soldier who has come to join the French cause. Fortunately, I am prepared with fifteenth-century currency, so I can pay for my room and board. After a solitary meal in my room that doesn't even begin to compare with Brother Thibault's fine cooking, I fall into an uneasy sleep, wondering where Nicolas is and if he has fared as well as I have.

With help from my iPhone alarm, I wake up at six-thirty in the morning and then hurry to our meeting place, trying to avoid being seen. Now I am waiting for Joan of Arc to meet with me, Katelyn Michaels from America, a place she has never even heard of, because it doesn't exist yet. It's insane, but unfortunately, I can never tell anyone about it, except for Thibault and Nicolas. Anyway, it's seven o'clock in the morning, and it's still dark outside. I scout the area to make certain that there's no one else here. After all, it wouldn't be fitting for Jehanne to be seen with me, especially since I'm dressed as a male. I'm not about to cut my hair (how would I explain that one to Dad and Adèle?), so I have on my slouchy cap. Fortunately, because of the cold February temperatures, there's no reason for anyone to be milling about this forlorn place so early. I enter the church, which has portions of its roof caved in, and find a place to sit on a fallen stone column in a dark corner.

It rained all of last night, but finally the heavens have halted their unwelcome downpour, and the mist is beginning to rise off the cold, damp ground. I'm so grateful Nicolas warned me about what conditions would be like, because underneath my tunic and leggings, I'm also wearing thermal underwear made of a mixture of wool and polypropylene that wicks away the moisture. That, along with my woolen cloak and my high tech gloves covered by wool gloves, keep me from shivering as I sit and wait. I'm also wearing Heat Holders, the newest thing in thermal socks, under my leather boots. I might look like fifteenth century on the outside, but the inner layers are all modern!

Even in the shadows, I see that Jehanne has a smile on her face when she enters and spots me. She too is enveloped in a cloak, but it is threadbare, and her worn leather shoes are hardly adequate to keep out the dampness. I wish I could offer her some of my modern, element-fighting gear, but I know that isn't possible. I can't rewrite history, so she can never be found wearing anything more out-of-the-ordinary than fifteenth-century male clothing. But she's going to be pretty miserable on this trip. It hasn't taken me very long to figure out that fifteenth-century France in the winter is wretched. I'd rather have snow and frozen ground than the constant rain and mushy terrain. No matter where you step, you sink five inches in the muck. It's horrific.

In spite of the cold, Jehanne's embrace is warm, and it is clear that she is grateful to see me. She may have thought that I was a figment of her imagination yesterday and that I wouldn't show up this morning. There's a lot of pressure on me. I've got to act, and act quickly, because according to her history, which I carefully studied again last night in my small but private room at the inn, she is supposed to be meeting with Baudricourt for the third and final time on the twelfth day of February, and today is the eleventh! It is during her visit with him tomorrow that he finally agrees to her request of providing her with an official escort to Chinon, so I only have a little over twenty-four hours to make certain that happens. I know what I have to do. It's something that Nicolas, Brother Thibault and I worked on before our departure, but I don't have much time to implement our plan, and there is no margin for error.

The first question I ask Jehanne is if she is acquainted with the soldier known as Jean de Metz. I know that he becomes one of her escorts on the journey to Chinon and also one of her most ardent supporters, but I'm not certain if she has crossed paths with him yet.

"*Mais oui*," she replies as she rubs her fingers together to keep them warm. "*Je le connais.* I know him. He is a squire in the service of Robert de Baudricourt. I know him and his friend Bertrand de Poulangy. They have both been very gracious to me. In fact, Jean de Metz told me yesterday that he would be pleased to accompany me to Chinon if and when I receive the permission from his commander.

He also agreed to find me appropriate clothing to dress as a male soldier, like you, and he assured me that his friend Bertrand would help as well."

"That's great, and hopefully, they can find you clothing that will keep you warmer than what you are wearing now," I reply. "You will also need sturdy boots to keep your feet dry. But I'm not here to speak of clothing. We've got more critical issues to discuss. We desperately need the help of Jean de Metz for my plan to convince Robert de Baudricourt to meet with you tomorrow to be successful. Do you think you could convince him to let me into the fortress today and to direct me to Baudricourt's sleeping quarters at a time when the commander won't be there? He won't need to know who I am, and you can assure him that no harm will come to the commander. In fact, if all goes as planned, Baudricourt will never know that I have even been there."

She looks at me strangely, and I quickly add, "Jehanne, you have no need to fear. I'm acting only under the inspiration given me by the Archangel. You don't need to know the details. In fact, it's better if you don't."

"*D'accord,*" she says as she stomps her feet and moves around in circles. Her teeth are chattering, and she reminds me of a frightened baby bird flitting a few feet off the ground whose mother has just abandoned her and who doesn't have the self-confidence to fly. "After the interaction I had with Jean de Metz yesterday," she continues, "I believe he might be willing to help me without asking too many questions."

"Jehanne," I explain, "we don't have any time for 'might' or 'perhaps.' We only have time for 'will.' You must convince him to help us. We have no other choice, and we have no time left."

"But how do you expect me to convince him to do something that could jeopardize his career?" she asks. "I do not know how I can do that."

"You have to have confidence in yourself," I insist. "If you want to save France, Jehanne, you have got to learn to have self-confidence. Otherwise, no one will ever believe you can do as you say."

"But, *mon amie*," she replies, "that is exactly my problem. I do not have any. On two occasions I have tried to convince Robert de Baudricourt of my mission, and twice, I have been a miserable failure. I do not know how I can do it."

Something my mother once said to me comes to my mind at that moment, like a life-saving packet floating down on its little parachute during the battles in *The Hunger Games*. Suddenly, it's just there for me to reach out my hand and grab. I know the perfect words to say to her.

"Jehanne," I begin, "if you want to have a certain quality, you must act as if you already have that quality."

"I do not understand," she replies. "That is the problem, Katelyn. I cannot even begin to muster up any self-confidence to act."

"Oh, yes, you can," I insist. "Pretend that you're playing a role. You are no longer Jehanne, peasant daughter of Jacques d'Arc. No, you are playing the role of a war-seasoned commander, full of confidence and self-assurance. And authority. You have the authority to command anyone, be they servant or king, to do your bidding. Forget about your own insecurities and act as if you are someone who has all the poise and conviction in the world."

"You truly believe that I could do that?" she asks.

"I truly believe it. Remember, Jehanne, you have been called by God to serve Him. He has complete and total confidence in you. He sees something deep within you that you cannot even see in yourself. And I promise you that if you continue to act as if you have that confidence, soon that quality will actually be yours. Soon, you will truly have that attribute."

"I will try," she says.

"No," I reply. "You will not try. You will do it. You will instruct Jean de Metz to let me into the chateau. Remember, you are *his* commander. Is there an entrance to the fortress that's more discreet than going in at the front gate?" I ask.

"Yes," she replies. "In the southeast tower of the fortress. The entrance is blocked by a storehouse for military provisions. What if I ask him to meet you there in the late afternoon? That will give time for Baudricourt to eat his noonday meal and have a rest, as is his custom. On the previous occasions when I met with him, it was well past three in the afternoon, and it was definitely not in his quarters. It was in a large hall where he handles his administrative duties."

"That would be perfect," I say. "I don't want anyone to see the two of us together, so could you leave a message for me to confirm the time? Leave it here for me under this stone," I say as I lift a small block that has fallen from the church wall.

"But how am I to leave you a message?" she asks. "I am ashamed to tell you that I do not know how to read or write. And unfortunately, that is not an attribute I can pretend to have." By this time, her fingers are red from the cold, and she is blowing on them.

I'm such an idiot. Of course I know that Joan of Arc is illiterate. It's so normal in my world to communicate through texting and email, that I just completely spaced out that inconvenient reality. In fact, I even know that the only written document in Joan's hand that has survived the centuries is her signature. For her communications, she used scribes, but this is not a situation where I can afford for her to ask anyone for assistance. "Can you write your signature or numbers?" I ask. I don't know if she's learned to write her name yet and I don't have enough information about her level of literacy to know if she can write simple numbers.

"Alas no," she admits with a sense of shame and I feel badly about having embarrassed her. "Do you have the ability to read and write?" she asks me.

Then a thought comes to my mind. *I am going to be the one who teaches Joan of Arc how to write her name!* I even have a copy of her signature that I printed out in my folder in the small backpack I brought with me.

"Yes, I can read and write," I answer, "but my case is unusual. I, a . . ." Well, okay, I'm not unusual at all for my century. Everyone in America and France in the twenty-first century knows how to read and write, but I can't tell her that. For her century, I *am* unusual, so I'll just keep it at that, because I really don't like lying to Joan of Arc. "I had an unusual upbringing, and I was blessed to learn those skills, but you have nothing to be ashamed of. Few young women of your station in life have those skills. But guess what? I'm going to teach you right now how to sign your name and how to write the numbers one to ten. That's all you will need. When you have messages or letters to send, all you'll have to do is ask someone to be your scribe and then sign your name. That's all you'll need."

"I fear I lack the mental acuity to learn how to even write my name," she says.

"Oh no," I assure her. "Act as if you have that mental acuity. Besides, I know you have it. You just haven't been given the opportunity to try."

I suggest we move to the front of the church where there is more light, and where we can use the old stone pulpit—which is still standing—as our writing desk. I remove my gloves, and then from my backpack, I pull out a pen and the printed page I brought with her signature.

Jehanne

"This is your name," I say as I show her the printout and point to each letter, mimicking the phonetic sound the letter makes, which in French is not so easy since half the letters are silent.

I take a blank piece of paper and write out the capital J. Then I show her how to hold the pen, and take her hand in mine and move it across the paper. Her fingers are frozen, and so I rub her hands in mine to warm them up and make the movement again. "Now you try." She marvels at the pen and paper I have brought, because even though I was careful to bring old-looking paper and a very simple fountain pen, by her standards, they must appear highly unusual.

And so it goes, with me writing out each letter and then having her copy and recopy it until she can form each letter correctly and can connect them all together to spell out her name. I mean, really. This is so cool. I just taught Joan of Arc how to write a signature that will go down in history! And she did it with frozen fingers.

"See?" I insist. "You are fantastic. You *do* have the mental acuity."

She smiles at me and says, "*Merci. Merci beaucoup.* No one has ever taken the time to help me learn. I am so pleased. I believe I have mastered it. Now, may we move on to the numbers, *s'il vous plaît?*"

"*Bien sûr,*" I reply and we repeat the entire process until she can adequately write each figure.

By this time, the sunlight is starting to filter in through the gaps in the walls and roof. On the floor of the church, the dappled rays look like a crossword puzzle of light. In spite of the increasing brightness and warmth, I'm starting to feel nervous, like someone is watching us.

"You must go," I instruct Jehanne. "I'll return here at one o'clock this afternoon and look for your message. Just write the number of the time I am to meet de Metz on this," I instruct as I tear off a small piece of paper, "and place it under that rock I showed you in the corner. Sign your name just as you learned so that I know the message is indeed from you. If he does not agree to meet with me, mark an X on the paper, like this," I say as I make an X on our practice sheet. "You will have to find or borrow your own writing tool, because if anyone notices you with this one," I say as I show her my pen, "they will find it odd." And then I add, "It's Breton."

After we have finished our writing lesson, I lead Jehanne back into the dark corner of the church. The hairs on the back of my neck are bristling. I look all around me to make certain that no one is watching us, but I neither see nor hear anyone. *It's just your imagination,* I tell myself. I see danger in every corner and Abdon in every face. But who wouldn't in my situation?

"And what shall we do if he is not willing to help us?" Jehanne asks, still not convinced after my little pep talk.

"He will," I reply. I have to stay positive for her. If Jean de Metz does refuse, I'm going to have to find a way into the fortress myself tonight. And then I add another injunction, appealing to one of the greatest qualities Jehanne does have: great faith. "Let us both pray that the Archangel will soften the heart of Jean de Metz, because it is vital that I find a way to get into Robert de Baudricourt's bedchamber. When you meet with Baudricourt tomorrow, I have a specific message that you must give him. This is very important, so you must get every detail straight."

I relay the message she is to give the French commander, and then have her repeat it back until she is able to get every detail correct.

"You must remember those exact words," I reiterate as I leave, "for the fate of France depends upon it."

Chapter 31

NICOLAS SHIVERED AS HE THOUGHT ABOUT Abdon having followed him into the time vortex. He could not banish the premonition that this was going to end badly for him, and there was nothing he could do to prevent it. However, before he could address the problem of Abdon, he had to complete his assignment to bury the sword, and he had to do it as quickly as possible. First, however, he had to make certain that this was indeed Sainte-Catherine-de-Fierbois. To further complicate his task, although the frigid night air testified to the fact that it was definitely still winter, he knew neither the hour nor the date.

He peered out the church door to see a village shrouded in darkness illuminated only by the moonlight and the dying flame of a candle sputtering in the transept. Judging by the waxing gibbous moon, he determined it must be about the eleventh or twelfth day of the month, but whether it was the month of January or February, he could not be certain. He had to proceed with caution, for it would not do for anyone to suspect that a stranger had come to the church to bury a sword that Jehanne La Pucelle would later claim to be that of the venerated Charles Martel. After closing the church door cautiously to prevent any noise, he slid the heavy bolt in place to lock it from the inside. It was a small church, and this was the only entrance, so Abdon or another interloper couldn't attempt to enter without Nicolas hearing.

His knapsack and its contents were strewn onto the floor in the middle of the church, and Nicolas recovered his belongings with gratitude. He could not carry out his assignment without the tools that Katelyn had sent with him. Then, he thought about the location of his time key. What had happened to it in the scuffle that followed his and Abdon's arrival? He hesitated to use the little headlamp Katelyn had given him because he knew the glow of the light could be seen from the exterior through the church's small stained glass windows, but he had no choice. He could not work in the dark. Katelyn had shown him how to place the stretchy band around his head and then flip a small switch to turn on the light. Someone had left a candle burning inside the church, so he hoped his headlamp would pass for candlelight.

With his small source of light, Nicolas tried to locate his time key. Where was the carved jobber's mark that Jean le Vieux had embedded into one of the church's stones to accommodate his key? His confrontation with Abdon had left him completely disoriented as to where he had arrived. He saw neither stone benches nor walls, and so he concluded that the jobber's mark must be on the floor somewhere. As he walked around the church, aiming the beam at the floor, he finally found it in the corner of the transept, near the sputtering candle. And glory of all glories, his time key was still sitting in the indentation. He breathed in a sigh of relief and thanksgiving that Abdon had not taken it. He adjusted his clothing so that he could place the key inside a hidden pocket of the undergarments Katelyn had provided for him. He already had several small coins in the pocket for emergencies. The pocket, located on the inner thigh of the leggings, would not be readily found if he was patted down by an enemy. It closed with some magical fastener she called "Velcro."

Nicolas looked at the statue on the wall of the transept. There was a large copper receptacle filled with sand sitting on the ground in front of it in which the single candle was burning. It was a statue of Sainte Catherine. A small marble plaque in the wall next to the statue stated in Latin: 'Donated to the Chapel of Sainte-Catherine in Sainte-Catherine-de-Fierbois by Louis, Duke of Touraine in 1391.' This was the confirmation he needed. This was indeed the church where Jehanne's envoy would find the sword in March of 1429. He retrieved the lighting wand Katelyn had given him to light several other candles in the copper basin. These inventions from Katelyn's world were so marvelous and certainly facilitated his task. He hoped that the flickering of the candles would mask the steadiness of the light from his headlamp.

Nicolas felt confident that the Archangel had sent him to Sainte-Catherine-de-Fierbois well before the time when the sword was to be found, and he could only assume that Katelyn had been sent to Vaucouleurs to help Jehanne convince Sir Robert de Baudricourt to pay heed to her message. Just as he had suspected, they had been separated.

He was grateful he had prepared Katelyn for such an eventuality, but that he was right about it did little to appease his sadness. It seemed like he would never be given the time or the opportunity to express his ardent desire to spend the rest of his life with her. It was a proposition that would require a great deal of convincing on his part, for how could he expect her to forsake not only her family but also the comforts and wonders of her amazing twenty-first century world to be with him? However, this was not the time to consider this conundrum. He had to focus on the task at hand, and so all of the passion he felt for his beloved Katelyn, and all of the anger he felt for the elusive Abdon, were channeled into one undertaking: burying Brother Thibault's handiwork, which was to become the sword of the Maiden.

It wasn't difficult to determine where to bury it, for Katelyn had told him 'twas to be behind the main altar of the church, and there was only one altar, beyond the transept in the apse. The floor of Sainte-Catherine was made of compacted dirt, which greatly facilitated his task. Katelyn had included a small spade and hammer along with a pair of thin, but remarkably warm and pliant gloves from her century to protect his fingers from the cold. That equipment, along with his own sword and Katelyn's headlamp, allowed him to accurately penetrate the soil that had been compressed by generations of pious priests and parishioners.

Fortunately, in spite of the winter chill, the soil seemed to have little water content, and it was not frozen. But it was solid. He did not want to disturb more of the ground than was necessary, and so he outlined a rectangle a bit longer than the actual sword, and then began painstakingly chipping away at the dirt, placing it on a large square of canvas he had brought for that purpose. It took him what felt like an eternity to carve out a section to about the depth of his hand, all the while tuning his ear to any sound of movement outside.

It was not productive to imagine what had become of Abdon, but he was certain the evil one was nearby, probably wondering what kept Nicolas inside the church. Hopefully, Abdon would assume Nicolas had taken shelter there for the night.

With the cavity finally sufficiently deep, Nicolas took the sword—disguised with Katelyn's realistic-looking rust—and in homage to both Brother Thibault and Katelyn's handiwork, he pressed his lips to its blade before placing it in its new hiding place. Although the work of digging the hole had been long and tedious, Nicolas soon realized that the real challenge was not to bury the sword, but to make it appear that the ground where it had been buried had not been tampered with in any way. He smoothed the ground, pouring dabs of water across it from one of Katelyn's water receptacles, then re-smoothed and compacted the soil over and over again. It was critical for there to be no question about the sword's provenance. He also knew that to tarry any longer meant that he risked being discovered inside the church. Then, there would certainly be unpleasant questions.

Finally, just as the spreading threads of dawn threatened to expose his presence, Nicolas judged his work to be done, and done well. He quietly gathered up his equipment, inwardly praising his sweet, dear Katelyn for having sent him with what she called thermal underwear and stockings—which he had donned before their departure—for the night of work in the frigid chapel with no fire to lessen the chill would have otherwise been unbearable. He was also grateful that she had insisted he take a portion of the foodstuffs she had brought from her time, for the compact little rectangle of pure goodness she called a protein bar not only tickled his taste buds, but also revived his lagging energy. Although he did not know what protein was, after tasting it, he was happy she had insisted that he take a dozen or so of the bars in his knapsack, giving him the admonition to spread them out, as they could sustain his life if he could not obtain other food. When he had everything stowed in his knapsack, including his gloves, the headlamp, and the bar wrapping, he pulled the drawstring to close it tightly and felt a sudden impulse to knot the string firmly. Then he blew out the candles in the copper basin, carefully disengaged the bolt, and opened the church's heavy door.

The thought briefly crossed his mind that perhaps the Archangel expected him to use his time key to return there and then to Mont Saint Michel after having done his part in burying the sword, but he pushed it away quickly. He could not abandon Katelyn. His plan was to make his way to Chinon and there wait for Jehanne to arrive. He and Katelyn had studied the maps and dates of Jehanne's journey from Vaucouleurs to Chinon. Although there was not much detail about the journey, it was known that she would pass through Sainte-

Catherine-de-Fierbois and attend mass, then travel on to Chinon, where she would send a messenger back for the sword before meeting the Dauphin. He felt it too dangerous to remain in the very small village of Sainte-Catherine not only because of Abdon, but also because his presence there could arouse suspicion among the locals. In Chinon, he could get lost in the city and await the group's arrival. Hopefully, Katelyn would be in Jehanne's entourage, traveling incognito as a young male soldier, just as they had discussed. It was the only thing he could think of doing.

If the altar and apse faced east, as most churches were laid out, then he knew he needed to head nearly straight west, the orientation of the church's doors, to reach Chinon. The one thing he knew for certain was that he needed to leave Sainte-Catherine-de-Fierbois sooner rather than later, and hopefully before Abdon could intercept him.

There was just enough light in the sky for Nicolas to perceive that the door opened up onto a small square and what appeared to be the main street of the village. Exactly where he did not want to be: exposed and vulnerable. He exited the church leaving the door ajar so as not to make any additional noise, and then pressed his body against the cold stone wall until he had moved around to the south side of the building where several other structures pressed in close to the church and offered him cover so that he could scurry away into anonymity.

But unfortunately, Nicolas's identity was not anonymous to everyone in Sainte-Catherine-de-Fierbois in the wee hours of that cold February morning. As he clawed at the heavy rope noose he felt being pulled tightly around his neck, his last thought before his breath was squeezed out of him was that his premonition that it would end badly for him had indeed been well-founded.

Chapter 32

THE NUMBER WRITTEN ON THE MESSAGE signed by Jehanne was "4," which I recovered from the abandoned church this afternoon. And so, here I am waiting for the soldier Jean de Metz to let me into Robert de Baudricourt's chateau fortress in Vaucouleurs. I am dressed as a man—well, I guess I really look more like a tall boy with my hair stuffed up into my slouchy cap. I have also pulled the hood of my cloak well over my head to hopefully leave my face in the shadows. There's no point in completely exposing myself to Jean de Metz. After all, I cannot appear in the historical accounts of Joan of Arc. I'm banking on the fact that Jean de Metz has already had his heart softened by the Archangel to help Jehanne, but also that he will never willingly admit to anyone that he allowed some unknown person to enter his commander's living quarters.

I have written instructions for Jean to take me to the bedchamber of Robert de Baudricourt—absent of the presence of Baudricourt, of course—and to leave me there alone for thirty minutes—adding the written assurance that no harm would come to the squire's military leader. I also added the confirmation that it is God's will that Jean de Metz support the cause of Jehanne La Pucelle.

At exactly four o'clock, the door in the southeast tower of the fortress opens a fraction, and I meet Jean de Metz face to face for the first time. He quickly pulls me inside the tower and closes the heavy door behind us. It's dark inside the fortress, but a torch inserted into a bracket on the curved stone wall allows me to inspect him more closely.

He is about my height, which I believe in medieval Europe is probably pretty tall, and he appears much younger than I expected, for according to the historical information he was probably about forty-one years old when he first met Jehanne in 1428. For a man living in fifteenth-century France, that's considered old. But he doesn't look old, and he's far more attractive than I expected. His wavy chestnut hair hangs nearly to his shoulders, and he has a strong, straight nose and a look of nobility about him. He has also been called Jean de Novelonpont, which is his city of birth, located about a hundred kilometers to the north of Vaucouleurs, near what in my time, is the border between France and Belgium.

I'm fully aware of the fact that many historians believe that Jean came to fall in love with the Maiden, but because of her virtue and goodness, he never told her of his feelings nor acted upon them. Some claim he never married—although I don't know if this has been proven—because of his unrequited love for La Pucelle. However, other historians speculate that he was, in essence, a spy for Robert de Baudricourt, sent to determine Jehanne's true or false worth. I'm not sure what his motivations are, but I choose to believe that he is and will continue to be devoted to Jehanne out of pure motives, heavenly motives. I'm counting on what I've read about his complete and total devotion to Joan of Arc, because right now, my life depends upon it.

I hand him the note I've written and then wonder if he is even literate. I keep forgetting that reading skills are not a given in fifteenth-century France. He takes it, studies it, and nods. Thank heavens. He can read. Without saying anything, Jean gestures for me to follow him. He removes the torch from the bracket to light our way through a network of dim and chilly corridors that smell of mildew and unwashed bodies. We must be deep within the fortress walls, because there are no windows that allow any natural light inside. Not my idea of a fun place to spend the winter. But hey, it isn't my idea to be here in the first place.

We cross the paths of several soldiers, but none question my presence, and I keep my face down, hidden within the shadows of my hood. We climb several flights of stairs, and when we approach the hallway where I assume Baudricourt's quarters are located, I'm concerned to see a guard sitting on a simple wooden chair next to a heavy wooden door. A small table sits next to the chair, and a single candle on the table lights the corridor. Jean places his torch in a bracket next to the door and then quietly addresses the guard who is now standing, while I remain several feet away, turned sideways so that the guard cannot see my face. As he leaves his post and goes in the opposite direction, I approach the door to Robert de Baudricourt's bedchamber. My heart is pounding so loudly I'm certain that Jean de Metz can hear the manifestation of my fear. Honestly, I have no idea if this is going to work or not.

"*Voilà,*" Jean whispers to me. "We are here. You have thirty minutes inside the commander's chambers, and then I will tap on the door, and you must exit. Please, you will have no longer than that. I have sent the guard on an errand, and there will not be any other opportunity for me to get you inside. I have no desire to know what it is you are doing, but if any harm comes to the commander, Mademoiselle Jehanne will suffer the consequences."

Jean looks down the corridor in both directions making certain that it's clear, and then he allows me to enter the sleeping quarters of Robert de Baudricourt. He closes the door behind me. I know what I have to do. This *has* to work, for I will not have another chance before tomorrow. I look at my watch, which I keep carefully hidden underneath the long sleeves of the shirt under my tunic. It is 4:07. I have until 4:37, although I'm not certain how Jean de Metz is going to know exactly when my time is up because there aren't a whole lot of wristwatches in the fifteenth century. Oh yeah, that's right. There aren't *any* watches, and I didn't see any clocks in the corridors. I guess people in this era have a better sense of time than those of us who rely on our electronic devices. I know they use the sun, but there weren't any windows in that corridor. Maybe he will judge the time by how much the candle burns down. I don't know. I'll have to ask Nicolas about that. If I ever see Nicolas again.

Before doing anything else, I take stock of the room. It is a cavernous chamber with a massive fireplace on the outer wall set between two windows. Hooray! Windows. Natural light. And additionally, a crackling fire is burning in the fireplace keeping the temperature inside the room comfortable. The barrel vaults that encase the windows are at least three feet thick, and all of the walls inside the chamber are comprised of un-plastered stone blocks.

However, in spite of its size, I am surprised at how simple the furnishings are. From what I've read about Robert de Baudricourt and his curt and inhospitable treatment of Jehanne, I somehow expected his quarters to express the opulence of someone who cherishes his power and station in life. I couldn't have been more wrong. Except for the warmth of the fire, this is a stark room without frills. Baudricourt doesn't seem to have a Mrs. Baudricourt, or if he does, she obviously doesn't share this bedchamber, for there isn't a hint of a female presence. There are neither tapestries on the walls nor rugs on the floor, and the furniture is sparse. A small canopy bed sits kitty-corner from the fireplace, and above the bed, a series of square stone blocks project out about four inches along the entire width of the wall, at graduating heights, almost like a very narrow staircase leading to the top of the wall. A small, low chest sits next to the bed. On the opposite wall, there is a basic table and chair and a tall wardrobe.

I look up to see that the chamber's ceiling is nonexistent, and judging by the blackened beams that span the space between the walls, I realize the ceiling was probably lost as the result of a fire. Above the three thick horizontal beams is the underside of a pitched wooden roof. The trusses and framework of the roof rest on a projecting ledge of stones that sits at the top of the fifteen-foot high walls. Except for the sheer height of the walls, this configuration is very good for my plan. In fact, it is better than I could have possibly expected, as long as my physical condition is up to the task.

I dash to the windows, which remain uncovered by any type of drapery, and carefully peer out to confirm that they look out over the inner courtyard of the fortress. There is no sentry path outside the windows, and no way to get into these windows from the outside of the chamber without a three-story ladder, so there's really only one way to get into this room, and that will make it impossible for me to use a line-of-sight remote control for my recorder. I'm going to have to use a timer, but I've come prepared for all eventualities.

And then it dawns on me. The climbing lessons I took. I'm going to be free climbing a stone wall. I wish I had the upper body strength of an American Ninja Warrior. For those elite athletes, this would be a piece of cake. They could do what I have to do in a matter of seconds, but for me, this is going to be a fifty-fifty proposition. Remember, they never really let me climb without my safety harness. I quietly carry the chair to the opposite side of the room, place it on the low chest next to the bed, and then say a prayer. I really need the Archangel's help right now, and I have faith that he will help me, because if he doesn't and I fall, it will be curtains for me . . . and curtains for Jehanne.

I remove my cloak and strip down to my skivvies: basically a very tight Lycra tank top—which compresses any suggestion of breasts I may or may not have (mostly not)—and tights. I don't need my 'male-soldier' tunic catching on anything and causing me to crash to the stone floor below. I also pull out the tattered knapsack I borrowed from Nicolas since I can't very well be flouting my high tech North Face backpack. From the knapsack, I pull out two flat electronic devices and program them to do their business, then place them inside my Lycra tank top, which is now not only holding in my poor excuse for female curves, but my devices as well. It's a frightening thought to realize that this entire mission could depend upon these two tiny 'magic boxes,' as Nicolas would call them.

From my precarious perch on the chair balanced on the wooden chest, I reach up until my fingers are wedged onto one of the projecting stones above my head. I pull my weight up with my fingers, then shift my weight onto my left foot, which has found a secure perch on a lower stone. Slowly, I bring up my right leg and put my weight on it. Then, I swing my left leg over to an adjacent stone, just lower than the one on which my fingers are clamped. Trying to breathe slowly, I manage to push up with my left thigh (my good thigh, unscarred from my last journey into medieval France), and then work my fingers up through the small cracks between the stones until I feel my fingers finding a grip on an even higher ledge. I move my right foot up to another projecting stone and continue the process. My right ankle is killing me, but I try to ignore it. With my chest and body pressed firmly against the stone wall, I work my way across the wall from right to left up the graduating projecting stones. When I have nearly reached the stone ledge at the top of the wall where my fingers will find safe harbor, I breathe a sigh of relief, thinking that this just might work, but a sharp pain in my ankle causes me to automatically look down, and I'm wracked by a wave of vertigo that makes me lose my balance.

And I fall backwards into oblivion.

Chapter 33

ALL WAS DARKNESS AND COLDNESS AND PAIN.

But just to recognize those sensations must mean that I am still alive, Nicolas thought.

By applying every ounce of willpower he could muster up, Nicolas finally managed to open his eyes. It was still darkness, coldness, and pain. His neck was on fire, and his chest felt as if one of the stone blocks from the abbey church had fallen on him. And there was something else: the most disgusting, putrid odor one could imagine.

He stretched out his hand and touched the surface beneath him. It was mud mixed with animal dung. A wet snout nudged his face. Soon he was surrounded by additional snouts, nipping at his frozen fingers and ears. He was in a wretched pig sty! He could hardly be in a more disgusting or demeaning place. Nicolas shooed off the irritated beasts and tried to lift his head, but the world started spinning, and he barely had the time to turn his head so that his vomit wouldn't fall directly on him. Not that it would have mattered. He was literally swimming in malodorous muck, and the regurgitated contents of his stomach could not have compounded the extent of his miserable situation in any way. He laid his poor, filthy head back into the mire and closed his eyes again. He wasn't certain how long he stayed like that, pitifully surrounded by pigs and sludge, and unable to do a thing to extricate himself, but it felt like an eternity. He might as well be dead.

Finally, he managed to move again. This time, rather than lifting his head, he turned on his side, keeping his head level with his body. He slowed his breathing and focused all of his attention on trying to recollect where he was and what had happened to him. And then, he remembered. He had come through the time portal to Sainte-Catherine-de-Fierbois, and he had buried Brother Thibault's sword in the little church of that town. Although it felt as though he had been lying in this hell-hole for an eternity, it could not have been as long as he thought, for the light of dawn was just seeping in through the chinks in the mortar of what he could now see was a ramshackle stone structure. Yes, he remembered clearly now. He had left the church in the predawn hours. Of course, there was also the possibility that he could have been lying here for an entire day, but he knew he would have been discovered by the owner of these pigs. As he tried to make sense out of his situation, he drew the only possible conclusion. Abdon had attacked him as he left the church, after he had buried the sword. Then like a lightning bolt, he remembered the feel of that rope coiled about his neck like a noose, and the breath of life leaving his body.

But where is Abdon? Does he truly believe I am dead? Does he think he killed me and then dumped my body here to rot and decay? To be eaten by the pigs?

There was something essentially alarming about this situation. More alarming than actual attempted murder, that is. Surely, Abdon would never have dumped Nicolas if he were still alive, and it did not make sense for Abdon to kill him in the first place. Although he was certainly evil enough and capable in every way of slaughtering other human beings, murder and revenge were not Abdon's primary motivators. As angry as Abdon might have been at Nicolas, this was not a case of revenge. No, murder and revenge were just side benefits of his twisted behavior. Abdon's primary motivation was to learn the secret of Mont Saint Michel, and to kill one of the only individuals who knew that secret did not make any sense. Unless it was completely accidental. Something was definitely amiss. Either Abdon believed he had accidentally killed Nicolas, or this was a trap.

And then Nicolas thought of another possibility. Could Abdon have abducted Katelyn? Did Abdon believe she knew the secret and he could get it out of her? But that line of thinking did not make any sense either, because Abdon had followed Nicolas, not Katelyn, through the time portal. There would have been no opportunity to abduct Katelyn. And what of Brother Thibault? No, that was not a possibility either, because Abdon would not have had the time to extract any information from Brother Thibault before following Nicolas and Katelyn to the abbey. He and Katelyn had been with Brother Thibault until the very last minute before their departure. Besides, Nicolas knew Thibault. He was a saintly man. He would never have betrayed either God or Nicolas. He would have suffered death before giving away the sacred knowledge.

Then Nicolas thought of yet another explanation. Perhaps Abdon was having difficulty controlling his new host. Perhaps it was the uncontrolled wrath of the host that had led Abdon to attack Nicolas nigh unto death. Nicolas knew nothing about Abdon's latest host, except that he spoke native French. He was definitely not a foreigner. He was not English, like Richard Collins, nor did he have the outward refinement of Collins, if evil could ever be called refined. Nicolas tried hard to focus on the face he had seen only in the shadows. As he honed in on those few seconds, he could remember some distinctive characteristics. Although the man had greasy dark hair, and appeared unkempt, his clothing had been of good quality. Then Nicolas remembered his hands. They were not the grimy hands of a simple laborer, and his French was not the French of a peasant.

No, in spite of his pockmarked face, this man definitely belonged to the French middle or upper class. He had been dressed as a follower of Saint James, but that had obviously been a disguise, just as Katelyn had suggested, which had allowed him access to Mont Saint Michel. By now, Abdon had probably discarded that pious clothing and changed his appearance. But the wildness of his spirit and the malevolence in his countenance could not be disguised. His dark face was embedded in Nicolas's memory. He would recognize him, regardless of his raiment. Nicolas had to find this man, and find him soon.

Nicolas thought of his time key. He lifted his hand and felt for it under his clothing. Yes, it was still there, and surprisingly, Nicolas's flesh actually felt dry, in spite of having been dropped into this soup of muck. Praise be to Katelyn for having had the foresight to provide him with such remarkable undergarments. They may just have saved his life.

Then, his thoughts turned to the fate of his knapsack and all the items Katelyn had sent to facilitate his assignment and sustain his life. Surely, Abdon had not left that for him. But once again, the Archangel had been beneficent. As he looked around him, Nicolas saw why the pigs had left him alone. They were gathered around his knapsack, which sat on a pile of dry straw in the corner of the low building. They were rooting around the bag, pawing it with their muddy trotters, clearly smelling Katelyn's protein bars. No wonder he had felt that inspiration to tightly knot his knapsack. He definitely had no desire to cast his pearls before swine.

But again. This made no sense. Why would such a malevolent soul as Abdon leave him with his knapsack, with the means to survive and continue on with his undertaking? If Abdon had believed that Nicolas was dead, surely he would have scoured his enemy's belongings to find not only his time key, but also to find any other hint that might reveal something about the Watchman's mission.

Truly, the only explanation was that Abdon did not have total control of his host.

Or, there was yet another possibility. This was an elaborate trap designed to entice Nicolas into showing his hand. If Abdon could get Nicolas to believe he had been left for dead so that he was less cautious, perhaps Abdon thought Nicolas would lead him to the answers he wanted. That meant Abdon was out there somewhere ready to follow Nicolas in an attempt to determine why he had been sent halfway across France in the middle of winter and to lead him to where Katelyn Michaels was. Nicolas had to act on the assumption that Abdon would be trailing him. He just prayed he could outwit his adversary.

Seeing his knapsack being trampled by the pigs gave Nicolas the motivation he needed to finally move his body. Slowly, oh, so slowly, he pulled himself to a sitting position, and although the spinning was still there, if he closed his eyes, he could pull his torso through the mud to the bit of higher ground where his knapsack had been abandoned. When he finally reached it, he found the straw there, unlike the straw in the rest of the sty, was fresh. After shooing the pigs away, Nicolas retrieved his knapsack and was surprised to find that it was dry and undamaged. He used the clean straw to begin wiping off his body. It did little for the stench, but it did remove the liquid muck. Now he felt like vomiting because of his own foul odor. Wretched, wretched Abdon. Nicolas could feel his anger towards the satanic envoy building into rage.

But rage would solve nothing. Nicolas had to remain calm. He had to be analytical and rational. Otherwise, he and Katelyn would not survive Abdon's latest onslaught. Anger was ungodly, although Christ himself had cleansed the temple in Jerusalem when his righteous indignation had been the motivator. So, Nicolas would use his anger righteously. He would do his very best to cleanse this earthly temple of all attempts by Lucifer's hosts to subjugate mortal men. He would protect the sacred trust that had been given to him, and above all, he would use this indignation to protect his Katelyn from the wrath of Abdon's latest ungodly host.

The pure power of this righteous indignation enabled Nicolas le Breton to finally stand on his own two feet, and in spite of his appearance, repellent odor, and spinning head, to bend and exit through the small opening of his pig sty prison.

With renewed confidence, he looked about. No one was in sight, except a few cows and goats, shivering in the early morning air. He was grateful that the heavens were clear and that it wasn't raining. He looked up to follow the path of the sun on the horizon, beginning its daily march across France's cold winter sky, and determined which way was west. Wherever Abdon had dumped him had been well out of the village of Sainte-Catherine-de-Fierbois, but Nicolas could see and recognize the steeple of the little church slightly to the east.

As quickly as he could, he took cover in a forest. Because of the deciduous trees that had all dropped their leaves, the forest offered him little cover, but up ahead, he saw a stand of pines and a green trail of undergrowth that looked promising. When he reached the pines, he found what he was seeking: a stream bed with a trickle of clear, clean water. It was sufficient. He followed it for a short distance until he came to a spot where the water formed a shallow pool, and where a bank of dry pine needles offered him the most protection. Although the water was as cold as ice, it did not matter to him. He refused to remain in these filthy clothes. He refused to allow Abdon to humiliate him in such a manner as to leave a lasting stench upon him. He refused to be victimized or demoralized by his enemy. Although he knew he would face the monster yet again, and although he knew that Abdon's power could never be underestimated, on this day, Nicolas le Breton refused to bear the marks of Abdon for a minute longer than necessary. Although he would have liked to build a fire, he did not want to take the time or risk the smoke exposing his location.

In spite of the frigid temperature, Nicolas stripped off every piece of clothing he had on. He removed his time key and coins from the pocket of his undergarments and set them on a dry stone. Even Katelyn's highly touted undergarments were saturated with the smell of humiliation, but they had kept his body dry, and so they had served their purpose. When he was completely naked, he pulled out a little bag sent by Katelyn for hygiene purposes. It contained products with which he was familiar from his stay in twenty-first century Mont Saint Michel: soap, shampoo, a toothbrush, and toothpaste. Praise Katelyn, once again, for he knew that this kind of stench could not be conquered by water alone. And so gritting his teeth, and breaking the ice off the stones that edged the little pool, Nicolas stepped into its freezing but cleansing waters. He scrubbed his skin until it was nearly raw, and threw handfuls of water onto his hair and face until he could work up a lather with Katelyn's shampoo. The hardest part was to submerge his head under the cold water, but when he was through, he felt renewed.

He pulled out a compact square of fabric, which Katelyn described as a miracle towel, and dried off his body, especially working it over his blond curls. It did work like a miracle, absorbing the liquid like nothing he had ever seen before. Then he removed the second set of clothing Katelyn had insisted he bring—'just in case'—and again praised her practical and inspired preparations. She had even included a duplicate set of the thermal undergarments, complete with secret pocket. He replaced his coins and key in the pocket and dressed. The only thing he did not have in duplicate was a heavy woolen cloak, but she had insisted he take a lightweight jacket—which took hardly any space in his knapsack—which she touted as having remarkable thermal properties like the underwear. By the time he donned it and the gloves, he had stopped shivering.

Wearing Katelyn's remarkable stockings, he knelt over the pool and scrubbed his leather boots until the fetid and caked mud had been removed. His final act was to brush the taste of vomit from his mouth with his toothbrush and toothpaste.

Truly feeling like a new being, and with renewed determination, Nicolas repacked his gear, cast aside his filthy garments for some unluckier chap to cherish, and then recommenced his journey.

He headed straight west, towards the city of Chinon.

And hopefully, towards Katelyn.

Chapter 34

I OPEN MY EYES IN PANIC. IT TAKES ME A FEW seconds
to realize where I am, which is lying flat on my back looking up at the
ceiling of Robert de Baudricourt's bedchamber. But it's from a
vantage point much closer than it would normally be if I were lying
on the floor. And if I were lying on that cold stone floor, having
fallen from my precarious perch on his wall, somehow, I don't think
I'd still be alive, or at least my head would hurt a lot more than it
actually does . . . which is still quite a bit.

I touch the back left side of my scalp where it does hurt, and my
hand comes away bloody. Yep, I've hit my head all right, but it isn't
smashed. It's just tender and seems to have a small gash. This hitting
my head business has really got to stop.

I turn my head to the side and can't believe my luck. I fell from
the wall straight onto the solid wood canopy that covers
Baudricourt's bed, and judging from the spot of blood on the corner
molding of that canopy, which projects up all around the edges of the
flat surface, that's where I hit my head. Unlike the flimsy fabric on
decorative canopies on twenty-first century beds, the commander's
canopy is made of a solid piece of hardwood, and even so, it looks
like I not only put a crack in my head, but I've put a crack in his
canopy as well. It makes me a bit nervous to move for fear of

splitting open the entire panel and falling through to the bed below. That will be a bit hard to explain to both Jean de Metz and Robert de Baudricourt.

I wipe off the tell-tale blood on the molding, and then extend my legs and arms trying to spread out the weight of my body evenly across the platform. I slowly inch my prostrate body to the edge of the canopy next to the wall, and grabbing the reinforced molding on the edge of the canopy, I pull myself up to a sitting position without causing an increase in the size of the crack. Phew, I think I've managed to avoid a catastrophe.

Then I gasp. I have momentarily forgotten about my time constraints. I look at my watch. It's 4:17, so I haven't been out long. I'd better get a move on it.

I force myself to focus on what I need to do. First, I check on my devices, and yes, they are still there inside my tank top, undamaged by my fall because I fell flat onto my back. The timer seems to be working correctly and the recording is still set to go off a few minutes after midnight. If I never have the opportunity to recover my devices, which is highly probable, then someone in some future time is going to wonder who on earth Baudricourt's decorator was. But that actually kind of lifts my spirits and makes me giggle. Can you imagine what the average fifteenth-century Frenchman would think if he came upon these gadgets from the future?

So once again, I set off on my Everest expedition, because honestly that's about how hard it seems to me about now, and I don't have a Sherpa guide or an oxygen tank to help me. I've never really been unduly afraid of heights, but once you've fallen, it's pretty tough to get back on the "climbing wall" if you know what I mean—especially when there is a time constraint involved—but I don't have the luxury of debating that issue in my mind. I've got less than twenty minutes to make this happen, and so I just have to do it.

I get back up onto the projecting stones directly above the canopy in the middle of the wall without further damaging the canopy. When I finally make it to the highest stone near the left side of the wall, I'm able to pull myself up onto the narrow stone ledge on which the trusses and rafters of the roof rest. But I don't have time to rest, so turning my body to face away from the wall, I manage to get into a sitting position and then swing my legs out over the wall. I bend my head over my knees to avoid hitting the rafters, and then scoot around the corner of the perpendicular wall until I reach the first overhead beam that spans the width of the bedchamber. It crosses directly over the foot of the canopy bed below.

This is the scariest part. I have to work my way out to the center of this beam and not lose my balance again. My breathing starts to accelerate, and I feel light-headed. There's a knot in my stomach and a hollow feeling in my chest. I close my eyes and force myself to breathe more slowly. Then the image flashes in my brain of a movie I just saw about Philippe Petit, the daring—or should I say crazy—young Frenchman who walked across the 130-foot gap between New York City's Twin Towers in the 1970s. And he did it on a steel cable only an inch wide! This beam is probably six inches wide, and I have only a fifteen foot fall, not a fifteen *hundred* foot fall, so for heaven's sake, I can do this. I *have* to do it. Too bad I didn't do gymnastics in high school, because this looks an awful lot like a balance beam, but then, my tall, skinny body kind of ruled out that sport for me.

I lean forward and hug the beam with both my arms and legs and start inching my way forward. I can't worry about the spider webs and dust that immediately invade my breathing space, and I choke back the coughing fit that threatens to expose my presence in this forbidden location. I also close my eyes. No reason to see how far down it is to the floor. Besides, I find that not being able to see actually helps focus all of my energy into feeling my way forward and connecting to that beam. After reaching what I estimate to be the mid-point of the beam, I finally open my eyes and hang on for dear life with my legs and left arm as I extract the timer and digital recorder from inside my tank top. I place them right in the center of the beam. They are connected by a short cord and they're both only about a quarter of an inch thick. I'm fairly certain they can't be seen from below. If anyone ever finds them, the batteries will be long gone, and the finder will have no idea of what these 'magic boxes' can do.

Once the gear is in place, I feel a huge sense of relief. The return trip doesn't take nearly as long as the trip out. I'm just glad it didn't turn into a one-way trip. When I finally get back down off the wall, I look at my watch. I have exactly five minutes left. I quickly put the chair that I'd placed on top of the chest to get onto the projecting stones back in its place on the opposite wall next to the small table. Then I look at the underside of the canopy to see if the crack is going to be a problem. Fortunately, it is hardly visible from underneath. I doubt very much Robert de Baudricourt will notice it, and if he does, hopefully he'll just chalk it up to normal wear and tear. I'd especially hate for him to accuse one of his servants of breaking his bed. I don't know much about him, and I hope he's not the type who would punish someone he believed committed my crime of canopy-cracking.

Then I scurry around the room to check out the beam from every vantage point. Nope, you can't see the devices on top of it. So even though Robert de Baudricourt is not going to see anything above his bed tonight, he's certainly going to be hearing something, and I hope it will sound to him just like it's coming from heaven, right through the roof and directly down to his bed. Although *I* know it's Brother Thibault's resonant voice, Baudricourt won't, and I hope he will be convinced by my little smoke and mirrors show. Yes, I hope he enjoys his midnight visitor.

Unfortunately, if he doesn't, I don't have a Plan B.

Chapter 35

SOMETHING WAS PULLING AT THE DEEPEST recesses of Robert de Baudricourt's consciousness, but his exhausted mind and body fought off the intrusion. It had been a long and frustrating day, and the morrow, February 12, 1429, threatened to bring even more of the same type of challenges. Morale was low among his small garrison of soldiers loyal to the French crown, for news steadily trickled in about the Dauphin Charles' ineffective leadership. And now, the English army's incursions into French territory, especially their siege of Orléans, had forced the Dauphin to leave Bourges and seek refuge in the fortress city of Chinon, as if by changing locations, the crown prince could somehow change French fortunes.

Baudricourt feared that the continued French failures to lift the siege at Orléans would eventually result in a mutiny among his soldiers. He had heard rumblings that many of his men now accepted the inevitability of an ultimate French defeat in this decades-long war and were considering switching sides to spare their lives, and the lives of their families. His close advisors had expressed to him the soldiers' feelings succinctly: they felt it was better to be under English rule and be alive than to die in the fight for a lost cause. And frankly, although Robert de Baudricourt faulted their loyalty, he could not fault their conclusions. Since the fortress in Vaucouleurs sat in Burgundian-held lands, and since the Burgundians had entered into their unholy alliance with the English in order to defeat their sworn enemies, the Armagnacs, the odds were stacked even further against him and his little band of soldiers.

If only the Burgundians and Armagnacs had been able to set aside their petty quarrels and power disputes and focus on fighting the English invaders, this war would have been over years ago. But unfortunately, Baudricourt's logic was not that of the Duke of Burgundy, who had forced the mad King Charles VI to sign the Treaty of Troyes in 1420. That evil excuse of an accord, entered into when Charles was obviously not in his right mind, meant that the French king essentially disinherited his own son, the Dauphin Charles, and recognized Henry V of England and his heir, Henry VI, as the legitimate kings of France. How could any rational Frenchman accept such a one-sided farce? As far as Baudricourt was concerned, the treaty had been entered into under duress and had no meaning. But being surrounded by the enemy did not help his argument. Having to fight off constant Burgundian attacks was not conducive to harmony among his discouraged French militia.

How was it possible to maintain order in the face of such odds? Although Robert de Baudricourt was loyal to France through and through, he couldn't help being disgusted by the Dauphin's vain and ineffectual attempts to thwart the invading English armies. It was almost a joke! While Charles may not be raving mad like his father, the Dauphin had none of the qualities of a charismatic leader who inspired trust, confidence, and most of all, loyalty. The man didn't even have the gumption to fight his way to Reims to be lawfully crowned King of France, to claim the throne that was *his*, not that of the young English monarch, Henry VI. The shallow Charles preferred to sit hidden among his courtiers playing games of coquetry and dalliance while what remained of France fought a losing battle.

And Robert expected his troops to give up their lives for such a lackluster leader? No, the discouraged commander could not fault them.

What France needed right now was plain and simple: divine intervention. Surely nothing but God Himself could change the course of this sovereign nation's failing fortunes. And that divine intervention had to start with Charles. It was no wonder Robert craved the oblivion that sleep brought, because there certainly seemed to be no answers for France's growing dilemma during daylight hours.

But sleep was not to be Robert de Baudricourt's good fortune that night. Once again, some noise or some force attempted to pull the commander away from his blessed oblivion. Finally, Robert recognized the intrusion for what it was. Someone or something was trying to get his attention. He opened his eyes and then heard the noise again. Someone was calling to him. Yes, someone was calling his name . . . his given name.

"Robert, Robert," the intruder called. "Wake up, Robert. Pay heed to this message from on high." Although the voice was not loud, it was deep and resonant, and it seemed to come from somewhere above him. Could someone have entered his bedchamber in spite of the twenty-four hour guard he had posted at his door?

He jumped out of bed and looked above the canopy of his bed, and then looked under his bed. No one. Then he looked all around him. The light from the dwindling flames still flickering in the fireplace was sufficient for him to see that there was no intruder in his sparsely-furnished room. He was not one for outward trappings.

He rushed to the wardrobe, the one place an intruder might hide, and opened its doors, but no, there was not another living soul in the chamber with him. He heard the voice again: "Robert. Robert, give heed to my words, for you hold the power to save all of France."

He remembered his thoughts as he had drifted off to sleep. He had concluded that only divine intervention could save France. Was this an answer to his thoughts and prayers? Would God answer an unworthy servant like himself? 'Twas inconceivable. He could not possibly be hearing voices from above! Besides, had he not himself recently ridiculed someone who claimed to have heard voices? Had he not himself cast out that peasant maiden who had made this very claim? What was her name? Je . . . Jehanne. Yes, Jehanne. She was the kinfolk of Durand Laxart.

But he could not deny what he had heard. And then it came again.

"Robert. Robert, give heed to my words, for you hold the power to save all of France."

How could he, a simple garrison commander, hold the power to save France? 'Twas simply not possible.

"Robert, I am the Archangel Michael, and I have been sent by God to chastise you for your unbelief. With you has rested the power to change the fate of France, and yet you have failed."

The voice was definitely coming from above, from heaven itself, piercing through the wooden roof of his bedchamber and cutting him straight to the heart. Although the fading fire had left his room chilled and forlorn, drops of sweat broke out upon his brow. His heart started racing, and he felt as though he would faint dead away. Somehow, he had aroused the wrath of God.

He fell to his knees with such force that he heard them crack against the stone surface. He had failed? How had he failed? He had done everything he could to keep his little garrison together, to remain loyal and faithful to a dying cause. Surely this was not happening. This was most certainly a dream. He slapped his face, but, still he knelt there, on the cold stones of his chamber floor, and now, in addition to a racing heart and bruised knees, he felt the sting of his own hand imprint upon his cheek. And still the voice spoke to him. This was no dream.

"Robert, Robert, give heed to my message. Twice God has sent you His emissary, and twice have you rejected her and her message. Have you no loyalty to France? Would you see her armies fail? Would you see the Dauphin abandon all hope of taking his rightful place as King of France? Is this your wicked desire?"

And then Robert found his voice. "No," he cried in anguish. "No, Sire." Robert was not certain how to address his heavenly visitor, but "Sire" seemed as good a choice as any. "I profess to you that I love my country. Never would I betray France. Never. Nor would I willingly betray God."

Silence. The voice did not respond, and Robert feared that no answer would be forthcoming. He feared that he would be consumed by fire right then and there. And then the same message was repeated.

"Robert, Robert, give heed to my message. Twice God has sent you His emissary, and twice have you rejected her and her message. Have you no loyalty to France? Would you see her armies fail? Would you see the Dauphin abandon all hope of taking his rightful place as King of France? Is this your wicked desire?"

"No," he pleaded, this time spreading his body out prostrate upon the floor. "No, I am loyal to France. And I am loyal to God's cause. What would you have me do?"

"I have good tidings for you, Robert. It is not too late for you. You shall have one more opportunity. Twice have you rejected God's messenger, but if you should reject her thrice, you will be in Satan's power."

"No, no, I shall not reject His messenger. Are you speaking of the girl? The maiden?"

There was a pause, and an ominous feeling of darkness enveloped him. Was it too late for him? Had he not only brought down God's wrath upon him, but God's condemnation as well? He waited, praying for guidance, and then that glorious, resonant voice spoke to him again. It was not a voice of harsh condemnation, but rather a gentle, loving tone. A tone of forgiveness . . . of redemption.

"Robert, you must listen to the maiden Jehanne, and grant her righteous request. In her hands, and her hands alone, rests the fate of France. It is God's will for France to remain a sovereign nation. You, Robert de Baudricourt, are called to assist Jehanne in her divinely appointed mission. Tomorrow morning, she will come to the fortress and ask for a third audience, which you shall grant. She will give to you a sign that she has truly been sent by God. This is the sign: she will bring you news of a battle near the town of Rouvray between the French and the English. 'Tis a battle that will take place tomorrow, a battle about which no earthly messenger could know.

"After she imparts this news to you, she will once again request assistance in her journey to Chinon to speak to the Dauphin. You will agree to lend this assistance by commanding your man-at-arms, Jean de Metz, to head up a small group of soldiers to accompany her and provide her protection. Bertrand de Poulangy should be included in this group. You will send Jehanne with a letter of safe conduct to be shown to any of the French troops who may hinder her journey. You will also charge her escorts to protect her safety and her purity at all costs. Furthermore, you will send a messenger with a letter of introduction to the Dauphin, in which you commend her and give him your strongest recommendation to heed her words."

"Is there nothing else I can do to assist the girl? The maiden?" he asked. After such an experience, he would have given any of his earthly valuables, any of his support to assist God's emissary. He would have escorted her to Chinon himself.

The voice replied: "Jean de Metz and Bertrand de Poulangy will assist her in her preparations to procure a horse and the appropriate male clothing for the journey. Jean has already proven to be my loyal servant."

Jean de Metz had found God's favor, but Robert hadn't? It was a blow to the man who had always been motivated by a desire to do what he deemed to be right.

"But I desire to assist as well," the humbled commander entreated. "I desire to be your loyal servant. I can offer her clothing and a horse. I can provide her with the money necessary to make the journey." At this point he stood on his feet and looked upward.

"You must do exactly as I have instructed. Jean de Metz will finance her journey as a token of his love of God, and this he should be allowed to do. It is not your responsibility. However, I have additional directives for you. After granting the Maiden's request, you must speak privately to Jean de Metz and inform him that he will be approached by a young soldier from Brittany. The lad's name is Kaelig. Outward appearances would lead one to believe that this soldier is a mere boy with nothing to offer by way of knowledge or ability, but just as it would be a grave mistake to judge Jehanne by her appearance, it would also be a grave mistake to judge Kaelig by *his* appearance.

"Instruct Jean de Metz to invite the lad to join his little army. Inform him in the very strongest of terms that he must allow Kaelig free hand during the journey to perform any task the Breton deems necessary, even if it appears strange or unusual. You must swear an oath with Jean de Metz, and he, in turn, must swear an oath with his group of soldiers that, under penalty of death, they will obey Kaelig's commands and that none of them will ever speak of anything Kaelig does or says, or of his friendship with Jehanne. Even if one day in the future, they are called upon to testify in the highest courts of the land, and even if that tribunal is conducted by the Church itself, this oath must *never* be broken. No word of Kaelig's activities or presence in your group may *ever* be made known, for Kaelig is God's own emissary sent to aid and assist Jehanne in her journey.

"Unfortunately, Jehanne has many enemies who will accuse her of having an impure relationship with this young soldier, when in fact, God, in his great mercy, has sent Kaelig to provide strategic direction and divine protection for the Maiden. Therefore, it is God's will that Kaelig's presence never be made known to anyone who could use the information for evil. Ever! Do you understand? So in a very real manner, you are making a covenant with God. Once you have given this information to Jean de Metz, and sworn the oath with him, you must never speak of Kaelig again, and after the journey is over, neither may Jean de Metz or his men speak of him. If you or they break this covenant, God's wrath will indeed be visited upon you. Will you swear this oath?"

"Yes, Sire. I swear that except for my explanations to Jean de Metz, I will never again speak of Kaelig the Breton. Of this, I solemnly swear."

There was another moment of silence, and then the Archangel spoke again. "Do you understand the nature of this oath? Can I trust you to instill in Jean de Metz the importance of keeping the oath?"

"Yes. I also swear that I shall make it very clear to him. I will inform him that his life and the lives of his soldiers depend upon their ability to keep this sacred oath."

"You have now committed to keeping this sacred trust," replied the Archangel. "Furthermore, you must now make an oath with me that you will never speak of my visit. Not even to Jean de Metz. Under no circumstances may you speak of the events of this night. These are the conditions for you to receive the grace of God's forgiveness. Do you accept these conditions?"

"Yes, Sire. I understand and I accept. I hereby swear to you that I will never speak to any man or to any woman about your visitation."

Robert was overwhelmed by the magnitude of his experience. The Archangel Michael had spoken to him! It was unbelievable. Exactly. Unbelievable. Even if he wanted to tell others that he had heard the voice of the Archangel, who *would* believe him? *He* had not believed the young girl's claims to have heard the voice of the Archangel and other heavenly visitors, and he himself had cast her out of his presence with the injunction never to return again. Shamed by his lack of intuition, compassion, and mercy towards the girl, he bowed his head in disgrace.

"That is sufficient," replied the heavenly voice, and then as if Michael had read his thoughts, he added. "In God's great mercy towards you, in a few days, you will receive official news about the Battle of Rouvray, news that will authenticate everything that Jehanne tells you about the battle on the morrow. This news will be sent to you to confirm in your heart that Jehanne has truly been sent by God and that her mission is divinely appointed. It will validate the fact that none of the events of this night were a figment of your imagination. Now, as your final act in this episode, you will order Jean de Metz to have all preparations complete so that Jehanne and her escorts can depart from this chateau on the twenty-third day of this month. That allows thirteen days for the preparations to be completed. Do you understand?"

"Yes. I understand."

"Good. Then may you ever be faithful, and may God grant you all of the righteous desires of your heart."

And with that, Robert heard a clicking and a whirring sound, and then there was complete silence. He had so many questions, but they went unvoiced, and unanswered.

He went to the door of his chamber to check on the guard. The guard, clearly unaware of the remarkable events that had just transpired within the chamber he was tasked to protect, sat with his head lowered, nodding between the states of wakefulness and slumber.

No matter. 'Twas not the guard who had allowed the heavenly visitor to enter his chamber. No, this was not a mortal encounter Robert de Baudricourt had just experienced. The guard could not have precipitated it or prevented it. Truly, God *was* merciful. Not only had the Almighty directed his messenger to visit Robert, but He had authorized Michael to forgive the headstrong man for his callous treatment of a young girl he could never have imagined to be God's emissary to save France. And even though he had many questions that remained unanswered, that France would, in fact, be saved, was no longer one of them.

He threw an additional log on the fire and sat in the wooden chair by his plain little table. It was no use to try to sleep now. No, he would spend these hours contemplating the incredible words he had just heard, and envisioning how this young maiden, Jehanne, and her Breton protector, Kaelig, could possibly save France. He would also write the missives the Archangel had requested: a letter addressed to the Dauphin to give heed to the message of the young maiden from Lorraine, and the injunction of safe passage to any French troops who might cross the path of Jehanne's little army.

And then, although Michael had informed him that Jean de Metz would provide Jehanne's horse and clothing, a thought came to Robert's mind.

Surely, the Archangel will not begrudge my giving Jehanne a token of my respect and a symbol of my faith in her. I shall give her my sword. Yes, every warrior, including the Archangel Michael, has a sword. This maiden is God's warrior, and so she has need of a warrior's weapon. Yes, the Maiden will need a sword.

Chapter 36

JUST AS KATELYN HAD PROMISED, WHEN Jehanne requested an audience with Robert de Baudricourt the next morning, telling his guards that she had news of great import, her request was not only granted immediately, but she was promptly brought into his presence without being obliged to wait. 'Twas a far cry from the manner in which the garrison commander at Vaucouleurs had treated her on the last two occasions. Jehanne had no idea of how Katelyn's intervention had changed his heart, but that it had was clear straightaway.

The commander was not alone. In fact, a small group of soldiers had been assembled. Next to the seated Baudricourt stood her friend and supporter, Jean de Metz, and she recognized another soldier, Jean's friend Bertrand de Poulangy.

Jehanne bowed before the commander and when she raised her head and looked into his eyes, she instantly recognized a difference in his attitude towards her. Whereas before he had looked upon her with disdain and dismissiveness, this time, his countenance hinted at a keen interest in what she had to say, and his deference to her displayed an unexpected degree of reverence.

"Mademoiselle," he began, "I am told you have news for me."

"Yes, Captain," she replied. "I am Jehanne La Pucelle, and I bring you news of another French defeat, which will be known as the Battle of the Herrings. The battle will take place near the town of Rouvray, just north of Orléans. 'Tis a battle that will occur on this very day, the twelfth day of February, 1429. Preparations for the conflict are beginning as we speak. My voices have instructed me to prophesy to you of its outcome, as a sign to you that I am indeed God's envoy."

"So you are prophesying of the outcome of a battle that has not yet taken place?" asked Baudricourt.

Jehanne initially thought the commander was mocking her, but as she looked at him, she saw softness in his eyes, and realized that he was in actuality confirming her claim, not ridiculing her.

"Yes, Captain, that is what I am about to do."

"Then proceed, mademoiselle, for I am anxious to hear what you have to say." He smiled at her encouragingly. Jehanne still could not process the transformation that had come over Robert de Baudricourt. Katelyn Michaels had called down heavenly powers to change the heart of this man.

She took a deep breath in preparation to repeat the words she had carefully rehearsed with Katelyn, including the specific names of the participants. Katelyn had underlined the importance of getting the names correct, for even if Baudricourt concluded that Jehanne had fabricated the details of the battle, for her to know the names of the actual participants, many of whom the commander would know, was next to impossible.

"A great convoy of three hundred supply wagons is now making its way to Lieutenant General John Talbot's English troops at Orléans," she began. "As you know, Captain, we are fast approaching the pre-Easter season of Lent when good Christians are required to abstain from eating meat, and so these supplies for the English garrison consist of foods appropriate for Lent, including enough salted herrings to sustain the English soldiers throughout this entire season of fasting. The convoy is being escorted by some six hundred English soldiers and a thousand Parisians under the command of Sir John Fastolf." She saw the commander knit his brows, and she wondered if she had made a mistake. But no, she knew the narrative by heart. She continued.

"In an attempt to lift the siege of Orléans, the French troops, under the direction of the Count of Clermont, along with several Armagnac militias, have joined forces with Sir John Stewart and his Scottish troops to cut off this line of supplies to the English. These combined forces total nearly six thousand. It would seem that with such numbers, the French should be successful in their quest, but alas, 'twill not be the case." Jehanne stopped, thinking of the devastating impact of yet another French defeat.

"Go on, Jehanne," encouraged Robert de Baudricourt. "I am amazed at the details you present. You have my complete attention. So what is to happen?"

"I am sorry to announce that this will yet be another unmitigated disaster for France, Captain, for the members of the convoy have been warned by the local English garrisons that hostile forces are amassing and preparing to attack. With this advance knowledge, Fastolf will order the English to group their supply wagons into a square, forming a solid barricade. While the French and their allies are waiting for their troops to be in position, the English will strengthen their protection by placing sharpened spikes all around their makeshift fortress to prevent the French cavalry from charging."

"Yes," muttered the commander. "'Twas a tactic the English used successfully at the Battle of Agincourt. Pardon me, mademoiselle. Continue."

"Using their field artillery, the Armagnacs will achieve limited success in blasting open several of the wagons, spilling their contents of salted herrings out over the fields, and hence give name to this unusual battle. When the Scottish troops attack the fortress prematurely, the French will be forced to cease their artillery bombardment out of fear of striking their allies. In the meantime, the highly skilled English archers and crossbowmen will use the cover of their makeshift fortress to launch a fierce attack of their own, bombarding both armies with a slew of arrows. Then, when the English realize the cowardly nature of the French troops—who are slow to join in the attack when they see the decimation of the Scottish ranks—the English will launch a counterattack. They will strike the French flanks from the rear, forcing them to flee."

"'Tis not a flattering picture of French courage, is it?" muttered Baudricourt.

"No, 'tis but a confirmation of the disarray of the French armies in general. Sire, the French and their allies will be sorely defeated. Whereas the English will suffer the loss of only four of their soldiers and several of their barrels of herrings, the French and Scottish losses will number nearly a thousand men-at-arms, including the Scottish commander, Sir John Stewart."

"Another dark day in the annals of this cursed war," added Robert de Baudricourt.

"'Tis the purpose of my visit here today," injected Jehanne, seeing the perfect opening to make her plea. "Without strong and inspired leadership, you and I both know that France's survival as a sovereign nation is impossible. Sire, you know why I am here. Twice have I made these declarations to you, and twice have you turned me away. But with God as my source of power and inspiration, I will repeat yet again my declaration without fear and without hesitation. God has commanded me to come to you today. Indeed, God has commanded me to save France. This kingdom belongs not to us, not even to the Dauphin, but to my Lord and God Himself, the very King of Heaven. My Lord would have the Dauphin be made King of

France and hold the kingdom in trust. I must go to the Dauphin, to convince him to allow me to take command of his armies so that I can make him King. I am the only hope for France . . . the only hope for the Dauphin. I say this without fear of repercussion or persecution, for how can I fear what God has commanded me to do? I do not know why and I do not know how, but with God as my witness and my protector, I know that it is possible. I petition you yet again to grant my request for an escort to Chinon. I petition you to write for me an incontestable introduction to the Dauphin Charles. If you once again deny my request, I shall call God's wrath down upon you."

After this powerful and daring diatribe, it was as if all of Jehanne's self-confidence and all of her pent up anger was drained, and she returned to her normal, humble persona, that of an ordinary peasant girl, without any special skills or military experience. Indeed, it was as if every ounce of energy she had within her physical body had been expended.

And yet . . . and yet. There, the words she had been longing to hear. Robert de Baudricourt's acquiescence.

"Yes, Jehanne. I hereby grant your request."

She looked up at him in shock. "You . . . you do?"

"Yes," he repeated. "Not only do I grant your request, but I will send you on your journey to Chinon in the company of two of my best squires, Jean de Metz and Bertrand de Poulangy. Jean, come forward," the commander ordered.

"Yes, Sire. What is it that you require of me?" Jean de Metz asked, addressing his commanding officer with all of the deference required of his station.

"I would that you gather a small group of soldiers to escort this young maiden to Chinon," replied Baudricourt. "And in everything you do, you will consider Jehanne's safety and particularly, her purity. You will do all in your power to protect her, for her mission is a sacred one, vital for the survival of France itself, and her person is equally sacred."

"Sire, I am honored to have been given this charge, for I too, believe La Pucelle's mission is a sacred one. However, inasmuch as she will be traveling through enemy territory, and additionally through districts laced with bandits and Burgundian brigands, I propose that she be given an exemption by the Church to dispense with her female clothing, for surely villainous men will be tempted to abuse her virginity should they come upon us. Sire, I propose she be outfitted as a young male soldier. I know that any deviation from appropriate dress is censured by the Church, and I would not wish for condemnation to fall upon La Pucelle for any perceived lack of decorum, hence the request for a dispensation. Have I your blessing to proceed with such measures?"

"I wholly concur with your assessment of the difficulties for La Pucelle to travel dressed in her female raiment," replied Baudricourt, "and I will do what is necessary to procure the required dispensation from the Church. I now give you and your colleague, Bertrand de Poulangy, the charge to procure clothing for her that would lead our enemies to believe that she is not a virginal female, but instead a young male soldier. I also charge you with providing her with a horse and gathering all of the supplies necessary for the journey. And this you will do as a testament to God that you honor and respect his servant."

"We will do so with willing hearts," confirmed Jean de Metz.

"Now, Jehanne," the commander turned then and addressed her in a quieter, more gentle tone of voice. "We have spoken of difficult things in your presence. We cannot ignore the fact that you are a maiden, and that you will not only be traveling in the company of men, but that there is a real possibility that you will be beset upon by those who would not only prevent you from accomplishing your mission, but who would also threaten your virginity. Do you understand that it is in your best interest to dress in male clothing?"

"Certainly, Captain," she replied. "This fact has already been made abundantly clear to me by my voices. I embrace the proposed solution, and I thank both you and your squires for their bounteous goodness and gracious support."

"I know, mademoiselle, that after so many months of waiting, you must be anxious to depart immediately on your journey, but it will take some time to gather all the necessary supplies. Therefore, I propose that you and your escorts gather here, in the courtyard of the chateau, on the twenty-third day of February. I will not only give you papers to ensure your safe conduct through French-held lands at that time, but tomorrow, I shall also send a messenger with a letter of introduction to the Dauphin so that he will know you are coming."

He then turned to Jean de Metz. "Is that timeframe acceptable to you, Jean?"

"Yes, Sire. We should be able to gather all we need for the journey by that time."

"Good," replied the commander. "Jehanne, you may leave now and begin your own preparations. However, Jean, I wish to speak with you in private. Will you please accompany me into my chamber?"

At that, Robert de Baudricourt and Jean de Metz left the audience room, while Jehanne watched on in complete and total astonishment. After months of unsuccessful petitions, all of Jehanne's requests had been granted in a manner of minutes.

Her long-awaited journey was finally to begin.

Part Four

Rejoice therefore that I have confidence in you in all things.
2 Corinthians 7:16

*Cast not away therefore your confidence, which hath
great recompence of reward.*
Hebrews 10:35

*L'homme, l'homme, l'homme armé,
L'homme armé doibt on doubter, doibt on doubter.
On a fait partout crier
Que chascun se viegne armer
D'un haubregon de fer.
L'homme, l'homme, l'homme armé,
L'homme armé doibt on doubter.
L'homme armé doibt on doubter.*

The man, the man, the man who's armed,
Beware of him, lest thou be harmed.
'Tis now proclaimed both far and wide
A sword should be at each man's side,
And a coat of iron mail
To protect thyself as well.
The man, the man, the man who's armed,
Beware of him, lest thou be harmed.

Old French Song from the Hundred Years' War Era

Chapter 37

NICOLAS'S JOURNEY FROM Sainte-Catherine-de-Fierbois to Chinon was without incident, which was not actually a comfort to him. He would have preferred to confront Abdon face-to-face, rather than to travel with the constant sensation of being followed and experience the persistent apprehension that, at any moment, he would be attacked from behind. It was utterly and entirely unnerving. Now, as he wandered the cramped and dirty streets of Chinon, Nicolas found himself ceaselessly on the lookout for his sworn enemy. He needed to find a safe haven where he could wait out the days until Katelyn arrived. Well, hopefully, she would arrive. He certainly prayed she would.

Before they had left Mont Saint Michel, Katelyn had insisted that Nicolas master the information about the Maiden of Lorraine in the papers from the internet she had brought with her. She felt it would be too dangerous to take the information with them in case they were attacked by enemy soldiers or Abdon during their mission. How could they explain having such information? He could not comprehend how the internet worked, but he was certainly grateful for it. It had helped Katelyn prepare herself in so many ways, like knowing how to stitch up his wounds. It had also provided not only a written history of Jehanne La Pucelle as well as copies of artists' renderings of the important events in her life. This invaluable information helped Nicolas to not only *know* her history, but also to *feel* her history.

Because of the information contained in those precious pages, Nicolas knew that Jehanne would leave the city of Vaucouleurs on the evening of February 23, 1429 in the company of six soldiers, including Jean de Metz and Bernard de Poulangy, two of Robert de Baudricourt's most trusted men-at-arms. He prayed that Brother Thibault's recording, made not only to "encourage" Baudricourt to grant Jehanne's request, but also to insinuate Katelyn—as the male Breton soldier Kaelig— into that elite group of Jehanne protectors, had been successful.

He thought about that evening in the safety of Jean le Vieux's cottage on Mont Saint Michel when the three had debated about the content of that recording, how they had carefully crafted each and every word. He thought of how Katelyn had insisted that portions of the message be repeated, in case Robert de Baudricourt did not awaken immediately, something that Nicolas and Brother Thibault had not even considered. He thought of how they had timed what they all believed would be the commander's replies to the "Archangel Michael's" powerful commands. Indeed, it had taken hours until Katelyn was satisfied with the recorded message, and the completion of the task did not arrive too soon for Brother Thibault's irritated throat. When the process was finished, the poor man could hardly speak.

Nicolas also knew that the long journey on horseback from Vaucouleurs to Chinon would last a mere eleven days, which, given the difficulties of the violent marauders, the inhospitable winter climate, and the muddy terrain, was quite an outstanding feat. One hundred leagues in eleven days? That was unheard of! It was a good thing Katelyn had mastered the art of riding, for that type of riding required great skill and ability. He knew the group would travel mostly at night in order to avoid the English soldiers and the vicious Burgundian marauders that peppered the land. He prayed that Katelyn's plan to dress like Jehanne, as a male soldier, would protect her. In fact, he constantly had a prayer in his heart for Katelyn's safety.

He could not help but wonder if Abdon could have traveled to Lorraine in pursuit of Katelyn, but he didn't see how that was possible. He once again praised Katelyn's wisdom in insisting that he carry no written information about Jehanne La Pucelle in his knapsack. If those papers had been in Nicolas's belongings when Abdon assaulted him, it would have had disastrous consequences. Nicolas had to constantly remind himself that even if Abdon existed in the future, he could not travel backward or forward in time, at least not without jumping one of the Watchmen at the perfect instant, as he had just done. So anything the Abdon of the future knew about this period of history or Jehanne, he would not know in 1429. No, Abdon could not possibly know that the Watchmen's mission was to support the cause of Jehanne La Pucelle from Domrémy. Abdon could not possibly know that Katelyn was most likely in Vaucouleurs preparing to make the eleven-day journey to Chinon.

That knowledge boosted Nicolas's morale temporarily, but after several hours of exploring the city under a steady mist of rain and plummeting temperatures, Nicolas finally realized he could go no further. He needed shelter and sustenance.

Even though he had the money to pay for food and lodging, he had not done so on his journey from Sainte-Catherine-de-Fierbois, a trek of about six leagues. Not wanting to leave a trace of his passage for Abdon to follow, he had avoided the villages during his journey to Chinon. He had survived on Katelyn's providentially-provided protein bars and an occasional raw egg snatched from the chicken coops of the inhabitants of the countryside, for which he left a coin.

After all, he was God's emissary, and he was not going to steal from the poor peasants who needed God's help the most.

He had slept either in stands of trees along the wayside or in abandoned barns or outbuildings, finding warmth and refuge in the compact but remarkably warm sleeping sack provided by Katelyn. He had even purloined a heavy woolen cloak to cover his twenty-first century jacket from one farmer's barn, for which he had also left payment. But up until his arrival in Chinon, he had not spoken to another human being. In fact, he had not even seen another human being up close.

Now, he was surrounded by people, but he did not know whom to trust. He had no idea of where to turn for assistance. As Nicolas looked up at the imposing chateau fortress on the hill above the city where the Dauphin Charles had taken refuge after leaving Bourges, he wished he could find refuge there, but he knew that was not possible. Although there was a prosperous merchant sector that sat just below the fortress on the banks of the Vienne River, he could find no food or lodging there, and the rest of the city seemed to be teeming with individuals who appeared to be in even more desperate straits than himself. However, that did not lessen the fact that he urgently needed a hot meal and warm shelter. He had hoped to find an obscure eating establishment, with the caveat that it offered fresh, wholesome nourishment, for Katelyn, with her twenty-first century perspective, had warned both Nicolas and Brother Thibault of the dangers of eating spoiled or undercooked food. But finding such a place had so far eluded him. He was exhausted both emotionally and physically, and he feared that without adequate food and rest, he would make a strategic blunder when Abdon finally appeared. For appear he would. That was a certainty. Abdon had to be here somewhere waiting for Nicolas to make his move. Waiting for Katelyn to appear. It was a dreadful thought.

As the rain turned to icy sleet, Nicolas knew he had to find shelter. Katelyn's clothing had kept him surprisingly warm up until now, but the pelting sleet now transformed his cloak into a soggy and smelly mess, and his feet and toes were wet and frozen. Nicolas finally spotted the bell tower of a church on the north side of the Vienne. Perhaps there he could find respite from the elements while he gathered his thoughts. Using the bell tower as his point of reference, he worked his way through the sordid, narrow streets, running with raw sewage and filled with animal refuse and soiled straw, made even more repulsive by the mud and standing water. The smell was horrific. It made him appreciate the orderliness of his Mont Saint Michel neighbors. Even during their most desperate hours, they had never lived in such squalor.

It was nearly dark by the time he reached the church, but it appeared the building was still open, for he saw several people enter and exit. Nicolas hoped he would find a compassionate priest who would offer him safe haven. After all, he was on God's mission. Surely the Archangel would provide assistance. As he approached the door, he prayed for God's guidance and help.

After his eyes adjusted to the dim candlelight, he quickly noted that he was not the only desperate soul who sought refuge within. Indeed the church, which compared in size to the abbey church in Mont Saint Michel, was filled with men, women and children who looked far more bedraggled than he. Most were kneeling at the pews in the nave facing the altar in the center of the transept, but others cowered in the structure's darkened recesses, hoping to be left alone to sleep. The priests could certainly not offer hospitality to every beggar and stranger who crossed the threshold of God's house, but perhaps they would not force these destitute pilgrims seeking sanctuary to leave on this wintry night.

Always on the watch for his adversary, Nicolas walked the entire length of the nave and transept, and explored each and every chapel in the apse of the cathedral. Several plaques revealed that this church was dedicated to Saint Maurice, a third-century Christian martyr from Thebes. *I pray I will not become a fifteenth-century Christian martyr from Brittany*, Nicolas thought. After completing his inspection, Nicolas returned to a small chapel that featured a statue of Saint Michael. Several candles burned in a basin placed before the Archangel. What better place to rest than here? He did not even have the energy to light a candle for Michael. Instead, he removed his soaked cloak, and pulled a small wooden chair over to the side wall of the chapel, so that he could rest his weary body against the cold stones. He tied his knapsack around his waist so that if anyone tried to steal it, he would wake up, and then he covered his entire body with the cloak. Within five minutes, he was asleep.

He wasn't certain how long he slept, but judging by the fact that the candles lit in homage to Saint Michael had not burned down, it could not have been for more than thirty minutes. At first, he wondered what had wakened him, but then he realized that someone was tapping him on the shoulder.

"Kind sir," said a compassionate-looking elderly woman leaning over him, "please wake up. I have been sent to help you."

Nicolas jumped up, immediately suspicious of this woman's motives. Was she trying to rob him? But then why would she be deliberately attempting to waken him?

"Are you not Nicolas le Breton, the Watchman?" she asked.

"Who are you to know my name?" he replied with harshness. Could this be one of Abdon's emissaries? "What do you know of me?"

"Calm yourself, my boy," she replied. "I am a simple widow lady who desires only to serve God, as do you."

Nicolas looked at her dubiously and drew away from her touch. He knew how insidious Abdon could be, and having some strange woman approach him who knew his name was more than disconcerting.

Sensing his discomfiture, she stepped away from him. "Please, let me explain," she continued. "I know that you are also one of God's servants, because this fact was confirmed to me by the Archangel himself," she said as she made a gesture towards the statue. "The Archangel Michael came to me in a dream. He showed me your face and told me your name. He also told me you were his servant, his Watchman, and that you were in need of help. He instructed me to come to the church this evening and that I would find you sleeping in his chapel. I have been instructed to take you in and feed you. Although I am a widow and have little of earthly value, I do have an extra room in my humble home where you can find rest, and I am willing to share what little sustenance I have, for surely God will provide for us. What say you? Will you come with me?"

Nicolas could not believe his ears. Was not this just what he had been praying for as he entered this place of sanctuary? Divine assistance? Was not this Michael's providential intervention? He thought of the story of the widow woman of Zarephath, who in spite of having only enough left for a final meal for herself and her son, had agreed to take in the prophet Elijah. Yes, surely this humble, old woman represented deliverance from his earthly woes.

Nicolas forced himself to lift his chilled and fatigued body from the wooden chair. His thoughts tumbled about his muddled mind like chunks of ice in a frozen pond cracking against each other. He tried without success to remember something important, something that nagged at him, but his exhaustion and hunger would not allow him the clarity of mind he sought. He looped the strap of his knapsack over his shoulder and once again donned his wet cloak.

"Yes," he replied. "Thank you for your generous offer. I will indeed come with you."

As the unlikely duo left the security of the cathedral, a tiny drop of doubt began melting the pieces of ice in his mind into warm pools of suspicion and mistrust, but the thawing did not come quickly enough to alter his decision. 'Twas as if Nicolas had no power to resist the tempting call of a hot meal and a warm bed.

Unfortunately, it was a decision he would sorely regret.

Chapter 38

AND SO IT WAS THAT AN UNEXPECTED CROWD of soldiers and supporters gathered in the courtyard of the Chateau of Vaucouleurs on the evening of February 23, 1429 to bid farewell to Jehanne La Pucelle and her small group of protectors. Although the evening hour of departure seemed unusual to those who had gathered, Jehanne had decided in concert with Katelyn and Jean de Metz that it would be judicious to travel during the nighttime hours and sleep during the day so as to lessen the odds of being threatened by the English and Burgundian soldiers, who were masters of the roads.

Jehanne and her escorts sat on their steeds amidst the growing group that seemed to sense something momentous was taking place. The Maiden's mount was a gentle but strong chestnut mare, which Jean de Metz had acquired for her for the sum of sixteen francs, her kinsman Durand Laxart having paid a portion. Jehanne had immediately built a bond of mutual trust and affection with the mare, and as the crowd pressed in to touch the Maiden, she stroked her steed's neck to assure her that these were not enemies trying to attack, but devotees trying to get their last look at the horse's rider.

For some five years before Jehanne had made her first public appeal to Robert de Baudricourt in Vaucouleurs, the inhabitants of the region had heard prophecies concerning a maiden in armor from the borders of Lorraine who would be sent to save France. Therefore, it was not unreasonable that when people learned that the maiden daughter of Jacques d'Arc from the village of Domrémy claimed to be God's emissary for that task, many residents of the Meuse River Valley believed she was indeed the Maiden of whom the prophecies spoke. Recently, Jehanne herself had done everything she could to confirm those beliefs. Adapting what Katelyn had taught her about acquiring a quality, she told herself, "Act as if you *are* that person, and soon you will be that person."

Consequently, when the news spread that Baudricourt supported Jehanne's cause and that La Pucelle was departing for Chinon, many residents of Vaucouleurs and the surrounding villages wanted to be there. Some even brought small gifts for the young maiden, whom they fondly called La Pucelle. It warmed her heart, and although she regretted the fact that her immediate family members were not there to see her off, she was grateful that Henri le Royer and the members of his family, with whom she had been lodging, were present.

Jehanne felt a great deal of love for these humble townsfolk. Jean de Metz told her that many of the residents of Vaucouleurs had donated resources to support her cause, but Katelyn had informed her that it was, in fact, Jean de Metz who had borne the bulk of the financial burden for the journey, and for this, Jehanne would forever be grateful. She prayed that God's blessings would be poured out upon this valiant servant. He and Bertrand de Poulangy had spent many hours in the past ten days collecting clothing for her, teaching her how to wield a sword, and instructing her how to ride a horse astride, something she would never have been allowed to do as a female.

When she had first dressed in the short tunic, the padded leather doublet, and the leggings brought to her by Jean and Bertrand, Jehanne felt extremely uncomfortable. But then, as she added the chest plate, the greaves that protected her shins, and her boots, she felt a sense of protection she had never had in female clothing. She had even allowed Katelyn to cut her hair into what her mentor called a 'bob,' and with the weight of her hair gone, she actually felt a weight lifted from the societal constraints of her gender. More than ever before, she felt like a warrior. God's warrior.

Besides Jean de Metz and Bertrand de Poulangy, her escort group consisted of Jean's squire, Jean de Dieulouard, a stocky young man with a sullen expression, and Bertrand's squire, Julien de Honnecourt, who stood out because of his unusual red hair. They also had in their small company Colet de Vienne, and his Scottish servant, known as Richard the Archer. The story of these two men was odd. Jean informed her that Colet was an official messenger from the Dauphin, and that both of the men had arrived on the nineteenth of February. When they heard about Jehanne's departure, they promptly offered to join her little army to accompany her back to the Dauphin. It was strange indeed. Was the Dauphin expecting her? Had God prepared him for her arrival? It was comforting to think such thoughts.

She had forgotten to ask Katelyn that question. During the past ten days of preparation, she and Katelyn (dressed as Kaelig) had been meeting privately in the garrison headquarters, encounters that had been facilitated by Jean de Metz. Occasionally, Katelyn invited Jean de Metz to join them, and he was fully aware of Katelyn's critical role in the upcoming expedition. Katelyn had given Jean the exact itinerary of their journey. During these private meetings together, Katelyn continually reiterated her charge to Jehanne to act as if she already had all the qualities she would need to be the commander of the armies of France. One of the qualities Jehanne did not have was courage, but now, as she sat astride her horse, she tried to act as if she were the most courageous woman in the world.

Just as Katelyn had prepared Jehanne with the details of the Battle of the Herrings for her interview with Robert de Baudricourt, she had also been preparing Jehanne for exactly what she was to do and say when she met the Dauphin for the first time, as well as teaching her the specifics about the current political and military situation in the beleaguered kingdom. Although Jehanne had insisted they would have plenty of time during the impending journey to prepare for her mission, Katelyn had informed her that she did not know how long she would be allowed to tarry. Her tutor had hinted of a more sinister enemy besides the Burgundians and English who would attempt to disrupt the mission, and for this unknown enemy, the usually brave and unfailing Katelyn seemed to have an inordinate level of apprehension, though she attempted to hide that fact from her young student.

Perhaps Katelyn herself was acting as if she were not afraid? Perhaps she too had her own weaknesses with which she was struggling, but she tried to act as if she did not have those weaknesses. It was an interesting concept, and it didn't lessen Jehanne's complete devotion to and admiration of her mentor. In fact, it gave her added hope that she could truly fulfill her assigned mission with all of her imperfections. And so on this evening, although she felt apprehension, she acted as if she hadn't a care in the world.

Quite frankly, it truly *wasn't* a time to be apprehensive. It was time to thank God for finally obtaining Robert de Baudricourt's support, and for providing her with this valiant group of men who had each requested to make this audacious journey with her. With Jehanne included, their little band numbered seven, and it would soon be eight. Katelyn, whom she now addressed as Kaelig, would be joining the group when they reached the abbey in Saint-Urbain, their first planned stop six leagues to the southwest. Katelyn had explained to Jehanne that she did not want her presence in the group to be witnessed by the local citizenry, for questions about her provenance might be asked. Knowing that her friend, mentor, and advisor would soon join the group—with the knowledge and approval of Jean de Metz—was of great solace and comfort to Jehanne.

At promptly six o'clock, Robert de Baudricourt called the group to order from atop a set of steps leading to the chateau fortress.

"Good people of Vaucouleurs who are loyal to France, we gather here to bid adieu to one of our own citizens, Jehanne La Pucelle from the village of Domrémy. This brave maiden has expressed her ardent desire to fight for the cause of France and to restore the throne to its rightful heir, the Dauphin Charles. She will be in the company of two of my most capable men-at-arms, their servants, and indeed, two of the Dauphin's own emissaries, in whom I have entrusted her safety and security. I now invite her escorts to raise their right hands and to swear with me a sacred oath."

Jehanne looked about her as her six protectors raised their hands. These men were vowing before God that they would protect her. It was overwhelming. Surely, her Lord was good and merciful.

The commander's voice boomed out over the crowd. "Do each of you hereby swear before God and these witnesses gathered here today that you will do everything in your power to conduct Jehanne La Pucelle well and safely to her destination, that you will protect her from any adversary, seen or unseen, and that you will likewise do everything in your power to safeguard and defend her virtue and reputation, even at the cost of your very lives, if necessary?"

"Aye, Sire, with God and these people as our witnesses, we do so swear," responded the six men.

"And this you do freely without any constraints having been placed upon you?"

"Aye, Sire, we so swear," the six men repeated together.

"Having so sworn, may each of you now ever be loyal to your oath, which you must consider as sacred and binding, and endeavor in all things and in all ways to fulfill your duties. If you do not, you risk the condemnation and wrath of God Himself, and I along with these people gathered here today will stand as witnesses against you. May God bless you all."

Then Baudricourt reached for a sword, which was leaning against the stone wall behind him. He descended the set of stairs and approached Jehanne on her chestnut mare.

"Jehanne," he said as he lifted the sword by the blade so that she could take the hilt in her hand, "I hereby commend you to God. Take this sword as a token of my support and esteem and as a source of protection to you on your journey. May God bless you and buoy you up. May He give you the strength and the ability to carry out your sacred mission. I now commend you into His hands. Go now, and come what may."

She now had her own sword, but because of Katelyn's careful tutoring, Jehanne knew there would be yet another sword she would soon wield, a sword more sacred than this, the sword of Charles Martel the great defender of Christianity. That sword, Katelyn had informed her, would have special powers to aid and assist her in fighting the English troops at Orléans. But until she had procured Martel's sword from the little church in Saint-Catherine-de-Fierbois, she would cherish this gift from Robert de Baudricourt, for surely it was a token of his change of heart towards her. It was yet another symbol of God's mercy and love for her.

The crowd cheered as Jehanne bowed in humility and gratitude before Baudricourt and then bid adieu to him. Then the small mounted group, led by Jean de Metz, began to work its way through the enthusiastic crowd toward the stone archway that led out of the walled city.

Jehanne heard a man standing next to the city gate call out a question to her. "Jehanne, how will you manage with all of the English soldiers everywhere?"

"Sir," she replied as she stopped the forward progress of her horse and looked confidently down into his eyes, something she would never have been bold enough to do in her female persona, "I am not afraid of the soldiers, for God is with me and my own band of soldiers. He will guide us along an unobstructed path, and if there are enemy soldiers along the route, I have my Lord God who will clear the way for me to get to the Dauphin. The very purpose of my birth is to accomplish God's will. I was born to do this. I have no fears." Then she moved on, and drew up alongside Jean de Metz.

"Well spoken," he said to her. And then as if he himself needed her assurance, he added: "Will you really do all you have said you will do?"

"My dear friend Jean, I know you must feel a degree of trepidation about this enterprise, for indeed, you have sworn your very life to protect me, so it is only natural that you would want to be reassured about my mission. But have no fear. What I am commanded to do, I will do; and my brothers in Paradise have told me how to act. It has been four or five years since my brothers in Paradise and my Lord—that is, God—first told me that I must go and fight in order to regain the kingdom of France. I have waited these long years to be able to do so. For this purpose was I born. I go now to save France."

With that, she dug her heels into her mare's flanks and galloped away from Vaucouleurs and indeed away from the Meuse River Valley, the only home she had ever known. It would be the last time she ever saw it. As her escorts followed suit to catch up with her, she turned and repeated her message to them, to the wind, and to God.

"I go now to save France!"

Chapter 39

MY JOURNEY TO SAINT-URBAIN, ABOUT twenty miles to the southwest of Vaucouleurs, was unpleasant, to put it mildly. I'd given the route for our journey from Vaucouleurs to Chinon to Jean de Metz, which is, of course, the exact route recorded in Joan of Arc's history, and Saint-Urbain was our first stop. Well before we left, I asked Jean to request that Robert de Baudricourt write to his relative, the Abbot Arnould d'Aulnoy, about giving us lodging and protection. I knew from the historical records that the abbot was pro-French like his cousin, so he was pleased to help. He pretty much had to help, because that's how it all played out in history.

Baudricourt told the abbot we'd also need supplies and care for our horses, for these steeds are going to have to do something really unusual. My few months of riding lessons certainly haven't made me an equestrian expert, but I do know that we're going to be traveling an average of thirty miles a day, and that's a pretty big deal. That's a lot of miles for a horse to cover in eleven days, so, we've got to make sure they're well-cared for and well-fed. The Abbot has arranged for us to lodge in the guest house of the monastery, and boy, is that looking good to me right about now. I can hardly wait until Jehanne arrives so we can get there. Right now, I'm waiting for her group as planned, in the woods not far from the abbey.

I left Vaucouleurs unseen and unnoticed some eight hours before Jehanne and her group, and though I'd prepared for this mission in so many ways, nothing could've prepared me for riding alone, virtually non-stop, for twenty-four hours in terrible conditions. I mean, it would've been better if it had been freezing temperatures and a snowstorm. At least the ground would have been hard. I've got a pretty great horse too, a chestnut stallion I bought from a farmer in Burey-le-Petit, but even he balked at our trek through swampy fields and muddy roads. There were times his legs sank up to his knees in mud. It was awful.

I'm sure it didn't help that my sword from Brother Thibault, sheathed in a gift of a hand-worked leather scabbard from Jean de Metz, was constantly pounding my horse's flanks, because I'm not very adept at galloping with a three-foot-long piece of heavy and deadly steel strapped to my waist. That's one thing they didn't teach me at Dixon's Riding Stables. I guess they didn't think that was a 'need to know' kind of skill.

Then, add the constant threat of attack from the English troops and their Burgundian supporters, who seemed to be everywhere along the route, and you get the picture. I had to make so many detours to avoid those guys, I felt like I was in the spin cycle of a washing machine. I think all those deviations must have doubled the twenty-mile trip. Thank goodness I have an electronic compass that works without satellite, or I never would have found Saint-Urbain. I'm just praying that Jehanne and the boys won't have as many close encounters of the third kind as I had with those alien invaders.

Although I had clear skies and reasonable temperatures for the first part of the journey, by the late evening, those clear skies had transformed into constant rain and absolute misery. Like I said, I would have preferred snow. As prepared as every good Scout should be (actually, I was never a Girl Scout), I brought a large plastic poncho that covered me and even part of Midnight. Yes, my valiant steed previously known as Dagobert has been renamed in honor of my fierce protector from Dixon's Stables. I know Dagobert isn't black, and I know he's going to have to get used to his new name, but somehow it gives me a sense of protection to call him Midnight. So, Midnight it is. He's going to have to learn to obey commands in English as well, because when I'm in panic mode, it seems only English words come out. That could be a problem when I finally join up with Jehanne and her Merry Men, for English words are not exactly what they're going to want to hear when they're trying to avoid English soldiers at all costs. I'm going to have to work on that.

Anyway, by the time I arrived in Saint-Urbain earlier this afternoon, after riding all night long, I was filthy, hungry, water-logged, freezing, saddle-sore . . . let's see, oh, yes, smelly, and just generally miserable in every possible way imaginable. And so was Midnight, although his saddle soreness came from actually having a saddle strapped to his back.

In spite of my many detours, I'm certain I'm still ahead of Jehanne's group because I gave myself plenty of time to get here ahead of them. Twenty-four hours ago, I had no idea of how miserable the wait would be, or I might have delayed my departure time. But the fact is, I couldn't do anything that would interfere with history, so I couldn't afford anyone seeing me join their group in Vaucouleurs, because Jehanne's departure is so well documented. No 'Kaelig le Breton' figured on the recorded history about the make-up of Jehanne's little band, and so when Jehanne, Jean, and I discussed it, we decided I'd simply leave ahead of them and then trot out from the forest surrounding the abbey when they arrive. Fortunately, there are hardly any records about Jehanne's journey after Vaucouleurs, except for the direct testimonies given at her trial by Jean de Metz and Bertrand de Poulangy themselves. And those two have sworn a sacred oath never to speak of my presence or actions.

I estimate they should be here in about two more hours. So, here I sit, covered in a plastic tarp. I'd love nothing more than to go to sleep about now, even on this muddy ground, but I can't afford to miss them, so I'm trying to see in the dim light if I can find any more information on my iPad about the journey that I've somehow missed.

I made Nicolas memorize everything he could about Jehanne, but I figured that I would take my iPad because there's just too much information to master, particularly about Jehanne's battles. That sounds crazy! Here I am talking nonchalantly about Joan of Arc leading the armies of France as if that information is completely normal for an average American teen to have mastered, but I not only have to *know* about it, I have to *facilitate* it. And if I get it wrong, it could result in my death or it could change history. And that can't happen. Actually, I'm not exactly sure what will happen if I do change history. That has always been an issue that's way too hard for my little brain to consider, so I just have to ignore it. Besides, if I change history, then isn't that what's supposed to happen? I can't figure it out. Way too deep.

But, back to my iPad. No one from fifteenth-century France, not even my most ardent enemy Abdon, will know how to access the information I have stored on my iPad.

Having my iPad also means having a solar recharging station and a solar battery charger. Technology has improved so much since my last trip back in time. Last time, I had a large foldable panel with solar cells that Nicolas had to spread out on the roof of Jean's cottage. Now, I can set out a little sensor in the sun, even if it's a slightly overcast day, and I get a few hours of added screen time.

I've brought every imaginable gadget I could fit in my backpack, which I could afford thanks to Dad's generous financial gift, including some little gizmos I think Jehanne will find helpful once she gets her sword. I won't really know for sure how or when to use them until the time comes. At least, that's how it happened last time. The Archangel expects me to be prepared and use my own cognitive skills. I'm so grateful for every item of clothing and protection I brought, and I hope Nicolas is appreciating his thermal underwear and his high-tech sleeping bag that weighs only a few ounces. I haven't had to pull out my sleeping bag yet, but I know that'll be coming soon. I'm just about ready to do it now just to get warm. But I'm afraid if I do, I'll fall asleep and miss my convoy. After all, I've been awake now for nearly thirty-six straight hours.

I also brought enough of those light-weight thermal sleeping bags for all members of the party. I'm going to have to convince them that we Bretons have somehow developed special fabrics from sheep's wool, or perhaps I'll just claim that all of my stuff is of divine origin sent to help God's emissary, Jehanne. I don't know how that's going to go over, but it's the best I can do, and hopefully there won't be too many questions. I stopped short of bringing a pop-up tent, but I do have two large tarps to give us protection from the rain as we sleep.

I wish I could have brought clothing and other gear for Jehanne to make her journey more comfortable, but I just couldn't risk it. Her manner of dress will already be a source of great persecution when Pierre Cauchon gets hold of her. He is the pro-English Bishop of Beauvais who is going to be instrumental in condemning my friend to death. I have to push those unbidden thoughts from my mind, because they are way too disturbing. Even more disturbing than thoughts about changing history. It's a delicate balance between too much and too little interference.

After searching unsuccessfully for any information I may have missed about Jehanne's journey, I finally give up. Besides, it's getting way too dark, and I don't want anyone to see my glowing screen. I also realize I've allowed my iPad to let my focus shift from listening for the sound of approaching horses, but it's really hard to hear horses' hooves in muck. It's not exactly the clip, clop, clopping you hear in the movies. I'm thinking I've got to be more vigilant, when suddenly I'm being grabbed from behind and pounded into the ground.

Chapter 40

NICOLAS HAD TO STOOP TO ENTER through the low doorframe that led into the widow's quarters. It was the first conscious action he had made since he left the cathedral. Like one of those electronic toys he had seen in the twenty-first century shops on Mont Saint Michel, he had followed the seemingly frail, old woman through the grimy underbelly of old Chinon without even a cognizant thought. He had not even asked for her name.

However, once he cleared the threshold of the little cottage, 'twas as if all his thoughts thawed at once. He remembered the notion that had been trying to push its way to the surface of his frozen brain: he had been afraid that his condition of hunger and fatigue would cause him to make a blunder when Abdon reappeared.

Well, unfortunately, that notion had been correct. He *had* made a blunder. He had made a colossal blunder. Lured into believing the seemingly kind widow's implausible tale, because of his pure desire to believe it and because he felt it was the Archangel's intervention, Nicolas had allowed himself to be duped by the master deceiver.

The minute he reached the center of the tiny room, he felt himself being projected flat on his stomach onto the hard dirt floor. The weight of his assailant kept Nicolas immobile, and his lack of strength prevented him from fighting back when the man wrestled his hands behind his back and tied them together with cording that cut into his flesh. Immediately Nicolas knew the truth. The elderly widow had not been sent by the Archangel Michael, but by Abdon.

"Well, we meet again, my friend," hissed the voice of Abdon's new host, as he flipped Nicolas over onto his back and shoved him against the cold stone wall next to the hearth where a pitiful fire was burning.

Two tallow candles sputtering on the mantel combined with the fire's weak flames to give a modicum of light so that Nicolas could examine his captors. Yes, it was the same greasy hair and pockmarked complexion he had seen in the church in Sainte-Catherine-de-Fierbois. And now as Nicolas took in what he had originally viewed as the tender face of a compassionate widow, the scales fell from his vision, and he saw her true nature. Where he had initially seen benevolence and godly devotion, he now saw cynicism and greed reflected in her beady eyes. Her paper-thin skin, which puddled in wrinkled folds under her eye sockets, stretched over the prominent bones in the rest of her face making her appear positively skeletal. She looked like one of the demon figures in the Weighing of Souls mural in his village church back home in Brittany. How could he have been so blinded? His desperate need for physical relief had obviously caused him to neglect his heretofore vigilant evaluation of his environment.

That lack of caution had brought him here as Abdon's captive in this depressing cottage, which reflected the squalor he had seen in the crowded city streets of Chinon. The odor of the rancid sheep fat from the candles and the mildew from the damp walls, combined with the nauseating smell of urine and human waste that permeated the entire neighborhood, caused him to gag. With no food or water in his stomach, the bile that rose in his throat just added one more element of misery to his already miserable situation.

It made him long for the fresh air of the countryside he had just left, even if it had been frigid. Even better were thoughts of the warm, cozy hearth of Jean's cottage on the Mount with the stimulating odors of Brother Thibault's latest epicurean creation. Having grown up in a small farming village, and then having spent the rest of his life on Mont Saint Michel, Nicolas had experienced few of the realities of city-living in fifteenth-century France. If this was what it was like to live in a city, then he would have none of it. Just sitting in this foul excuse of a dwelling was torture in and of itself.

"Pay me what you promised, man, and I will be gone," the old woman's cackle brought his attention back to his captors. "None shall know what has transpired here this evening."

Nicolas would not have been surprised if Abdon—for he still didn't know the actual name of Abdon's new host—simply killed the only witness to the Watchman's abduction. It actually gave Nicolas a sense of hope when he watched Abdon pull a few coins from his pocket and place them in the withered hand of his co-conspirator and then shove her out the door into the stormy night.

"Well, Abdon, I see that as usual, you are preying on the weak and destitute souls of the world to do your evil bidding," Nicolas could not refrain from saying. It was almost as if he no longer feared his adversary now that he could actually see him face to face, rather than sensing his lurking presence in the shadows. "I do not know who this new host is that you have found, but he appears worthy in every way of your wicked nature and abhorrent behavior."

"Yes, we are a good fit, are we not?" replied Abdon. "And although you call my behavior abhorrent, to illustrate that, *au contraire*, I am a man of excellent comportment, allow me to introduce you to my new incarnation, Nicolas. Meet Philippe Montrouge. I am a tailor and clothier to the nobility from the great city of Paris, and I am at your service, sir." Abdon/Montrouge bowed deeply in front of

Nicolas's sitting form, sweeping his arm in front of his waist in an exaggerated gesture of obeisance. No longer was Abdon or Montrouge wearing the simple pilgrim's raiment, but rather a fine black tunic with gold embroidery and embellishments, reflective of his newly-revealed profession.

"Ah, Paris," retorted Nicolas, "the hotbed of Burgundian turncoats and intellectual sissies. And a clothier. You dress the nobility while the weak and impoverished dress in rags. Put clothier to the wealthy and Paris together, and surely you have two of my favorite things!"

"You *are* droll, Nicolas," replied Abdon, "but I must admit, you are also rather brave, or should I say brazen, to make such disparaging remarks about your humble host, for you are not exactly in a position to criticize, now are you?"

"Do with me what you will, Abdon. I no longer fear your retaliation. Or do you prefer to be called Montrouge? I cannot tell which would irritate you more, to be called by your eternal moniker as a reminder of your inability to keep a human host for long, or to be called by your new name of Philippe Montrouge, as a reminder that you have to bounce to and fro from host to host. Yes, I admit that Richard Collins was a formidable opponent, but alas, like your other hosts, he has passed the way of all flesh, just as Montrouge will soon do as well. So, what shall it be? Abdon or Montrouge?"

At this, Philippe Montrouge kicked Nicolas as hard as he could in the gut, but the only reaction he elicited from Nicolas was a slight grunt.

"As I already informed you, *Montrouge*," Nicolas said emphasizing each syllable of Abdon's new name, "do with me what you will. You may kick me, beat me, even torture me simply by continual exposure to the odors of this hellish abode, but you will never get me to impart any information to you."

"And as I inferred to you, my dear Nicolas, before I left you that first night in the church at Sainte-Catherine-de-Fierbois, I am not planning on extracting information from you by such crude methods as mundane torture. Although I will enjoy exploring new methods of causing human suffering, that will only be for my own recreational purposes and enjoyment. No, my pathetic little stonecutter, I am planning on using you as bait to capture the real object of my desires, Mademoiselle Katelyn Michaels. And I am not as convinced as you seem to be that you will be able to stand by and watch me torture *her*. Yes, you seem to be a man of some ill-founded compassion and loyalty, and I sense that your personal emotional connections to the lass—regardless of how ill-placed they are—will preclude keeping the resolutions you seem to have made about divulging certain information, so we shall see what transpires when Mademoiselle Michaels arrives."

"Unfortunately for you, Montrouge," Nicolas countered in his best attempt to bluff, "*your* ill-founded conclusion that Mademoiselle Michaels will somehow miraculously appear in Chinon so that you can kidnap and torture her is laughable."

"Say what you will," replied Montrouge, "but we shall soon see who will be laughing. In fact, I feel the need for a little laugh right about now."

With that, Montrouge's raucous snickering filled the one-roomed cottage as he savagely kicked Nicolas in the face.

"And remember, Nicolas," Montrouge added, "this is just for my own entertainment and amusement. Nothing more."

With his hands tied behind his back, Nicolas had little defense against the vicious assault. He ducked his head and drew his knees up in an attempt to cover his face and torso, but the battering continued until his nose began to bleed. Then Montrouge pulled off the Watchman's boots and socks so that his bare feet sat flat on the ground. One by one, Montrouge stomped on his captive's toes until the blessed veil of unconsciousness finally sent Nicolas into dark oblivion.

The blessing in that darkness was that Nicolas could no longer hear that insidious and malevolent laugh or feel pain.

Chapter 41

BY THE TIME JEHANNE AND HER WARRIORS arrive in the abbey forest in the outskirts of Saint-Urbain, I'm an absolute basket case. Even though I've had several hours in which to treat my wound, stop shaking, and curb my uncontrollable outbursts of tears, I'm still trembling and incoherent. It has to be abundantly clear to them now that I'm no military genius, but I have to just gird up my loins and calm down. Right now!

The reason I'm completely undone is because my life has just been threatened for the seventh time. But even worse, I nearly had to kill a man. Many times during these past months, I've considered the possibility that I might be called upon to take a human life in order to perform my mission. I've asked myself if I could actually go through with such an irrevocable act. I've come to the conclusion that I *would* be able to kill any of Abdon's incarnations if my life or other lives were in danger, but could I kill a non-Abdon mortal? I knew full well at the beginning of this particular mission that I'd be operating in an even more dangerous and life-threatening environment than last time. After all, this is war, and I'm smack dab in the middle of it. There's nothing nice or pleasant about war. People get killed and people kill other people. That's what war means.

As I ponder these concerns, the thought comes to my mind: if and when I have to make the decision to take a life, I will either have reached the point where I can do it, or God will provide me with a means of escape, as He has just done.

And so in a new state of calm, I begin my explanation in French to Jehanne and my new expedition companions. "While awaiting your arrival, I was attacked by a man in the woods over there." I point to the spot behind me where the body now lies. "I am uncertain as to whom exactly he is, but he tried to slit my throat." I confirm this by showing them the blood-stained gauze bandage I've managed to tape across my neck. "I couldn't fight him off, and just when I thought I was lost, my horse reared up and pounded his hooves into the man's head, and I was able to wriggle out of his grasp. Midnight trampled the man to death."

I see the color leave Jehanne's wind-reddened face. She looks—like me—as if she is ready to puke.

"Jehanne," I say, trying to provide a logical reason for her not to have to see the gruesome and bloody scene, "we need a watchman." Ironic that 'watchman' is the word that slipped out of my mouth. "Please remain by the path, hidden in the trees here by Midnight, and be on the lookout for anyone approaching. This man could have associates, and if so, they could pose a problem for us. Hoot three times like an owl if you see anyone, and we'll come to your assistance immediately."

"Certainly, Kaelig," she replies as she awkwardly dismounts, clearly unaccustomed to riding astride in full military dress, and even more unaccustomed to being exposed to the dangers of traveling through such dangerous lands. The color comes back into her face as she wrestles with the horse's bridle straps, and then she leads her chestnut mare into the protection of the hardwood forest that surrounds us. I notice she keeps her distance from where I tied up Midnight. Maybe she thinks that instead of being my loyal protector, he's really a vicious man-killer. Though she can't be seen by anyone coming down the trail from a distance, the deciduous trees don't give her or us much cover. We have to perform our distasteful task as quickly as we can, especially before dusk completely overtakes us.

"Come," I say to the rest of the men. "Leave your mounts here and follow me."

When we reach the grizzly scene, I muster up every ounce of self-control I have to keep myself from gagging. It wouldn't be a good thing for the men to see me like this, so I focus on unfolding the camping shovel—like the one I sent with Nicolas for more noble purposes—which I'd removed from my pack before the group's arrival.

"Can you identify who he might be?" I ask. I hadn't been brave enough to examine the body for any identifying clues. Jean de Metz picks up the knife, stained with my blood, which sits on the moss-covered ground just inches from the body. He also picks up a handful of moss and wipes away my blood, then examines the knife.

"Well," he says, "judging by this dagger, I would say it is of English make."

"Aye," confirms Richard the Archer as he takes the dagger into his hands and examines it before returning it to Jean. "I have seen this type of dagger among the English troops before," Richard adds in broken and heavily accented French that's even worse than my own. Then while Bertrand de Poulangy and his servant Julien roll the body over and examine the man's clothing, Richard walks towards a thicket of walnut trees that stands about a dozen yards from where we're standing.

"There is nothing on his body to identify him," Bertrand says. It takes all the discipline I have to keep from looking at what I know is a bashed-in face and focus on Bertrand's words instead. "He has none of the outward trappings of a soldier, and he certainly is not wearing any body armor, but that doesn't mean much. Except in times of battle, few soldiers on either side of this conflict would don heavy armor. But he must have a horse nearby that could offer up additional clues."

Just as he says those words, Richard comes rustling through the underbrush leading a horse. "I think I have confirmed our suspicions," he says as he unties an odd-looking weapon from the horse's saddle. "This is definitely an English crossbow. I should know, because it was on one of these that I honed the skills that have given me my name. I am certain we shall find additional confirmation that he is an English soldier in here," he adds as he pats the bulky pack on the horse's back.

"Even if he *is* an English soldier," I ask, "why would he want to kill me without even bothering to learn my identity? For all he knew, I could have been one of his fellow countrymen, or at the very least a Burgundian supporter." I jump as the crackle of a tree branch behind me startles me. Anxiously, I whip around and see Jehanne approaching. She has left her assigned post, and I immediately conclude that the dead man on the ground has some buddies in the area. But with a look of impatience, not fear, she joins our small group, looks at the body, including the bashed-in face, and addresses us calmly, but confidently. Even the timbre of her voice sounds different to me.

"Gentlemen. You are members of *my* army now, and that means you are members of *God's* army. We are at war. It is of little import who this man is, for war means that there will inevitably be a loss of life. Besides, God is in charge of His army, and if He saw fit to protect Kaelig from this enemy, then this man *had* to die. One life is little to pay for the sovereignty of our great nation. What *is* important is that we dispose of his body immediately, so that there is no scandal attached to this journey. All of you now commence digging a hole and bury him deeply so that wild animals will not dig up his body. We will take his horse and belongings, for God would not want us to waste any offerings He places before us. This additional steed will carry our packs and lighten the loads of our own mounts. Should anyone recognize the horse, we will simply reply that we found him in the forest unattended, which is indeed the truth. And of this incident," she said as she indicated the body with her hand, "we will never speak again."

I look at her in complete and total shock. Is this the same insecure and self-doubting girl I'd first met in the chapel of the Vaucouleurs fortress? No. Double no! This is no longer an uneducated, helpless maiden standing before me, but an assertive and bold leader. I look around me at the men. They seem to be just as surprised at I am at her forceful and self-assured words.

Julien de Honnecourt takes the camp shovel I'm still holding in my hands and immediately begins testing the ground for a favorable spot to dig a grave. The others unsheathe their knives and cutlasses and begin digging alongside Julien.

As Jehanne and I look on at the flurry of activity, she grabs my arm and pulls me aside. I feel her fingers trembling on my arm.

"Did I do well?" she asks. "Was I convincing? Did I act self-assured? Could they see that I was shaking like a leaf?"

"Commander," I address her for the first time. "You did not have to *act* self-assured, because you *are* self-assured. Even the most experienced battle commander has moments of fear and trepidation, but you've surprised me beyond my own expectations. You are ready, Jehanne," I revert to her given name, "You are now ready to save France."

Chapter 42

THAT MOMENT WAS THE TURNING POINT for Jehanne. Katelyn Michaels had been right. If she wanted to have a certain quality, she must act as if she already had it. It had worked! When she first heard that Katelyn had been attacked in the forest near the Abbey of Saint-Urbain and that a man had been killed, Jehanne had cowered behind the heavy armor she was wearing, as if somehow the metal protection could create a barrier between her and reality. She could not face the horrific scene she knew the others were trying to erase. Then, as she stood there, shaking in the forest, waiting for Katelyn and the men to return, she realized that if she was indeed who she purported to be, the one prophesied to save France, she would not be standing there alone while her small army faced the actualities of war without her. No, she would be there with them.

So repeating in her mind Katelyn's injunction, she tied up her horse and boldly walked towards the grizzly site where the men gathered around the body. Acting as if she were the most confident leader in the world, she unflinchingly gave them her instructions. She could see the subtle change that came over her men as she faced them with self-assurance and firmness. Her men. Yes, they were now *her* men, not Robert de Baudricourt's men, or Jean de Metz's men, not the Dauphin's men, and not even Katelyn Michael's men. They were *her* army, and as Katelyn had pronounced, she was their leader. It was a life-changing moment.

Later that evening in the seclusion of Jehanne's bedchamber in the abbey's warm guest house, she and Katelyn met privately to discuss the events of the day and to plan the next day's journey. For a brief moment, both women allowed their masks of bravery to slip, and together, they shed a few tears. However, they were not tears of despondency but mostly tears of gratitude at having been given the fortitude to carry on. The Archangel had never told either of them that their quest would be easy, but together, they had found a way to work through things that, under normal circumstances, would have induced panic and despair. In spite of having been mocked and ridiculed, no one had ever tried to take Jehanne's life, so she could not imagine how difficult it must be for Katelyn, but Katelyn assured her that it was not the first time, and unfortunately, it would most likely not be the last time her life would be threatened.

"Knowing I am in the service of God gives me the courage to carry on," she told Jehanne, "and I am just grateful I didn't have to take the life of that man. I recognize God's mercy in that regard."

"Yes, I can understand that," Jehanne admitted. "It is something I have thought about with great apprehension. Will I be called upon to take a human life?"

"Jehanne, whatever God needs you to do, He will also give you the ability to do it," Katelyn assured her, "although I don't believe your mission will require that of you. But just think about what you *did* do, today, Jehanne. You were amazing. You saw how your men reacted."

Even Katelyn recognized that they were now Jehanne's men. Katelyn's unsolicited praise helped increase her burgeoning confidence.

"My work here is nearly done," Katelyn continued. "I just have to tell you a few things about your visit with the Dauphin when he finally agrees to see you in Chinon. He's going to try to trap you."

"What do you mean?" Jehanne asked, and Katelyn carefully explained everything that Jehanne needed to know to avoid the traps that Charles would set to try to discredit her.

When Katelyn had finished her explanation, she said, "You are ready to forge ahead on your own now, Jehanne. I have taught you nearly everything you'll need to be successful in your mission."

At that, Jehanne's panic returned. "Oh, no, Katelyn, you cannot leave me yet. I still need you. I am not ready to do this without your help. I might have sounded authoritative today, but I have no idea how to command an army. I need your wisdom, your experience, and your knowledge."

"Jehanne," replied Katelyn. "We have spoken of this many times. In general, your presence will not be required on the front lines of battle. Like mine, yours will be a role to inspire and motivate your soldiers, as well as to assist your commanders in outlining military strategies. Remember how I told you I was unconscious during the Battle of Mont Saint Michel? I didn't even lift a weapon, but I was able to sufficiently inspire the Montois to carry out my plans so that they were victorious even without my presence. They did it. Surround yourself with military experts and courageously study and consider all the options, and the Archangel will assist you. The answers you seek will be given to you."

"It is true that I have always trusted in my voices," Jehanne replied, "and I *do* have faith that they will reveal military strategies to me, for surely I cannot develop any type of battle plans without their assistance, but I certainly do not know how to inspire and motivate an army of men. How do I do that?" she asked her mentor, sincerely hoping for a concrete answer. "Yes, I have tried to act with confidence, as you have instructed me to do, but I still do not understand how to inspire an entire army."

"You can and you will do this, Jehanne," Katelyn replied. "It is because of your special spiritual nature that you have been called of God for this great mission, not because of your knowledge of military strategy. Use your strengths, Jehanne, the strengths that you already have deep within you."

"But what are my strengths? I am a simple peasant girl who loves God. That is all. I am true and faithful to my Lord. That is my only strength."

"Exactly," replied Katelyn to the puzzled girl. "That *is* your strength, and that *is* what is needed right now in this corrupt kingdom, Jehanne. If the armies of France want God's help to defeat the invading usurpers, then they must be worthy of God's help."

"I don't understand what you are saying. How can I help them be worthy of God's help?" Jehanne asked.

She saw Katelyn draw in a deep breath. She stopped for an instant as if she were thinking, and then she began her explanation. "Jehanne, these are difficult things to speak of to one as pure as you, but it's time to cast off the shadows and speak of things as they truly are. You have a devoted Christian soul, but unfortunately, the troops of France don't share your pious nature and firm beliefs. Right now, after years of being led by uninspiring kings and corrupt commanders, the French army is in complete disarray. There is no discipline among the troops. They're a vulgar and drunken lot. They're spineless and lack even a bare minimum of bravery. Their language is foul, and those who openly worship God are few and far between. Many have descended into a level of depravity and lewdness that defies description. Why, I've even heard that prostitutes follow the troops, euphemistically called 'camp followers,' distracting them and introducing debauchery and disease among their ranks. Some of these men are thieves and murderers, even plundering from the poor peasants they're charged to protect. Do you think God would grant such a lot victory over their foes?"

"No, you are right, Katelyn. Those things are an abomination and cannot be rewarded from on high. But how might I, just an inexperienced girl, cause such men to change their behavior?"

"You're learning to be bold and self-assured, Jehanne, and now you must use this newfound boldness to do what God expects you to do. You must call these soldiers to repent of their evil ways and to stand up valiantly and righteously for France. As an envoy of God, you *must* remedy this situation, for God can't bless those who serve the adversary. And even if we speak of purely non-spiritual conditions, no army with such a lack of discipline can defeat the better-trained and more disciplined English troops. I know you can do this, Jehanne, because you're entirely and whole-heartedly devoted to God. This is your great internal strength. In spite of being mocked, you've never denied the source of your inspiration. With the same faith and courage you've already shown, call the troops to repentance. Clean up their ranks with boldness and courage and restore discipline and a sense of purpose among them. This is why you've been chosen by God."

Jehanne was shocked at this revelation. For these many years, she had wondered why she, a simple uneducated child, had been given such an impossible task. She had wondered how she could possibly carry out the things God had commanded her to do. And finally, Katelyn had given her the answer. Her voices had not come to her because she was of noble birth with a standing to command the loyalty of her countrymen. They had not come to her because she was a military protégé or genius. They had not come to her because she had remarkable skills in oratory. No. They had come to her because she had a deep and abiding faith in God and devotion to His word. This was her greatest strength: her unfailing faith. Katelyn's explanation made perfect sense. God wanted France to throw off the

English yoke. And she, Jehanne, the humble maiden daughter of Jacques d'Arc, had been called as one of God's servants to help her beloved country become worthy of His assistance.

"I do not know what to say," she admitted. "I am overwhelmed."

"Do you recognize my words as truth?" asked Katelyn.

"Yes, for the first time since I heard my voices, I have a clear vision of why God has called me to this noble task. Although I cannot provide knowledge or unusual skills, I *can* give Him my undying devotion and faith. This, then, will be my charge. With boldness, I vow to call the ranks of French soldiers to repentance."

"Now I've got to be honest. I'm afraid that you're going to be disappointed in many ways, Jehanne," said Katelyn, and Jehanne noticed that a tear was forming in Katelyn's right eye. "You won't be successful in purifying the entire nation of France, not even its future king, but it will be enough for God to lend His assistance."

Jehanne was not certain what Katelyn meant by that comment. She watched as that single tear worked its way over Katelyn's eyelid, and then her friend quickly wiped it away as if she were trying to prevent Jehanne from seeing it. Was Katelyn visionary? Was she prophesying of future events?

"Do you know of things to come?" Jehanne asked her mentor.

Jehanne could tell that Katelyn regretted her statement, for her mentor turned her head away for an instant, and then began her explanation. "I speak from past experience . . . from my experience with the forces of evil. As much as we'd like everyone to engage in the battle against evil for holy and pure reasons, neither I nor you can change people's true nature or motivations. We can only do our best, and I know that you'll do your best. I've said enough on this subject. I'll leave it to you now to find a way to carry out your undertaking. I have every confidence in you, Jehanne. When you face the armies of

France and instruct them to abandon evil, never forget to be as bold as you were today. Will you promise me you'll do that?"

"I will. In fact, I will make an oath to you of this," replied Jehanne.

"I don't want you to make an oath with me, Jehanne, only a promise of your willingness to do your best. Your oath will be with God, not with me," insisted Katelyn.

"Be that as it may," replied Jehanne, "but I wish you to be my witness of this sacred oath, for you have been my dearest tutor and friend. You have been the only one, besides my voices, who has had complete and undying faith in my abilities to accomplish my mission. You have buoyed me up and shown me the pathway I must follow. You have been my inspiration and my confidante in all things, and I now wish you to know that the things you have said to me today will be my watchword and my guide."

And so with Katelyn as her witness, Jehanne made an oath to God that she would go forward with boldness to accomplish His will.

Jehanne could see that Katelyn now had not a single tear, but streams of tears working their way down her cheeks. In fact, she was sobbing as she took Jehanne in her arms and held her closely to her breast. The feeling of fraternal love and support that flowed from Katelyn's arms to Jehanne's heart added further strength to her conviction. She could and would become that Maiden who would save France, the one of whom it had been prophesied.

"And so, my beloved friend," Jehanne finally said. "When must you leave my side?" She did not beg for Katelyn to stay with her, for now she knew that this was no longer Katelyn's mission, but hers alone.

"The Archangel has impressed it in my mind that I should travel with you as far as Chinon. Once you arrive, you will request an audience with the Dauphin. You will also send for the sword I told you about in Sainte-Catherine-de-Fierbois. I will be with you to help prepare you for that interview with the Dauphin and to teach you about the sword's miraculous properties. I'm confident that with the sword you'll be able to inspire your men to lift the siege of Orléans, and then, after that, you'll be able to clear the way for the Dauphin to get to Reims. But this will be your mission to accomplish. Not mine."

They had already spoken in some detail about the sword, the sword that Katelyn told her was the weapon used by Charles Martel to defend Christianity. As a sacred offering to the next great warrior God sent to fight for France, Martel had buried the sword in the church at Sainte-Catherine-de-Fierbois, and according to Katelyn, it was the sword that Jehanne would use to finally lift the siege of Orléans and defeat the English armies there. It was that battle that would give the armies of France the confidence to follow Jehanne in all her campaigns to liberate Reims.

"Yes, Katelyn, you have shown me that a maiden of seventeen can lift a siege. You did it at Mont Saint Michel, and now it is my turn to follow in your footsteps," replied Jehanne. "But," she continued, "where will you go after you leave me in Chinon?"

"There's a young man I must locate," Katelyn explained. "I'm not certain where he is, and I'm concerned about his well-being. When I find him, we'll return together to Mont Saint Michel. But, Jehanne, I want you to know this one thing: never forget that I'll be with you in spirit. Your journey is *your* journey. I can't be with you because that isn't God's will, but never, ever think you're alone, because neither I nor God will ever abandon you. Ever."

With those words, Katelyn left the room, and Jehanne was left to ponder what challenges awaited her. She felt more strongly than ever that Katelyn Michaels had a visionary gift.

But I know she'll be with me. She'll be with me to the end of my journey.

Chapter 43

I'M PRETTY DARN PROUD OF MYSELF FOR finally figuring out what I needed to say to Jehanne to motivate her to the max. I had read her story so many times, and I knew that she had actually rarely led the armies of France into battle. In fact, when it came to military leadership, Jehanne spent most of her time arguing with the French generals about strategy. She always wanted to boldly attack, regardless of the circumstances, and maybe that was because I had taught her to act boldly. But she usually lost those arguments.

However, when it came to inspiring the troops, or the people of France in general, she was a master. Yes, she had been wounded in the shoulder in the assault on the Tourelles during the Battle of Orléans, and also in the foot during the unsuccessful bid by the French to re-take Paris, but according to the testimony of some who served in her army, her primary concern was the spiritual well-being of her troops.

It is well documented that she rebuked her men for their anti-Christian vices—gambling, drinking, swearing, theft, immorality—and that she was absolutely livid about the so-called "camp followers" who traveled with the troops. She even physically chased prostitutes out of the military camps on occasion. Tradition has it that that's how she broke the sword that Robert de Baudricourt gave her. Many of the soldiers had mistresses who lived in the camps, and Jehanne demanded that the soldiers either marry their companions or forced the women to leave. Jehanne even insisted the troops attend mass and go to confession regularly, proclaiming that because of their debauchery, God was allowing their enemies to be victorious.

So why did it take me so long to figure it out? I'm not sure. I'm just slow, I guess. It makes such perfect sense. To be responsible for the spiritual well-being of the French soldiers was the perfect motivator for Jehanne. Because of her tremendous devotion to God and the Christian morals that were a part of that devotion, I finally woke up and realized that *this* must be her cause. It was a role she could unflinchingly play. And it worked. I guess the Archangel is patient, because he allowed me to figure this one out on my own.

I also almost blew it when I hinted that Jehanne would be disappointed in her efforts to bring spiritual strength back to the French. That's when she questioned me about whether I could see future events. Wow, what an unfortunate slip of the tongue. I lost it there for a second because I just couldn't help but think of how horrific it is going to be for her to have the very people she helps, turn their backs on her and refuse to intervene when she is put on trial.

The whole time I've been with her, I've had to block out the reality of her future. I can't deal with it because I can hardly bear the fact that I can't warn her. I can't prepare her or do anything to prevent what I know will take place in just over two years. I can't change history. Jehanne has to die. She *has* to become a martyr for the tide of French weakness to finally be turned.

It makes it even harder for me to do this because I really like this girl. I honestly care about her. I mean, she is, quite frankly, amazing. It wouldn't be so hard for me knowing her fate if she were a self-righteous jerk. But she's not. She's one of the kindest, most sincere people I have ever met, and although she's pretty naïve, I can't fault her for that, because just six months ago, I was even more naïve than she is. I couldn't have cared less about current events in the United States, or the world, for that matter. I couldn't have cared less about the war between good and evil in general. No, I was consumed with my own little world. Who was going to ask me to prom? What did so-and-so say about so-and-so? How could I get Mom to buy me the latest gadget I'd found? How could I punish Dad for leaving us? I had been purely self-absorbed and self-centered. Jehanne is so far from being self-centered it isn't even funny. Nothing she has ever done has been out of a selfish motivation, and since she was a child, she has been consumed with what is happening to her country. How many girls her age would have those preoccupations? None that I know of—except for her, of course.

And she doesn't even realize how amazing she is. Jehanne has all of the qualities of the *Wizard of Oz* heroes wrapped into one. She has Dorothy's loyalty and persistence, the Good Witch Glinda's compassion, the courage of the Lion, the heart of the Tin Man, and yes, even the brains of the Scarecrow. She learns quickly and retains nearly everything. Jehanne even has Toto's bite. She will do well rebuking the soldiers, because this girl has a lot of righteous indignation, which comes from her pure devotion to God. In every way, this girl is remarkable, and it humbles me to think that I was given the responsibility to help her carry out her mission.

Last night, when I made that unfortunate statement, I'd been particularly thinking about the Dauphin Charles. Now obviously, I don't know the guy personally, and I hate to make snap judgments, but I've read a lot about him, and unlike Jehanne's, his integrity is less than stellar. I've already informed Jehanne that he's going to try to fool her when she goes to see him for the first time in the great hall at Chinon, and I've done everything I can to describe Charles so that she can pick him out of the crowd. I'm also praying for the

Archangel's help on this one because although I can give her the description of the Dauphin from history books, I don't have a photograph of the man, just photos of paintings of him. And honestly, the guy is *not* eye candy. So I hope she'll pass the first test. She has to. It's part of history.

As for the second test Charles has planned for our maiden from Lorraine, here it is in a nutshell: the Dauphin is going to request a private meeting with her after she identifies him. He tells her that he will believe she has been sent by God if she can answer the question he has in his heart, a question he will not even reveal to her. Jehanne will pass this test with flying colors because she's going to tell him what his question is and then answer it to his satisfaction because I gave her the question and her answer last night. Charles will be convinced that she has been sent by God and will be delighted to hear that God wants him to be King of France. I mean, who wouldn't be? But just to placate his critics, the Dauphin will send Jehanne to Poitiers to be questioned by a slew of skeptical theologians. They will hassle her for three weeks or so and give her a taste of what is to come at the end of her life when the Burgundians and English bring her to trial. Eventually, the clerics in Poitiers will give their approval, and she will be allowed to join the troops in Blois to prepare for the Battle of Orléans.

After the successful lifting of the siege in Orléans, and then success in the following campaigns as well, Jehanne will accompany Charles to Reims in July of this very year for his coronation. He will have her at his side while he is crowned King of France in an elaborate ceremony. The amazing Jehanne, who is responsible for paving the way for the Dauphin to be in Reims, will kneel at his feet and confirm that he is God's anointed to rule France. But that just doesn't seem to be enough to buy that man's loyalty.

To this day—actually I mean in the twenty-first century—the French love to blame the English for killing their national heroine, but the truth is, there's plenty of blame to go around. I know Jehanne has to die to become a martyr, but it just makes me so angry that she did all she did for a man like Charles. I'll let God sort that part out.

I certainly can't tell Jehanne about any of this, and I shouldn't have hinted that her path would not be easy. She'll learn that soon enough. But there is some good news. Some really good news. For the first time since I got here, I truly believe she is ready. She can do this on her own. Well, I mean, without my help or Nicolas's help. She will still have God's help, and I know the Archangel will assist her, but my job here is almost done.

I hadn't been lying to Jehanne when I told her I had received the impression that I was to leave her when we got to Chinon. It's true. I literally heard the words in my mind: "Your mission is complete once Jehanne has received her sword." And so I know I must travel with her to Chinon and teach her what to do with the sword. And then after that? I'm not sure, but one thing is certain. I have to find Nicolas. I'm getting desperate to find him, and my hope beyond hope is that he will be waiting for me when our little band arrives there.

After a good night's sleep, in what I realize will probably be my last comfortable quarters for some time, I wake with a sense of renewed urgency. Not only am I anxious to get Jehanne to Chinon to begin her mission, but I'm also anxious to find Nicolas. I miss him so badly, I can't bear it. Our time together before we left Brother Thibault was so short, and we were so busy that we didn't have the chance to talk about our future together. If we have a future together. But just as I can't think of Jehanne's future, I cannot think of my own future. I must put it out of my mind and focus on my responsibility to get Jehanne safely to Chinon.

This journey is about to begin, and I know it's not going to be an easy one. I'm going to let Jean de Metz worry about following the itinerary I've given him, for he and his men seem pretty capable of figuring out how to get places. But I do have to keep him on schedule. After all, we have a critical deadline. We have to travel nearly thirty miles a day. I realize that it's now up to *me* to make certain there *are* no incidents. My mission isn't over. I am still the one who has to protect Jehanne while traveling some three hundred miles, much of it through enemy territory, and if these enemies have any clue who I'm protecting, they will do everything in their power to prevent her from arriving in Chinon.

Suddenly, I feel terribly apprehensive, and it's not just about Jehanne's safety. A darkness fills my soul that actually scares me. It's the same sensation I've felt every time I've been in the presence of Abdon, regardless of who his host has been. I look around to see if there is anyone in the room with me, but of course, there isn't. A torrent of questions assails me. Can Abdon flit around in his spirit form? Does he know I'm here with this incredible woman who will change the destiny of France? Does he realize she spells doom for his English allies, those who would destroy Mont Saint Michel? I rehearse in my mind everything Jean and Nicolas taught me about Abdon. I know he can't travel through time, and I also know he can't read my thoughts. I don't think he can follow me around in a non-corporeal form, but does he always have to travel in a physical body? If so, how did Abdon get to America and into the body of the horse, Thunder, if he can't move through space?

I don't have any answers. I need Nicolas. I need Jean le Vieux. I need Brother Thibault. I feel desperately alone, and I can't even talk about it to Jehanne. No, I can never let her know about unseen enemies who might be out to destroy her. She has enough to worry about with her human enemies. Unfortunately, she has enough to worry about with her human supporters!

And then an even worse impression comes to my mind. Something is definitely wrong. Something is wrong with Nicolas. That he is in Chinon, I have no doubt, and that he is in danger, I also have no doubt. I have to get to Chinon and find Nicolas. And then the truth dawns on me.

I don't know how he managed it or how he knew to go to Chinon, but I know that Abdon is also there.

And I know he has Nicolas.

Chapter 44

AS THE GROUP RODE AWAY FROM SAINT-URBAIN at dusk the next day, Jehanne's heart was pounding. With gratitude, she realized it was not from fear, but elation. For the first time since she began hearing her voices, she felt hopeful. The manner in which she should accomplish her mission had been logically and lovingly mapped out for her by Katelyn Michaels.

Jehanne was not naïve enough to think the way would be easy. In fact, even though Katelyn was still with her, there was no guarantee that *this* journey to Chinon—before her mission even began—would be easy. However, she soon learned how merciful God had been by sending Katelyn to accompany her, because not only was her companionship and encouragement invaluable, she had brought with her many remarkable items and devices that made their burdens lighter.

With strict instructions that these objects had been supplied by God to assist His maiden warrior and should never be spoken of outside of their journey together, Katelyn in her Kaelig persona—for Jehanne's men still did not suspect she was a female and she was always careful to keep her long locks covered by her cap—provided each member of the party with tiny, fireless lamps. They bore unusual stretchy straps which allowed them to secure the lamps to their foreheads. Jehanne and the others found them miraculous, and although the light they emitted was not bright, it was enough to help them weave their way through the thick, damp forests through which they chose to travel. As Jean had suggested to Katelyn, it was much too dangerous to travel in the open fields.

When they set up camp the next morning after riding all night long, Katelyn showed them how to choose the ideal location between two solid trees with enough space for sleeping. She had them gather dry pine needles or moss to place on the ground and then she covered that cushion provided by nature with a rectangle of stiff fabric she called a tarp. She had the men tie a stout rope between the trees over which Katelyn placed another tarp to create a triangular shape. The two edges of the tarp were held in place by stones the men gathered. The tarp repelled water keeping them dry better than any canvas Jehanne had ever seen. Katelyn also produced a very light-weight sleeping sack for each member of the party, which she explained would help them retain their body heat and stay dry in spite of its paper-thin composition, thus providing much-needed warmth and protection from the bitter elements. They covered the odd fabric of their sleeping sacks with wool blankets provided for the trek by Jean de Metz and the villagers of Vaucouleurs.

The little group quickly fell into a routine they followed with little variation each day. They traveled all through the darkness of the nights, counting on Jean and Bertrand to lead the way, following Katelyn's carefully prepared itinerary, and then set up camp every morning, with each member of the party assigned a certain task to increase their efficiency.

From Saint-Urbain, they travelled by way of Auxerre and then on to Gien, passing perilously close to the Burgundian garrisons at Clairvaux, Pothières, and Mézilles. One of their biggest challenges was crossing a succession of icy, swollen rivers including the Marne, the Aube, and the Seine, which added to their misery. They were always wet.

With the amount of rain that pounded them as they rode all night, the tarps and sleeping sacks were lifesavers, for at least during their eight hours of sleep, they stayed relatively dry, making the lack of a warming fire more palatable. To fit under the tarp and to conserve body heat, they all slept next to each other, with Jehanne always sleeping between Jean de Metz and Katelyn. Although Jehanne had privately expressed concern to Katelyn about sleeping in such close quarters with members of the opposite sex, Katelyn had assured her that God had removed any unholy or impure thoughts from the minds of her male companions, and that both women would be safe. The men had complete faith in Jehanne, and she in turn had complete faith in them.

When dawn arrived each day, Katelyn gathered the lamps from every member of the little militia with the injunction that only she would be the guardian of the devices. She seemed particularly worried that one of the lamps might fall into enemy hands if the group was set upon by enemies. Jehanne understood Katelyn's apprehension about losing one of the miraculous lamps, for hers was indeed a sacred charge. If there was one thing Jehanne had learned in her young life, it was that one did not trifle with sacred matters.

Each morning, a campsite was scouted out where they could sleep during the day. They tried always to find an area in the thickest part of a forest, preferably a pine forest, which provided the soft pine needles and more protection than the deciduous trees. Katelyn also insisted that the site include a source of water not too far away. They had brought enough provisions with them from Vaucouleurs to sustain life for two weeks, although they seldom felt satiated, for their circumstances precluded bringing fresh food. They had also brought oats for their horses. The abbot in Saint-Urbain had added even more to their supplies, particularly additional provisions for the horses.

With their cured meats, variety of cheeses, and bread, they were able to take nourishment without the necessity of building a cooking fire, although a hot meal and the warmth of a fire would have offered blessed relief from the biting cold. However, both Jean and Katelyn had warned Jehanne that visible smoke and the smell of fire would be a dead giveaway to their presence. They insisted that in spite of the wintry weather, they build a fire only when absolutely necessary. One of the benefits of sleeping during the daylight hours was that they were immobile during the warmest part of the day, rather than the coldest. Although the forest canopy blocked out the direct heat from the sun (if ever that reluctant orb showed its face), the canopy also blocked out the light, which made it easier to sleep in broad daylight, and it also helped block out the rain, which seemed to be their constant companion.

The group ate two meals a day, one before they slept, and one after they slept, and Katelyn gave each of them a rectangular sweet biscuit to eat as they were riding at night, which she said would help keep them alert and give them added energy. Occasionally, she distributed other unusual foodstuffs at mealtime, and all of the members of the party looked forward to seeing what new epicurean delight she would produce. To Jehanne and her men, Katelyn's offerings were like manna from heaven.

Once in a while, if Jean and Bertrand felt it safe, one or two of the men were sent to obtain fresh provisions from nearby villages as well as hay for their horses. At Jehanne's insistence, they always paid for their supplies and never stole or plundered.

Jehanne noticed that Katelyn seemed to particularly connect with the Scottish servant of Colet de Vienne, Richard the Archer. She mentioned that she had learned some English and liked to practice her language skills with him, even though Scottish, not English was his native tongue. However, the two could communicate in the tongue of their enemies and both mentioned that it might come in handy at some point during their journey. Richard was a giant of a man, stout, tall, and strong as an ox. For some reason, Katelyn took to calling him Olg, telling the others she had a severe aversion to the name Richard. Soon all the members of the troop began calling him Olg as well.

Each morning when they set up camp, and after all the water for their needs had been gathered, Katelyn asked Richard for assistance in placing four unusual devices, about the size of an egg, in the trees around the outside perimeter of their camp. She called them 'motion sensors.' Katelyn had produced so many extraordinary items that Jehanne finally stopped asking about them, and just accepted the fact that the Lord in His mercy had provided bounteous blessings for her protection. As with all the other miraculous items, Katelyn warned the group that they must never speak of them to another soul. These motion sensors served a dual purpose. Without fire to ward off animal predators, the slumbering travelers were fodder for the wolves and wild boar that roamed the forests. And as Jehanne knew full well, the forests were full of human predators as well, both Burgundian and English troops. Should anyone or anything approach their camp, the device would make a squawking noise startling any intruders. Katelyn never allowed them to camp as closely to the water source as the others would have preferred, for she said that the forest animals coming to drink would set off the motion sensors needlessly.

If the noise itself didn't drive away the predators, it was sufficiently loud to wake the men, who always slept with their weapons at hand. Although an occasional beast was startled by the devices, so far the group had blessedly not been bothered by any uninvited guests of the human variety.

In addition to the motion sensors, Katelyn required each member of their party, including herself and Jehanne, to serve as a watchman for one hour during their nine-hour period of sleep. She had some type of timing mechanism like a miniature clock that counted off each hour so that there was no guesswork involved. On the hour, each watchman would wake his or her successor and pass on the timepiece. This way, each member of the party was guaranteed eight hours of sleep each day. Although Jehanne, who was constantly anxious to get closer to her destination, felt the nine-hour sleep period was too generous, Katelyn insisted that this amount of sleep was imperative to counteract the stress and fatigue that resulted from riding nearly ten leagues a day in darkness and near-constant rain.

They used the horse acquired from the English soldier to carry all of their bedding and gear that needed to stay dry, and each evening as they packed up to leave, this bundle would be covered by the tarps so that when they set up camp the next morning, they had dry bedding. Katelyn also provided each of them with a very thin hooded cape to wear as they rode, which she called a poncho. It was transparent like glass, but pliable, and although it provided no warmth, it protected them from the bulk of the deluges. Without Katelyn's extraordinary amenities, their journey would have been nearly unbearable, as winter turned to spring and the heavens wept down upon them.

Along with the rain, the mud was also their constant companion, and Katelyn insisted they clean themselves as best they could in the creeks, ponds, and streams near their camps with the tiny bars of soap she had brought. In fact, she was brutally insistent about the men adopting unusual measures of cleanliness, which she claimed would help them avoid illness and infirmity. She required each of them to wash their hands before they ate and after they relieved themselves to prevent contaminating their meager supply of food and to prevent the spread of disease. She even provided them with a soft paper to wipe themselves after answering nature's calls, and maintained that they were never to perform those bodily functions near their water source. These were new and surprising concepts to the men, and some of them grumbled about the rigorous requirements, but Jehanne scolded them and reminded them that Kaelig was God's emissary, sent to keep them safe. Did they truly intend to defy God?

Katelyn also insisted they choose their water sources carefully, running, clear streams being their best option. Bertrand and Colet were assigned to procure water, and she taught them the importance of scouting above the area where they filled their vessels to make certain there were no dead animals or animal waste contaminating the water. The horses were always watered below the spot where their water was collected. Because they could not build fires to boil the water, which she said killed tiny unseen organisms that could make them sick, she required them to pass every drop they drank through a pliable bottle she called a water filter.

While the others set up camp, the two squires, Jean and Julien, were charged with caring for the horses. This was also of great concern for Katelyn. She instructed them to brush their coats daily and carefully clean their hooves, and if she had time in addition to her own camp duties, she cared for her own horse herself. She was adamant that the squires tether the horses on high ground as devoid of mud as possible. Jehanne also understood this concern, for they were completely dependent upon these hard-working animals, and she viewed them as God's creatures that deserved kind and loving attention.

In fact, for the most part, Jehanne did not interfere with 'Kaelig's' instructions. She trusted her friend implicitly and knew that all of these precautions were meant to keep her safe. However, there was one point of mild contention between them. Each day, Jehanne expressed her ardent desire to attend mass in the village and town churches by which they passed. "If we can, we shall do well to hear mass," she urged Katelyn, but both Katelyn and Jean de Metz discouraged her, for fear of being recognized. When Julien was sent on an advance scouting trip, he brought back the surprising information that news had spread throughout the land of the female warrior dressed as a male soldier fighting for the French cause. Consequently, extreme caution was their byword. Katelyn reminded Jehanne that all it took was one Burgundian cutthroat, and her mission would be over. However, in Burgundian-held Auxerre, Katelyn relented and allowed Jehanne, covered by a hooded cloak, to attend mass with Jean de Metz.

It was monotony, not the enemy, that was their greatest challenge, for their hours were consumed with dreary repetition: eat cold food in the rain, ride in the rain, sleep in the rain. Jehanne chided them if they complained, stating that their monotonous routine was much preferred over fighting or fleeing enemies. She frequently reminded them that since they were being guided and protected by God, they needed to express more gratitude.

When the group passed Gien, south of the besieged city of Orléans, they relaxed their guard somewhat, for they were entering lands largely loyal to the Dauphin. They headed southwest to the Loire River Valley, just south of the Loire River itself. On the morning of their ninth day, the first thing to change was the weather, and that was a good thing. They removed and stowed their rain ponchos and basked in the clear skies and warm sun.

However, as they were scouting for a place to make camp, they unexpectedly entered a clearing, and before they could withdraw, a voice rang out at them.

"Halt. Who goes there?" an unmounted soldier asked in perfect French. This was a French, not an English, soldier. However, was he Burgundian or Armagnac? Was he their friend or their enemy? That he was not a soldier loyal to the Dauphin became immediately evident, for in the clearing behind him, a banner bearing the diagonal blue and gold stripes of the coat of arms of the Duke of Burgundy boldly flew. The others had seen it as well, for Jehanne saw Jean de Metz whisper something to Katelyn. Then subtly, Jehanne's beloved protectors had not only surrounded her but pushed her chestnut mare to the back of the group so that she could not be seen. Katelyn and Jean de Metz placed themselves front and center, and then Jehanne watched as Olg quietly directed his mount directly to the left of Katelyn.

"We see by the banner that you are our comrade, and not our enemy," replied Jean de Metz. "We are relieved, for we too are forced to travel across these lands. But what are you doing here alone in French-held territory?"

"I am the one asking the questions, not you," replied the soldier gruffly. "And I am not alone. And as for what we are doing in this region, 'tis none of your affair. Who are you and where are you headed?"

"We bear an important message for the Duke of Bedford from the garrison commander in Bordeaux," Jean de Metz replied. "Let us pass." Jehanne forgave her protector for speaking this untruth and marveled at how quickly he had fashioned a plausible answer. Bordeaux was in the English-controlled Duchy of Aquitaine straight to the south, a territory that was separated from the northern-held English territories, so had they truly been traveling from Bordeaux to the Duke of Bedford's stronghold in Reims, they would have had to cross directly through this sector. She prayed silently for the soldier to believe their claims and allow them to pass peacefully, but she felt no such assurance. Instead, she had the distinct impression that this was going to end badly.

"Then show me your papers of safe-conduct," the enemy soldier insisted. He lifted a bow and arrow that he aimed at the cluster of mounted men, but he did not approach any closer. "Now," he instructed, "only one of you dismount, and bring me the orders."

Jehanne saw a subtle non-verbal message pass from Katelyn to

Olg, followed by Katelyn's reassuring hand gesture meant for Jean de Metz.

"Olg," Katelyn ordered. "Show the man our papers."

The Scotsman dismounted and handed his reins to Katelyn. Jehanne knew that Richard did indeed carry the papers of safe-conduct, but they were from Robert de Baudricourt.

"Now remove your weapons and drop them to the ground."

Olg unsheathed his sword, and placed it on the ground for the Burgundian to see.

"Your dagger as well, sir, for a man of your constitution is probably not content to bear only a sword, as is clearly demonstrated by the crossbow I see strapped to your saddle."

Richard lifted his cloak to reveal an additional scabbard over his doublet, from which he removed a short dagger. He placed it on the ground as well.

"Very well," replied the Burgundian. "I wish for the rest of you to back up into the trees, and I heartily advise none of you to attempt to withdraw a weapon or to charge on your steeds, for if I see or even suspect such an action on the part of any one of you, your comrade-in-arms will have an arrow placed neatly in his heart. Do not make the grave error of underestimating my skills as an archer either," he added, "for I could hit a pinecone in yonder pine," he nodded towards the forest with his head, "and your companion here presents a much larger target."

"Now, sir," the Burgundian addressed Richard, "remove the papers and show them to me."

"I have the papers here in my doublet," Richard replied in English as he reached to an inside pocket and removed the sheath of papers. "Oh, pardon me. I suppose you do not speak the language of the Duke of Bedford, now, do you?" he continued in his heavily accented French. "He will certainly chastise you for this very undiplomatic greeting we have suffered at your hands."

Although her companions had done a good job of blocking her from the soldier's view, Jehanne could still see the Burgundian's face through the gaps. She saw him visibly relax at hearing English spoken.

Brilliant, she thought. Katelyn had been correct about English coming in handy. With those few words in English, the Scotsman had allayed the Burgundian's suspicions.

"No, I do not speak English, and so how am I to believe that what you are speaking is indeed that language?"

"Because we are both English soldiers who have been placed in a Burgundian regiment as advisors," replied Katelyn in French, attempting to make her voice sound as low-pitched as possible. "Do you not recognize our English accents?" To Richard, she addressed additional words in English, which Jehanne did not understand.

"I demand that you speak only French," their adversary ordered, but his tone seemed less harsh.

"As you wish," replied Richard as he extended the papers in front of him.

"Why are you treating us like common criminals," asked Katelyn, with firmness but not harshness, "when we are clearly on your side of this conflict?" Jehanne recognized what Katelyn was attempting to do, both drawing the soldier's attention away from Richard and attempting to develop a bond of trust.

"Have you not heard the rumors?" the soldier asked. "A maiden warrior from Lorraine is said to be traveling to Chinon with the ludicrous mission to place the French pretender on the throne. We are here to stop her." And then, as if he regretted saying too much, his tone became more severe again. "Now," he said to Richard, "advance very slowly. Step by step."

Jehanne shuddered as these words were spoken. It was true what Bertrand had said. Rumors of her journey west had spread, and the

Burgundians were emboldened to enter French territory to prevent her from arriving in Chinon. They were in dire straits.

"And, you, my young man, could very well be that maiden," continued the Burgundian to Katelyn. "Your voice is particularly high-pitched, just like a female's, and I cannot fathom why the English would send such a young soldier as you to serve as an advisor to us. You are nothing but a lad. You could hardly have any experience in matters of warfare." Jehanne felt the blood drain from her voice at the Burgundian's words. Now her friend's female identity, as well as her own, were in danger of being uncovered.

Jehanne was amazed when instead of reacting with fear, Katelyn laughed, while Richard began to walk forward slowly.

"You think I look like a maiden, sir?" she asked. "First of all, have you ever seen a maiden of my height and build?" She sat tall in the saddle and then opened her cloak to show that there were no signs of voluptuous female anatomy. "And from Lorraine, you say? I admit I have tried these many months to perfect my French, but I fear I will never pass for a native of Lorraine. As for my voice, I also admit that it has caused me some anguish, but alas, my poor father had a high-pitched voice, and I am afraid I inherited his curse. And as for my apparent lack of experience, you would be wrong there as well. I have what some would call a brilliant military mind. The last battle strategy I planned was an unmitigated success. So think what you will."

The Burgundian's focus was split between Katelyn on her horse and the advancing Scotsman. When Richard was about two body lengths from the Burgundian, he suddenly lowered his head, and, with a speed that was simply unfeasible for a man of his size, he charged the Burgundian, who did not have the time to react. Richard head-butted him with such force that he flew through the air, along with his bow and arrow and then fell back to the ground. Jehanne gasped in horror at the sound of his skull cracking open as it hit a large rock, but she swallowed the gasp as quickly as it left her mouth. Once again, the realities of war were being made forcibly clear to her.

"*Dépêchez-vous.* Hurry, Olg," ordered Jean de Metz. "There must be a Burgundian garrison near here, and the forest will soon be teeming with his companions. They will know we are here. Return from whence we came. *Maintenant.* Now!"

With that frightening injunction, Jehanne and her small band of determined but exhausted warriors rode back towards the rising sun, with only one thing in mind: to get as far from that clearing as they possibly could.

Chapter 45

EVERY NOW AND THEN, NICOLAS regained consciousness. As if he were a common thief or murderer, Philippe Montrouge had bolted him to the wall of his cottage prison with a heavy iron chain attached to a leg shackle around his left ankle. That too-tight leg iron bit into his skin like a flesh-eating predator, and the agony of his festering and swollen ankle was enough on its own to cause Nicolas to lose consciousness, not to mention the additional pain from his toes, some of which he knew were broken. It had taken some time for him to open his eyes, as they were so swollen from the vicious kicks Montrouge had administered that first night. The blood that had oozed from his nose had finally dried up, but it was still so swollen that he had to breathe through his mouth. He could only imagine how horrific he must look, and he was glad that Katelyn was not there to see him in this condition.

If Nicolas was lucky, Philippe Montrouge would not be there during his brief moments of lucidity. In fact, thankfully, Montrouge was seldom there. He clearly had other quarters in Chinon, for there was no other room in this cottage. Because his captor had not tried to get Nicolas to talk during those savage beatings, Nicolas could only assume that Montrouge somehow divined that Katelyn was on her way to Chinon. He clearly planned to snatch her and use her for leverage to get Nicolas to talk. It was a horrifying thought. Could Nicolas honor the sanctity of his sacred knowledge while watching Montrouge perpetrate the same type of attacks on Katelyn that he had exacted on Nicolas?

He thought often of his beloved mentor, Jean le Vieux, who had been called upon to sacrifice his only son to keep the secret safe. Nicolas did not know if he could withstand that type of torture. Yes, he knew he could be tortured unto death himself, but he did not trust in his ability to helplessly watch his beloved Katelyn receive the same type of inhumane treatment. He did not think he would be as strong as Jean had been, and it was his prime motivator to escape. Consequently, in Montrouge's absence, Nicolas managed to choke down the stale bread and fetid stew that were left just within his reach. The foul fare was barely enough to sustain life, but it was all he had, and Nicolas needed to regain his strength. He had too many reasons to live, the most important being to protect Katelyn.

In his adversary's absence, he also relieved himself in the wooden bucket that had been placed on the hearth, its odor adding even more putridness to his already rank environment. But instead of focusing on the impossible nature of his predicament, Nicolas began thanking God for the small blessings. Jean had always taught him to look for the positive rather than dwelling on the negative.

At least he had a bucket for his private needs. At least he was protected from the elements, although Montrouge had never built another fire to temper the cold that gnawed at him continually. At least his clothing, which had been soaked from his night in the rain and sleet, had actually dried out from the fire in the hearth that first night. Even though Montrouge had removed Nicolas's belt, which could have been used as a weapon or a tool with its metal buckle and prong, he still had Katelyn's remarkable undergarments, for without them, he feared he would have succumbed to the temperatures in his

351

weakened state. And at least Montrouge had not disposed of his stockings or short leather boots after removing them to crush his prisoner's toes. Although it had been agonizing, as soon as he was able, Nicolas had put them back on to protect his feet from the cold and to keep the swelling under control. He had even managed to work the stocking under his leg iron, which offered some relief by covering the open flesh wound and protecting it slightly from the sharp-edged shackle.

At least he could still crawl, although walking, even if he tried to balance his weight on his heels, was still too painful because of the damage Montrouge had done to his toes.

And at least Montrouge had not found his time key. It was still there, inside the hidden pocket on the inner thigh of his undergarments. Katelyn had been right. Montrouge must have looked and looked for that key. He must have gone through all of Nicolas's belongings and checked out all of his outer pockets for the key, wondering if he could use it himself to travel through time and space, the way the Watchmen did. Nicolas did not believe it was possible. He was quite certain that only the owner of the key could use it, but after Abdon had traveled through the vortex by grabbing onto Nicolas, all that Nicolas thought he knew about the key was in question. He still did not believe the key could be used without the owner, but he did not want to find out. Besides, even if Abdon could not use the key, he could dispose of it so that Nicolas could never use it again.

But most importantly, at least Nicolas could still think rationally. And at least he still had the cognitive ability to formulate a plan. Every waking moment was spent in trying to find a means of escape.

One of his main concerns was that he had lost all track of time. He could have been here for a few days, a week, a fortnight or even a year. It was impossible for him to tell, because his periods of lucidity were few and far between. Nicolas had been careful to keep track of the date before his arrival in Chinon, and he knew that he had arrived in the city on the very date that Jehanne was to have left Vaucouleurs, the twenty-third of February. If Katelyn was with Jehanne and her little troop, then he did not believe he could have been held captive here for more than ten days at the most, and surely Philippe Montrouge was spending his time watching for Katelyn to arrive in Chinon. But that also meant there was very little time left.

And if Katelyn was *not* with Jehanne, then it did not much matter how long Nicolas had been held captive, for in that case, Montrouge would never find her. Perhaps Katelyn had already completed her mission and had returned with her time key to Mont Saint Michel, or even back to America. If so, Nicolas might remain here captive indefinitely, or at least until Montrouge gave up the hunt and decided to return to Mont Saint Michel to try to wrangle the secret of the Mount from Brother Thibault. In that case, Montrouge might kill Nicolas, or he might use him for leverage with Brother Thibault. Either way, it was of little importance. The only important thing was Katelyn's safety. He *hoped* Katelyn was safely back home, for although he was desperate to see her, he knew that seeing her meant that her life—as well as *his*—was in jeopardy. And if she *was* with Jehanne's group, she would unfortunately have no way of knowing that a trap had been set for her. She would have no way of knowing that Abdon had accompanied Nicolas through the time vortex. It was not a possibility that any of them had ever considered.

So during his moments of clarity, Nicolas tried every conceivable means to escape, but up until now, that had proven to be impossible. He had tried loosening the iron loop anchored in the wall that held his chain, but Montrouge had craftily removed every single item from the room—including Nicolas's knapsack—with the exception of the wooden waste bucket and the occasional wooden bowl that held his rank stew. Montrouge did not even allow Nicolas to have an eating utensil, so except for his bare hands, he had absolutely nothing to use as a tool. Montrouge had even removed the metal handle from the waste bucket and although Nicolas had tried removing the iron bands that held the bucket's slats together, he simply could not pry them loose, as he had no way of getting leverage under the tightly forged iron.

He had considered using both the bucket and bowl as a weapon to hit Montrouge in the head, but he feared they were too light to do any more damage than to enrage his captor enough to kill Nicolas in the ensuing counter-attack. He could imagine Montrouge's rage at being covered with Nicolas's excrement.

Nicolas had extended the leg chain to its full length in every direction in the room, but he could not reach either the door or the single small window covered by wooden shutters. He thought about attempting to choke Montrouge with the heavy chain, but once again, he acknowledged the fact that he did not have the strength to wrestle him to the ground. No, Nicolas could not afford to attack unless he was certain to kill or disable, and he simply did not have the strength to win a hand-to-hand combat. He needed a weapon. He checked the fireplace for a cast iron fireback or grate, but even those had been removed.

For the first few days, Nicolas had tried calling out for help, but the walls of the cottage were as thick as the length of his arm, and with the window and door covered by solid wood, it would have been difficult for anyone to hear his cries unless they were standing right next to the cottage. And besides, even if anyone did hear his call for help, it was no guarantee they would come to his aid. Nicolas had seen the abject poverty and squalor of this city, and it appeared to him that the people of Chinon had only enough energy to worry about themselves and their own family members. None but the woman who had duped him with her feigned kindness had offered him any assistance upon his arrival in the city. He knew he could not count on anyone besides himself to get out of this situation.

And then one day—he knew it was day and not night, for he could see tiny spots of light break through the chinks in the aged wood of the window shutters—a thought impressed itself in his mind. Whether it was his thought, or an idea mercifully placed there by the Archangel, he could not tell, but it did not matter. He crawled to the fireplace and began methodically sifting through the ashes that had been left from an untold number of fires. His hands and face were covered with ash, but that was a small price to pay for his reward: three wrought iron nails, the only remnants of old building timbers or furniture that at some point had been used as firewood.

It was gratifying to Nicolas to have something to focus on besides his concern for Katelyn, his pain, his hunger, and the menacing cold. He worked with renewed enthusiasm and optimism, and his periods of lucidity became longer and longer. At first, he attempted to unlock the shackle on his leg with the nails he had recovered, but he had little success. Then he shifted his focus on loosening the iron ring that anchored the chain into the cottage wall. He had to do it carefully so as not to expose too large an area of damaged plaster for fear of Montrouge discovering his handiwork. He had finally gotten to the point where the rubble stone was exposed beneath the plaster. The bolt was fixed into the mortar between two stones. Hour after hour he chipped away at the plaster and mortar, carefully and regularly collecting the white powder onto his jacket and spreading it among the ashes in the fireplace so there was no outward evidence of his labor.

When Nicolas heard Montrouge unlocking the latch to the door, he quickly shook out the powder from his jacket, placed his nails in his doublet pocket, and lay on his stomach with his eyes closed. The success of his escape depended upon Montrouge truly believing he was helpless and unconscious until he was able to free himself from the leg shackle.

"Well, well, Nicolas," Montrouge said as he entered the room, "I see you are insentient as usual. Or doing a good job of pretending. No matter, my friend."

Unfortunately, Nicolas knew what was coming next. It was all he could do to refrain from reacting when Montrouge approached him and kicked him in the ribs. That he was able to appear unfazed in spite of the waves of agony that washed over him was purely because of Katelyn. He had never forgotten her account of being on the Godon ship and pretending to be unconscious when one of her captors punched her in the leg with no warning. If she could hold it together with no warning, he could do it knowing it was coming. But it came with a cost. The flood of nausea that hit him threatened to reveal his state of full consciousness, and it took every ounce of self-control his battered body could muster up not to retch right there and then.

"Yes, my friend," continued Montrouge, as if the two were having a cogent face-to-face conversation, "you are to have a brief reprieve from my ministrations. I must refrain from incurring too much damage to your pitiful body because I need you to be awake and alert." At this, he kicked Nicolas lightly in the head, but when there was no reaction, he continued on with his diatribe while Nicolas continued to feign unconsciousness.

"The time has come for you to wake up, Nicolas. You see, we haven't much longer to wait. My scouts bring me word of a maiden warrior fighting for the cause of France who is making her way towards Chinon as we speak with a small band of protectors. I have a fairly good hunch that the female in question is none other than your beloved Katelyn Michaels, for surely she is the only female warrior with whom I have ever been acquainted. As difficult as it is for me to admit, she certainly displayed an uncanny military prowess by deceiving my troops—or should I say Richard Collins' troops—during our last encounter. That was an unfortunate outcome in many ways, not the least of which was the complete disintegration of my authority over those cowardly English soldiers, and the ultimate demise of my cherished host. As much as I appreciate the service of Philippe Montrouge, I must admit that I still yearn for Collins' body. His was a worthy mortal body, and I am not one bit pleased that your associate Jean le Vieux chose to give his life to protect Mademoiselle Michaels. No, I do not forget easily, my friend. I have waited over four years for vengeance, and I shall have it." As if in spite of his statement to the contrary, Montrouge simply could not refrain from inflicting more pain, he kicked Nicolas again in his ribcage. Nicolas did not know how long he could continue his act, but being able to glean any bits of information from his assailant made the pain bearable.

"I am still uncertain as to why you two have left your station on the Mount. Yes, I am quite anxious to learn more about what you are up to traipsing about France, so far from your post. And of course, my main motivation remains the same: to finally uncover your little secret that will change the course of my existence forever. Finally, I believe the time has arrived when I shall have some answers. I cannot wait to see how surprised and thrilled Mademoiselle Michaels will be when she finds such a warm welcome for her here. And since she has never had the privilege of meeting Philippe Montrouge, I will have the advantage over her. Yes, I shall offer her my kind hospitality, and then, voilà, I will be so pleased to reunite you two lovebirds. Imagine her delight upon seeing her dear, sweet Nicolas. How lovely it will be to watch the two of you interact as I torture her limb by limb, bit by bit until you beg to give me the answers I so desire. Such fun awaits us, my friend. So please, it is time to shake off your lethargy. I have even had the good grace to bring you a fine meal to impart the strength you will need to watch your beloved Katelyn suffer a fate worse than death. Yes, what delightful amusement there will be. I shall return in a couple of days, my friend, and then let the games begin." With this, Nicolas heard Montrouge leave the wooden bowl on the floor, along with a leather pouch of drinking water, and leave the room, locking the door behind himself.

Just as it had taken every ounce of self-control Nicolas had to refrain from reacting to being kicked in the ribs and head, it took every ounce of self-control he had to curb the rage he felt at hearing these words. But once again, he counted his blessings, for this visit had indeed been a blessing. He now knew more than he had known since Montrouge had taken him captive.

First of all, Abdon did not know anything about Jehanne, and that was a relief, for Nicolas understood how critical it was for her to succeed in her mission to save France. The fate of Mont Saint Michel was inescapably tied with France throwing off the yoke of English occupation and remaining a sovereign nation.

Secondly, Abdon mistakenly thought that the Maiden Warrior whose fame was spreading throughout the land was Katelyn. He would not be expecting Katelyn to be disguised as a male soldier, and that fact might just be enough for Nicolas to get to her first.

Thirdly, Nicolas finally had a timeframe with which to work. Jehanne and her group were arriving within the next few days. Nicolas now knew what he had to do. He had to work all night to free himself, or he and Katelyn were doomed.

And finally, miracle of miracles, in an attempt to get Nicolas coherent enough to begin the torture again, Montrouge had actually left Nicolas a decent meal. But Nicolas didn't plan on being tortured again.

Not this time, anyway.

Chapter 46

JUST AS I HOPED, OLG WAS MAGNIFICENT. Olg the Magnificent. Now that's a novel name. When I couldn't bear to call the Scotsman by his first name, which is the same as Abdon's last host, Richard Collins, I remembered my brother's *Dungeons and Dragons'* Scottish ogre, and that became my nickname for Richard the Archer, even though he's certainly no ogre. He's just a gentle giant of a guy with a heart as big as his body. For a fleeting second, I think of Jackson and of how proud he would be to see his Scottish giant outwit the enemy. But I cannot think about Jackson now. He belongs to another life, another time. *Dungeons and Dragons* is a game of war, and this is real war. Seeing the Burgundian soldier's head split open on that stone was not virtual. It was real. And it is also real that Jehanne is in grave danger, so now I have to focus on how we're going to get her to Chinon.

Thanks to Olg, at least we still have that option. Yes, Olg just possibly saved all of our lives. I almost blew it by giving him a big hug in front of everyone, but I have to act like a male, and I don't think that would be considered appropriate behavior in fifteenth-century France. I guess I'll have to do it in private, because Olg is the only member of our group, besides Jehanne, who knows the truth about me. Well, at least the truth about my being female . . . and also the truth about my not being Bretonne, which even Jehanne doesn't know. In fact, he figured both of those things out right away.

"My heavens, lassie," he had said to me in private in the forest outside Saint-Urbain when I first joined up with Jehanne's little group. "All it took was one look at your face after nearly being killed by that Godon, and I knew you were a female. I do not know why the others have not yet divined that fact, but ol' Richard knows a woman when he sees a woman! And furthermore, I know you are not Breton, for I have learned a few Breton words in my journeys, and when I threw them out to you, you did not respond. So, where are you really from?"

"You are right," I replied reluctantly. "My native tongue is a variation of English, but I am from an island far from England, and I am *not* English," I exclaimed. "I am loyal to Jehanne through and through."

"I believe you there," he replied in his version of English, "for I have seen the way you protect and respect her. I want you to know, your secrets are safe with me. I will defend them and you to the death."

I knew at that moment that I could trust him with my life. The next day, I even told him why I couldn't call him Richard. Well, I didn't tell him that Richard Collins was the physical incarnation of one of Satan's evil spirits, but I did tell him that a man named Richard Collins, a lecherous English commander, had once tried to kill me. And I told him the truth about where his nickname came from: basically that my little brother had an imaginary friend, a Scottish giant named Olg. I think he found it endearing, and he took to the name immediately..

So needless to say, Olg and I have developed a great friendship. I can totally be myself with him, even more so than with Jehanne. We can speak English together, even though Old English is as different from American English as fifteenth-century French is from modern

French. Still, it feels good to speak my native language and let my hair down with Olg. Literally let my hair down. The other men have yet to see me without my slouchy cap that covers my hair, but Olg has seen it. My very stinky hair. Honestly, I can hardly stand it. Anyway, I know Olg *will* protect me with his life. I've told him, though, that if it ever comes down to it, he has to choose Jehanne before me. I have told him that her success is critical for the world in general. Her life must be protected at all costs.

Anyway, back to the present. After our unfortunate encounter with the Burgundian soldier, we rode several miles back to the east, and then Bertrand scouted out another route further south—and further away from English-held lands—for us to get to Sainte-Catherine-de-Fierbois tomorrow. According to the record, Jehanne will stop there and attend mass, but she won't send for the sword until she gets to Chinon.

Now, we are hesitating about stopping to sleep, but after discussing it with Jean and Bertrand, we decide it is too dangerous to continue during daylight hours with Burgundians in the area, so when we reach the center of a thick pine forest, we decide it is a good place to stop. We have encountered no one in this forest.

We set up camp quickly since we have lost so much time, but I pay particular attention to the placement of the motion sensors. Olg lifts me onto his shoulders so that I can place them in the best possible locations. This could be our most critical night, I mean day. We are all exhausted, hungry, and nervous, so after we eat our usual fare of stale bread, cured ham, and moldy cheese, I pull out all the stops to lift everyone's spirits: a bag of Skittles. It's like I've given them liquid gold . . . in rainbow colors. And it works. Everyone's spirits are lifted . . . except for mine.

I'm worried about Jehanne, and I'm worried about Nicolas. And I feel filthy. I'd like nothing more than to have a bath, and especially to wash my greasy hair that's been stuck up in my equally greasy cap for nearly two weeks. Since it's the first day we've had since leaving Vaucouleurs that has actually been reasonably warm, I decide I'm going to do just that. There is a clear stream that empties into a pond about five hundred yards from our camp. When all the men are asleep, except for our assigned watchman, I'm going to slip away and bathe.

Then I remember the last time I was dying to take a bath in fifteenth-century France and I hesitate. That hadn't ended so well. Reluctantly, I decide it isn't a very smart thing to do, but I'm just so darn stinky. Then I think of Olg. Yes, I'll ask for his help. I trust him with my life, and I know he'll be super vigilant. Last time in Mont Saint Michel, I'd foolishly slipped off alone thinking I could take care of myself, that I was invincible, and I'd ended up being kidnapped by the Godons. Now, I know I'm not invincible. I've learned to think twice before acting because so many lives depend upon my decisions.

After we clean up from our meal and the others settle down to sleep, I tell Bertrand, who has first watch, the truth. I'm going to take a bath in the pond taking Olg as my protection. He looks at me like I'm crazy. Now I know bathing isn't a priority here, particularly in winter, but honestly, I wish I could get the whole lot of them to take a dunk as well, because they are all pretty rank. But these guys already think I'm crazy because I insist they wash their hands, so I'm not going to push my luck. I have a moment of concern knowing that we'll have to disable the motion sensor in order to get to the pond, but with Olg guarding the sector, it will be just as secure, if not more so, and both of us have our weapons with us, my sword and his bow.

After I disable the motion sensor, we make our way to the pond. It almost feels warm, and I am so excited I can hardly restrain myself. Well, it's the beginning of March, so it's not that warm, but compared to the weather we've been through, this feels like Tahiti to me! I have a fresh change of underwear and even thermal underwear that I can hardly wait to get into once I'm clean, and I've brought a little sundries kit in a mesh bag, like the one I had in Mont Saint Michel. It has small bottles of shampoo and conditioner, shower gel, a shower scrunchie, a tiny hair brush, and one of those miracle microfiber towels that hardly takes any space but absorbs lots of water. I also have a razor, but I don't think this is a good time to worry about shaving my hairy legs. That'll have to be for later—when I'm with Nicolas. If I'm ever with Nicolas.

Olg sits down on a large boulder facing away from the pond, which gives him a good view of anyone or anything approaching. I entrust him with my sword—Brother Thibault's remarkable sword lovingly made for me—and I make him promise under penalty of death that he will not watch me disrobe. However, I still take the precaution of doing so behind some scrub oak. I mean really. Men are men. I'm not completely naïve.

Once I'm naked, I feel surprisingly vulnerable, as if that ridiculous tunic and doublet I've been wearing can actually provide me with adequate protection. Instead of tentatively wading into the freezing water inch by inch, leaving myself exposed, I just dive right in and get the shock over with immediately. And is that water ever a shock. Tahiti it isn't after all. But it's clean, and it isn't frozen. And it isn't sea water, like the last out-of-doors bath I took in France. I swim out to a spot that's slightly shielded from Olg's view until the water comes to my shoulders.

I look all around me, inspecting every bank of the pond, but all is quiet and peaceful. Still, because of my nervousness left over from my bath in the Mont Saint Michel Bay, and because of the cold, I don't waste much time in lathering up my hair. I dip under the water to rinse it, and then lather it up a second time, and rinse thoroughly. I apply a generous dose of conditioner because my rat's nest is going to need extra help and leave it on while I scrub my entire body with the shower gel and scrunchie. My skin is freezing and nearly raw, but it is clean raw and freezing. I immerse myself a final time to remove all of the conditioner and body wash, and then head straight back for the bank, where I've left my clothing.

I made it. No Godon sailors or Burgundian soldiers to abduct me here. Quickly, I put on my clean underwear, thermals, and socks and I breath a sigh of relief. Just that brief time naked makes me realize that it's no fun being a woman in war-torn France. I turn abruptly when I hear a sound in the brush on the opposite side of the pond, and I call out quietly to my friend.

"Olg, did you hear that?"

"A doe," he answers. "Just catching a drink, but she dashed away very quickly when she saw us." Olg is now facing the pond, and I'm glad I stayed in the shielded portion of the pond for my bath. There wasn't much he could have seen from his vantage point.

Now fully dressed and with my boots on, I emerge from the scrub oak trying to get the brush bristles through my tangles.

"Just sit here with me while I brush my hair," I ask him. "I can't really head back into camp with this showing, now can I?" I say as I stretch out the wet, snarled mass.

He laughs and places my sword next to me. "Take as much time as you need."

"Thank you," I say as I brush. "I just can't tell you how much I needed that. I appreciate your help . . . and your friendship."

"You are welcome, Kaelig," he says, "although 'tis not your real name, now is it?"

I decide it's time to tell him my real name. "No," I say, "it's really Katelyn. Katelyn Michaels, but you can't let that slip. You have to always call me Kaelig."

"Katelyn," he said. "A beautiful name, but 'tis one I have never heard before."

"Typical of my island," I explain. Yeah, typical of that twenty-first century island called America.

"And Michaels?" he asks. "Is your father named Michael?"

"No," I answer, "but my protector is named Michael. Long story," I say as I finish brushing my hair. We sit in silence as I quickly braid my hair and loop the braid on top of my head, and then pull on my cap. I wish I could have washed the darn cap. Then I hear another sound in the forest. Twigs breaking.

"Shhh," Olg says as he stands up. He looks all around us, but then sits back down. "Probably just the doe finding her friends," he says. "But I will feel more secure when we get back to camp."

"Let's go then," I say as I stand up and replace my sword in my scabbard, which I've actually kind of gotten used to. I feel naked now without it. "Thanks again, Olg. You are a true friend. Even Jehanne doesn't know that I'm not from Brittany. I didn't want to scare her. You know, I didn't want her to think I was an English spy or something. It's so nice to be able to speak in my native tongue."

"Although I do find your English odd, I too enjoy speaking English, for I have mastered that language much more than French," he says as we head back to the camp, "and I too appreciate your friendship. I have said it before," he added, "but I will say it again. I told you that I would protect you with my life, and I will."

"And I repeat, that if there is ever a choice to be made, you must first protect Jehanne. It is critical, vital, that you protect her before me, although hopefully, it will never come down to that. Tomorrow morning, we should reach Sainte-Catherine-de-Fierbois, and the day after that we'll be in Chinon. Our journey is almost over."

We quietly work our way through the trees and brush and get back to camp.

"Bertrand," I whisper as we approach. "I'm already awake, so I'll take the second watch. You and Olg both go sleep now," I instruct them. He and Olg quietly crawl (well, as quietly as Olg can crawl) under the tarp tent, which the crew now knows how to install like experts, and soon, I hear Olg's snore out-blast all the rest of them combined.

Other than the rumbling from under the tarp, all is quiet except for the occasional bird who happily announces that winter is nearly over.

For the first time, I have a few minutes to think about the past several weeks. Operation Maiden's Sword is almost completed. As soon as we get to Chinon and Jehanne takes possession of the sword, I can turn my attention back to the focus that now has me preoccupied. Finding Nicolas. I try to push away those impressions I'd had that Abdon is in Chinon and that somehow, he has captured Nicolas. It just doesn't make any sense. Abdon would have no way of knowing that Nicolas went to Chinon. In the future, he obviously knows I go back to help Joan of Arc, because he tried to stop me twice, but I know Abdon can't travel back in time. There's just no way that Abdon in 1429, regardless of what form he has taken, could know anything about Joan of Arc or Chinon. It just isn't possible. I'm just being paranoid about our security.

Security. And then I remember! As paranoid as I might be about Abdon, I just made a terrible mistake concerning the security of this camp. I failed to reset the motion detector after Olg and I returned from the pond. I jump up to go wake him so we can go reset it, but, as I shake Olg, I realize that this one lapse in my cautiousness may have just caused this mission to fail, because it is already too late.

Chapter 47

SHOUTING AND THE SOUND OF CLANGING metal woke Jehanne from a deep sleep, but she could not move because Julien was lying on top of her, covering her mouth with his hand.

"Quiet, Jehanne," Julien whispered in her ear. "Do not get up or utter a word. We are under attack. Take this," he whispered as he placed a dagger in her right hand, "and use it if you need to. I am going to conceal you under the bedding, and you must not move."

Jehanne pulled her left hand up to cover her mouth and nose to create a space so she could breathe as Julien piled several blankets over her. He also bunched up some of the blankets on either side of her to camouflage the fact that there was a body under the mound. Then she heard Julien lean over and whisper to her again, "Remain in here, no matter what. Do not come out until we tell you 'tis safe." She felt, rather than saw, Julien leave the meager protection of their tent.

Outside, she could hear grunts and the sound of metal hitting metal, which she now knew was the sound of sword clashing against sword. With her heart racing so loudly she feared it would betray her presence, she silently called upon Saint Michael for protection, not only for herself but for her little army of valiant soldiers. Particularly Katelyn. She had come so far after so much tribulation, and she knew she could not have done it without Katelyn's assistance. Surely, the Archangel would not allow them to be harmed this close to their destination.

After her prayer, she turned her attention to the sounds of the battle outside the tent. She realized she was holding her breath until she could distinguish Katelyn's voice in the fracas.

"Jean," she heard Katelyn scream, "behind you!"

Katelyn was alive. Jehanne released her breath and then had to pant to fill her starving lungs with oxygen. It was torture to remain here and not come to the aid of her companions, but she was not foolish enough to think she could really be of any assistance. She was not versed in sword fighting, and she would just become a distraction for her protectors. Even though she would have willingly sacrificed her life to save one of her friends, she also knew she did not have that choice. She had been chosen for a higher purpose, and regardless of her personal feelings, she could not fail God. She had to do everything in her power to fulfill her destiny. When she had done what she was sent to do, God could do with her as He wished. As long as she could assist the Dauphin in his quest to be crowned in Reims, that was all she hoped to achieve. Nothing else mattered.

As a way to cope with the sacrifices being made by her friends to protect her at all costs, Jehanne blocked out the reality of the battle from her senses. She did not listen to Colet de Vienne cursing. She did not hear the recognizable sound of metal on metal changing to a less-recognizable tone when metal hit bone. She did not feel Olg's great bulk trampling along every edge of the tarp in an attempt to prevent the enemy from diving into the heart of her hiding place. She did not hear the squires Jean or Julien shouting out that the horses had to be protected at all costs, or the sound of branches breaking and the pounding of horses' hooves. She did not see the sunlight that filtered through the tarp and her wool coverings blocked as Olg's ever-present hulk dashed in and out of the rays. She did not pick out the sounds of Bertrand or Jean de Metz crashing through the brush in pursuit of their assailants, or the howling of unknown voices, in pain and shock. She did not see Katelyn duck her head into the tent to make certain Jehanne was still there and still safe. She did not even hear Katelyn scream, or feel the thud of a body hitting the ground just a hand span from her feet. She did not smell the coppery odor of blood seeping into the ground all around her.

No, instead, Jehanne focused on her voices. Her voices had guided her and protected her thus far, and she heard them now telling her to have faith and be still. She obeyed the voices. She had faith and was still, but she also found her mind reviewing her short life.

From the time she was a little girl, Jehanne had never aspired to anything greater than being a wife and mother, like her own beloved mother. She had always fully expected to follow in her mother's footsteps, and consequently, she had carefully learned the skills necessary to be a productive and frugal homemaker. But even at that young age, there was something that was more important to her than thoughts of motherhood. It was her devotion to God. And then the voices had come, and she had cast off all thoughts of her future. Her only motivation was to obey her voices. Did it mean she no longer wanted to be a wife and mother? No. In fact, when Katelyn had spoken of the man she loved, Jehanne had felt a twinge of envy. But she knew that until her mission was complete, she had to remain virginal and pure. This is what God expected of her, and she had submitted her own desires to God's will. Her future was in God's hands, and come what may, she would follow the path she had been given.

At that moment, she knew she would survive this ordeal, and others to come. In her mind's eye, she even saw crowds hailing the new King Charles VII in a magnificent edifice she knew must be Notre-Dame de Reims. She saw herself kneeling at his side.

However, as she sought to see beyond that glorious vision, as she struggled to envision babes in her arms, or a husband at her side, she saw only dark prison walls closing in upon her. She heard a harsh, unpleasant voice ordering her over and over and over again to answer his questions, and she felt the heartache of humiliation and scorn, which threatened to eat her from the inside out.

And then, she smelled smoke.

Chapter 48

IT WAS ALMOST DARK WHEN NICOLAS finally succeeded in loosening the bolt in the wall with his iron nail to the point where he could pull it out, even in his weakened state. Ironically, it was the potato and pork stew Montrouge had left that had actually renewed his strength enough to accomplish the task. Unfortunately, however, his makeshift nail tools did little to loose the leg shackle locked onto his left ankle with a warded lock. Without the properly shaped key, there was no way to open the lock. He needed to procure a saw or rasp to cut off the leg iron and the chain attached to it, but he had to get out of this cottage prison first, even if his shackles provoked questions.

It was an effort to get to his feet with his swollen ankle and broken toes, but there was no time to dwell on his injuries, particularly as daylight was nearly gone. He pulled the chain attached to the leg iron up underneath his leggings so that the remainder of the chain came out at his waist, and then he wrapped that length of the chain around his waist in an attempt to camouflage it. With his doublet pulled over the bulk, at least no one would instantly remark that he was an escaped prisoner dragging a leg iron and chain.

He turned his attention to getting out of the cottage. His heart sank when he realized that the wooden shutters and door, although they could be locked from the inside with an iron bar, were also locked on the outside. Philippe Montrouge was not taking any chances with his prisoner. There was no glass pane in the window, just the wooden shutters, but Nicolas judged that even if he could break through the wood of the shutters, the window was not large enough for him to slip through. For security reasons, most peasant homes had very small windows so that intruders could not get in. His only choice was to exit through the door.

Montrouge had said he would be back in a couple of days, but that could mean anything. Nicolas did not have time to waste. He had already finished every morsel of the bread and stew, and there were only a few drops of water left in the animal skin pouch.

He sat down and made an assessment of everything he had to work with: a wooden bucket without a handle filled with his own waste, a wooden bowl, a leather water pouch, his clothing, and the chain attached to his raw and swollen ankle. He prayed to the Archangel for guidance, for he felt incapable of finding any answers.

He felt impressed to turn his attention to the door. It was made of several vertical slats of wood, with a wooden cross brace across the top and bottom of the door. An iron bar attached to a swiveling mechanism bolted to the left doorframe swiveled upwards so that the door could be opened from the inside, and then to lock it again, the bar swiveled back down into a horizontal position across the middle of the door to fit into a metal U-shaped brace bolted onto the opposite side of the door frame. If he could dislodge the metal anchor that held the bar to the left side of the doorframe and thereby free the bar, he could use the bar as a lever to pry the door open, hopefully breaking through the exterior lock. And if he could not break through the lock, then perhaps he could use the lever to pry the wooden slats apart.

This was his answer. He had to work that bolted anchor plate out of the door frame. Once again, he turned to his little nails. It was now almost pitch black, and he had to work by feel. The task was tedious and his fingertips were raw, sore, and cold, even though he kept his gloves on, but he worked all through the night, chipping away little by little at the solid wood that held the four bolts of the anchor plate. It would have been much easier if he'd had a smaller pry bar to pry the anchor off the wall, but that was not the case, so on he worked, feeling the effects of severe deprivation. He could survive with not enough food, but not having enough water was taxing. He longed to drink every drop in his little pouch, but knew he needed to space out his sips. He rewarded himself with a sip after what he judged to be each hour. In spite of the fact that it was cold, he was sweating from the exertion, and as he had learned from Katelyn, sweating caused the body to become even more dehydrated, and it was critical to replace the lost water, or one could die quickly from lack of water.

Just as his thirst was becoming unbearable and he was losing all feeling in his fingers, it dawned on him. He did have a smaller pry! His time key was made of pewter, and it was still hidden in the secret pocket of his thermal underwear. The coins were too small and thin, but the time key was nearly as large as his palm. He removed his gloves and reached under his breeches until he felt the key.

Pewter was a softer metal than iron, and he did not want to risk damaging his key, but he found that if he applied pressure evenly along the edge of the metal oval with his hands, the key did not bend. He removed his gloves so that he could feel exactly what he was doing and to ensure that he did not bend the key. He repeatedly pried under all four sides of the rectangular plate, and little by little, he felt the greedy wood give up its treasure.

At last, the anchor plate fell to the ground, as did Nicolas in total exhaustion. But he only allowed himself a moment of respite before he moved on to the next step: prying the door open. For this, he drank his final sip of water, and replaced his gloves. Gloriously, prying the door open with the heavy wrought iron bar proved to be the easiest thing Nicolas had done all week long.

In complete disbelief that his ordeal was finally over, the injured, cold, thirsty, starving, and exhausted but grateful Watchman left his prison, just as dawn broke.

Chapter 49

I AM MORTIFIED. THE BURGUNDIAN ATTACK on our camp was entirely my fault. I had been so wrapped up in my own world, wanting so badly to bathe and then getting lost in my thoughts, that I'd forgotten to reset the motion sensor. I had failed to be vigilant while I was on watch. The enemy should have never made it past the motion sensors, let alone within two feet of Jehanne. But, no. Incredibly, they slipped into camp right through the sector where I'd failed to reset the sensor. I mean, what are the odds?

The only thing that keeps me from a total breakdown is that thanks to Olg, we all survived the attack. That incredible man was Jackson's ogre and the Energizer Bunny all wrapped into one, and trust me, even though he's known as Richard the Archer, the man really knows how to handle a sword. And for a giant, he can really bust a move, as I saw when he fought off every attack around the perimeter of the tent where Jehanne was hiding. When he'd promised me he'd fight to the death for me and Jehanne, he hadn't been kidding. Thank heavens it hadn't been to his death—but instead to the death of our enemies.

Oh, the rest of us helped, and I have to admit, I did some pretty fancy swordplay myself, thanks to the impression that I needed fencing lessons. At least I wasn't a detriment to our little army. I was actually able to hold my own, which allowed Olg free rein to get his job done. And he really did it. We figure there were about twelve men who attacked. They must have left their horses some distance away and then quietly slipped into camp on foot. Olg singlehandedly dispatched half of them, and the other men and horses—yes horses, for they also joined the battle—took out four more. Two of the Burgundians escaped, but they were both badly wounded, and I don't think they're going to make it very far.

With the battle over, I feel an overwhelming sense of gratitude to the Archangel once again for the fact that I personally didn't have to take a life. It was almost as if Olg was aware of my moral dilemma. He was there at every opportune moment to remove that horrible prospect from me. It was bad enough for me to have to be in the midst of that battle and realize that simply because of alliances made by their superiors, those Burgundian soldiers had to die. In the aftermath, I can't help but think of their wives and children. Their mothers. It's horrible. Their loved ones will probably never know what happened to their sons, fathers, and husbands. This is a very sobering experience. It's one, unfortunately, that I will never be able to put from my mind. But this is war, and war isn't pretty. I've heard people say that before, but until you've actually had to live through it, you don't have a clue what that really means.

Still, I can't help but think how amazing it is that among our little band of eight, we didn't lose one soul, and except for a few cuts and bruises, we are all pretty much okay. If that isn't a witness that God is with us, I don't know what is.

During the battle, Jehanne stayed under the tarp as Julien instructed her to do. When I call into the darkness under the tarp and tell her that it's now safe to come out, she pushes aside the blankets and emerges to the scene of mayhem and death. I wonder how she will respond, but I soon learn that I have underestimated her once again. This woman is strong. After inspecting the carnage, she stands tall and addresses all of us.

"Thank you all for your valiant service," she says as she looks each one of us in the eyes. "You have once again confirmed to me that you have been called of God to assist in His work, for this is not my work, but God's. I desire each of you to know that I did not cower under the bedding there simply because I feared for my own life. God has made it abundantly clear to me that I must let nothing stop me in my mission to save France. I must journey to Chinon, I must speak to the Dauphin, I must take him to Reims, and without each of you doing everything in your power to protect me, that would not be a possibility."

Then she turns her praise heavenward, thanking God for His mercy in protecting us. Her words are eloquent and moving, and I cannot help but marvel at her power and the strength of her personality. She speaks with authority, and in spite of her humble beginnings, she speaks with such magnetism, it's like our souls are bound to hers. This is her gift from God, and it is certainly one that I don't have. I might be adept with electronics, and that certainly helped me save Mont Saint Michel, but Jehanne has charisma and knows how to captivate an audience.

For centuries to come, historians and writers will try to dissect how she did what she did. I know that, because I've read what has been written about her. But now, I know the truth. No, she's not a military genius. No, she's not a brilliant strategist. No, she's not even a hardened warrior. But absolutely yes, regardless of how her non-believing critics will try to spin her story, Joan of Arc *is* a humble servant of God with a remarkable ability to convey her message with such authenticity and genuine passion that you can't *not* believe her. I know her secret, because I know her. I know Joan of Arc. She is a force to contend with, and she is ready.

As I stand watching her, captivated by her authority, she kneels and silently prays over the dead soldiers, touching each of them individually with a reverence that defies description, gently closing the eyes of those that remain open. I see tears streaming down her face as she does this, and I feel tears streaming down my own face and down the faces of the others as well. Her soldiers. Her male soldiers. Jehanne's sorrow and compassion are so heartfelt and so genuine, that she infuses that compassion and transforms the hearts of all those around her.

The hardest reality for me is that I can never tell the truth about Joan of Arc. This experience is something I'll have to keep in my heart and cherish privately. At least I'll be able to tell Nicolas and Brother Thibault about it, but how I long to shout from the rooftops that I've been in the presence of greatness.

"These men," Jehanne finally says as she stands, "although fighting for an unjust cause, have given their lives doing what they felt was their duty, and we owe them our deepest respect. Each deserves a proper burial. We must do this quickly, in case those who escaped send in reinforcements, but we must nevertheless do it correctly."

There is something cathartic for me about helping to bury those men. It is healing for the trauma of the battle. It is done with complete reverence and respect. First, Jehanne has us take all of their weapons and lay them aside. Other than the weapons, she does not allow the men to take any of their belongings, clothing or equipment. We don't just dig a pit and throw their bodies in on top of each other. No, in spite of our concern about an imminent attack, Jehanne insists we take the time to dig individual graves, side by side in a row, and we feel a calmness come upon us that could only be divine comfort. The bodies are not roughly thrown into the holes, but are carefully placed, facing upwards towards heaven, with their arms crossed over their chests. These men are treated with dignity. After each grave is properly covered with dirt, and after the soil has been compacted so the animals won't dig up the graves, Jehanne has us gather small stones, which she then instructs us to place on each grave in the form of a cross. These are Christian men, and they are given a proper Christian burial, even if they have no priest to give them absolution. Jehanne gives them her own absolution.

She then turns our attention to the weapons, and asks each of us to chose at least one item, as a reminder, she says, of the savagery of war, and also of our responsibility towards the fallen.

"'Tis not a trophy of your victory," she insists, "but a token of your responsibility for the deaths of these men, for cutting them down in the prime of their lives. The arm you have taken is a reminder that you should pray each day for the life of the soldier whose weapon you now bear. Pray to God that, in His mercy, He will forgive that soldier for his transgressions and that He will also forgive you your own trespasses. 'Tis a reminder that you should never kill out of lust for blood, but out of a sacred commitment to fight for a righteous cause . . . for God's cause."

Wow. What a humbling experience. I look around me, and see all of my comrades-in-arms bowing their heads. These men have complete faith in Jehanne. They respect and revere her. They trust her. They would do anything for her. Her goodness and devotion to God do not come across as fake or self-righteous. No. We feel her goodness. We feel her faith. It permeates us. It makes us all want to be better, to do better. I don't know about the others, but for me, this is a transforming moment.

Jehanne chooses first. She takes a sword, the simplest of all the swords available. It is now her sword to go along with the one Robert de Baudricourt gave her and a companion to the one she will shortly receive. *The* sword. The reason Nicolas and I came. I wonder if she really needs the third sword, for I've seen that she doesn't need gimmicks to save France. But then I realize that not all people will have the same openness to her spirit as we do. We chose to come with her. We've been in her presence constantly. We've watched and observed her. We have genuine feelings of affection for her, and we do not reject the possibility of divine assistance. Others, however, might not be so susceptible to spiritual matters. They'll need more convincing. They might need some type of proof. They will seek for a sign, and in my very last act of this mission, I am going to help Jehanne give them what they want.

Olg jabs me gently in the ribs. It's my turn to choose. Humbly, I choose a sword, not just as a token of my responsibility, but also out of necessity. During the course of the battle, my cherished sword from Brother Thibault literally shattered into two pieces when a Burgundian soldier lunged at me and struck my sword with the most forceful blow I've ever experienced. I was so stunned that I momentarily froze. That's when Olg saved my life, driving his own sword through my assailant's back, just as the Burgundian was lifting his arm to come in for the deadly thrust. The weight of the dead soldier pushed me flat on my back, practically on top of Jehanne under the tarp. To make matters worse, his blood dripped all over me. And Olg did that while holding off another soldier with his dagger. Divine intervention. That's all I can come up with. God placed Olg there to save me and Jehanne.

After we complete the ritual of choosing our weapons, it's time to make a decision about what to do next. I have the advantage. I know exactly where Joan of Arc is supposed to be tomorrow, so I speak up.

"I know we are all tired," I say, "and we need sleep badly, but I think we should break camp and head straight to Sainte-Catherine-de-Fierbois. I feel confident that we will find protection and shelter there for the night, and tomorrow, Jehanne, you will be able to attend mass."

Actually, according to the history books, she will attend three masses tomorrow. It is her way, I know now, of expressing her gratitude for having been spared today.

Everyone readily agrees with my suggestion, and we quickly and efficiently break camp. Olg helps me retrieve the motion sensors, including the one I failed to reset. I hope we won't need them again. I pack them away in my backpack, feeling grateful that my one lapse did not cost any of us our lives.

I pay special attention to Midnight as we all mount our horses and ride straight west. I pat his shoulder to let him know that I am aware of his sacrifices for me. Like the rest of us, he hasn't eaten enough or slept enough, but this wonderful horse has served me well, literally protecting my life. And he did it again today, inciting the rest of the horses to attack the Burgundians in their paths in an astonishing manner, which even these seasoned soldiers have never seen. Surprisingly, none of the horses seem to be faltering now. Perhaps they sense the end of their journey is drawing near. They seem to have been given extra strength.

In fact, in spite of our fatigue and wariness, we all seem to have been given extra strength, extra endurance to push through our exhaustion. I am sobered by the realities of war—which I totally missed on Mont Saint Michel—and I am certainly tired, but I am also exhilarated. We survived an attack when we were outnumbered without one of us being injured, and tonight we will be in Sainte-Catherine-de-Fierbois. And then the day after that, we will be in Chinon.

And there, I hope, I will find Nicolas.

Part Five

I have fought a good fight, I have finished
my course, I have kept the faith.

2 Timothy 4:7

King of England, and you, Duke of Bedford, who call yourself Regent of the Kingdom of France . . . give heed to the King of Heaven, and deliver to La Pucelle, who is sent here by God, the keys to all of the good cities that you have taken and violated in France. She has come here sent by God to reclaim the [throne for] the royal family. She is ready to make peace, if you agree that her cause is just and if you will abandon France and pay amends for your occupation.

And if you are not prepared to do this, wait for word from La Pucelle, who will shortly come to see you to your great misfortune. King of England, if you fail to heed these demands, I am the Chief of War, and wherever I cross your men in France, I will force them out, whether willingly or unwillingly. And if they refuse to obey, I will slay them all. I am sent here by God . . . to drive you out of all of France. And, if they wish to obey, I will show forth mercy . . . You have no other option, for you have not received the right from God to rule France, for King Charles is the true heir . . .

If you refuse to believe this news delivered from God by La Pucelle, we will strike you wherever we find you, and we will cause such an awful din that there has not one like this been heard in France for a thousand years . . .

Excerpts of a letter Joan dictated and sent to the English commanders at Orléans when she arrived in Blois.

Chapter 50

TO HER UTTER ASTONISHMENT, JEHANNE was treated almost like royalty upon her arrival at Sainte-Catherine-de-Fierbois, even though the hour was late. Several of the village men rushed out to greet the bedraggled group of warriors, asking if she was La Pucelle. After her reply in the affirmative, it was as if the heavens opened.

The villagers, proud of their great religious heritage, were grateful to welcome yet another defender of the faith. Her reputation as the Maiden Warrior guided by God had preceded her, and the villagers seemed willing to embrace her claim. They were quickly taken to the rectory, where the village priest and his housekeeper came out with open arms, offering them food and lodging.

"Welcome, welcome to Sainte-Catherine-de-Fierbois," the curé cried out to them as they dismounted. "This village has a long-standing tradition of welcoming great warriors who have fought for God's cause, and so we are humbled by your presence here, for we have heard of your divine charge, Mademoiselle Jehanne. Your fame has spread throughout the land. You are now our honored guests." He quickly directed the men of the village to take their horses and instructed them to respectfully care for those valiant steeds that had borne God's anointed.

When Jehanne asked about God's warriors who had passed before, the curé proudly told her of the fabled grandfather of Charlemagne, Charles Martel, who was said to have buried the sword used in his great victory over the Moors in 732 at the very spot where the church now stood. It made Jehanne's heart skip to realize that she would soon wield this sword.

However, Jehanne was unfamiliar with the second cause of the villagers' inordinate pride.

"Please allow me to show you our greatest treasure," said the priest, as he invited the group to enter the church. He directed them to a little alcove where a beautiful gold reliquary stood behind glass.

"These are the only relics in all of France from Saint Catherine of Alexandria, who was martyred in Egypt nearly a thousand years ago," he explained.

As Jehanne touched the window with her hand, she was overcome with emotion, for Saint Catherine was one of her beloved voices. She knew her story well from the village curé in Domrémy. At the tender age of fourteen, Catherine was converted to Christianity and in turn converted hundreds of others. The little group of Christians was persecuted by the emperor of Egypt, Maxentius, who summoned fifty of his most learned philosophers to refute Catherine's arguments. Several of them, however, were converted by her eloquence and were immediately put to death. The emperor then had Catherine scourged and imprisoned, but even in prison, she converted another two hundred souls from among those who came to visit her, including the emperor's wife. When Catherine refused to forsake her newfound faith, the furious emperor had the virgin beheaded. It was said that eight hundred angels had borne Catherine's body to Mount Sinai, where she was interred. A great monastery was later built over her grave as a shrine to one of Christianity's early martyrs. Jehanne couldn't help but wonder. If she had been in Saint Catherine's position, would she have had her same courage when faced with the threat of death?

"How was such a small church as yours blessed with such an illustrious treasure?" she asked the curé. The priest told her of the other great Christian warrior who had become a patron of their village.

"These priceless relics were a gift from the celebrated knight Jean le Maingre Boucicaut, the former marshal of France. He felt it fitting that these relics be brought here because of the name of our town."

"I fear I have not heard of the man," admitted Jehanne.

"He was born in nearby Tours and was a valiant hero of the joint French-Hungarian crusade against the Ottomans some thirty years ago. While in the eastern lands, Maréchal Boucicaut made a pilgrimage to Mount Sinai to the tomb of Sainte Catherine, where he obtained the relics. He revered her as a martyr and prayed to her. 'Twas he who graced our little church with these precious relics. Many miraculous healings have occurred for the parishioners here because of them."

"Does Maréchal Boucicaut reside here?" she asked. "Could I visit him and thank him for his generous gift? I, too, revere Sainte Catherine. She is dear to me, for I have been guided by her sacred voice, and I would consider it a privilege to speak to one who has actually visited her tomb."

"Alas, my daughter, no. Like you and all of us here today, he too was caught up in this despicable war with the English. He was captured by the Godons at the battle of Agincourt and taken captive to England where he died eight years ago. Fortunately, his remains were returned to his people, and he is buried in the Saint-Martin basilica in Tours, not far from here. Perhaps you could pay homage to him there. You also have him to thank for your quarters tonight. 'Twas he who provided the funds to build our rectory."

"Thank you for your kind hospitality, Monsieur le Curé. I can speak for all of my men in thanking you," Jehanne said. "We have slept upon the damp ground for many nights, and 'twill be a pleasure to sleep in beds."

"Then please allow my housekeeper to show you to your quarters so that you may freshen up before we dine," the curé suggested. "We shall call you down to supper in about an hour. As we speak, the gracious farmers of our village are bringing sustenance so that you might all eat your fill, and their wives are assisting my staff in preparing a fine meal for all of you."

"Father, you have been so kind, and you must find me taxing, but I have one more request. I must ask a special service," Jehanne said to the priest as he directed them back to the adjacent rectory. "Have you a man in the village who could ride this night to Chinon to deliver a missive for the Dauphin Charles? I am anxious to advise him of our imminent arrival."

"Certainly, mademoiselle. I know just the man. He has a fine and fast steed, and he is devoted to God's cause. I shall send for him immediately. When he arrives, I shall have my housekeeper inform you."

"We cannot thank you enough for your kind and generous welcome, Father. We shall remember it always," replied Jehanne.

The housekeeper led them up a flight of stairs to four small and sparsely-furnished rooms. To them, the rooms seemed luxurious, for they each boasted two small beds and a table with a wash basin and a mirror. Although Jehanne wanted nothing more than to invite Katelyn to share a room with her, she knew it would not be fitting, as none but she and Olg knew that Katelyn was a female. Instead, she assigned Olg to share a room with Katelyn and then invited the men to carry one of the beds from her room into the largest room, where Colet, Jean, and Bertrand would sleep. The squires Jean and Julien shared the last and smallest room.

After she had dictated her message for the Dauphin to Jean de Metz, Jehanne retreated to her room for a moment of privacy. She sat at the table and washed her hands and face, covered with the grime of the journey and even the blood of the Burgundian soldier who had attacked Katelyn. Although she had not participated in the battle, she had been the focus of the battle. She had helped bury her enemies and had prayed for their souls. She looked into the mirror at the boyish reflection that faced her. Did God now consider her to be one of His warriors?

Two great Christian warriors fighting for God had left such powerful legacies in this little town, and the relics of one of Christianity's first martyrs sat in its church. Jehanne wished she could leave these humble and welcoming people with some lasting gift, not only to thank them for their hospitality, but also as a witness that she too, was a Christian warrior fighting for God's righteous cause.

She could not build a rectory or bring back relics from the Holy Land like Maréchal Boucicaut, and she could not leave them the sword that stopped the invading Saracen armies like Charles Martel. She could not convert hundreds to Christianity and seal her conviction with her life like Saint Catherine. She certainly had nothing to offer in the way of material things. Would her passage here in Sainte-Catherine-de-Fierbois even be remembered? She knew from Katelyn that as soon as they got to Chinon, she was to send for the sword of Charles Martel. Would actually finding his sword be her legacy for the people of Sainte-Catherine-de-Fierbois? Would it testify to them and to the rest of France that she had truly been sent by God?

With her desire to give back, and also out of deep gratitude for God's assistance throughout their journey, Jehanne had an idea. Katelyn, who always seemed to be inordinately concerned about the date and their exact itinerary, had informed Jehanne while she was dictating her letter that they would tarry the morrow and the following night in Sainte-Catherine-de-Fierbois to await the Dauphin's reply. An entire day and another night in this hallowed place! After their long journey, and after not having been able to attend mass except in Auxerre, Jehanne wished to spend the entire day in grateful worship.

When Jehanne and her companions were called down for supper, she asked the curé if he would consider celebrating not one but three masses on the morrow, inviting all of the inhabitants of the town to attend at least one of those celebrations so that she could mingle with the good townsfolk and thank them personally for their hospitality.

"'Twould be an honor and a privilege," the curé replied. "And I shall invite my assistant and my colleagues from the neighboring villages to assist. And now, please follow me to the dining room. Tonight, we shall dine together, and tomorrow, we shall worship together and thank God for your safe arrival."

That night, for the first time since leaving Saint-Urbain, Jehanne and her companions not only enjoyed a hot meal, but they ate their fill. The only thing that marred the evening for Jehanne was Katelyn's absence. While Jean de Metz, Jehanne, and Katelyn had been working on the message for the Dauphin, Katelyn had informed Jehanne that she wanted to eat privately in her room, and Olg had taken her up a plate.

The good women of Sainte-Catherine-de-Fierbois had outdone themselves. Although it was the middle of Lent—with Easter to fall on the twenty-ninth day of March—the villagers had donated fresh fish caught from the Vienne River, and it was served with roasted cabbage and turnips. In addition, they were served fresh crusty bread and a variety of savory cheeses, which were now allowed during Lent. It was a contrast to the stale bread and moldy cheese they had been eating. The meal was topped off with an apple tart, the likes of which

Jehanne had never before tasted. It was even better than her mother's.

The delectable meal, combined with thirty-six hours without sleep—and a battle in between—left the group physically exhausted. After supper, they did not tarry to visit with the clergyman and villagers but excused themselves with the promise that they would be more social on the morrow. With hardly more than a *bonne nuit*, the seven weary travelers separated, and each fell into a much-needed and well-warranted sleep upon a bed that felt heaven-sent.

As Jehanne hoped, the following day was one that brought a fullness of joy. Once again, the only thing that cast a shadow of sadness on her was that Katelyn did not join her and the others.

"Do you not wish to express your gratitude to the Almighty?" Jehanne asked her that morning when Katelyn informed her she would not be accompanying her to the church.

"Oh, no," Katelyn explained. "It is not that, Jehanne. As I have told you before, I do not wish for my presence with you to be known. The less people see of me, the better it is. So don't worry. My absence has nothing to do with my lack of devotion to God and everything to do with trying to keep a low profile . . . to keep out of sight. I am only trying to do God's will. Remember how I told you that you are never to speak of me? If I am with you all day, people will remember me, and that is not what God or the Archangel desire. That's why I didn't eat with you and the others last night, and I'll repeat that same pattern tonight. Please have Olg bring me up some food as he did last night, for I don't want the housekeeper to see me, and if you have to say anything to anyone, just tell them that one of your comrade-in-arms is under the weather . . . not feeling well," she amended. "I have also asked all of the men to return the sleeping bags and anything else I've given them. I'm sorry I can't let you keep these items, but there would be too many questions, so I'll have to ask you the same thing."

After Jehanne returned Katelyn's marvelous objects, she expressed her disappointment, but also her understanding of Katelyn's situation. She explained to the other members of their party why Kaelig would not be joining them and reminded them not to speak of Kaelig or of 'his' absence. She also instructed Olg to discreetly take her food that evening.

With that issue resolved, the rest of the party adjourned to the church next door. The news of the masses and of La Pucelle's presence had spread, and the village church was already full when they arrived. Jehanne was astonished when she realized that the villagers were clamoring not only to see her, but also to touch her and to speak with her. Initially, it bothered her, for she did not feel worthy of such adulation, but she came to understand that it was because they saw her as an emissary of God. They were honoring her mission, and they were honoring God, not her as an individual. She gloried in sitting in the little church nearly all day long as she greeted people who seemed to delight in her presence, and to celebrate with her fellow travelers and the humble citizens of Sainte-Catherine-de-Fierbois, not just one, but three masses. She always glorified God and His goodness in her heart, but this day, she cherished being able to praise God openly with her full voice.

That evening after the party had retired, the rider who had been sent with Jehanne's letter to Charles returned with the Dauphin's reply. Jehanne was wakened by the curé's housekeeper, who knocked lightly on her door, handed her the letter, and then withdrew.

Jehanne in turn knocked on Katelyn's door, and with no one up and about to witness the subterfuge, Jehanne invited her into her chamber.

"'Tis here," Jehanne said with enthusiasm. "His letter! The Dauphin has actually replied to my request. The day has finally come. Shortly, I will be in his presence and can finally deliver God's message to him. Will you read it to me please, Katelyn?"

"Jehanne," Katelyn replied, taking the letter and breaking the Dauphin's seal, "I just want to warn you. He's not going to make it easy for you. Don't get your hopes up, because I have the strong feeling that he's going to make you wait a while before he sees you."

"Katelyn, why are you being so negative?" Jehanne asked. "You are the one who has instructed me about being confident. Surely, you are not chiding me for my confidence?"

"Oh no, not at all," Katelyn replied with a sheepish look on her face. "But like you, I am guided by my voices, and they wish you to know that you must be patient. Don't give up, but be patient and don't get discouraged. He's going to see you, but it might take a couple of days."

"Well, then," replied Jehanne, "now that I am prepared, let us see what he says."

"Okay, here goes. 'Mademoiselle,' " Katelyn read, " 'It was with interest that I received your request for permission to enter Chinon. I can hardly refuse entrance into the city, for surely you must know that I am a benevolent ruler who respects the freedom of each of my subjects, be they male or even female, and as you have indicated that you have come from Lorraine, I can only surmise that you and your companions are weary. So you are certainly welcome to enter Chinon and here find respite from your travels. Truth be told, word of your journey and of your imminent arrival had already reached our fair city before I received your communication, and I am happy to inform you that a generous innkeeper has offered to provide housing for you and your traveling companions.' Then he goes on to say who that generous host is and where you can find him . . . blah, blah, blah," Katelyn explained as she scanned through the letter. "Okay, now, here we get to the heart of the matter: 'As for your request for an audience, I am certain that you understand that I am a very busy man with many important affairs of state that occupy my time. I will send you word if and when I deem an audience with you is in the realm of possibility.' And he signs it Charles VII."

Jehanne could feel her blood begin to boil. After what she had just been through, this was how she was to be received? She calmed herself and said, "So, Katelyn, if I understand it correctly, the Dauphin will allow me into Chinon because he is a benevolent ruler who allows even his female subjects great freedom. He offers me the hospitality of someone else, claims to be the king already by calling himself Charles VII, even though he has yet to be anointed in Reims, and then has the gall to state that he is too busy to see me because he is involved in important matters of state. Is that correct?"

"That's about it," Katelyn replied. "That's why I tried to warn you to be prepared. Don't worry. I promise you, once you get to Chinon, it will take a couple of days, and then he'll agree to see you. After everything you've been through, what are a couple more days in the eternal scheme of things?"

"You were right, and I was wrong," Jehanne admitted. "I truly thought he would see me immediately. I even thought he would send an escort here to Sainte-Catherine-de-Fierbois. It is so frustrating. I hear that those important matters of state he spends so much time with are nothing more than flitting about among his courtiers playing games of chance and being entertained. Sometimes, I do not understand how God has chosen him to lead France. There, I have said it, and I regret having said it. Katelyn, do not repeat those words to anyone. Please!"

"You don't have to apologize to me," Katelyn assured her. "I won't even tell you what I think about him, but guess what? He's all God has to work with right now. He's the lawful heir to the throne, and for heaven's sake, look at us, Jehanne. We aren't exactly what most men would call brilliant war strategists, are we? But we're also all that God has to work with right now. Whom God calls, he qualifies, so you're just going to have to give the Dauphin a break . . . a chance. When you get to Chinon, just keep asking for an audience. Don't give up."

Jehanne felt her stomach drop at these words, for it sounded as if Katelyn would not be there with her to assist and encourage her. "What do you mean, *I* will just have to keep asking for an audience? You will be at my side, assisting me, will you not? You told me you would not leave until I received the sword."

"Jehanne, I've been thinking about this, and I'm not going to ride into Chinon with you tomorrow. I'm going to leave early in the morning, long before your departure. I don't want to draw any attention away from you, and I especially don't want to attract any attention to myself. What if there are some perceptive people in Chinon who suspect that I'm not who I claim to be? What if they think I'm female? There could be questions, and I don't want to distract anyone from giving you the full attention you deserve. Besides, I told you I have another mission in Chinon, to find Nicolas. I will not be staying with you at the inn in Chinon."

"Nicolas? Is that the name of the man you love?"

"Yes, Jehanne. That's his name."

"Are you going to marry him?" It was not difficult to see how Katelyn's eyes lit up when she mentioned the name of the man she loved. It testified of an intense but different kind of love than what Jehanne felt towards God. A pain pierced Jehanne's heart momentarily, but then it passed.

"I . . . I'm not sure what's going to happen between us, but yes, I think we will eventually get married. I don't know when or where, but first, I have to finish my mission with you and help you with the sword."

"But what about the sword? How am I to obtain the sword? I need your help, Katelyn."

"No, Jehanne, you don't. When you get to Chinon, you are going to cross paths with someone you've never met before, someone who identifies himself as an armorer from Tours. You will make a point of asking him in front of others if he has ever met you before, and when he confirms that you've never met, ask him to ride back to Sainte-Catherine-de-Fierbois. Instruct him to gather the curé and his assistant, as well as the other priests who attended mass with you today, and the villagers as well, for it's important for there to be witnesses. Then, instruct the armorer to state that because of their kind hospitality, they are to once again receive a great honor from God. He must tell them that you've received divine authority to procure the sword of Charles Martel to assist you in your fight to free the nation of France from the Godon invaders. This will be your legacy to them, Jehanne. Their little village will forever be known because you found the sword of Charles Martel there, and with it, you saved France."

These words seared into Jehanne's soul. It was as if Katelyn had read her mind about wanting to leave a legacy for the people of Sainte-Catherine-de-Fierbois. She would honor them with a legacy after all, but it would not be by *leaving* them something, but by *taking* something already precious to them, something which had never been found. The irony was remarkable. Because of her, the legendary sword of Charles Martel would be found, but instead of being left to them, she would use it to accomplish a higher purpose.

"And where will they find it? Where is it, Katelyn?" asked Jehanne.

"Have your envoy invite the priests to dig into the ground behind the altar of the church. That's where they'll find the sword. It will be covered with rust, testifying to the fact that it has lain in the ground for seven long centuries. Instruct him to tell the clergymen to wipe the sword with wet cloths. Incredibly, the rust will fall away, and the sword will appear as if it were brand-new, as a witness of its divine power. Like the relics of Sainte Catherine, the sword has miraculous properties. Once it has been cleaned and seen by the villagers, direct the armorer to come with haste to you at the inn in Chinon. Do you understand?"

"Yes, Katelyn, I understand. And then will you teach me how to access its power?"

"Yes, I'll come see you after you've had your audience with the Dauphin. By then, you'll have the sword. I'll show you how to use its power, Jehanne, and then I'll have to say goodbye to you and our little band of merry men."

"Can you not linger with me longer?" Jehanne asked, as the tears now flowed freely down her face. "What will I do when you leave? How will I know what actions to take?"

"You'll have your voices, Jehanne. But the time will come when even your voices will abandon you. Even the Archangel's voice will be silenced. Just remember when that happens, that it too is God's will. But you'll know what to do. I've said it many times. You're ready for this. You don't need any more assistance or instruction. Even if you never receive another direct message from the heavens, know that you are ready."

"So you are telling me that not only you are going to abandon me, but that my voices will abandon me as well?" asked Jehanne, trying to stem the flow of her tears. "They have guided me from the beginning, and you say they will leave me? I cannot do it without them, Katelyn."

"Yes, you can, Jehanne. You know they spoke to you, and you can't deny that fact. Just know that even if you feel all alone, God has not forsaken you. He will allow you to show your devotion by carrying out His will without any assistance from anyone. But never despair, Jehanne. I've already assured you that I will be with you in spirit, and more importantly, God will never be far from you. He'll give you the strength to do hard things and to face every trial." Katelyn's voice faltered as she said that last word. "You *are* strong enough. You *can* do it. I'll be gone when you get up in the morning, but I promise I'll see you in a couple of days. Show the letter from the Dauphin to Jean, and he'll get you to the inn."

After Katelyn left, Jehanne cried herself to sleep. Yes, it was true that without Katelyn, she had mustered the courage to travel to Vaucouleurs, and so without Katelyn, she could fulfill her destiny, but having one devoted friend who knew the truth about her had been empowering. She had leaned on Katelyn's strength, and now she would have to rely on her own strength. And now it seemed that at some point, even her voices would abandon her.

But in spite of her tears, she knew she could do it. She was ready.

Chapter 51

FROM HIS HIDING PLACE IN THE WOODS east of Chinon, along the north bank of the Vienne River, Nicolas watched for Jehanne and her companions. He also watched for Philippe Montrouge.

Word had spread through the city like wildfire. The Maiden Warrior from Lorraine, about whom rumors had been circulating for days and even weeks, was said to have spent yesterday in Sainte-Catherine-de-Fierbois. She had sent a letter on ahead to Chinon asking for an audience with the Dauphin, and the city was all abuzz with the news.

Nicolas had fortuitously found a blacksmith's forge early that morning in the southeastern outskirts of town and stopped to have his leg iron removed. That unusual request was facilitated by a small gold coin and a promise that the blacksmith could keep the heavy chain as additional payment as long as no questions were asked. Fortunately, the smithy seemed much more interested in the news about the Maiden than about learning why Nicolas had a leg shackle.

"'Tis said her letter stated that she had traveled from Lorraine to come to his aid and to deliver him good tidings," he informed Nicolas.

The smithy was also anxious to share the rumor that La Pucelle, as everyone was calling her, claimed to be the prophesied virgin who would save France.

"'Tis it not exciting? Do you think this maiden could actually do it?" the smithy asked Nicolas.

Nicolas, not wanting to be any more memorable than possible, which was already difficult considering he had a chain attached to his leg, refused to engage in the speculation, but his heart began pounding upon hearing the news. Was today the day that Jehanne would arrive in Chinon?

"I cannot say, kind sir," Nicolas replied. "I have not heard of this maiden, as I have been illegally imprisoned for some weeks by common criminals who have attempted to extort monies from my family. I was fortunate to escape their evil grasp, and now all I wish is to rejoin my family. But, please, may I ask you, what day it is?"

"Why, 'tis Friday," the smithy replied. "The week has nearly ended."

"And do you also know the month and date?" Nicolas asked.

"Happily, we have left the bleak days of February behind, and we have started Lent. 'Tis March, sir, but as for the exact date, I cannot tell you. Perhaps my neighbor, Madame Renard, could enlighten you. I think, if you have another of your golden coins, she could also provide you with sustenance, of which you appear to have some need, for she occasionally provides meals and lets rooms for travelers. I dare say she would even dress your injured ankle." At that moment, the leg iron fell free, and with it, Nicolas felt the weight of the world fall away as well. This was to be a good day, in spite of Abdon's presence.

Nicolas *did* visit the smithy's neighbor and learned from Madame Renard that it was the sixth day of March. It was a miracle that he had escaped on the very morning that Jehanne, and hopefully Katelyn, would be entering Chinon. He acknowledged the

Archangel's assistance in this fortuitous timing. The kind Madame Renard, commenting on Nicolas's sorry physical state, also filled him with a warm meal worthy of Brother Thibault's culinary skills and gave him his fill of cool, clean water. She offered him a tankard of her famous ale, but he declined, wishing to keep his head and faculties clear. He could not afford to have any of his senses dulled with Abdon out there somewhere, remaining a serious threat to both his and Katelyn's safety. Nicolas knew that Montrouge would be furious when he discovered his captive's escape, and his rage was unpredictable. He might just as soon kill the two Watchmen out of pure spite as try to discover their secrets.

He then asked Madame Renard if she would be willing to provide board and lodging for him and a companion for a few days.

"As you have noted," he said, making up the story as he spoke, "I am in a sorry state. I was set upon by some unscrupulous highwaymen, but fortunately, they did not find my hidden stash of coins. I have sent for my younger brother," he explained, knowing that Katelyn would be traveling in male clothing, "but I cannot be certain when he will arrive. He is coming to help care for me and accompany me back home. I am hoping he will arrive today. He will be on horseback. Can you accommodate his horse as well?"

"Yes, my husband has a small barn with a horse and a milk cow in the back. Oh, he will grumble, but as long as you can pay a fair price, he will take in your horse and treat him well. He is actually a good man, mind you, but he does not want others to know that. And as for the rooms, I have two lovely little bedchambers in the attic," she said. "The staircase is narrow, and the steps shallow, but two young people like you and your brother could navigate them without a problem," she said as she led him to the attic, holding tightly to the handrail so that she would not fall.

"The bed in each room is large and could accommodate both of you," she said, "but the rooms themselves are rather small, so you might prefer to have individual rooms. As much as I like you, young man, I would have to charge you double if you took both rooms because my husband would blow his cork at any sign of generosity on my part." Between her high-pitched laugh and her shortness of breath from climbing the stairs, she sounded a bit like a rooster with consumption.

Nicolas actually felt the corners of his mouth turn up at the banter of this pleasant woman who had shown him so much kindness. He glanced into the two rooms, which sat on opposite sides of a narrow hallway. Although he could stand straight up in the hallway, the identical rooms sat under the pitched eaves of the roof, so he had to bend once inside, but they were cheerful rooms, each with a gable window that brought in natural light and improved the space. The beds sat under the slope of the eaves.

As much as Nicolas wanted to take just one room—not for financial reasons, but because his most ardent desire was to share that bed this night—out of respect for Katelyn, he made the only choice possible.

"These will be perfect. I'll take them both," he said, asking her what the cost would be per night for both room and board for two. He counted out the amount she asked for and put the coins into her outstretched hand and then entered one of the rooms. With her watching, he slowly lowered his body onto the simple chair next to the hand-planed table. A pitcher of water and a washbowl sat on the table.

"I would like to freshen up a bit," Nicolas said, "and then I will shortly be going out to meet my brother, but I wonder if I could trouble you for one more thing, Madame Renard. Could you bring me some boiling water and a clean piece of muslin or linen that I could use for bandages? Of course, I will be happy to remunerate you for your kindness."

He did not ask for Madame Renard's help in dressing his ankle injury, having had the importance of properly sterilizing and dressing flesh wounds drilled into him by Katelyn. Besides, he did not want to explain that the festering wound was the result of a leg shackle. Unfortunately, without his knapsack, which had been confiscated by Montrouge, he no longer had any of Katelyn's special cream or sterile gauze to properly care for the oozing wound.

When Madame Renard brought the water, Nicolas stripped and washed his filthy body as best he could. He wished he had a clean change of clothes, for hopefully he would be seeing Katelyn this day and he did not want her to see him like this. But Montrouge had left him with only the clothes on his back.

Once he had bathed, he turned his attention to the ankle wound. It was definitely infected, a word he had learned from Katelyn, but until he could find her and her twenty-first century medicines, there was nothing he could do but clean it with the sterile water and bind it with the clean muslin. Hopefully, he would find Katelyn soon and she would still have some of her healing salve.

After scrubbing himself, applying the clean bandage, and with a full stomach, Nicolas felt better than he had in two weeks. He informed Madame Renard that he would return at some point during the day, and she sent him off with a linen bag full of bread and cheese, and his water pouch refilled with water, chiding him for attempting to walk in his condition.

"Unfortunately," he explained, "my brother will not know where to find me if I do not meet him on the road into town, so I have no choice."

"Well," she replied, "I hope he comes soon so that you might be able to rest your broken body. I wish him and you Godspeed."

Nicolas left the city limits as quickly as his broken toes and throbbing ankle would allow him to move. He knew that the road along the river to the east of Chinon was the route the party would take from Sainte-Catherine-de-Fierbois, and Nicolas wanted to be the first one to greet them to see if Katelyn was among their ranks. He *had* to be the first one to greet them, because otherwise, Katelyn was doomed. However, he stayed in the trees north of the road to work his way east, not wanting anyone to see him, least of all Philippe Montrouge. He found a place where he could sit on a fallen log and where he had a view in both directions but where his presence was hidden by the branches of several small evergreens.

Now, as he sat and watched, Nicolas rubbed his ankle unconsciously, trying to anticipate Abdon's next move. Would he too be waiting along this thoroughfare for La Pucelle's arrival? Nicolas knew it would be some time before Jehanne's group actually arrived, since the records stated that she would enter Chinon around noon. Judging by the shadows, it was now only about nine o'clock in the morning. It was a clear, sunny morning, thankfully free of rain, but in spite of the good weather, except for a few farmers tending to their beasts, he saw no one about. Consequently, he was surprised when he saw a rider approaching from the east at high speed. The rider was clearly on an urgent mission.

He squinted as he saw the figure coming closer and closer. Although it appeared to be a man, there was something about the rider's mannerisms that caught his eye. Then he recognized her cloak and her cap. Yes! Unbelievably, it was Katelyn. Heaven be praised.

He had to calculate his approach carefully, in case Abdon or any of his minions were around. Nicolas did not wish to jump out into the middle of the road to stop her, for it would be a dead giveaway that this was Katelyn Michaels, not some unknown male rider.

As fast as he could, Nicolas gathered all of the pinecones he could find in his forest refuge. If he could hit her hard enough and with enough pinecones, she might stop, but if he missed, he would be forced to call out to her. He could call out the male Breton name, Kaelig, which they had agreed she would use, but it was so close to her real name. Then it dawned on him. He would use the words—she had called it a mantra—that she had mentioned back in her hotel room in the twenty-first century: no time. He could call out the words 'no time' and it would stop Katelyn in her tracks.

As she got close enough for him to hit her, he unleashed the pinecones, but he was still weak after days of penury and torture. She did not even slow down, and so finally, as she pulled abreast of him, he called out as loud as he could the words only she would recognize.

"No time!"

He saw her pull up abruptly and look to her right. She was riding a handsome chestnut stallion, which surprisingly, seemed to be well-fed and well-groomed. He threw another pinecone that hit Katelyn squarely on the head, which allowed her to spot him amidst the underbrush and evergreens. When his eyes met hers, it was if he had received an electrical shock. It was over four years of longing fit into one second of pure joy. In some serendipitous twist of fate, or should Nicolas say divine intervention, they appeared to be the only two people on this road at this particular moment in time. Two people whose fate had been intertwined through war and across space and generations of time, finally finding themselves together again.

"Shhh," Nicolas indicated with his finger, and then motioned for Katelyn to exit the road and ride into the trees as quietly as she could.

As she dismounted, he took her into his arms. It was unbelievable, monumental, and wondrous, in spite of his bruised ribs and battered body. He breathed in the essence of her and touched her face, but as much as he wanted to linger, he knew they needed to get as far away from the road as they possibly could. Philippe Montrouge would be waiting some place along the route for Jehanne's arrival.

"Katelyn, my darling," he whispered, "I am so happy to see you. But true to our code words, we have 'no time' for proper greetings.

We must get off of this road as quickly as possible. Abdon is in Chinon and is awaiting the arrival of La Pucelle."

"What? He's here? Are you kidding?" she said, as she unstrapped the pack that sat on her horse's back. Her modern backpack was covered with a fifteenth-century blanket. Katelyn began to put it on her back, but Nicolas stopped her.

"No, you take the reins, Katelyn, and I'll carry the pack and sit behind you. But we must hurry."

"Nicolas, you look terrible. What happened to you?"

"We will speak of it later. But please, we must leave now."

Katelyn mounted and then extended her hand to Nicolas, who was adjusting the backpack so that it didn't put too much pressure onto any of his ribs, which he suspected had been broken by Abdon's vicious kicks.

"Tell me about Abdon," Katelyn whispered.

"I shall, but first, tell me about Jehanne. Have you been with her? Is she coming as planned?" he asked as he tried to swing his leg over the horse without too much grimacing. Fortunately, the horse did not seem to mind the extra weight. Nicolas settled into his perch behind Katelyn's narrow saddle.

"Yes, she's on her way," she said, as he put his arms snuggly about her waist. "She's pretty amazing, by the way, but I'll tell you all about her later." The feel of her back against his chest was like healing balm, helping him forget the pain of the pack as it pounded against his ribs. "She and the others are about two hours behind me. Nicolas, I can't tell you how relieved I am to see you. I didn't know how on earth I was going to find you, and I've been so worried about you. It just about killed me when we got split up."

"It was fortunate that I prepared you for that reality," he said. "It was the Archangel who gave me that impression."

"Yeah, I was pretty miffed, but it wasn't a total surprise, thanks to you. Anyway, were you able to get the sword buried?"

"Yes, Katelyn. Just as you instructed, behind the altar of the church at Sainte-Catherine-de-Fierbois. And I think I did an excellent job of making it look as if the compacted soil had never been disturbed."

"Fantastic. You're amazing, but are you okay? You look positively emaciated and your face is covered in bruises. Your nose looks terrible, too." She shifted the reins into one hand and then reached her arm backwards over her shoulder to touch his face.

"I am okay now that I have found you. But Abdon jumped on me in the abbey just as I was turning my enseigne. I traveled through the time vortex to the church in Sainte-Catherine-de-Fierbois, and he came through with me. I did not know it was possible, but that is what happened. I shall tell you of my adventures in due time, but what about you? Where did the time key take you? Has everything gone as planned? Are you well?" He poured out the questions as if he had only one chance to get them out.

"Yes. I've got to say that I've been blessed," she answered. "I was taken to Vaucouleurs just as Jehanne arrived for her last attempt to see Robert de Baudricourt. Honestly, I couldn't have done it without the Archangel's help and inspiration. Every preparation he inspired me to make before I came to France was critical to the success of this mission, including the rock climbing and fencing lessons. Then, he helped me figure out how to help her emotionally. Things just fell into place. Jehanne is ready, Nicolas. She's going to be able to do this. It has been so cool to be with her and help her. I'll tell you all about it, but right now I've got to recover from the shock of hearing that Abdon's here. I had a really bad feeling that you were in trouble, that he captured you. I was right, wasn't I?"

"Though I wish I did not have to share that terrible news with you, I fear it is true, Katelyn. I only escaped from him this morning. That is why I want to stay as far from the road as possible. Head straight north through this forest a bit, and we will then turn back towards the west. I think we will be able to avoid him and probably many others who will be coming to meet the famed Maiden Warrior, including, I am certain, the Dauphin's personal guards."

"Are we going into Chinon then?" Katelyn asked. "Do you have a place where we'll be safe?"

"Yes, I have secured lodging with a kind woman I met by divine providence, for I too have received the assistance of the Archangel. I told her I was bringing my brother back with me. I hope that meets with your approval. I knew you would be in male clothing."

He felt her ribs expand, as she had a sharp intake of air, and then she let her breath out slowly.

"Your brother, huh? Yeah, I get it. But right now, I'm not feeling much like your brother, Nicolas."

"Katelyn, I thought it only proper to ask for two rooms." He did not know what she would reply to that, and for a while, they rode in silence.

"I'm just grateful you found us a safe place," she said, avoiding the issue of the two rooms. "I already told Jehanne I wouldn't stay with her at the inn. I didn't want to draw any attention to myself, you know, because of interfering with history and all, but now it sounds like it's even more critical not to be near her because of Abdon. I promised Jehanne I'd stay in Chinon until she gets the sword, so I can help her with my bag of tricks, but after that, I think our mission is over, Nicolas."

"I agree. I think we have accomplished what we were sent to do. Truth be told, I wish we could leave today, because I know Abdon will be ever-present. We will have to be careful, Katelyn, but I agree that we must stay until she has the sword. After all, that was our mission."

"How on earth did you know I'd be coming early today?" she asked.

"I did not know," he admitted. "I knew that today was the date on which Jehanne was to arrive in Chinon. Even if I had not known it from the historical record you required me to memorize, I would have known it from the townsfolk. Everyone is speaking of La Pucelle, the maiden who is on her way to see the Dauphin. Frankly, I just hoped you would be with Jehanne and her group, and I wanted to get here as early as possible and as far from the city as I could to get ahead of Abdon. He has heard of this Maiden Warrior, and thinks *you* are La Pucelle, Katelyn. That is the only advantage we have over him. I am so grateful I was here and that you were early. We may have escaped his grasp today, but I can assure you, 'twill not be easy to stay away from him, for I fear I have angered him a great deal." He winced and audibly groaned when Katelyn knocked his foot as she kicked her stallion's flanks.

"Nicolas, what did he do to you? What happened to you? How did he capture you?" she asked. "And how did you get away?"

"I will tell you about it when we get to our lodging," he said, "but until then, keep your head down and ride as quickly and as quietly as you can."

"Let's stop and trade places," Katelyn suggested. "Since you know where we're going, it'd be better for you to guide Midnight to our destination."

"Ah, Midnight. You have named your horse Midnight," he said.

"Yeah, Midnight," she said, "and just like his American counterpart, he's already saved my life!"

"I cannot wait to hear of your adventures, Katelyn, and as much as I would love to guide your noble stallion, I fear I would be unable to properly motivate him, as my feet are injured. Abdon gave me a memorable gift. He broke my toes, and I fear that if we cannot avoid him as we enter the city, we will both have more injuries to lament."

It was a good thing Nicolas could not envision at that moment the severity of the injuries Abdon was yet to inflict on him.

Chapter 52

WE ENTER CHINON FAR TO THE NORTH of the Vienne River to avoid the main road into the city, as Nicolas suggested, and it works. No Abdon, no royal guards, no enemy soldiers, no questions. Then we head back south to the Renard residence, reaching it from the rear. A neat and sturdy barn sits behind the house, and as we dismount, a man walks towards us. He looks to be in his sixties, has a scowl on his face, and he's carrying a pitchfork. I hope he's friendlier than he looks.

"You must be Monsieur Renard," Nicolas calmly says as he dismounts. I can see him wince as his feet touch the ground, but he's trying hard not to let his pain show.

"That is who I be," the scowling man replies without offering any other information.

"Did your wife tell you that she let out your rooms and that our horse is in need of care and shelter? We will pay a fair price, of course." I can see the man's scowl visibly relax as Nicolas says the word 'pay.' I dismount as well, and pat Midnight reassuringly. He has already killed for me, but I don't want him to kill my host.

"Yes, young man," Monsieur Renard affirms. "She done told me, all right. That woman manages to take in more strays than the Dauphin takes in flatterers. But as long as you can pay, I have no objections." He looks at Nicolas as if he is waiting for something. "With strangers a comin' and a goin' now that our poor excuse for a king has taken refuge here, I am not wont to lend my services until I know a body can pay," he adds.

"Certainly," replies Nicolas. He turns away from the man, and reaches inside his trousers, probably to that secret pocket I showed him in his long underwear. He looks at me as I watch him. I can't help but grin. My unashamed gaze is making him uncomfortable, and that makes me smile.

"I hope this will be enough of a guarantee to engage your kind services, sir," Nicolas says as he turns back to the man and hands him a small coin.

"Aye," says Monsieur Renard, "just as long as this here coin has a twin." Wow, this guy doesn't mince his words. Nicolas's description of the 'kind woman' who had rented us rooms obviously doesn't apply to her husband. I reluctantly hand him Midnight's reins after Nicolas gives me a reassuring nod.

I take the pack that Nicolas has placed on the ground, and though I know he wants to take it from me, I also know that right now, I'm in a lot better shape than he is. Besides, I'm not a helpless woman. I'm his little brother.

As we approach the house, Madame Renard comes out to greet us. I'm glad to see that she, unlike her husband, has a smile on her face.

"Ah, welcome back, Nicolas. I see you found your brother. 'Twas faster than expected, *n'est-ce pas?*"

"Yes, Madame Renard, this is Kaelig. He did arrive earlier than expected."

I nod my head in greeting, reluctant to speak because of my imperfect and accented French. How do we explain that we're brothers when I don't sound anything like Nicolas? He seems to understand, for immediately he says, "I'm afraid Kaelig is suffering from aphonia and cannot speak." I have no idea what aphonia is, but I assume I'm either mute or have laryngitis. I hope it's just the latter. Anyway, I'll have to ask him about that later.

"I assure you that Kaelig is grateful to you for taking us in, as am I. If it meets with your approval, we would like to stay three nights in your kind care."

"'Twould give me great pleasure, gentlemen," she replies, as she leads us into her home. "I have three sons of my own, and they have been gone from the family home for many long years, so 'tis wonderful to have young people under my roof again."

"We appreciate your hospitality," Nicolas replies and then adds, "Kaelig and I have both been without sufficient sleep for several days, and I think we shall retire now for a rest. I have the bread and cheese you gave me for lunch, but tonight, we would appreciate a hot meal, if that is possible."

"Absolutely," she replies. "As we are in the Lenten period, 'tis fish tonight, but tomorrow and Sunday are feast days, so I can offer you more substantial meals. And 'twill give me great pleasure to cook for men who actually appreciate my culinary skills," she says, as she looks accusingly at her husband.

"That will be wonderful. Thank you," Nicolas says as he leads me up a steep and narrow staircase. The steps are only about eight inches deep, so I really have to struggle to keep my balance while wrestling with the backpack. Nicolas reaches out to help me, but I won't let him. I mean who helps his little brother walk up stairs? I don't think you'd see me doing that with Jackson unless he was seriously injured. Besides, I know Nicolas *is* seriously injured. I'm grateful I still have most of my first aid supplies, because I think I'm going to need them.

When we reach the hallway at the top of the stairs, he opens the door, instructing me to take that room, and now that we're out of Madame Renard's sight, I take his hand and draw him into the room.

Without even thinking about how it might appear, I gently push him on the shoulders so that he sits down on what is supposed to be my bed.

"Okay," I say to him in English, before he misreads my action. "I can tell by the way you're moving that you've got some pretty extensive injuries, and it's not just your toes." I can hardly hold in my anger. This is what Abdon did to him. I'm anxious to hear more about Abdon's newest host, but right now, I just want to take care of Nicolas. "Strip to your skivvies, Nicolas. I need to see what that monster did to you."

"Katelyn," he protests. "I am okay."

"Oh, for heaven's sake," I say, "I've seen you in your underwear before, so just do as I say. In fact, I'll do it." As I gingerly strip off his clothing, I'm not prepared for the shock. His torso, front and back, is black and blue. It's all I can do to keep my cool. I press gently on his ribs, and he winces in agony. He definitely has some breaks. I can't believe he can even breathe. I once cracked a rib from a fall when I was skateboarding as a kid, and I could hardly take a breath. I'm amazed he was able to ride today.

"He kicked you, didn't he?" I ask the obvious as I discard his clothing onto the floor, and he nods his head.

"Katelyn, get my enseigne and other coins from the pocket of the long underwear," he asks.

I retrieve the metal objects and take the opportunity to examine the jobber's mark on the back of his enseigne. I think, like mine and Jean's, that his is also a Hebrew letter, but I haven't memorized the alphabet, so I'll have to check it out when I get back to my computer. I sear the mark into my brain so that I'll remember it.

T

I recall meeting with Herr Dreyer, the German teacher back home, and thinking then that the symbol on Nicolas's key was the final clue I needed to make a word from the letters on our enseignes. I'll have to work that out later. Right now, I've got more pressing issues, like can Nicolas survive all this damage to his body? I worry there could be internal bleeding, maybe a ruptured spleen, from so much abuse, but all I can do is take care of the injuries I see and rely on the Archangel.

"And what about this bandage on your ankle? What's this from? Tell me what happened to you," I say as I press him gently down onto his back so that I can lift his equally bruised legs up onto the bed. I gingerly remove the muslin bandage from his ankle to uncover a festering open sore that covers the entire front part of his lower shin. While he begins his account of all that's happened to him since we got separated, I get my first aid supplies and begin to clean and dress the wound, which he insists he just cleaned this morning. It is covered in fresh pus, and I slather on the Neosporin.

As Nicolas tells me about Abdon's new host, Philippe Montrouge, and about being taken prisoner by him, I can hardly keep from crying. Here I've been complaining about eating cold food, sleeping on the hard ground, and surviving an attack from a few Burgundian renegades while Nicolas has been systematically tortured and starved day after day.

His toes are so bruised that they're practically black, and several are misshapen. As he groans in agony, I do my best to realign them and tape them so that hopefully the bones will heal properly. I try to appear unfazed for his sake, but it's all I can do to keep myself from gagging. I've never seen so many injuries on one person, and I can't believe he actually survived this kind of trauma. This must be what it's like to work in an emergency room, but while it's one thing to take care of injuries, it's an entirely different thing to take care of injuries on a person you love. I can hardly bear it. I can see why doctors are told not to care for their own family members.

When he explains how he managed to escape this morning, I finally lose it. I don't want to hurt him, but I just want nothing more than to take him in my arms and offer him any comfort I can. But his body is so battered that I hardly dare touch him, let alone hug him.

After I've bandaged his toes, I turn my attention to his face, and I feel him relax. His nose looks like it's been broken, but there's not much I can do about that now. He closes his eyes as I gently apply the remainder of my Neosporin to the newer abrasions, and then I run my hands over his head and scalp. I find a bunch of lumps covered in dried blood. As carefully as I can, I lift his head and try to clean away the blood with some baby wipes. His breathing is slowing down, and he looks as if he's practically asleep.

There is only one positive thing about his condition that I can see. For some reason, the only part of his body that has been spared are his hands, and it seems as if that is yet another of our many tender mercies, because he could never have escaped if his fingers had been broken.

I can tell that he's completely and totally spent. He used every ounce of energy he had left to find me, and I know he stayed alive to protect me. He's just incredible.

"Nicolas, I am so sorry," I whisper the only words I can as I take his hand in mine. "I'm just so grateful you survived and that you had the presence of mind to find me. Now, you've got to sleep. That's the best thing you can do for your body to heal."

I cover him with a blanket folded at the foot of the bed, and then I lower my head and touch my lips to his. It's the first time I've initiated a kiss, and he opens his eyes and pulls my face in closer. It is not a passionate kiss, for my beloved Nicolas is not capable of passion in his current condition, but it is a kiss that conveys more love than I ever imagined possible. This is the man I love. I know it, and I also know that I want to be with him for the rest of my life. There will never, never be anyone but Nicolas for me. I don't know what that means right now, because I also know I have to go back to my father and Adèle, who are waiting for me on Mont Saint Michel. I have to go back to my mother and Jackson in the United States. I could never hurt them by just disappearing. I have to at least finish high school, and then, whether it's in the fifteenth century or in the twenty-first century, Nicolas and I will be together. We *have* to be together. There is no other possibility.

Even though I know I'm legally married to him in the eyes of the Catholic Church and the townsfolk of Mont Saint Michel, I need to marry this man in a ceremony that feels legally binding to *me*. I need to feel married, and I need to have my parents' blessing. I know it won't be easy. After all, I'm only eighteen years old, and they don't have a clue I'm in a relationship. There's nothing about it on my Twitter account or Instagram. I mean, how can I tell them why I even know Nicolas in the first place? And honestly, I'm going to tell them that I'm marrying someone I've only known for a few months? At age eighteen? I can just hear my parents' arguments now.

"Katelyn, nobody knows who they are at eighteen years of age. It's impossible," my pragmatic father will say. "That's the mistake I made. Your mother and I were too young when we got married. Besides, what about your education? What about swimming in college? That has always been your dream. What about your future? You've said and done plenty of crazy things in your life, but this takes the cake. It's simply ridiculous, and I won't let you throw your life away." He certainly can't criticize me for following my heart, since that's exactly what he did with Adèle, so he'll just focus on the rational and logical approach.

My mother, on the other hand, will go ballistic. She has already lost her husband to some unknown Frenchwoman. "Katelyn," she'll say, "how can you possibly abandon Jackson and me to marry someone you've only known for a few days (because, of course, she doesn't know just how long I actually *have* known him). A Frenchman? Are you kidding? You don't even know this guy. What is it with the French and our family, for heaven's sake? They must be mind-controllers. You're going to throw your life away for some Frenchman that doesn't even have any college education? At least you could choose a doctor or a lawyer, but no, you're just going to follow your heart. Just like your father. You're going to leave me just like your father did? I can't bear it."

Frankly, I can't bear it either. I can't bear hurting them, but I have no choice, because it's even harder for me to consider my life without Nicolas in it. I know I'm only eighteen years old, but honestly, I feel like I've lived double that number of years in the past six months. In fact, right now, I feel like I'm about eighty instead of eighteen. For heaven's sake, I've saved Mont Saint Michel from one of Satan's minions, and not the cute yellow kind. I've escaped from Richard Collins and the Godons. My life has been threatened by Abdon and by plenty of enemy soldiers, both English and Burgundian. I've been gravely injured and had to work my way back to good health. I've seen people die, and I've even had to help bury my assailants. Worst of all, though, is that I've seen a man I deeply loved and respected, Jean le Vieux, give his life to save mine. But Mom and Dad don't know any of that.

And now, I've seen what it took for Nicolas to stay alive to save my life as well. I don't need five or ten more years to figure this out. Nicolas is my destiny. I don't know how I'm going to get my parents to understand it, especially if I have to go back in time and leave them to be with Nicolas. But none of those issues are more important than the fact that I love this man, and I know beyond a doubt that I cannot live without him.

"Katelyn," he whispers from his semi-sleeping state, "I love you. One day we will be able to talk about our future, but for now, I just have to tell you how I feel. I love you." With that, he turns his head and falls into a deep and silent sleep.

I need to make certain that the sword is delivered to Jehanne, because I've got to get Nicolas back home.

Chapter 53

THE DAUPHIN KNEW THAT LA PUCELLE WAS not pleased about his delay in granting her an audience. She had arrived in Chinon at noon with much fanfare and excitement on the part of the townsfolk. However, the supposed 'Maiden Warrior' immediately began to assert a foolhardy, unwarranted authority. She had sent to him immediately to grant her an audience that very afternoon, but his advisors thought it imprudent to accede to her demands straightaway.

Before her arrival, when her missive to him had arrived from Sainte-Catherine-de-Fierbois, he had gathered his advisors.

"I need your counsel," he had told them. "I am aware that news of La Pucelle has spread throughout France, and I do not wish to give her more attention than necessary, but neither do I wish to raise the ire of my subjects. I wish to read to you her audacious communiqué."

" 'Sire, I have journeyed a hundred and fifty leagues from Lorraine to come to your aid and I bear you many good tidings,'" the Dauphin had read. Immediately, his counselors had informed him that she had obviously dictated the letter, because they had heard from reliable sources that the girl herself was not even literate.

" 'I come not of my own volition,'" he had continued, " 'but I am sent here by God to come to the aid of this great nation of

France, which has been beset with enemies and false claimants. I come to you with two mandates from the King of Heaven. The first is to raise the siege of Orléans, for I am come to lead your armies as Chief of War. In whatever place I find the English in France, I will make them leave it, willingly or unwillingly. And if they will not obey, I will have them all killed; I am sent by God, the King of Heaven to, body for body, drive the English out of all of France.'"

"Ah, all she wishes is to be your Chief of War? That is certainly unassuming," Duke Jean II d'Alençon, the Dauphin's cousin and one of his military commanders, had said sarcastically. "So, she is going to do what none of us trained generals have been able to do after decades of fighting? This maiden who can neither read nor write? 'Tis laughable. Read on, Sire."

" 'The second mandate is to lead you, my King, to Reims for your coronation and anointing, for I am come to uphold the royal bloodline of France. The Kingdom will be held by you, King Charles, the true heir; for God the King of Heaven wills it, and so it is revealed by the Maiden. I know you are the rightful heir to the throne, and as such, though I have never seen you, I shall recognize you immediately, though you be surrounded by your subjects, for the great God of Heaven has given me the clarity of mind to know and recognize your face.' So then she goes on to insist that I grant her an immediate audience upon her arrival in Chinon. What think you all?" Charles had asked.

"What gall, what impudence," Simon Charles, the master of the Court of Requests, had said. "Who does this child think she is to order you about as if you were *her* subject? Sire, what message would you be sending to the people if you grant her access to you immediately? That you believe her claims? That you are desperate for the help of a simple peasant girl? No, 'twould be a grave mistake to show weakness of any kind. Grant her entrance to the city, yes, but not an audience. At least, not directly."

"One of Chinon's innkeepers has kindly offered her and her group lodging at his expense, so you can offer her hospitality in the city without having to grant her an audience," Count Louis de Vendôme had said, "and we will not even have to open our coffers. You will appear generous to your subjects but not foolhardy."

"Yes," his other counselors had agreed. "Allow her to enter Chinon, and invite her to stay at the inn, but do not grant her an immediate audience. Wait for a day or two, and then you can grant an audience."

Charles had sent her his reply with the rider from Sainte-Catherine-de-Fierbois, stating that Jehanne was welcome to enter Chinon and enjoy the hospitality of the local innkeeper, but without any promises of acceding to her demands of an audience. That had been easy enough to do, but since then, things had become more complicated. By separate route, a messenger from Robert de Baudricourt arrived, bearing the commander's written endorsement of La Pucelle's mission and his strong encouragement to the Dauphin to give heed to the Maiden's message.

Then, the captain of the King's guard arrived with more astonishing news. "I am told that the commander of the French forces defending the besieged city of Orléans has heard the news about La Pucelle. Today, two of his emissaries passed through enemy lines to obtain more information about the girl. They are anxious to hear your assessment of her, Sire, and are looking for help from any quarter."

Late Friday afternoon, after refusing to grant her an audience that day, the Dauphin once again gathered his advisors, some of whom had paid impromptu visits to the inn where the maiden was staying, just to get a glimpse of her.

"Sire," Duke Jean II d'Alençon announced, "I have seen the maiden, and she is nothing but a girl dressed in male clothing. She appears neither intelligent nor skilled in the arts of war. I cannot fathom what all of the fuss is about. However, 'tis true that the city is abuzz about her and her supposed mandate from God, and 'twould be a mistake to reject her out of hand, for some of your subjects might infer that you reject God Himself. I suggest you first have the clerics and a chosen group of men of the Church examine her. Let them decide if she is worthy of your time."

"Yes, that is precisely what I shall do," the Dauphin replied. "If the clerics feel she is a fraud, then I have not sullied my reputation by entertaining her strange notions, and if they find her story credible, then I have only done the bidding of God's anointed servants."

"But I have another idea, as well," the Dauphin continued. "If the clerics deem her worthy of my time, I shall grant her an audience on Sunday afternoon. Then I will show her for the fool she is by using her own words against her. In her first missive, she claimed that she will know my identity though she has never met me. 'Twould be easy to pick me from a crowd, for my manner of dress and the deference with which others treat me would give away my identity immediately. But what if I exchange clothing with one of my courtiers, place him on my throne in the audience hall, invite a crowd of people to join us, and then order them not to pay me any special heed or reverence? Surely, in those circumstances, she will not know me, and then I will have a legitimate reason to discredit her assertions."

"Masterful," invoked one advisor, Lord Raoul de Gaucourt.

"Genius, Sire," cried Guillaume Gouffier, Lord of Boisy and chamberlain for Charles.

"Worthy of your superior intelligence," said Jean d'Alençon.

"Yes, Sire," stated Louis, Count of Vendôme, "'tis the perfect solution. But I must admit that I am hoping the clerics find no fault in her, for I, for one, am interested in what the lass has to say. If there is anything she can do to help us fight off the scourge of these hated Godons, we must not discount her without careful consideration."

"'Tis decided, then," the Dauphin announced. "Louis, send the clerics to interrogate her, and if she passes their examination, arrange for a large gathering of my courtiers, local nobility, and my men-at-arms to meet on Sunday afternoon in the Great Hall. There, I will change places with one of my courtiers, and the maiden shall be put to the test."

However, the Dauphin's counselors did not know that Charles had a more private and personal test to which he would subject La Pucelle. And her answer to this test, which was the desire of his heart that he had only expressed to God in secret prayer, was about to change the world.

Chapter 54

IT WAS A CLEAR SUNDAY AFTERNOON IN early March. The waning sunbeams lit the creamy white façade of the royal fortress, creating a brilliant reflection in the Vienne River. It took Jehanne's breath away. It was as if she were bathed in heavenly light. She took it as a sign. This was the most important moment in her seventeen years of life. Today, she would either convince the Dauphin that she had been sent by God, or he would send her away in disgrace.

As she crossed the bridge alone, wound through the narrow streets of the town, and then headed towards the steep passageway to the entrance of the chateau fortress, she thought of everything Katelyn had said to her, and she prayed for the guidance of the Archangel. Jean de Metz and the other men had volunteered to go with her, but she had rejected their offers, stating that this was something she had to do on her own, just as Katelyn had advised her to do. She could no longer lean on them or on Katelyn for assistance and advice.

As she approached the bottom of the hill, a middle-aged man emerged from a guardhouse.

"*Bonjour, mademoiselle. Je m'appelle* Simon Charles. I am Master of the Court of Requests," he said. "I assume you are the maiden Jehanne La Pucelle?"

"That is correct. Since you are the Master of the Court of Requests, you are well aware of the fact that the Dauphin agreed to give me an audience today, and as you see, I have come alone, for I fear neither you, nor him, nor his many cohorts. I come with a message from God to be delivered directly to the King, for that is his true title. Will you please escort me into his presence?" she ordered in a firm voice, acting confidently, as Katelyn had taught, even though she quivered inside with fear.

"Yes, mademoiselle, that is why I am here waiting for you. I will take you up to the fortress where you will be met by Louis, the Count of Vendôme, who is waiting to usher you into the audience hall." Without another word, Simon Charles led Jehanne up the hill through a series of gates, drawbridges, and watchtowers. When they finally reached the plateau, she relished the warmth of the sun on her face, which renewed her confidence and gave her added confirmation that God was with her. A small flock of black sheep nibbled on the tender blades of green grass planted in neatly sectioned rectangles surrounded by gravel pathways. She noticed that leaf buds were beginning to form on the trees that dotted the grounds. Spring was nigh. A waft of the sweet smell from a clump of purple crocuses instilled her with a sense of burgeoning hope and the confirmation in her soul that her long winter of doubt and dejection was over.

As they walked, Simon Charles informed her that the fortress was composed of three separate sections, Saint-Georges, Le Milieu (so called because it was the middle section), and Coudray. The royal apartments were in Le Milieu. These three sections were connected by bridges. He also gave her some background about the man she was about to meet: Louis, born of the noble Bourbon family, the Count of Vendôme and Castres, her escort.

"I believe you will find," he said, "that although you have never met Count Louis, he will be one of your ardent supporters. He most gladly supports anyone opposed to the English occupation, for there is no love lost between him and the Godons. You see, he was captured by them at the Battle of Agincourt and held in England for several years. He is a great supporter of the Dauphin and the Duke of Orléans, and he has expressed his willingness to meet you. I know he will have an open mind about you."

With that bit of encouraging news, Simon Charles tapped on the ground-level door of the royal apartments. Out stepped a regal-looking man in his middle years: Louis of Bourbon, the Count of Vendôme.

"Welcome, Jehanne La Pucelle," he said as he bowed to her in a surprising show of humility. "I have the privilege of escorting you into the audience hall to meet the Dauphin. Please, come with me," he said as he placed her hand on his arm and led her into a vast hall. He did not seem to mind the fact that she was dressed as a male but instead treated her with the decorum warranted for a woman of noble birth. Jehanne liked him immediately.

There must have been over four hundred people packed into the hall. Katelyn had warned her that many of the Dauphin's supporters would be there to watch the 'spectacle,' but she had no idea that there would be this many people. The Count removed her hand from his elbow, bowed to her slightly, and then pushed her forward into the crowd. As the people became aware of her presence, all eyes turned and immediately focused on her. A corridor in the center of the crowd immediately opened up, leading to a dais on which a man in regal dress sat on a throne.

She did not even bother to approach the pretender but started looking through the wall-to-wall people. She worked her way through the crowd to the perimeter of the hall, sometimes standing on her toes to improve her view. And then, there he was, a younger version of the painting Katelyn had shown her. He was dressed in simple clothes unbefitting a king, but she knew nonetheless. She met his eyes, and the Archangel confirmed it to her by a burning in her bosom that she could not deny. This was the man for whom she had sacrificed her happy life with her family in Lorraine. This was the man whom God had foreordained to lead France during the era when the English yoke would be forever cast off. He did not look especially commanding or noble. He did not appear authoritative or formidable, but then, neither did she. What was it Katelyn had said? Whom God calls, He qualifies.

She approached him and took his hand in hers and then fell to her knees in obeisance.

"In God's name, noble prince, it is you and none other. Noble Dauphin, I am called Jehanne La Pucelle, and the King of the Heavens sends a message to you through me. You will be anointed and crowned in the city of Reims, and you will be the lieutenant of the King of Heaven, who is King of France."

The Dauphin looked at her in astonishment and began peppering her with questions as the onlookers clustered about them, straining to hear the exchange. After answering several of his questions simply and to the best of her ability, Jehanne finally said, "Noble Dauphin, I perceive that there is a pressing matter about which we must speak in confidence. Perhaps 'tis best for us to leave this assembly and entertain these concerns in private."

At this, the Dauphin knitted his sparse brows together and looked at her with what she surmised as pure amazement. Charles nodded to the man standing at his elbow, whom Jehanne later learned was his chamberlain, Guillaume Gouffier, Lord of Boisy. Gouffier led the Dauphin and Jehanne through the throng, which quickly separated to allow the trio free passage out of the packed hall.

"Guillaume," the Dauphin said when they found themselves in a quiet hallway, "I wish to speak with this young woman alone in my study. Please see to it that we are not interrupted."

"But, Sire," Guillaume replied, "are you certain you do not require my presence? Do you truly wish to be alone with this unknown visitor . . . without any protection?"

"Not to worry," the Dauphin said. "No harm will come to me. Please ensure that we are not interrupted." With that, Guillaume led the two through a short hallway until they had reached the study. He opened the door and bid them enter.

"Sire, I shall be just outside should you require any assistance."

"Thank you, Guillaume. Now leave us," was the Dauphin's only reply.

After the Dauphin closed the door firmly, he ushered Jehanne to the far end of the well-appointed room, away from the door and listening ears. However, he remained standing and did not offer her a seat. The sun, dropping closer to the horizon, beamed directly in through the undraped window, imprinting the checkerboard pattern of the paned window onto the stone floor. Dust motes glittered as they moved in and out of the patch of light, adding an even more ethereal feel to the already transcendent setting.

Jehanne could hardly take in the fact that after all of these years of preparation, after all these months of trying to get someone to pay her heed, after all the doubters, naysayers, and critics who had denounced her claims as childish rubbish, and after her long and arduous journey from Lorraine, she was finally here. She had succeeded. All the years of hardship, of preparation, all the teachings of her voices, and all of Katelyn's preparation had led to this one pivotal moment in time. This was her one opportunity to convince the Dauphin that she had indeed been sent of God to assist him. And Charles himself had invited her into this secluded setting to converse with her in private.

In a single second of time, she poured out a hundred supplications for divine assistance and a thousand expressions of gratitude for God's aid in bringing her this far. She prayed a million prayers for the courage to do all she had been commanded to do, and a trillion pleas for the strength to face the persecutions she knew would be poured out upon her. And in the next instant, she felt the peace and love of Almighty God surround her, protect her, strengthen her, and enlighten her. She *could* do this. She *was* ready, just as Katelyn had told her. And she *could* do it all on her own.

"Now, what is this pressing matter of which you speak?" the Dauphin asked her sharply. As Katelyn had warned, she perceived that Charles was doing everything in his power to somehow trap her in her own words.

"You misunderstand, Sire," Jehanne said with a new-found boldness. "'Tis not *I* who has the pressing matter to discuss, rather 'tis your Royal Highness who has the pressing matter to discuss. I know, noble Prince, that deep in your heart, you wish to question me about a deep concern of your heart. A private concern. A concern about which you have spoken to no other human soul. I am ready to give you the answers for which you have fervently prayed."

Again, Jehanne read upon his face a look of pure, undiluted astonishment. At first, he appeared as if he were about to protest, but then she saw a softening in his eyes, as if the warming sun hitting his face had also warmed his resistant heart.

He looked down at his feet and rubbed his hands together, as if that action would somehow give him the courage to be completely candid. At last, he spoke.

"I grant you confirmation of what you state, mademoiselle. One might argue that you have the gift of discernment, but are you divinely inspired? That, I do not know, but I will reserve my judgment for now. It is true that I have a matter that constantly presses upon my heart and mind. Some time ago, I offered a private prayer to God. If you are truly a messenger from the Almighty, if you truly hear the voices of His servants, then surely this would not be asking something impossible of you. I wish for you to tell me what I asked for in that prayer."

"Certainly, Sire," she replied without a second's hesitation. "Not only can I tell you exactly what you asked for in that prayer, but I can even tell you when you offered that prayer. It was on All Saints Day, the first day of November in 1428."

As Jehanne contemplated the Dauphin's reaction, she saw a slight tic in his right eye, contracting the muscle in his eyelid at regular intervals. He looked at her, trying to keep the look of total disbelief off his face, but it was easy to read. However, he did not acknowledge whether or not she had been right about the date, which Katelyn had told her to memorize.

"Continue," he said, looking at her with such intensity that she felt as if his eyes would burn holes in her own. The tic was still there. "And for what did I pray?"

"Gentle Prince, you asked God to allow you to gain the throne if you *are* the rightful heir, the legitimate son of your father, King Charles VI. And there is one more thing. You also asked God to punish you for all of the suffering caused by your efforts to claim the throne if you are *not*, in fact, the rightful heir."[3]

With these words, the Dauphin spontaneously fell to his knees, and Jehanne, not wishing to be guilty of one of the ultimate improprieties of standing higher than the king, also dropped to her knees.

"I have never told a single soul about that prayer," Charles admitted. "I have never wanted anyone to know that I have any doubts about my parentage. Since you have not only told me exactly

---

[3] For more information about why the Dauphin was so worried about being the legitimate heir, read *Katelyn's Historical Commentary* at the end of the book.

that for which I prayed, but also the very date on which I uttered that prayer, I have no choice but to believe that you have indeed been mandated by God Himself to come to my assistance. And now, I ask you for God's reply to that question," he said, as he took Jehanne's hand in his own, as if by touching her, he could somehow influence her answer. "Am I truly the son of King Charles?"

"Sire, you *are* his son. You *are* the rightful heir to the throne of France, just as I told you in my dispatch to you, for God Himself has declared it. The Kingdom will be held by you, King Charles, the true heir; for the King of Heaven wills it, and so it was revealed to me. I am sent here by God Himself to save all of France from the traitors and false claimants who would have it ceded to England. I am come to uphold the royal bloodline of France and you, my King, are the rightful heir. With your support, I will raise the siege of Orléans, thus clearing the route to Reims of your enemies so that you may be consecrated there, where previous kings of France have received God's mandate of heaven. There you will be anointed with the holy unction and receive the Divine Right to rule. For this to be achieved, you must straightway make me your Chief of War, as I so entreated in my dispatch. I must be sent immediately to Orléans, there to perform my duty in lifting the siege."

At this, Charles rose and pulled Jehanne to her feet, as well.

"Thank you, Mademoiselle Jehanne," he said with a warm and sincere smile on his face. Jehanne could see that her message had completely transformed him. It was as if her words had permeated him with a peace of mind that had always been missing, infusing his very essence with an energy that changed his entire countenance.

"You have truly given me a new hope in what I otherwise found to be a hopeless world," the Dauphin continued, "but I beg you to comprehend that although I now fully embrace your message and your mission, I must proceed with caution. My acceptance of you may be ill-perceived by my advisors and supporters, particularly by my generals and military commanders, as I am certain you can well imagine. You must remember that my father—and do not misunderstand how grateful I am to know that he was indeed my father—was one who unfortunately suffered from fits of madness, and I must do all in my power not to let my behavior in any way appear to be judged as a manifestation of madness to others. I must proceed in a logical, not a reactive, manner. So, in order to appease them, I would ask for your patience for a few weeks longer. My advisors have suggested to me that in addition to the clergymen who questioned you here in Chinon yesterday, you be sent to Poitiers, there to be examined further by the clergy of that fair city. In the meantime, I wish for you to stay here at the chateau so that we may have further discussions about your proposed objectives. Will you agree to this?"

"Sire, I have waited many long years to deliver my message and to begin my campaign against the English. I suppose I can wait another few weeks, but you must understand that I am anxious to join the troops at Orléans. It is God's will that I go there in haste."

"Yes, mademoiselle. I shall keep this constantly in mind and will do all in my power to expedite matters."

"There is just one more thing, Sire. I have traveling companions who await me at the inn where we have been so kindly lodged. May I be allowed to send for them? I do not propose extending your kind hospitality to lodge them here, as they are several in number and most are wont to return to their own homes, but I do wish to thank them for their service and to bid them adieu now that our journey is over."

"Certainly, mademoiselle. I will place you in the hands of the master of my household, Guillaume Bellier, and instruct him to send for your companions. Please, take a seat while I send for him."

Charles opened the door and gave the message to Guillaume Gouffier to send immediately for Bellier, while Jehanne sat on an ornately hand-carved chair appointed with silk cushions, the likes of which she had never before seen.

"Thank you, Sire. My men have served me loyally, and I would not want them to leave without my being able to express my love and appreciation for their many sacrifices."

"Mademoiselle," the Dauphin said, as he turned back to Jehanne and sat down in a chair facing her, "there is another point of interest about which I would like to speak. My advisors tell me that there was some fuss this morning in town about a sword. A sword that you sent for in Sainte-Catherine-de Fierbois? They tell me that you declared to the gathered townsfolk that it is the sword of Charles Martel. I am at a loss to understand this news. Can you explain your claims to me?"

"Certainly, Sire. What I said this morning is true. I am in possession of the sword that belonged to Charles Martel. With this sword, I will lift the siege at Orléans."

"And how is it, may I ask, that you have acquired such a relic as Martel's sword?"

"Sire, my voices instructed me how and where to find the sword. Martel himself buried it behind the altar of the church in Sainte-Catherine-de Fierbois as an offering to God for having assisted him in defeating the enemies of God and of France."

"Your voices told you where to find the sword?" the Dauphin asked with a measure of incredulity.

"That is correct, Sire, just as they told me of the concerns of your heart. As you well know, Charles Martel was a great defender of our faith and of our nation. With that sword, he defeated the Saracen invaders who threatened all of Christendom, and with that same sword, I shall drive out the English invaders. With it, I will call down the very powers of God Himself."

"My dear," he replied, "I am beginning to believe that you are capable of just about anything, in spite of your less-than-inspiring appearance. I shall instruct Guillaume to consent to all of your requests," Charles said, as a knock on the door announced the arrival of the master of the household, Guillaume Bellier, "and I am looking forward to seeing this famous sword."

"Gouffier and Bellier, please come in." The Dauphin rose and invited both his chamberlain and the master of the household to enter. "I wish for you to meet Jehanne La Pucelle. I have heard her message for me, and I want you to know that I do not discount it out of hand. While we continue our discussions, I desire that she be housed in the Coudray Tower with every necessity and convenience she might require. I also desire that she be custom-fitted with clothing and protective armor that would befit one of my top military advisors. Please assign her a page to assist her with her needs as well. I think little Louis de Coutes would be appropriate. Furthermore, she wishes to send a message to her men-at-arms housed in the inn to visit her here forthwith, and I insist they be treated with respect and deference. Do you understand?"

"Yes, Sire," they both said. "We understand."

"Then dispatch the messenger immediately. Have him tell La Pucelle's men to come unarmed but to bring Martel's sword. Now, I know there will be talk and speculation about her presence here," the Dauphin continued, "and I would expect you to quell any rumors or criticism. She is my invited guest, and as such, you owe her the same kindness and respect that would be given to me."

"Yes, Sire," replied Gouffier, as he bowed his head. "Bellier, see to her needs immediately. Would you please follow him, mademoiselle? Guillaume will get you settled and provide refreshment for you as well, and I shall send a messenger to invite your friends to come at once. And we shall see to your . . . wardrobe as well."

"Thank you," Jehanne said as she headed towards the door to follow Guillaume Bellier. With the same given name as his superior,

Bellier was a short man with a terribly scarred face, but his appearance didn't seem to damper his confidence. It was a good reminder for Jehanne. Her less-than-commanding appearance did not matter, as long as she acted with confidence, just as Katelyn had told her. Thinking about Katelyn, she turned back to Gouffier and said, "Would you instruct your messenger to tell Jean de Metz to make certain that *all* of my men-at-arms are to come?" Jean would understand by that message that Jehanne wanted him to summons Kaelig to join them.

"*All* of your men. Certainly," confirmed Guillaume Gouffier.

"Thank you," she replied and turned once again to the Dauphin before leaving the room. "And thank you, Sire. I express my deepest gratitude for your kind hospitality, and I look forward to our future conversations. I would also be pleased to show you Martel's sword at your earliest convenience," she said, bowing to him.

"As shall I," he replied. "And I look forward to seeing the sword. Now, if you will excuse me, I must return to my guests."

With that, Jehanne took leave of the Dauphin, marveling that with the simple information given to her by Katelyn, she had succeeded in persuading the future King of France to pay her heed. Her great quest to escort Charles to Reims was about to begin. But first, she had to turn the page on her preparatory period, and that meant bidding adieu to her loyal companions, and more importantly, to her mentor, Katelyn. It would be difficult to say goodbye to all of them, but especially to Katelyn, for her friend had hinted that this would be their last encounter.

It was a good thing Jehanne did not know at that moment that in addition to this imminent visit with Katelyn at the Chateau of Chinon, she would, in fact, see Katelyn Michaels a final time. That final time would be in much less favorable circumstances.

Chapter 55

IT WAS A CLEAR SUNDAY AFTERNOON IN early March. The waning sunbeams lit the creamy white façade of the royal fortress, creating a brilliant reflection of it in the Vienne River.

As Nicolas sat on the south bank of the river, hidden from view under the bridge, he waited for Katelyn and her traveling companions to appear. He contemplated the awe-inspiring scene and felt an overwhelming sense of gratitude to be alive. The nearly three days of rest under Madame Renard's roof had made a world of difference to him. He had regained his strength from her fine home cooking and from Katelyn's gentle care, and although his broken ribs and toes were still painful, he could actually walk without too much agony. But the beauty of the setting did little to assuage his apprehension.

He tried his best to take in deep breaths of the healing spring air to fill his lungs as Katelyn had encouraged him to do. She told him it would keep him from getting a lung inflammation and that it would calm his body. He just hoped his lungs and feet would support him for this final test. As he waited, he thought about the past few days, which were somewhat of a blur for him.

Although he had slept most of that time, as if his body needed that extra sleep to mend, he had nonetheless reveled in those moments when he was awake and Katelyn was at his side. Perhaps not wanting his mind to be distracted from the business of healing, Katelyn had not spoken of their relationship or of what might lie ahead for them in the future. Instead, as she sat by his side and tended to his injuries, she told him the highlights of her adventure since arriving in Vaucouleurs and about her traveling companions on the journey to Chinon. He sensed there was more she did not tell him about that journey, but there would be time for that later.

She also entertained him with amusing stories from her childhood, trying to give him a flavor of what life in the twenty-first century was like, but always dwelling on positive things. Although he had only briefly met her younger brother, Jackson, Nicolas felt as if he knew him well from Katelyn's stories. His fondest desire was to personally become acquainted with not only Jackson, but with Katelyn's parents as well.

However, when Nicolas tried to speak of such matters, Katelyn changed the subject, telling him they would have plenty of time to discuss their future when they returned to Mont Saint Michel and when he was restored to health. He knew she was trying her very best not to dwell on anything negative, for she had told him the power of positive thinking helped heal the body faster. Nonetheless, she *had* asked Nicolas to give her a detailed description of Abdon's new host, Philippe Montrouge.

While Nicolas slept, he knew that Katelyn had stayed busy. She acquired another set of clothing for him, quite different from what he had been wearing when he came through the time vortex. Madame Renard had been very helpful in this quest. Katelyn expressed her desire to stay at her 'brother's' side, and their hostess had enjoyed the excitement of haggling with someone else's money to obtain the specific list of items Katelyn gave her verbally. From the town market, she had procured a nice assortment of used clothing including a pair of leather boots several sizes too large, to accommodate Nicolas's bandaged feet. She had also purchased a sleeveless leather jerkin to be worn over a linen shirt, and a long, hooded cape made from wool dyed dark green. At least Philippe Montrouge would not recognize Nicolas by his clothing.

Katelyn had also explained to Nicolas that she had been exchanging messages with Jehanne and Jean de Metz, facilitated by a young stable boy who worked for the Renards. Earlier that day, Katelyn had received a message informing her that Jehanne had been summoned to the chateau to meet with the Dauphin and also that the armorer from Tours had delivered the sword from Sainte-Catherine-de-Fierbois. But the messenger had not been the only one talking about the sword. When Katelyn went down to fetch their lunch, Madame Renard was all agog about the magical sword that had been brought to Chinon for Jehanne La Pucelle. Perhaps wanting a bit of the limelight himself, the armorer had made quite a spectacle in the town square, announcing that the clerics of the little church in Sainte-Catherine had unearthed the sword of the revered Charles Martel after following the Maiden's instructions. As he brandished the gleaming sword about, he explained how with a simple wet rag, the village curé had removed seven centuries of rust from it as La Pucelle had promised. He then invited Jehanne to join him there in the square, where she publicly proclaimed that with the same sword Martel had used to drive out the blasphemous Saracens, she would lift the siege at Orléans and deliver France from its unhallowed invaders.

Then, earlier that afternoon, another message arrived for Katelyn. She was summoned by Jean de Metz to join him and Jehanne's other traveling companions to visit her in the royal chateau where the Dauphin had invited her to stay. Katelyn was to meet them as quickly as possible at the bridge in town crossing the Vienne River, and she was to come unarmed. The only weapon they were allowed to bring was the now-celebrated sword.

"This is it, Nicolas," Katelyn stated with a tremble in her voice as she rifled through her knapsack. "This will be my last visit with Jehanne. The sword has arrived. I'll show her how to use these gadgets and how to attach them," she said as she held up a drawstring leather pouch containing several items she was taking to Jehanne, "and then I've got to say goodbye to her. It's going to be hard, but it also means we'll be able to go home tomorrow."

"And what is home for you, Katelyn? Is it Mont Saint Michel with me?"

She bowed her head and said, "Nicolas, there are so many things we have to discuss—my role as a Watchman, the secret you still haven't told me, what lies in the future for us—but for now, let's concentrate on finishing our mission. Right now, my concern is whether or not we can go back to Sainte-Catherine-de-Fierbois and return together to the mount with your time key. If Abdon came through the vortex while he was touching you, will it work for us as well? Otherwise, I've got to either go back to Vaucouleurs or just ride directly to the Mount."

"We'll go to Sainte-Catherine together and try it," Nicolas told her as Katelyn pulled on her boots, floppy cap, and cloak. "But that is not the big concern, Katelyn. There is a much bigger issue, and that is Abdon. I am coming with you to the chateau. I am not going to let you out of my sight again." He stood and began pulling on the outer clothing Katelyn had procured for him, but he felt a blackness overtake him after standing too quickly. He sat back down to avoid letting Katelyn see his discomfort.

"Nicolas, it's too dangerous," she insisted. "First of all, you're in terrible condition, and secondly, if Abdon is out there, he'll recognize you more easily than me. From what you told me, he thought *I* was the maiden warrior. I'm sure he was there waiting for me when Jehanne entered Chinon, and when it turned out that I *wasn't* Jehanne and that I wasn't even traveling with her group, he must be refocusing his efforts on finding you. He doesn't even know that I'm here with you."

"Katelyn, I appreciate everything you have done to help me heal as quickly as possible," Nicolas said as he tried to subtly lower his head between his knees and then slowly raise it again, "but now it is time for me to leave my sick bed, get my wits about me, and return to the affairs at hand." He stood slowly and put his hands on her shoulders.

"Suddenly everything is clear to me, Katelyn," he continued. "Unfortunately, this is not over. Have you thought about the possibility that Abdon might target Jehanne? Think about it. I have never before left my post on the Mount, and so he has to know there is a compelling reason for me to do so. And he knows *you* left with me as well. He must have been following us in the village the night we left the Mount for him to have jumped on me right as I turned my key in the Guest Hall, so he knows you traveled through the vortex, too. Add that to the fact that I just happen to be here in Chinon at the same time as the famed Maiden Warrior and that a legendary sword has just been brought from the church where my time key took me. He *has* to know there is a connection. I am certain he has deduced that Jehanne plays a vital role in our undertaking here. He knows that it all ties into our responsibility to protect Mont Saint Michel. And you know him, Katelyn. He has no scruples. He would just as soon kill as not, so if he thinks Jehanne's death would hinder our assignment as Watchmen, he will just do away with her. 'Tis not only your safety I fear for, but Jehanne's, as well. I feel the strong impression that I need to come with you, not only to protect you, but to protect her. We are so close to our goal. We cannot falter now. We cannot allow any harm to come to her."

Katelyn stopped her preparations to look at him. "You're right," she agreed. "I hadn't even thought about Jehanne being a target, but you're absolutely right. We can never underestimate Abdon. We've got to protect Jehanne. We've got to prevent anything from happening to her before she accomplishes what she was sent here to do."

"Now you understand how serious this is, Katelyn. We cannot leave Chinon until we have found Philippe Montrouge and stopped him. Otherwise, Jehanne will always be in danger, and I fear the only way to stop him is to kill him. There is no other choice. If we don't kill him, he will kill Jehanne. I know it. I feel it in my heart. With Montrouge dead, it will take time for Abdon to cultivate a new host. By the time he does, Jehanne will have finished her mission. We have to find him, Katelyn."

He had not wanted to frighten Katelyn with this reality that had come to him so suddenly, but there was no time for mincing words. Nicolas saw the color drain from her face. He could only imagine the thoughts that were tumbling through her mind. She had been through so much, faced so much, but she had never willingly taken another human life. He prayed he could spare her that eventuality.

"Once again, you're right," she conceded. "As much as I'd like to just leave and go back to the Mount, you're absolutely correct, Nicolas. Abdon's not stupid. I'm sure he's figured out that if the French are victorious over the English, Normandy will be liberated, and the Mount will finally be safe from the English desire to destroy it as a symbol of anti-English defiance. And I'm sure he's heard Jehanne's claims to be the one to drive the English from France, so even if he doesn't find us, he would want to kill her. But we don't have time now to strategize. I've got to go right now, or I'll miss my opportunity to meet with Jehanne and help her with the sword. We've got to be smart about this. Follow us at a distance. If Philippe Montrouge or anyone else shows interest in our group, you need to be there to have our backs."

She stopped, as if she were analyzing something in her mind. Then, she jumped up from her chair and headed for the door. "I'll be right back," she explained. "I just thought of something in my room I've got to give you." She was gone for just a few seconds and then returned with a blue bag of gear he had seen before.

"You know how I told you I felt inspired to bring this stuff from home. Now I think I know why. I hope you won't need to use it, especially in your condition, but in case you feel it's necessary, I'll do my part," she said, and explained exactly what she would do to help.

As he tied the bag to his belt under his cloak, Nicolas said, "We must leave separately so Montrouge will not see us together. I shall leave first and take position under the bridge on the south side of the river where I will not be seen. From there, I will be able to see you meet with your companions on the other side of the bridge and watch for anyone following you."

"I agree," Katelyn said, finishing up her own preparations to depart. "Nicolas, keep your hood over your head, and for heaven's sake, try your best not to limp. Montrouge will be expecting you to be hobbling after everything he did to you. And Nicolas, remember what I told you about my traveling companions. They would do anything for Jehanne, and for me, for that matter. Especially Olg. He's the only one who knows I'm female. You can rely on him to help should Abdon show his face. While we're walking up to the chateau, I'll give him a heads up—I'll warn him about Montrouge. Here, you take my sword. I won't be allowed to enter the fortress armed anyway. Go now," she said.

"Katelyn," Nicolas said as he looked at the sword she had handed him, "this is not the sword Brother Thibault made for you. What happened to it, and where did you get this one?" He suddenly knew that Katelyn's journey from Vaucouleurs had not gone as smoothly as she had told him.

"I don't have time to tell you the details now," she said, "but I kinda broke Brother Thibault's sword while fighting a bunch of

Burgundian soldiers. Obviously, we won. This sword came from them."

He looked at her with amazement. Katelyn had been so concerned about his condition that she had not wanted to hamper him with the truth. Had she been forced to take a life and not even told him about it?

"And the answer to your question is 'no.' I didn't have to kill anyone. Not yet, anyway, but this isn't over, is it?" she said.

Before opening the door, he touched Katelyn's cheek and kissed her softly on the lips. "Go with God, *mon amour*, and be careful."

Now from his position under the bridge as he sat and observed the small group of men waiting for Katelyn, he thought of that brief kiss. There was never enough time with Katelyn, just as she had said. There was never an opportunity for him to tell her how she had transformed his life. There was no time to speak of their future. He prayed a silent prayer for her protection.

Shortly, Katelyn—in her Kaelig disguise—appeared and greeted her companions. As he observed them, he tried to pick out each of the men as she had described them to him. Olg, the Scottish archer whose real name was Richard, was easy to identify, a giant of a man who seemed particularly happy to see Katelyn. The two squires, Jean de Dieulouard and Julien de Honnecourt, were also easy to pick out because of their age and because Katelyn had told him that Jean was stocky and Julien had red hair. It was more difficult to differentiate between the three older men. However, from the way the others seemed to accept one of them as their de facto leader, he deduced that the man was Jean de Metz, the man of whom Katelyn had spoken so highly and who had been the first to lend his support to Jehanne. Since he knew Colet de Vienne had been sent by the Dauphin to Vaucouleurs to meet Jehanne and therefore was probably very familiar with Chinon, Nicolas determined that he was the one pointing out the direction for the group to go. That left the third man, who had to be Bertrand de Poulangy.

Nicolas was quite proud of himself for having deduced their identities from a few simple observations, but he did not have much time for self-congratulation. When the group began to walk north towards the bluff on which the fortress sat, he had to push himself to his feet to cross the bridge so as not to lose sight of them. Looking carefully around in every direction, he kept his head down and moved forward, gritting his teeth as he tried to walk without limping.

As he followed the little group from a distance, he scanned the streets for any sign of Montrouge or anyone else that seemed to find interest in the troop of foot soldiers heading towards the promontory on which the fortress stood. When Katelyn and her friends reached the eastern side of the bluff, from which the well-guarded road led up to the fortress entrance, he allowed himself to relax. From his vantage point, he had seen no one fall in behind the group or indeed express any more than a passing interest in the group. He watched as one of the royal guards stopped the party to question Jean de Metz, and then allowed them to pass. No one would be allowed up that road to the fortress entrance without first having been granted clearance. It appeared that he did not need to worry about Katelyn or Jehanne, at least until Katelyn headed back down into the town after her visit.

Nicolas found a spot in the shadows where he could rest his weary body against the side of a seemingly well-frequented tavern from which he had a clear view of the approach road. The location was carefully thought-out. His lingering presence would most likely be attributed to a state of inebriation. He would be seen as one of those unfortunate men who had had too much to drink too early in the day and had to sleep it off before returning to his badgering wife. He could sit there for hours and play the drunk while he kept a careful watch on the only means of egress to the royal chateau.

Unfortunately, from that vantage point, Nicolas would never see the threat that still hung over him, Katelyn Michaels, and Jehanne La Pucelle.

Chapter 56

IT'S A CLEAR SUNDAY AFTERNOON IN early March. The waning sunbeams light the southern façade of the royal fortress, creating a brilliant reflection of it in the Vienne River. It is a magical image that will stay seared in my mind forever. However, I don't have time to appreciate it because I see Jean de Metz, Colet de Vienne, Olg, Bertrand, Jean de Dieulouard, and Julien de Honnecourt waiting for me on the north side of the bridge. And though I try not to be too blatant about it, I can also see the shadow of Nicolas sitting under the bridge. His presence is reassuring.

As I reach my former traveling companions, they greet me with enthusiasm. They all seem happy to see me, particularly Olg, who clearly wants to take me in his arms and give me a hug. Fortunately, he restrains himself.

"It has happened, Kaelig," says Jean de Metz with enthusiasm. "The Dauphin has listened to Jehanne's message and has invited her to stay in the royal fortress. Our journey has not been in vain. She has sent for us to bid us adieu."

"Yes," I say. "It is wonderful news. I am so happy for her, and I can't wait to tell her so in person. I'm afraid it will be the last time I see her, for it is time for me to return to my home. What about the rest of you? What're you all going to do now?" I ask.

I listen to their various replies, most of which are, like me, to return to their homes. As Colet leads us through the winding streets of the town, the conversation turns to Jehanne and the story of her miraculous sword, which Jean is carrying. They are so anxious to tell me all about it, and I can't help but smile from ear to ear. Then, Jean de Metz actually hands it to me.

"You carry it, Kaelig," he says. "You deserve this honor. You deserve to deliver it to Jehanne, for we would never have made it on this journey without your guidance." He hands me the sword, which I gladly carry in spite of its impressive weight.

But honestly, I'm moved by Jean's words. *I* would have never made it without *his* guidance, but I'll take his praise at its face value because honestly, he really has no idea that I actually *do* deserve to deliver this sword to Jehanne. None of these men know, and I'll never be able to tell them or anyone else that the already legendary 'Sword of the Maiden' stemmed from all of my research, Brother Thibault's excellent craftsmanship, and Nicolas's stealth. And of course, the Archangel's inspiration. It will just have to be our little secret forever. But darn it! Sometimes I wish I could tell someone about all the cool things I've been able to do. That's the curse of being a Watchman. I save Mont Saint Michel, I help the iconic Joan of Arc fulfill her destiny, I even deliver a sword I had made that will go down in history, and I don't get to tell a soul. It's not even that I'm trying to brag or anything. It's just that it's so amazing, but I can't tell anyone. Not even Jackson. But God and the Archangel know, and that's really all that matters.

While my friends' chatter about the sword fills the streets, my thoughts shift from that happy subject to the sickening subject of Abdon. I can't decide whether to break this festive mood by warning them about Abdon or not. These exuberant men have been through so much, and they deserve to go back to their homes after their unselfish service. I hesitate about involving them in a problem that concerns me and Nicolas. Finally, I decide that I will only speak to Olg about the possible threat that Nicolas spoke of earlier.

"I need to talk to you, Olg," I say as I pull him to the back of the group, trying to think of how to word my warning. "I think you know that I've been caring for one of my dear friends here in Chinon, Nicolas le Breton. He was attacked by an evil man named Philippe Montrouge who is trying to kill us. Long story. Anyway, that's why I haven't been at the inn with the rest of you. We've been trying to stay out of sight. Nicolas believes that Montrouge might target Jehanne because she's my friend. I just want you to know about Montrouge in case he tries to interfere with our visit this afternoon."

I then share with Olg his description, as given to me by Nicolas. Although I haven't seen Philippe Montrouge, Nicolas's description reminds me of Severus Snape of Harry Potter fame. Too bad Abdon won't turn out to be essentially good, like Snape. Anyway, I think I'll know Montrouge by the Snape sneer, if and when I see him. But, I sure hope it's not today, because today, I take the final step in the mission Jean le Vieux gave to me in a dream: "Learn of the Maiden, Katelyn, and take her the sword."

I've certainly learned of the Maiden. I've learned of her character, her courage, her faith, her determination, her unfailing devotion, and her loyalty. I could go on and on and on about her qualities. But now, I just have to 'take' her the sword, and that means showing her how to use my enhanced miraculous sword features to give her a little boost for the battle of Orléans. Then Nicolas and I have to deal with Abdon (which I don't want to think about), and then we can be on our way back to the Mount.

Honestly, it seems like months, like years, like decades, like centuries since my dad helped me up the stairs with my bags at the Du Guesclin Hotel. How can I go back and greet him and Adèle on *their* next morning when I've been through weeks of turmoil? How can I possibly act like I've just seen them the night before? It's going to take some pretty good acting. Oscar-caliber acting. I try to put the thought of my reunion with Dad and Adèle from my mind. It's premature because as much as I want to ignore it, we still have the Abdon problem to take care of.

I look at the fortress looming above us and try to focus on it instead. The great irony of this place hits me like a ton of bricks. In the eleventh century, the fortress became the property of the Counts of Anjou, and Henry II, who founded the English Plantagenet dynasty, was not only the Count of Anjou and Duke of Normandy, but he was later crowned King of England. He ruled half of medieval France, all of England, and parts of Ireland and Wales from this very spot. He loved this place and lived here until his death. In fact, he and his famous wife, Eleanor of Aquitaine, are buried in the Fontevraud Abbey, just a few short miles from here.

Yes, how ironic that the Dauphin Charles, the Valois heir and enemy of the Plantagenets is now taking refuge in this same fortress today, because the feud between the Plantagenets and the Valois dynasties is at the very core of the Hundred Years' War.

As we approach the guard stationed at the bottom of the road that climbs up to the bluff, I think of how this royal fortress, now in the hands of the House of Valois, is the ultimate physical representation of what this long war with England has been about: a war between cousins who have fought over the right to rule France for not just a hundred years, but actually for several centuries.

And right now, as much as I dislike Charles for his refusal in the future to save Jehanne, I've got to be on his side. That means I have to set aside my personal feelings about him.

After Jean de Metz speaks with the guard, we are checked for weapons, and Jean explains why I have the sword. I hope, because I am openly displaying it, the guards won't check inside my pockets where I have my mini bag of tricks. But it seems the guard has been informed of our arrival and of the one weapon we are allowed to bring, and he allows us to pass without inspecting me further.

We wind our way up the narrow road lined with sentries and pass what Colet de Vienne tells us is the Saint-Georges fortress. I look behind me and spot Nicolas at the bottom of the hill, trying not to look too obvious about his interest in us. He's sitting outside what looks like a tavern. I'm grateful there hasn't been any sign of Abdon. There's no way he'll be able to get to the chateau with all of these guards, so it appears I'll be able to carry out this part of the mission in peace.

When we reach the moat across from the watch tower and the main fortress, I turn a final time and nod my head briefly at Nicolas far below to let him know I'm okay. Although it appears he's sleeping, I know he's watching my every move. Jean announces our arrival at this final guard station, and after we are checked a second time for weapons, the drawbridge over the moat is lowered. As I walk across the drawbridge and under the portcullis, a feeling comes over me that is hard to describe. It reminds me of that first time I crossed the drawbridge under the portcullis on Mont Saint Michel. It's that same sensation of déjà vu. My body involuntarily shivers, and for a second, I feel it's a warning of something sinister. I shake it off and convince myself that it's just a feeling of awe. I'm in this amazing place where the future king of France is currently residing. I mean, really. Who gets to do things like this?

This is it. I'm not saving the Mount, but I'm helping to save a nation.

Wow. The scope of what I'm doing hits me as we are escorted inside the fortress. Indirectly, I realize, I *am* saving the Mount once again by helping to save the nation that will protect Mont Saint Michel for future generations.

A guard leads us under the arch of the bell tower and then up another incline until we reach the crest of the promontory. I realize immediately that from the south, you can't envision how large this place is, because you see only the south side of the battlements and its buildings. But there is an entire section on the north side, which consists mostly of open grounds and small outbuildings. The entire top of the bluff is surrounded by defensive battlements. To our left, the stone battlements block our view of the valley below. There are no buildings on this southern stretch of the defensive wall. I notice a set of narrow steps that lead up to the top of the wall, and I get up the nerve to ask the guard if we might be permitted to climb up to see the vista. After all, this might be the best vantage point I'll ever get of medieval Chinon. Besides, I have a more important reason to look at the view.

The guard is grumpy about my request, but at the urging of the other men, particularly Colet de Vienne, he finally gives in. We climb up the narrow set of steps one at a time, and I purposely go last so that no one can see me hide Jehanne's sword in a little alcove or pull two items out of my pocket once my hands are free. When I reach the ramparts, I find everyone marveling at the panorama that opens up before us to the south. The sun is slowly setting in the west, and in the distance, the rolling green hills are dotted with villages and church steeples.

I lean over the wall and look down, and I immediately understand why this location is such a perfect strategic location for a fortress. The stone battlements sit atop a sheer cliff that drops straight down to the town below. You would have to be a skilled climber, much more skilled than I am, to scale that unforgiving rock face without gear.

Then my eyes are drawn to the Vienne River. Colet, whose last name is a reminder that he originated from this river region, points out the bridge where we met earlier, and then explains to us that the Vienne runs northwest from here to feed into the Loire River. The calm, flat surface of the river's waters soothes my nerves. I take a minute to sear this view into my mind, just as I had earlier when I saw the reflection of the chateau from the opposite side of the river.

I peruse the rooftops of Chinon below, which remind me of tiny Monopoly buildings. When I see a church tower below to the right, I ask Colet if it is the Church of Saint Maurice.

"Kaelig, I am surprised you are so familiar with our little town," he replies. "That is exactly what it is. It is not a particularly large or famous church, but I have warm feelings about it, since I spent many an hour there at my mother's knee as a child."

I have nothing against Saint Maurice or his church, but I don't have the heart to tell Colet that, to me, the church represents treachery. That's where the old woman tricked Nicolas into following her into Abdon's torture chamber. Unlike Colet, I will never have warm feelings about that church.

The guard grows impatient, and we agree that our little sight-seeing venture must come to an end. One by one, we descend the steep steps. Again, I go last so that I can do what I climbed up here to do. No one looks back at me, and besides, it only takes me an instant, and then I hurry to retrieve the sword, and catch up with the others.

Our escort leads us straight west towards the setting sun, and Colet points out the royal lodgings to our left, overlooking that same steep cliff we just saw. But we don't stop there. Evidently, Jehanne isn't quite ready to be housed with the royal family. Ahead, I see several towers, but to get there, we have to cross a deep rift in the plateau. A heavy stone bridge crosses over to this section, which Colet informs us is called the Coudray fortress.

At the very end of the bridge is a stone tower, which I estimate to be about four stories tall. This must be it! This is where Jehanne is staying. There's a lower door that goes directly into the tower, but there's also a set of stairs on the outside of the tower that leads to the second floor, and that's where our escort takes us. When we get to the top of the staircase, he knocks on a door into the tower. As it is opened, he moves aside, bows at us as we enter, and then goes back down the stairs to return to his post.

The door is opened by a short man with terrible acne scars, or maybe they're scars from the plague, although I actually do know the plague was long before he was born. Chicken pox, maybe? Regardless of his horrible complexion and short stature, he seems very self-assured.

"Ah, so you are La Pucelle's associates," he says, as he escorts us into an open circular space equipped with several chests, some chairs, and a large table. There is also a fireplace where a young man who looks to be about Jackson's age is building a fire. It feels quite chilly in here, especially since we no longer have the warmth of the sun shining down on us.

"Allow me to introduce myself. I am Guillaume Bellier and this young man stoking the fire is Louis, who has been assigned to be La Pucelle's page. Please, come in."

This is so weird because I've read in Jehanne's history about both of these men. I know Bellier is the master of Charles' household, and the story about the page, Louis de Coutes, is even more incredible. I know he was fourteen years old when Charles assigned him to be a page for Jehanne. It seems Charles 'borrowed' him from Lord Raoul de Gaucourt, one of the Dauphin's advisors, for this assignment. However, providing a page for Jehanne was just another sly move on the Dauphin's part. Louis's real job was to keep an eye on La Pucelle for Charles and to report back directly to him about any unusual occurrences. In other words, he was the Dauphin's spy. I also know from the original sources that Louis was called by several names—Minguet, or Mugot or Imerguet—and that he served Jehanne until August 1429 (or will serve her until August of this year, even going into battle with her). Louis eventually testified (or will testify) in her rehabilitation trial, as well. It's so weird to speak of the past when it's still in the future for me here.

So here I am actually meeting these people in real life that I've read about. It's so bizarre. Little Louis has no idea that while he's trying to warm up Jehanne's lodgings, his name will be remembered in six centuries simply for the kinds of things he's doing right now! And he doesn't seem to be too skilled at fire-making, so maybe he's a better spy than he is a page. But, I can't say anything to Jehanne about him. Besides, he ends up being her faithful supporter in the end.

I turn my attention back to Bellier, who is speaking to us.

"This is the antechamber for La Pucelle, but her actual quarters are just one floor up. I will take you up to her immediately and give you some privacy for your visit. Louis and my staff will also be bringing up some supper for you. When you are finished visiting and eating, you will find Louis in his quarters on the ground floor of the tower. Go back down to the ground floor via the outside steps, and his door is just to the left of the staircase. Louis will escort you back to the guardhouse."

I see the staircase that ascends, this time on the inside of the tower rather than on the outside. I also notice a large chart on the table that looks like a type of blueprint or map of the fortress. My curiosity gets the best of me, and I casually stroll over to look at it. The three sections of the fortress are clearly marked, and looking at the schematics laid out like this helps me get my bearings. I pick out the exact location of the ramparts we climbed to see the view, and of the Coudray Tower where we are now. The thought pops into my mind: *If I need to, I think I can navigate this place even in the dark.*

I carefully examine the map of this, the westernmost Coudray Fortress, separated from the Château du Milieu by the natural chasm. The only access is by the bridge we crossed. I note that the northwestern side of this section is isolated. The Coudray Tower blocks this portion from the view of the royal lodgings. For some reason, I think this might be important, but I'm not sure why.

I try to put such thoughts from my mind and follow the others who are being led by Guillaume Bellier up the stairs to Jehanne's room. There is a door at the top, and after Bellier knocks, Jehanne enthusiastically opens it.

"Greetings, my beloved friends. Come in, come in," she says as she invites us into her quarters. Once we are inside, Bellier says goodbye to us and leaves.

"Oh, Kaelig, I am so happy you got my message to join the others," Jehanne says as she sees me come in last.

"Jehanne," I say as I bow to her deeply, "I was told to deliver the sword to you." She has no idea of just how true that sentence is, even though she knows that without me, she would never have this sword. She takes it lovingly in her hands, bows in return, and then places it reverently on top of her bed. "Thank you, Kaelig. I shall always remember that you brought it to me." She looks at me with a twinkle in her eye. It's a private joke that none of the men here can appreciate.

I turn my attention from her and the sword to my surroundings. The room's furnishings seem pretty sparse. I'm sure this room is nothing like the royal lodgings, but it's a lot better than sleeping on the ground, and the fire is actually burning in here. Bellier has seen to it that we have a table and chairs set up for us, as well as eating utensils, and I find that I'm actually hungry. A lot has happened since I had Madame Renard's lunch. Instead of sitting, I go stand by the fire to warm my chilled hands. After all, I've been carrying that cold metal sword.

"Before we talk," Jehanne says, "I wish to take you up to the top of this tower so that you can appreciate the strategic location before the sun goes down. It is remarkable," she says, as she leads us up the staircase, which takes us up to the lookout platform on top of the tower. We have a view in all directions. As I look over the waist-high wall that surrounds the open-air platform, the drop on the east side plunges down to the bottom of the ravine crossed by the bridge. It's a long way down, and it makes me dizzy. I feel so cold, as if an arctic blast has surrounded me. As the light begins to dim, Jehanne suggests we head back down, and once again, I linger. This time, I will have to be very subtle, for I don't want to draw any undue attention to this building, but I have no choice. I'm not sure what's going to happen, but I've got to be prepared . . . just in case.

When I get back downstairs, I go to the fireplace again while the rest of the men sit and focus on Jehanne as she gives her account of her meeting with Charles that afternoon. I can't help but grin as the others ooh and aah as she tells them of the Dauphin's subterfuge and her ability to recognize him immediately. She looks over at me knowingly, as she tells the story. Everyone is eager to jump in and ask questions.

The fire is finally thawing my body, but the greatest source of heat comes from the inside, fueled by the warmth of the comradery I feel all around me. These fine men and this remarkable young woman have been my companions for several weeks through some pretty hard times. I will miss them all, especially Jehanne and Olg. It is so surreal and so bittersweet. I will never see any of them again, and I can't do anything about it. I have to force myself not to let my tears sneak out of the hiding place where I try so hard to keep them, but it's hard.

When supper is brought up by Louis and several female servants, including a plentiful supply of ale, I politely ask one of the women if I might have water instead. The woman looks at me like I'm crazy, but she complies. I not only hate the ale and cider that is always offered to me, but the last thing I need is to have my judgment clouded in any way. After all, I know Abdon is out there somewhere, and I've got to get back to Madame Renard's tonight. I hope the evening will proceed without incident, but I continue to feel anxious.

Soon the effects of the ale turns the others' mood even cheerier as the men enjoy what is to them a remarkable feast. I have to admit, it's the best meal I've had since leaving Brother Thibault's table. Everyone marvels at the variety of food as they chug down more ale, and as we share memories of our journey, both good and bad.

After an hour or two of frivolity, Jean de Metz finally stands and announces that it is time for us to leave. Reluctantly, we begin to say our goodbyes. Jehanne embraces all of the men warmly, thanking them profusely for their service, and then announces, "I need to discuss some final important matters with Kaelig and Olg. I think it is best for the rest of you take your leave now, and they will follow later."

Jehanne is wise asking Olg to stay behind with me. She knows she can't say that she wants to be with me alone, for that would be viewed as inappropriate, since they all still think I'm a male. I'm sure she's also thinking of my security, and Olg will help me get home safely.

As I also bid the men goodbye, I realize that this will be my final farewell. I am fond of each and every one of them, Bertrand and Colet, and the squires Jean and Julien, but I am particularly indebted to Jean de Metz. I thank him for all of his help and especially for the honor he gave me of bearing the sword today. I can't think about the goodbyes too deeply, because young male soldiers fighting for the honor of France do not cry. I literally have to bite the inside of my cheek as I shake their hands and bid them adieu.

The three of us accompany the men back down to the antechamber, and then we close the door behind them as they clomp down the outside staircase. We hear them knocking on Louis's door below. He joins the noisy group and escorts them to the guardhouse at the exit of the fortress. I pray that when he returns, Louis will not notice what I left on the top of the tower.

After the others leave, I ask Olg to wait for me in the anteroom because I can't allow him to see what I've got up my sleeve. He knows the truth about my friendship with Jehanne, and he isn't offended when I tell him I have some final matters of business to discuss with her. Jehanne and I go back up to her room where it is finally time for me to explain to Jehanne how to use her 'enhanced' sword.

"Jehanne, now that you have the miraculous sword, we're going to make it even more miraculous," I say as I sit on the side of the bed and open my little leather pouch. I pull out two rolls of electrical tape in gray and brown, a flat 1,000 lumen LED flashlight, a tiny MP3 player the size of a pen drive, and two iFrogz Tadpole speakers, the smallest Bluetooth speakers I've ever seen.

I've thought about how on earth I'm going to explain this to her, and so I just go with terms I hope Jehanne will understand. "I have been sent with these remarkable relics for you, which I am going to show you how to use and how to attach to Martel's sword. I think you should only use them during the battles to lift the siege of Orléans. People will be anxious to see the sword before that, so don't put them on except when you are in combat, and then remove them. The truth is that because you have no experience in warfare, you will unfortunately find that the French generals and soldiers won't have confidence in your ability to lead them. These relics are going to help you change those attitudes once and for all." I can't let her know that Orléans will be one of the only campaigns where she fights on the front lines . . . or that she will be wounded in the taking of the Tourelles. But that campaign *will* be the turning point for her.

After she gets over her initial shock at what my incredible 'relics' do, I spend the next half hour showing her how to place and attach the flashlight and the MP3 player with the brown electrical tape on either side of the sword's grip so they can be easily activated by pressing down on the buttons on the tops of the devices, one with her thumb and the other with her index finger. I teach her how to activate and attach the speakers under the cross guard with the gray electrical tape. While we practice, we have to turn the volume down on the MP3 player, but I show her how to turn the volume to its highest level for her little sound and light show. It won't be as magnificent as *my* sound and light show on the Mount, but it will be sufficiently astonishing for those in her immediate vicinity.

When Jehanne feels she has mastered their use, I make it very clear to her that she must protect the devices carefully until they are to be used, and that once the Orléans campaign is over, she must crush the relics and throw the pieces into the Loire River so that no one will ever find their remains. Until they are to be used, I instruct her to keep them in the leather pouch and to wear it around her neck hidden beneath her clothing.

However, before she has a chance to attach the pouch around her neck, I hear Olg running up the stairs. He taps on the door and whispers, "Katelyn, the page Louis is outside with an envoy of the Dauphin to see Jehanne. You had better come down so that you are not found with her alone." As I open the door, I hear Louis and his companion enter the room below. At least Olg is upstairs so that it will not appear that I am alone with Jehanne. I tell Olg and Jehanne to go down, and I whisper to Jehanne that I will hide the pouch under her bedding.

As Olg and Jehanne enter the room below, I hear the page's words.

"Mademoiselle, the Dauphin has sent for the best armorer in the region, Colin de Montbazon, to fit you with a custom set of armor. He will arrive tomorrow, but the tailor is here now to make you a set of clothing fit for a warrior. Could he take a few minutes of your time to take some measurements?"

"Certainly," I hear Jehanne reply.

"Then I will leave him here with you now, mademoiselle. Should you need any further assistance, please fetch me in my quarters downstairs," Louis says, and I hear him going back down the steps outside the tower.

I feel grateful that Jehanne is not already wearing the pouch under her clothing since the tailor will be measuring her body. Then another thought pops into my mind. Jehanne doesn't yet have a scabbard for her sword, and I know from her history that she has one made by the Dauphin's tailor or armorer. I don't remember which, but I decide to take the sword down to be measured. I pick it up from her bed and descend the stairs, but for some reason, when I reach the bottom of the staircase, I leave the sword in the shadows on the final step before entering the room.

When I enter the antechamber, the thought of the leather pouch and Jehanne's sword immediately leaves my mind, because I am greeted by the sneer I knew I would recognize instantly.

Unfortunately, even with the heads up I gave Olg, he does not recognize him as readily as I do, and before I have the opportunity to react, Philippe Montrouge has a knife at Jehanne's throat.

Chapter 57

ONCE KATELYN AND HER COMPANIONS disappeared from his view into the safe confines of the fortress, Nicolas relaxed somewhat. There had been no sign of Montrouge, and for that he was grateful. But he was also not naïve enough to think that Abdon's new host would simply fade into the background. No, he was still out there somewhere, and Nicolas could not let his guard down for one second.

He prayed that he would be allowed to maintain his post here beside the tavern. He had a clear view of the access road to the chateau and could see anyone coming or going. After he had been sitting there for about an hour, some of the tavern's unruly clients exited the establishment and tried to engage him in a conversation . . . or perhaps just an altercation. When they saw him in his semi-prostrate position, they began hooting at him, and then one of them actually kicked him. Fortunately, it was in the thigh, missing any of his major injuries. Nicolas simply acted as if he were totally inebriated, and fortunately, they soon left him alone.

As the sun set and the sky began to darken, Nicolas sat up straighter and focused his eyes more diligently on the road. He was completely alert when he spotted Katelyn's traveling companions coming back down the access road and past the lower guardhouse.

Katelyn was not with them, nor was Olg. At first, he began to panic, but judging by the jovial nature of the men, he determined that all was well. Katelyn had probably asked Olg to wait for her while she instructed Jehanne about the sword.

Nonetheless, a sensation of uneasiness washed over him that seemed to grow by the minute. He was uncertain if the apprehension was simply a result of not seeing Katelyn come back down, or if the Archangel was trying to impress something upon his mind. And then he saw the figure in black approaching the guardhouse at the bottom of the entryway to the chateau. Even though he could not see the man's face, it didn't matter. He didn't need to see him. He knew. It was Philippe Montrouge, and even more surprisingly, the guards were giving him access to the fortress.

Without drawing any attention to himself, Nicolas slipped into the shadows of the town streets. The entrance road to the fortress sat on the far eastern end of the promontory, and Katelyn had told him to go to the southern battlement. As quickly as his poor feet would take him, he worked his way behind the very last row of buildings in the village before the cliff rose up to the hilltop fortress. Katelyn had told him she would try to choose the safest place for him to come up over the ramparts, where it would be least likely for him to be observed. And there it was, the eerie greenish light, aptly named a glow stick, which Katelyn had told him would mark his path. During his forays into the twenty-first century, Nicolas had already learned of the many marvelous uses of the product she called duct tape, and it seems it had once again done its job of holding the unusual beacon to the wall.

Working his way directly below the marker, he climbed up the brushy hill as far as he could go before the rock took over, and then grateful that his hands and arms were largely uninjured, he launched the grappling hook attached to the rope. It took several attempts before the hook found purchase on the edge of the rampart walls.

On Mont Saint Michel, while Brother Thibault was finishing the swords, Katelyn had said she felt impressed to teach him some of the climbing skills she had been learning, and so she took him out at night when they would not be seen, and practiced climbing up the back face of the abbey wall below the West Terrace, using the gear she had brought. Tonight, he had no climbing partner to belay him, and he had no way to anchor the rope, so he knew he would just have to 'walk' straight up the wall with the help of the rope. His main climbing aid was pure adrenaline. He did, however, attach the little mechanism Katelyn called an ascender to at least keep himself from slipping back down the free-hanging rope. He also knew it would be awkward to climb up with Katelyn's sword around his waist, but he had no option. He needed to be armed.

His arms supported most of his body weight as he pulled himself up the cliff face, using his feet planted on the wall to guide him and to give him some added support. Katelyn had been right to insist he stay in bed the past few days to regain his strength and heal. He knew that without the rest, hearty food, and tender care, he could not have made this climb, even with all the adrenaline in the world. He was exhausted when he reached the top, but knowing how dangerous it was to change the resistance on the rope, which might allow the hook to shift positions, he maintained his weight to the very last second until he could pull himself over the edge.

Once over the top, Nicolas collapsed on the top of the rampart. With the battlements on each side of the wall, he could not be seen unless someone actually climbed the steps where he was. It took him a moment to recover from the strenuous climb. Then he pulled up the rope, looping it as quickly as he could and stowed it back in the bag still attached to his waist, along with the grappling hook. Carefully, he raised his head above the wall and leaned over to remove Katelyn's glow stick and duct tape, which he also shoved in the bag. Katelyn had told him the light would fade after about twelve hours, but there was no reason to leave any sign of his passage behind. Once he had caught his breath, he tried to get his bearings, aided by the waning gibbous moon. To the right, or to the east, as he faced away from the wall, sat the guardhouse and entryway to the fortress, and to the left, or west, was a cluster of buildings he assumed to be the royal lodgings judging by the flickering lights in the windows. This part was going to be trickier.

Rather than standing and exposing his entire height, Nicolas sat and scooted his way down the rampart steps. He knew he had to move to the north, away from the wall, to look for Katelyn's next marker, which she had told him she would place to identify Jehanne's quarters. When he reached the gravel walkway at the base of the stone wall, he looked around carefully to see if there was anyone in sight, particularly Montrouge, but all was quiet.

Nicolas got on his stomach and pulled himself across the gravel to an area where he could hide behind trees and shrubs. Moving as quickly as he could while at the same time staying low, he reached a point where he was opposite the brightly lit royal quarters. A guard walked back and forth in front of the length of the building, and light glowed in nearly every window. With the light, it was going to be more difficult to see Katelyn's marker, but then as he turned his head to the right, he saw the tiny green glow up in the air to the northwest of the buildings he was facing. This was a relief, because he did not know how he would have circumvented the guard to get into the royal lodgings.

Using the same method of stealth to avoid being seen by the guard, he continued to work his way towards the western end of the promontory. When he got closer, he realized that the marked building was a round tower, and that to get to it, he had to cross a bridge over a ravine. No one was about, and all seemed calm inside the round building, but Nicolas knew better. Abdon was in there. Of that, he was certain. On his hands and knees, he crawled across the bridge so that his silhouette would not be seen above its side walls.

A torch had been placed in a bracket at the bottom of a staircase on the outside of the tower, and Nicolas pressed himself back into the shadows as a young man exited a door in the middle of the tower and descended the stairs. The lad opened a door into the ground level of the tower, went inside, and closed the door behind him. After that, all was quiet. This was probably a page assigned to Jehanne who had unwittingly escorted Montrouge up to Jehanne's quarters. Katelyn would not have left the glow stick on the top of the tower if Jehanne were housed on the bottom floors.

Nicolas was fully aware of the fact that he and Katelyn had been placed in a very difficult and dangerous situation. Here they were, in the very heart of the Dauphin's sanctuary, one of the most famous sites in current day France, and they were not supposed to intrude in history. There was no mention of an attack on Jehanne in the historical accounts of the Maiden's visit with the Dauphin, and so this predicament had to be handled judiciously. On the other hand, it was clear that Abdon in the form of Philippe Montrouge was here, and that his aim was to thwart their mission, which meant either killing Jehanne or Katelyn . . . or both.

Confrontation was inevitable, but for their mission to be a success, this confrontation had to take place without coming to the attention of the Dauphin or his many servants and guards. It seemed an impossible task. Nicolas could not help but wonder if he and Katelyn had *already* altered history, but he could not approach the present situation from that assumption. He had to act as if their mission could still be saved.

Nicolas moved quietly from his location on the bridge over to the staircase, trying to stay out of the light of the burning torch. He did not see any other guards about. Not even thinking about the pain in his feet, he crept up the stairs as silently as he could. When he reached the door leading into the tower room, he could hear voices within, but they were not screaming voices. Whatever was happening inside, Katelyn was either unaware of Montrouge's presence or identity, or she too was realizing the importance of not alerting anyone in the fortress to an altercation.

Nicolas removed his sword from the scabbard. He knew Katelyn was unarmed because *he* had her sword, the sword he now knew had once belonged to a Burgundian enemy. However, Jehanne's sword made by Brother Thibault, which everyone was now calling Martel's sword, was probably inside somewhere. He hoped that Katelyn knew where it was. He eased the door open a crack. What he heard chilled him to the bone, but at the same time, he was amazed at Katelyn's ability to stay calm under fire.

"So Mademoiselle Katelyn, your friend's life is of such little value to you that you would let her die rather than tell me what I so wish to hear."

"Abdon, I am willing to tell you exactly what you want to hear, but I need some kind of guarantee that you will let Jehanne go, and right now, I don't feel you can give me that. So *you* tell me why I should trust you'll do what you say. And if you so much as put a nick in her neck, all negotiations are off the table!"

Philippe Montrouge was trying to ply the secret of Mont Saint Michel out of Katelyn in exchange for Jehanne's life. Jehanne was to be used as leverage in Abdon's evil game, just as he had done with Jean le Vieux on two occasions, the first time using Jean's son as leverage, and the second time using Jean as leverage to get Katelyn and Nicolas to give up the secret. But Jean had sacrificed himself instead.

There was just one problem with this scenario playing out right now in that room, and he and Katelyn were the only ones who knew what it was. Katelyn did not know the secret. *This* is why the Archangel had insisted she not know. Nicolas realized that if Katelyn had known the secret, she would never have allowed her friend's life to remain in jeopardy. She would have told Abdon, not because she was weak, but because she would not have been willing to compromise Jehanne's safety. And if she had known the secret and told Abdon, he would have killed Jehanne anyway. He was not bound by any code of honor. He had no honor. Satan and his minions had no honor. They wanted only to do evil and to persecute anyone who tried to serve God.

The fact that Katelyn did not know the secret meant that she was forced to find a way to negotiate with Montrouge, to prolong the confrontation, and that is why Jehanne was still alive. Katelyn's ignorance had, in fact, saved Jehanne's life. Now, it was up to Nicolas to find a way to end this, and as hard as it was for him to accept it, Jehanne was the only player involved who was indispensable. She had to be saved at any cost, even if it meant his life or Katelyn's life had to be sacrificed.

It was an impossible choice, but his mentor Jean had made it, and Nicolas wondered if he could make it as well. One thing was for certain, he was going to do everything in his power not to have it be Katelyn. He *had* to protect Jehanne, but he also had to protect Katelyn.

Not wanting to give away his presence until he had determined what to do, Nicolas continued to listen.

"If you so much as touch either Jehanne or Katelyn, I will smash you to smithereens," Nicolas heard a heavily accented voice proclaim. This had to be Katelyn's friend, the Scottish archer Olg. It was a relief knowing he was there. Certainly, there was a way for the two men to outwit and overpower Montrouge, if Nicolas could just think of it.

"I have all the power here, Mademoiselle Michaels. There is no time for negotiations. *I* am the one holding a knife to your friend's throat, so *you* have no clout."

"Not true, Abdon. I know you too well. Whether it's as Philippe Montrouge, Richard Collins, Gothman, or even that nasty stallion you used to try to kill me, I know your true nature. Don't think you can fool me. You would just as soon kill Jehanne as not, so don't you see that *I'm* the one with the power? I know if I tell you the secret while you're holding a knife at her throat that you'll just kill her anyway. You've got to offer me another way to resolve this."

Nicolas marveled at Katelyn's ability to make the correct analysis under the circumstances. She was amazing. He could only imagine how her mind and heart must be racing.

"By the way," Katelyn continued, "I'm sure you're not interested in having all of the Dauphin's men rush you when I start screaming, which I will certainly do if you injure Jehanne in any way. Remember, her page Louis is just downstairs. He'll hear me immediately. Oh, you might kill Jehanne or me before the guards get here, but Olg and the guards will be all over you in a heartbeat because Jehanne is under the protection of the Dauphin. He will not look kindly on some intruder who comes in the guise of a tailor to dress her and who ends up killing her instead. No, you'll be dead in a second, and then you'll have to start all over with another host, and I know that takes time. And you still won't know the secret."

Nicolas, who had wondered how Montrouge had infiltrated the fortress, finally understood. The Dauphin had sent for a tailor to make a new set of garments for La Pucelle, and according to what Montrouge had told Nicolas earlier, Abdon's host *was* a tailor by profession. A tailor to nobility. It was brilliant.

"I suggest we make an exchange. You let Jehanne go, and you may take me hostage instead." Katelyn continued.

Nicolas felt his heart drop to his feet. Katelyn was willing to sacrifice her life to save Jehanne.

"Aren't you the little heroine?" Montrouge hissed sarcastically. "Just like your friend Jean. You would sacrifice your life to save a friend. 'Tis touching indeed."

"Oh, no, you misunderstand," Katelyn insisted. "I'm not planning on letting you kill me. It's still the same deal. You let Jehanne go, take me as a hostage instead, but then we still find a way for my safety to be guaranteed before I tell you the secret."

"No," replied Montrouge. "Now I am the one who does not trust you! I know you Watchmen well. You think you are so valiant in maintaining your so-called sacred trust, so taking you as a hostage would do me no good. You would not tell me anything, and I would just be forced to kill you. That would be a waste of my time, would it not? No, I know you are willing to sacrifice yourself, mademoiselle, but I still believe you care too much about your friend here not to let *her* die, so there will be no exchange."

They were at an impasse. Nicolas did not dare rush Montrouge, because the chances were far too great that he would kill Jehanne first. And then all would be lost. Finally, it came to him. It became clear to Nicolas that there was a way, and one way only, to guarantee the safety of both Jehanne and Katelyn. There was a way to end this without drawing the attention of the Dauphin's guards. It was not what he had planned for, it was not what he had hoped for, but there was no choice.

"Yes," Nicolas said as he entered the room with his sword unsheathed and held out defensively before him. He quietly closed the door behind him and said, "There *will* be an exchange. *I* will be your hostage."

"Well, well, well, Nicolas," Montrouge said with a malevolent sneer. "I wondered when you would be showing up to save your little princess. Isn't that just the sweetest thing? Katelyn is willing to sacrifice herself to save the Dauphin's new little pet, whoever she is, and you are willing to sacrifice yourself to save Katelyn. You people are just so touching. Really. But unfortunately, I do not possibly see how the exchange can be made without you and this giant here trying to rush me, so that would be a no." Montrouge tightened the knife at Jehanne's neck, and Nicolas saw a drop of blood running down her neck. He was afraid that Olg would react before he managed to make the switch.

Nicolas saw the look on Katelyn's face. It was one of combined relief and horror. Jehanne, on the other hand, looked completely peaceful, as if she were not even present in the room, but had tuned into a higher sphere. Nicolas hoped it was true. He hoped her voices were speaking to her in a calming manner, for this situation could easily turn deadly if she panicked.

"Stop the pressure on Jehanne's neck immediately, Montrouge, or this is going to end badly. I have the solution. You just have to be patient and let me show you. But we are going to do this in an orderly manner, and as Katelyn has already told you, we are going to do it in a way that will draw no attention to us. Katelyn, get out your duct tape. You must have it in your pocket."

Katelyn looked at him, imploring him in that look to find another way, but there was none.

"Katelyn has this marvelous product with which to effectively bind a prisoner. We shall bind both Olg and Jehanne so they cannot attack you or escape to get help."

"Yes," interjected Katelyn, looking at Nicolas as if to impress this into his mind, "and then you, Nicolas, and I are going to take our discussion outside to the northwest side of the fortress, away from the guards and the royal lodgings, and away from Jehanne's page downstairs."

Katelyn removed the roll of gray tape from her pocket and handed it to Nicolas.

"I think having you as leverage is to my advantage, Nicolas, because I believe Katelyn's feelings for you are stronger than her feelings for that laughingstock of a girl warrior—Jehanne, is it?—but if you think for one instant I would trust you to bind the prisoners, than you must have pottage for a brain," spat Montrouge.

"Oh, I am not proposing to bind them myself," said Nicolas. "I know you would not trust me to do it. I am going to roll this over to you and let you do it yourself."

"Yes, and while I focus my attention on the girl, you and Olg will attack. I think not."

"Well then, let Katelyn bind Olg first, so that he will not present an immediate threat to you, and then you will be able to check the bindings yourself," Nicolas suggested as he handed the tape back to Katelyn. He was as concerned about Olg as he was about Montrouge. Nicolas could sense how difficult this situation was for Katelyn's friend. This giant of a man had no desire to negotiate with the crazed tailor holding Jehanne captive, and Nicolas knew he had to neutralize Olg if he wanted to avoid a disaster. He could hear Katelyn's whispers in English, trying to reassure her friend to trust Nicolas and to do what he said.

"First, however, I am going to slide my sword over to you, and then the three of us are going to remove all of our outerwear so that you will see we have no other weapons," Nicolas said as he scooted the sword with his foot across the floor to Montrouge. Nicolas removed his cloak, the scabbard, and the bag of climbing gear around his waist, and slid them both over as well. "I have no other weapons. And Olg and Katelyn were checked by the guards when they entered the fortress. They were not allowed to enter with weapons, but they will still take off their outer clothing to prove that to you." Montrouge looked on as both Olg and Katelyn removed their bulky outer garments. Katelyn even removed her cap, letting her hair fall down past her shoulders.

"Katelyn, take a chair over to Montrouge so that Jehanne can sit down. Olg, you sit down as well," Nicolas said as he pulled up a chair next to him. "Move slowly, and make no sudden movements." With great reluctance, Olg sat down.

Montrouge kept his eyes on the two men until Olg was seated, and then he pushed Jehanne down into the chair Katelyn had placed in front of him. With Jehanne now sitting, Montrouge was able to pick up Nicolas's sword and scabbard and clumsily attach them to his waist with one hand while maintaining the knife at her throat and watching the others.

"Now Katelyn," Nicolas continued, "put a piece of tape over Olg's mouth so he cannot call out. Then bind his feet, and bind his hands behind the chair. Do it well. When you've done that, bind him to the chair around the chest. When you are done, move away." With reluctance, Katelyn did Nicolas's bidding, apologizing to Olg as she complied. Nicolas could read her mind. She, like him, could see no other way out of this predicament. She knew this was the only way to protect Olg and Jehanne, so she bound him tightly. Olg subtly tried to break through the tape, but to no avail.

"Katelyn, now I want you to bind my hands behind my back. Do it tightly. I know you will be tempted not to do it securely, but I will turn around and let Montrouge watch you do it. Montrouge, do you want to check Olg's bindings, or do you trust that Katelyn did it correctly?"

"Since I have no idea of what this material is that she used, I cannot judge if it will withhold your or Olg's attempts to break free, and I am certainly not going to let go of Jehanne to check. But, I will allow Katelyn to bind Jehanne as well. Come forward slowly," Montrouge instructed as he brusquely pulled Jehanne's hands behind her chair. "Do the hands first." As he spoke, Montrouge moved around to the side of Jehanne's chair so that Katelyn could tape her hands while he still held the knife firmly at her throat. When Katelyn had finished with Jehanne's hands, she moved slowly back to the front of the chair.

"Bind each foot separately to the leg of the chair," Montrouge instructed. When Katelyn had finished taping Jehanne's feet, she backed away from the chair and Montrouge tried to pull Jehanne's hands apart.

"Well, whatever this strange binding is, it seems to be secure," Montrouge admitted, as he tugged on Jehanne's hands. "Cover her mouth like you did Olg's, so she cannot scream." Katelyn did his bidding and then backed away again. "Now Nicolas," Montrouge ordered, "back up to me slowly and stand at arm's length from Jehanne, and we will make the exchange. Any attempt to kick me or attack me, and I will kill the girl warrior instantly." Nicolas slowly backed up.

Montrouge stood on the opposite side of Jehanne so that Nicolas could not reach him with his feet, and then in one sudden movement, Montrouge jumped over behind Nicolas, grabbed him by the neck and thrust the knife into his side. With his hands bound behind his back, Nicolas was unable to react, as much as he would have liked to. He could have tried to hit Montrouge with his body, but he simply did not dare risk Jehanne's life.

Unbelievably, Nicolas realized there was still a glimmer of hope. What Montrouge did *not* see while he was focused on his maneuver to change hostages was that Katelyn had backed up to the steps leading to Jehanne's quarters upstairs and had reached for something in the shadows, which she hid behind herself before moving back into full view. Nicolas saw a brief glint of the object and knew what it was. It was the sword . . . Jehanne's sword. He had no idea how Katelyn could manage to keep it hidden. After all, a sword was not a small knife, but he clung to that tiny particle of hope. It was all they had.

"And so now, my friends," Montrouge spoke to Katelyn and Nicolas, "we will continue our discussion outside. And you two," he addressed Olg and Jehanne, "sit here quietly and do not struggle.

Once I have obtained what I came here for, I will release Katelyn and Nicolas, and they shall return to free you. No need to fuss."

"Please," Katelyn jumped in, "do as he says, Jehanne and Olg. I'll be back, so don't make any noise to arouse Louis. Honestly, it's best this way. No one can know about this incident, so trust me on this. Stay quiet and wait for me. Please nod that you understand." Both Jehanne and Olg nodded, grudgingly, certainly, but they nodded nonetheless.

Nicolas could see the look of urgency on Katelyn's face as she implored her friends to stay quiet, and he prayed they would listen to her counsel. Regardless of what happened to him, Jehanne had to be protected at all cost. Furthermore, no mention of this incident could be recorded in the annals of her history. He knew the chances of this situation ending well for himself were unlikely. Katelyn did not know the secret of the Mount, which Abdon sought so desperately, and so he could not envision how he would come out of this alive unless Katelyn could somehow keep her sword hidden and use it to their advantage. His fate was in her hands . . . and in God's hands. He silently prayed for divine intervention.

"Now, Katelyn," Montrouge instructed, "I wish for you to precede us, but I want you to keep your hands behind your back, and I want you to go backwards down the stairs so that I can see your face at all times. Proceed very slowly. No sudden movements, or your beloved Nicolas is dead."

Nicolas was stunned. This was an immediate answer to his urgent prayer. He had wondered how Katelyn would be able to keep the sword hidden behind her, and Montrouge himself had provided the way. Surely, the Archangel was watching over them. She would have to navigate the steps very carefully so that when she bent her knees, the sword would not be visible, but it was possible.

Katelyn opened the door with her free hand and backed out of the room, taking one step at a time. He and Montrouge followed just as slowly. Katelyn must have been holding the hilt of the sword up as high as she could with the tip of the sword just hitting above her knee, for Nicolas could see no tell-tale sign of the weapon. The fortitude and resourcefulness of this woman he loved never failed to amaze him. To think he had found her a spoiled and shallow brat when he had first met her. The transformation in her character had been nothing short of miraculous since she had received her calling as a Watchman. Perhaps it was not as much a transformation of character as it was an awakening as she had begun to discover her true potential.

Now as Nicolas looked at Katelyn with a yearning that ached to the depths of his soul, he wondered if these were to be his last moments on earth to gaze upon her face. So much remained unsaid, and so much remained undone. Katelyn was his wife in the eyes of the Church, but he had never had the opportunity to make her his wife in the true sense of the word. They had never lived together as husband and wife. He had never been given the opportunity to bring children into the world with her. Regardless of his calling as a Watchman, Nicolas knew in that moment that he was ready to follow her anywhere to become her husband, even to her time, but now there was no more time left for them. Their time had expired. There was no time in the fifteenth century and no time in the twenty-first century. Instead of their ally, time had become their curse. Their mantra of 'no time' had unfortunately been accurate.

When they reached the bottom of the steps, Montrouge whispered for Katelyn to continue to lead the way, still walking backwards. By moving around to the back of the Coudray Tower, they moved immediately out of the light of the torch, and they put the tower between them and the royal lodgings. It was completely dark, and no one was about. With only the moon to guide her, it seemed that Katelyn knew where she was going. She backed up to the very edge of the fortress, behind a large clump of scrub brush that further blocked them from the view of anyone who might be walking the grounds. When she reached the battlement wall, Katelyn stopped.

"Move away from the ramparts, Katelyn," Montrouge instructed. "Nicolas and I shall take that place next to the wall. I hope you will remember what happened to the last person I held in this position. Oh, yes, 'tis true that my incomparable host, Richard Collins, died in that unfortunate fall off the abbey's Western Terrace, but so did your old friend, Jean le Vieux. I hope you have had sufficient time to ruminate on that unfortunate incident, Katelyn, for after all, it was entirely your fault, you know. I would hope you do not wish to repeat that episode. If you try anything, I shall simply push Nicolas over the edge and *voilà*, another death of a loved one for which you will be responsible. So now, how do you propose we proceed?"

As Montrouge talked, Nicolas turned his head unobtrusively to see what lay beneath the wall. In contrast to the wall he had scaled on the opposite side of the grounds, this fortification wall rose waist-high directly above ground level. Unfortunately, Nicolas could not see well enough in the moonlight to judge how far the drop was or what the terrain below was like. He could only pray that an eventual fall would be cushioned by brush or soil, rather than unforgiving rocks like on the opposite side of the promontory.

"I must have a guarantee that you won't kill either me or Nicolas once I've told you the secret," Katelyn replied, "and I'm not talking about a verbal guarantee, for as I have already told you, I don't trust one thing you say. You have to be able to guarantee that we'll be able to walk away unharmed."

"What do you suggest?" Montrouge asked. He still held Nicolas in a chokehold with the knife pressed into his broken ribs. The pain was excruciating.

"I will back away from you both," Katelyn suggested, "and you release Nicolas, Montrouge. I will allow you to still be within inches of him, so that you can get to him if you don't like what I have to say, but once I tell you what you want to know, Nicolas and I can both run, and you will leave these grounds immediately."

Nicolas tried to determine what Katelyn was trying to tell him to do. He believed she meant for him to run as soon as Montrouge released him, and that is what he did. The minute Montrouge lightened the pressure on his neck, Nicolas bolted with all the energy he had, but Montrouge was quicker and stronger than the man he had nearly beaten to death. Montrouge did not have the time to remove his sword from the scabbard, but he head-butted Nicolas in his ribs to slow him down. The pain nearly caused Nicolas to lose consciousness and prevented him from taking any further evasive action. He was incapable of fighting back when he felt himself being lifted by Montrouge. He was still coherent enough to hear Katelyn rushing towards them, but before she could intervene, Montrouge had managed to lift Nicolas up to the top of the wall, and then he felt the hand of the malevolent Abdon's human host, thrust him over the edge.

Nicolas knew he was falling through the emptiness of space, but by the time his body hit the darkness below, he no longer felt anything.

Chapter 58

ONCE NICOLAS HAS FALLEN, THERE IS nothing I can do but pray that somehow he has miraculously survived the fall, but I won't know his condition until I get rid of Montrouge. There are no qualms now in my mind about killing. This being is evil beyond words, and I don't hesitate for a second.

With Jehanne's sword in my hand, I lunge at him with a fury like nothing I've ever felt. I am completely and totally crazed with anger. I guess this is what vengeance feels like, and it isn't a good feeling. But right now, it's a necessary feeling. Montrouge is caught off guard. First of all, he had no idea I was armed, and secondly, he doesn't know I've been taking fencing lessons. This isn't my first swordfight. Although I didn't kill anyone, I held my own when those Burgundians attacked us on the way to Sainte-Catherine-de-Fierbois, and then, I wasn't motivated like I am now. One of us is going to die right now, and it isn't going to be me!

Montrouge just barely has time to whip out his sword and jump out of my path. The irony is that he took that sword from Nicolas, the sword I had taken from the Burgundian soldier, which I had given to Nicolas that afternoon for his protection. Now here I am, fighting against my own sword. If I hadn't given it to Nicolas, I wouldn't be in this predicament. But it's too late to change that now.

I put my trust in Brother Thibault's craftsmanship. I am using the sword of the Maiden . . . Jehanne's sword. Even though I know it doesn't have any special powers, Montrouge doesn't know that. And another thing he doesn't know is that I will *not* lose this fight.

"Jump if you like, you despicable coward," I say, "but just so you know, I am using La Pucelle's sword, the legendary sword she found in Sainte-Catherine-de-Fierbois. I'm sure you've heard about it. It once belonged to Charles Martel. It's the sword he used to defeat the enemies of God. It has miraculous properties, so you are doomed, Abdon."

He lunges at me from my left, but with an alacrity that even I can't explain, I am able to sidestep his thrust, and with both hands on my sword, I wind up and swing back to the left with all my force, landing a hit right in his thigh. Even in the darkness I can see the dark stain that begins to seep through his finely cut breeches, and he can't refrain from crying out in pain.

"You little witch," he hisses. "If you think I am going to let you do this to me again, you are badly mistaken. Prepare to die."

I almost laugh at his words. It is as if hearing that exact quote from *The Princess Bride* gives me new energy. It is as if my sword *is* magical. "My name is Inigo Montoya. You killed my father. Prepare to die," I whisper at first, and then repeat it louder and louder until he can hear every word. He looks at me like I'm crazy, and frankly, I am. But as I swing my sword back and forth to that mantra, my concentration becomes more focused, and my defensive moves become more and more improbable. It is as if I can read his mind. I know every move he is going to make. Over and over he jabs and thrusts at me, but emboldened by my newfound inspiration, I dance and twist and rebuff every savage attack.

Then *I* go on the offensive and as I gradually drive him back towards the battlements, I see him start to panic and make mistakes. I touch him in the arm, then the scalp. He does not cry out, as he did when I connected the first time, but I can feel his wrath. He turns, and in one instant, the moonlight reveals his eyes. For just one second, I can see those eyes, and it is all the time I need. They are black and sinister and evil. They are malevolent and vile. Those eyes are a testament to every wicked and revolting act this creature has perpetrated. It is as if time stands still. It is as if God grants me this one eternal instant to understand why I must kill this mortal host and why my hands will be clean of Montrouge's blood. His eyes are seething with anger at me, whereas my anger is focused on winning this battle because of my love for Nicolas and Jehanne and Olg and Jean le Vieux. His anger is focused solely on his hatred for me. That is his big mistake. His motivation is ungodly, and mine is righteous indignation. He is fighting because of hate, and I am fighting because of love.

With a final guided thrust that comes not of my own strength or skill, but from some divine source, I pierce Abdon's host, Philippe Montrouge, straight through the heart. It kills him instantly. For some reason, I look at my watch, which I wear in spite of the danger of it being discovered. I can't help it. I always feel compelled to know the time. And right now, I need to know what time it is. I just killed a man, even if he wasn't really a man, and I need to know the time. It is 9:35 p.m., and five minutes earlier, the man I love was pushed over the ramparts by the man I just killed. Five minutes out of an eternity. Five minutes in which my life has been forever changed.

After all the anguish I have felt about being put in the situation where I might have to kill, I feel no regret. I would have done it again and again and again to save Nicolas and Jehanne from Abdon. I realize now that there are times when even that most egregious of all sins in the eyes of God is necessary to prevent evil from triumphing over good. But unfortunately, it is too late. I killed Philippe Montrouge too late to save Nicolas.

I rush to the wall to search for Nicolas below. It is too far down for me to jump, but the moonlight illuminates his body lying on a clump of bushes right below the wall. Miraculously, the bushes cushioned his fall, and that gives me a glimmer of hope. As I squint my eyes to focus better, I think I can see movement in one of his legs. My heart skips a beat.

I lean as far over the wall as I dare and call out to him softly, but when he doesn't respond, I know I have to get Olg to help. Wiping the blood from Jehanne's sword onto Montrouge's luxurious overcoat, I turn and run back to the tower, conscious of the need to get to Nicolas, to quickly dispose of Montrouge's body, and to escape from the fortress without questions being asked. Olg will help me do all three of these things.

The torch is still burning, but there is still no sign of Louis as I scamper up the stairs as quietly as I came down them. When I enter the antechamber, the look of relief on the faces of both Jehanne and Olg is unmistakable. I place Jehanne's sword on the table, careful not to put it on top of the map of the fortress so that it doesn't mark it with Montrouge's blood. Now I know why I had looked at those plans so carefully.

I go directly to Jehanne and pull the duct tape from her mouth.

"Katelyn, what happened?" she frantically asks me. "Where is Nicolas? And what about Montrouge?"

"Montrouge is dead. I killed him, and I killed him with your sword, Jehanne. You'll have to clean it before anyone sees it," I say. Then I dash back to Olg, pull the tape off his mouth, and begin to rip the tape from his hands. He'll be able to help me free Jehanne.

"Good," she says. "'Tis God's will. That man was evil and would have thwarted God's work. What about Nicolas?"

"Nicolas is injured," I reply, hoping that I'm right—that he really is just injured and not dead. "Montrouge threw him over the ramparts. I don't know how badly he's hurt. Olg, can you help me? We've got to get to him as quickly as we can."

"You know I will help you with anything you need, Katelyn," he replies.

"Get Jehanne free," I instruct, "while I gather our things. Jehanne and Olg, you can never speak of what has happened here tonight. Never. Your safety and my safety depend on it. This all goes back to the battle of Mont Saint Michel. It has nothing to do with you, Jehanne. Philippe Montrouge used you as leverage to get to me and Nicolas. He had a grudge about being on the losing side of the battle on the Mount, and he wanted me and Nicolas to pay because of it. Now that Montrouge is dead, you'll never have to worry about him again. But you can't say anything about it. Do you understand?" I ask as I put my cloak and cap back on, tie the bag with the climbing gear around my waist, and gather up the outerwear belonging to Olg and Nicolas, as well as all the remnants of the duct tape.

"Yes," they both reply.

"Good. Jehanne, I need your help," I say, as I think about the grappling hook and climbing rope. We can't leave those items on the fortress wall, or there will be questions for Jehanne. "Come with us right now. We'll be fast so you can get back to your room before anyone comes to check on Montrouge." I hand Olg his cloak, and he puts it on as we exit the room.

Once we're down the stairs, I lead the way through the darkness. When we get to the ramparts, I instruct Olg to throw Montrouge's body over the wall while I get the grappling hook and climbing rope out. I also throw down Montrouge's knife and my sword—the sword Montrouge took from Nicolas and used to fight against me—that were on the ground next to his body. I look around quickly to see if there are any other indications of our struggle.

"But what do I say to Louis about Montrouge?" Jehanne asks me. "He was supposed to be my tailor. How do I explain his disappearance?"

"Tell Louis he insulted you by trying to touch you inappropriately, and so you sent him packing . . . that you sent him away. Just say he was embarrassed about the incident and didn't want Louis to know about it. Then ask for another tailor to be sent. Olg and I are going to see to it that his body is never found," I say, as I try to remove the traces of blood on the ground with my foot. Then I attach the grappling hook to the rampart wall.

"We aren't coming back, Jehanne. At least, I'm not. I'll send Olg back when Nicolas and I are out of danger. But for me, this is goodbye. I've got to go back to Mont Saint Michel. You know everything you need to know. The pouch with your gear for the sword is under your mattress. You know what to do with it. You are going to amaze the entire world, my friend, and I'll be watching, but I'm afraid we'll never see each other again. As I have told you before, I'll always be with you in spirit.

"As soon as both Olg and I are down and off the wall, you need to throw this hook and rope down to us. Then, run back to your room immediately. When Louis comes to check on you, tell him that your friends left after Montrouge." I'm trying not to cry as I throw my arms around her to hug her goodbye.

"Katelyn, thank you. You not only saved my life today, but you also saved my soul by helping me carry out God's will. I know that without your help, I would not be where I am today. You will never know the depths of my gratitude. *A dieu, mon amie et que Dieu te bénisse à jamais.*"

In some ways, I'm glad we don't have time to prolong this goodbye. I hate goodbyes, and I hate even more knowing how this goodbye ends. In four short months, Jehanne will not only lift the siege at Orléans, but will succeed in getting the Dauphin crowned in

Reims. Then, in a little over two years, she will seal her life's work with her own blood.

Our goodbyes are tempered by the most important thing on my mind right now, and that's getting to Nicolas. After Olg and I rappel down the wall and Jehanne has thrown down the hook and rope, I give the gear to Olg to store, and I head for the clump of bushes where I saw Nicolas's body. He's still there and now he is motionless, but I can hear his labored breathing. He's alive! He fell on the only possible spot that could have saved his life. Another blessing from the Archangel. I need Olg's help to get him off the bushes, but first I have to clean up the scene.

Quickly, I turn back to Montrouge's body. Without looking at his face, I undo my scabbard and secure it around my waist and then find the sword and knife I threw down, putting one in the sheath and handing the other to Olg. Just as I didn't want Gothman's brass knuckles, I don't want a war trophy from Philippe Montrouge either. I need no reminders of Abdon. Olg hands me the climbing bag, which I tie around my waist, and he pulls Montrouge's body under the bushes to hide it from plain sight.

"Olg," I say, "you've got to help me get Nicolas back to our rooms, but what are we going to do with the body?"

"Katelyn, I'll come back tonight and bury him after Nicolas is safe. Do you still have that spade?"

"Yes, of course. And thank you Olg. You are amazing. I don't know what I'd do without you here." It's true. What would I do without this man? He has saved me from so many predicaments. I will be eternally grateful. For the first time since we met, I give him a hug.

I spread out Nicolas's overcoat on the ground, and then together, Olg and I gently pull Nicolas off the bushes and lay him on the cloak. I pray that he has no spinal cord injury because we have no other choice. I can't wait for the EMTs to move him carefully onto a stretcher, or I'll be waiting six hundred years. I just have to go with my gut instinct and pray that the Archangel continues to watch over him. His breathing is steady, but I can't get him to respond.

I wonder if we should try to make a stretcher with our cloaks, but before I even have a chance to think about it, Olg wraps Nicolas in the cloak, throws him over his shoulder, and heads down the hill towards the town. I follow Olg into the darkness.

Fortunately, at that moment, I don't know just how dark it is going to get for me.

Chapter 59

AS JEHANNE HUMBLY KNELT AT THE FEET of King Charles in the magnificent cathedral of Reims, scenes of what had led her here flashed through her mind: the first time she heard her voices, being rejected by Robert Baudricourt, meeting Katelyn Michaels who forever changed her destiny, the journey from Vaucouleurs to Chinon, recognizing the Dauphin in the crowd of his courtiers, obtaining her sword and having Katelyn show her how to use those marvelous relics, the examinations to which she was subjected in Poitiers before the Dauphin allowed her to join the royal troops, and then Orléans itself.

Yes, Orléans. That was the turning point. She was not naïve enough to think that this long war with the English was over, for Paris still had to be liberated, but in those few moments as she knelt, Jehanne relived the prelude to Orléans and the battles there that resulted in the lifting of the siege.

Her mind raced backwards, and she thought of that day, that glorious day when her brothers, Jean and Pierre, arrived from Domrémy to join their sister in her quest to liberate France. It was a confirmation to her that her mother and father not only finally understood, but also supported her cause. It brought her great joy and great comfort to be with her brothers. They filled the void in her life that had been there since Katelyn had left.

There were others who also helped fill that void. The Dauphin allowed her page, Louis de Coutes, to join her in the campaigns that led up to Reims, and she found him to be a loyal and faithful supporter.

True to Katelyn's word, Olg had also returned to her, explaining how he had buried the body of Philippe Montrouge in the vast forest surrounding Chinon, and how he had assisted Katelyn and Nicolas with their departure for Mont Saint Michel. He arrived astride the chestnut stallion Midnight, Katelyn's final parting gift to him, but he brought other troubling news: Nicolas seemed to be suffering from dropsy of the brain. Jehanne was heartsick for her friend, but there was nothing she could do other than pray for the young man's quick recovery.

Then Jehanne's mind turned to the day she met the commanders of the army at Blois prior to setting off for Orléans. It had been daunting, but Jehanne remembered the lesson Katelyn had taught her: 'act with confidence and you will be confident.' The group included Lord Gaucourt, whom she had already met in Chinon, Jean V de Bueil, Lord Louis de Culan, Jean de la Brosse, Baron Gilles de Rais, La Hire, Poton de Saintrailles, and dozens of others serving in lesser roles. Completing the group was Regnault de Chartres, the Archbishop of Reims. He had presided over her intense examinations in Poitiers and then insisted on accompanying her to Blois. She still wasn't certain whether she trusted him.

During those preliminary days with the army in Blois, although she acted as if she were completely comfortable in the presence of these aristocratic commanders, Jehanne preferred being with the members of the religious orders, the simple servants of God. Twice a day, she assembled the priests of the company for prayer and hymn singing. In her attempt to clean up the camp as Katelyn had suggested, she allowed no soldiers at these gatherings unless they had confessed that day. As preparations were made for the attack on Orléans, she became particularly close to Brother Pasquerel, an Augustinian monk who became her own personal confessor.

Besides using that time in Blois to prepare spiritually, she commissioned a large banner and smaller pennant to be taken into battle. Olg suggested she call upon his fellow countryman, a Scottish artist by the name of Hamish Power, to design the standard. It depicted Christ holding the world, with an angel on either side, surrounded by a field of fleurs-de-lis. She came to love the banner, and indeed, it had become more important to her than her weapons of war. It became her replacement for the marvelous sword from Sainte-Catherine-de-Fierbois, which was no longer in her possession. That sword had never truly been hers. It was Martel's . . . and Katelyn's. She had just been allowed a brief stewardship over the sword, which may have allowed her to change the world.

As Jehanne knelt on the cold stone pavement in the Reims cathedral, she thought back to the day when the generals finally announced that the royal army was ready for battle. She would never forget the spectacular scene near the end of April when they left Blois for Orléans. The army was four thousand men strong, with sixty heavy wagons and more than four hundred head of cattle. As the titular commander of the royal armies, Jehanne gathered all the priests and had them lead the company, singing hymns and praising God. She followed them astride her horse, dressed in the full set of armor commissioned for her by the Dauphin, and carrying her banner. Behind her were the mounted military leaders, largely members of the nobility in their fine garments and gilded armor, followed by the troops on foot, bearing the colorful standards of the various aristocratic houses to which they were associated. It was an extraordinary pageant designed to impress and intimidate the enemy.

Unfortunately, that initial expedition had not ended well. Her advisors, perhaps in an attempt to force her into a symbolic, figurehead role rather than an actual military leadership role, led her to the town of Chécy, past her intended destination and on the opposite side of the Loire River from where the English commander, John Talbot, and his troops were stationed. This was the same Lieutenant General Talbot who humiliated the French in the Battle of the Herrings. Jehanne had already dictated a scathing letter to the King of England, the Duke of Bedford, and Lord Talbot at the end of March in which she ordered Talbot and his men to go back to their own lands or be wiped out, as decreed by God, the King of Heaven, but to no avail. She was particularly anxious to defeat the man who refused to listen to God's messenger.

Jehanne was furious when she met the on-site French commander, Lord Jean de Dunois, the illegitimate half-brother of the Duke of Orléans, who admitted that he was the one responsible for the decision to have the army stop in Chécy. He claimed it was safer and wiser to take her beyond the mark on the wrong side of the river rather than face the English enemy directly. She chastised him soundly in God's name. "The counsel of God our Lord is safer and wiser than yours. I bring you better aid than ever came to any soldier or city because it is aid from the King of Heaven," she had told him. As she spoke those words, the wind changed, suddenly favorable for launching boats to carry her and the other commanders across the Loire. Divine intervention, some said.

Unfortunately, however, there were not enough vessels to ferry the entire army across. The decision was made for the main army to return to Blois where they could more easily cross the Loire and then make their way back up to Orléans on the north side of the river. Jehanne deplored all of that wasted effort, which could have been avoided if someone had just shown her a map! *She* would have asked the question about crossing the river *before* the army had ever left Blois.

While waiting for the remainder of the army to arrive, Lord Dunois convinced Jehanne to go with him into the city of Orléans where, she was told, the inhabitants awaited her arrival with great anticipation. The English had cut off the city on three sides with a chain of fortified buildings and fortresses connected by a series of trenches. However, on Friday, the twenty-ninth day of April, Dunois snuck Jehanne into Orléans through the unprotected side. They entered the city after dark as much to avoid a mob scene by the good citizens of Orléans as to fool the English enemy.

Even so, she was greeted by a large group of *Orléanais* expressing such joy and gladness to see her that she was overcome with emotion. They pressed in to touch her on her new white steed, a gift from the Dauphin. It was a level of adulation that made her uncomfortable, but she recognized it for what it was, a spark of hope that God would assist France and liberate Orléans. While Dunois and the other military leaders watched in dismay, the townsfolk hailed her as their liberator, expressing faith in her ability to throw off the hated English yoke.

She and her men were housed for several days in the home of Jacques Boucher, a prominent citizen who was the treasurer for the Duke of Orléans. During her stay, the good citizens of Orléans nearly broke down his door on several occasions, so desirous were they to catch a glimpse of her.

Once in Orléans, Jehanne tried to convince Dunois that they needed to immediately commence liberating the string of English fortresses one by one, but he insisted they wait until the full army arrived.

Feeling helpless and anxious to begin this confrontation, Jehanne sent her second message to Lord Talbot in which she reiterated her earlier demands, stating that the King of Heaven would send greater strength to her than the English would be able to bring against her in all of their assaults. She warned him that if they would not leave the city, God would drive them out of France, and that there would be a great clash of arms in Orléans such as had never been seen in France in a thousand years. Katelyn had taught her to be bold, and so she did not mince her words.

The heralds who delivered her message were received by the English with disdain. The first was illegally imprisoned, and the second was sent back with a message calling Jehanne vulgar names and ordering "the cow herder" back to her farm.

That evening, Jehanne made a third attempt to deliver her message to the English, this time in person. There was a small French-held island in the Loire from which she could actually communicate with the English soldiers in the bridge towers known as Les Tourelles. She called out to their commander, Sir William Glasdale, ordering him "to surrender in the name of God," but once again, vulgar language was spewed back, this time with the added threat that Glasdale would take great pleasure in personally burning Jehanne himself.

The next day, the first of May, was the Sabbath, and hostilities were suspended for "the truce of God," but it did not stop Jehanne from trying to communicate with her enemy from a different location. However, the results were the same. That same day, Dunois left for Blois to check on the status of the army. Rumors were flying that without Jehanne in their midst, many of the French soldiers had deserted.

Finally, on Wednesday, Dunois arrived with the much-awaited army and also with the news that the English commander, Lord Fastolf, was arriving from the north with reinforcements and supplies for his garrison. Jehanne demanded to be informed of events, but ignoring her request, Dunois launched an attack without her knowledge on St. Loup, one of the English-held fortresses outside of

Orléans. To this day, nearly three months later, it still rankled Jehanne when she thought about how Dunois had attempted to keep her ignorant of his plans. However, higher powers woke Jehanne in the middle of the night, and she knew. This battle was to be the pivotal moment for her and for France.

She had already prepared her sword with the relics Katelyn had given her, and after being helped to don her armor and mount her horse, she headed directly for the Burgundy Gate that led to St. Loup, with both her sword and banner in hand, accompanied by her faithful band of followers, including her brothers, Brother Pasquerel, and her page, Louis.

As she and her companions galloped through the gate towards the battle, for the first time in her life, Jehanne saw the rude realities of war: scores of wounded French soldiers being helped back into the safety of the city walls, men with horrific lacerations attempting to hold their flesh together with filthy hands, even soldiers with severed limbs bleeding uncontrollably until the loss of blood drained them of life. Jehanne's group was told by those returning from St. Loup that the French were losing the battle. The English were better equipped, more disciplined, and more numerous, and they might as well turn around before they, too, were mortally wounded. *This* was Jehanne's chance to turn the course of the conflict.

When Jehanne and her men reached St. Loup, the scene was even more horrific. Soldiers moaned in agony as their entrails spilled out upon the muddy ground and corpses stared up to heaven with lifeless, sightless eyes that would never again look upon the faces of their beloved wives and children. They were visions Jehanne would never forget, though she dreamed a thousand dreams of light and joy. Those images would haunt her forever, imprinted into the darkest recesses of her mind. She would never again see a wounded soldier without the hair on her neck rising in a frisson of terror. But they were images that also motivated her in a way she never thought possible.

As they approached the fortress's bell tower, Jehanne handed the banner to Louis and instructed him to hold it as high as possible. Then she fearlessly grabbed her sword, and pressed her index finger and thumb on the buttons of the attached relics, as Katelyn had taught her to do. Immediately, a beacon of light sliced through the darkness, and the sound of thunder and rushing air pierced through the sounds of striking swords and desperate cries. She began to shout that she was coming to save the French, and her small group of men joined in the chanting. Soon, the French soldiers assaulting the fortress began to shout as well, renewed in their determination to conquer their objective.

In a change of momentum rarely seen in the annals of war, the French under Jehanne's leadership rallied boldly, and the English defense began to collapse as the soldiers—frightened at the unearthly spectacle of La Pucelle inspiring her troops—lost their courage. The fortress was taken after a vicious three-hour battle. During those entire three hours, Jehanne held her magnificent sword aloft, strengthening French resolve, and inspiring her men to victory.

After the battle was over, Jehanne dismounted and tended to the wounded, and offered sanctuary to the English clergymen, some of whom may have actually been soldiers hiding behind the pious robes of the Church. Jehanne did not care. She offered hope and relief to all. Although she had threatened to kill every Englishman in France, her heart broke when she instructed the men to tally up the counts. Forty English prisoners were taken, and over a hundred were dead. She wept with compassion for all the dead, being particularly devastated that they had died without confessing their sins.

As the French soldiers rallied around her, proclaiming how miraculous her intervention had been, she chastised them. "'Tis not my intervention," she said as she pointed heavenward, "that turned the tide tonight, but the intervention of the great God of Heaven. I am only His servant, sent to do His will. I hereby declare in His name that within five days, the current siege laid to Orléans will be lifted if you will but express your gratitude to Him and confess your sins before Him."

She then instructed all those present to kneel and thank God for the great mercy that had been poured out upon them, after which she called upon Brother Pasquerel to listen to her confession, and then to the confessions of the rest of the company.

Later, Jehanne learned that Lord Talbot's reinforcements sent to St. Loup had been stopped by the six hundred troops of Lords Coulences, Graville, and Saint-Sévère. Talbot was forced to order the retreat of his men, leaving his isolated forces at St. Loup on their own.

News of the battle soon spread. Jehanne's miraculous capture of St. Loup was the first ray of hope in an otherwise dreary century of French hopelessness.

Now, as she knelt in Reims beside the man she had made king, Jehanne thought about the four days following the Battle of St. Loup. She had continued her courageous campaign to lift the siege, buoyed up by her marvelous sword, which she used judiciously, and by her battle standard, which she used unceasingly. She never left her soldiers during the assaults, exhorting them to take heart and never to retreat. And with her as their leader, they never did fall back.

In spite of her total trust in God, while she was helping to raise a scaling ladder during the Battle of the Tourelles, an enemy archer found his mark. The arrow penetrated Jehanne's flesh between her neck and shoulder. The pain was intense, but she was comforted by her voices, and her injury only served to increase her compassion for the wounded on both sides of the conflict.

At first, her troops were dispirited by the fact that she was wounded, but after emerging from the vineyard where she had been taken for treatment, she took her sword in hand once again and placed her banner in the hand of a Basque soldier with instructions to hold it high. In spite of her injury, she called her men to action with power and authority. Even though she was wounded, she witnessed firsthand how the English panicked as they saw and heard her approaching, as if the very heavens had illuminated her uplifted sword, and as if the armies of the Almighty were rushing down to assist her. When the wind rippled her banner and it touched the wall of the tower, it was as if God Himself commanded her men.

"All is yours now," she ordered. "Enter!" And so it was. The Tourelles were reclaimed for France. Orléans was liberated.

Yes, as Jehanne knelt in Reims next to the man God had called her to assist, she silently thanked Him in turn for having assisted her in accomplishing this task. She had lifted the siege of Orléans not by personally shedding blood, but by motivating and inspiring her men. She thought of how she, in turn, had been inspired by all those whom God had sent to prepare her for this moment. Those who had gone before her . . . all those who had made their own sacrifices to help her, Jehanne La Pucelle, fulfill her destiny.

There were so many, including her father and mother, her little sister Catherine, and big brother Jacquemin, who had loved and supported her and believed that she truly heard divine voices, as well as her brothers, Jean and Pierre, who continued to support her even now. She thought of her new friends, her page, Louis de Coutes, and the Augustinian monk, Brother Pasquerel. She thought back to her kinsman, Durand Laxart, who had taken a chance and agreed to take her to see Robert de Baudricourt in Vaucouleurs, and then Baudricourt who in turn had supported her request for help to travel to Chinon. She thought of those amazing traveling companions, Jean de Metz and Bertrand de Poulangy, Colet de Vienne and the squires Jean de Dieulouard and Julien de Honnecourt. She thought of Olg, to whom she had entrusted the sacred sword—the sword of Charles

Martel—after the siege had been lifted, after the bells of the city had pealed out their victory cry.

But most of all, Jehanne thought of Katelyn. There were not enough words to express how much Katelyn Michaels had inspired her, but she knew. And Katelyn knew.

"Wherever you are, my dear friend," she whispered silently as the bells of Notre Dame de Reims echoed the pealing of Orléans' bells three months earlier, both celebrating the beginning of a new era in France, "I pray that you are well, and that your Nicolas has recovered. I pray that you will know of my great appreciation for your friendship and mentorship, for without your tutoring and inspiration, I would not be here today. May you find eternal happiness with your beloved Nicolas, for you truly merit all of God's richest blessings."

With that whispered injunction, her thoughts returned to the present. She stood now, holding her banner aloft, as she examined the towering walls of the great cathedral covered in the banners of the principal Armagnac families who had supported the Dauphin's cause. The *Sainte Ampoule*, that holy vial of anointing oil, was escorted to the cathedral by four of Jehanne's military commanders on horseback, Lords Saint-Sévère, Culan, Rais, and Graville. Solemnly, they handed the vial to the Abbot, Jean Canard, and accompanied him into the cathedral. The Dauphin was knighted by the Duke of Alençon, and the Archbishop anointed him with the holy unction, the Divine Right to rule, and in the last symbolic gesture, the clergyman placed the crown upon Charles' head.

With tears in her eyes for all that had led her to this very moment, Jehanne knelt and threw her arms about the king's legs.

"Noble King," she cried, "now is accomplished the will of God, who wished me to lift the siege of Orléans and to bring you to this city of Reims to receive your holy anointing, to show that you are the true king, and the one to whom the kingdom of France should belong."

The onlookers cheered in jubilation, and spontaneously the crowd began chanting the word "Noel," in remembrance of Clovis, who had been crowned with this very oil on Christmas day nearly a thousand years earlier. The sound of the trumpets heralding the new king echoed through the vast space like a heavenly chorus. Many, like Jehanne, cried tears of joy. Surely this was *her* crowning moment as well. All of her efforts, all of her trials, all of her disappointments, all of her suffering, and all of her self-doubts had been worth it, and all of France seemed to concur.

What Jehanne did not know, however, was that there was one Frenchman, a clergyman, who was singing neither her nor the new king's praises, one man who did not shout "Noel" with the enthusiastic onlookers, one man who did not shed tears of joy at the coronation. In fact, this Burgundian bishop had been driven from city after city as the royal army retook control of what he considered to be *his* country. Seething with hatred for this upstart of a peasant, this self-proclaimed prophetess, this girl warrior who declared herself to be a conduit to God, he had even been forced to hastily retreat from Reims when the Armagnacs took control of the city as the Dauphin arrived. This man would never forget what Jehanne had done, and he would never forgive her, for her successes had meant the defeat of the Anglo-Burgundian faction to which he had pinned his hopes for power and prestige. He would never forgive her for forcing him to leave his home region or his diocese.

His name? Pierre Cauchon.

Chapter 60

AS THE HOURS TURNED INTO DAYS, AND THE days
into weeks, and the weeks into months, even the usually jovial
Brother Thibault began to lose hope. It was bad enough that he had
to observe Katelyn fall deeper and deeper into a state of despair, but
now he felt the gloom of despondency fall upon himself, as well.

Although Nicolas could eat and swallow when fed, he did not
open his eyes, and he did not speak. Katelyn mentioned how
concerned she had been after his fall that he might have incurred
what she had called a spinal cord injury that could impair his
movement, but he had no trouble moving his limbs and extremities.
What he could not do, however, was squeeze the hand of his friend
or caress the face of the woman who loved him beyond measure.

Thibault suffered greatly, hearing Katelyn cry herself to sleep on
the straw pallet he had set up for her next to Nicolas's bed. She told
Thibault she could not bear the thought of him waking up and not
finding her at his side, and so day after day, and night after night, she
sat next to him. She rarely left his room, even to eat, usually opting to
force down her meals as she watched for the slightest change in his
condition. Occasionally, she would allow Thibault to feed Nicolas so
she could have a much-needed break.

The only bright spot for his grieving friend came one hot afternoon in late July when Katelyn was visited by a giant of a man, a Scotsman whom she addressed as Olg.

"Brother Thibault," Katelyn said as she invited the man inside, "this is my dear friend, Olg. He was my secret guardian the entire time I was with Jehanne. He knew immediately that I was a woman, and it was so good to know I had someone to count on. He's the one who helped me get Nicolas off the mountain when Abdon threw him over the ramparts. In fact, he rode with me all the way to Sainte-Catherine-de-Fierbois, carrying Nicolas in his arms. I can never thank him enough for all he's done," she said, as tears ran down her face.

Brother Thibault took the man, who was even larger than himself, into his arms and gave him a bear hug.

"We men of a certain size need to stick together," Thibault chuckled, the first authentic laugh that had left his mouth in some time. "Thank you, kind sir, for taking care of this remarkable woman. I felt so badly that I could not be there to safeguard her, and I am grateful to know that you took my place as her protector. Come in, come in, and sit down. I have just made a fine chicken stew, and I fear that Katelyn and Nicolas hardly eat enough to keep a flea alive, so I am glad to have a hearty eater to share it with."

"Nicolas is eating?" asked Olg as he took a seat at the table. "That sounds like good news, Katelyn. How is he?"

As Katelyn's face clouded, Thibault jumped in and answered. "We manage to get enough food down him to preserve his life, but I regret to tell you that there has been little improvement in his condition since you last saw him."

Thibault saw Olg squeeze Katelyn's hand.

"I am so sorry, Katelyn," Olg said. "I was hoping for better news."

"I was, too," she said, as the tears continued to flow.

"Come, my dear," said Thibault. "Sit with us and eat. Later, you can take Olg up to see Nicolas, but for now, sit and enjoy the company of your visitor."

Thibault could see that in spite of her great affection for Olg, it was still difficult for her to give him any of her time, which had been solely dedicated to Nicolas.

"Yes, Katelyn, come and sit with us. But first, I have a commission to complete." The man stood again and removed his scabbard. From it, he withdrew a sword that he placed ceremoniously in Katelyn's hands. Both Katelyn and Thibault recognized it immediately. Five stars graced its finely-honed blade. It was Jehanne's sword, the sword Brother Thibault had made for La Pucelle.

"Olg, what happened?" Katelyn said with a sense of panic in her voice. "Why are you bringing this to me?" Brother Thibault watched as she inspected the sword's hilt. It carried none of Katelyn's gadgets, nor the electrical tape Jehanne had used to attach them.

"Do not fear, Katelyn. Jehanne used the sword as you instructed. I have been with her. I was with her as she helped lift the siege at Orléans with this sword."

"So it worked?" Katelyn asked with the first excitement Thibault had heard in her voice since her return. "I mean, did it . . . was it . . ?" Brother Thibault wondered how she was going to explain this to Olg. How much did the giant actually know about Katelyn Michaels?

"I do not understand exactly what you mean," Olg said, "but this sword certainly has special powers, if that is what you mean. Or, perhaps it is Jehanne who has special powers to render the sword miraculous. But I saw it. I was there. I am a first-hand witness. 'Twas as if the sword emanated the sound and light of heaven, as if it focused the powerful sounds of the thunder and wind itself. This remarkable sword inspired and motivated the royal armies of France and completely disconcerted and confused the English."

"But why have you brought it to me?" Katelyn asked.

"I am returning it to you at Jehanne's request. She told me to relay this message to you, Katelyn. She said that this sword, along with your mentoring, enabled her to demand respect from the armies and military leaders of France. After the campaign at Orléans, she came to understand that her role was not to kill with this sword, but to inspire others. And that she has done. That is why I am returning it to you. She has chosen now to carry a banner rather than to risk taking a human life."

For an instant, Thibault worried if the reference to taking a human life would be another source of pain for Katelyn, who had been forced to kill Philippe Montrouge with that very sword, but on that score, he was wrong. Instead, Katelyn lovingly rubbed her fingers the length of the sword, and then placed it on the mantel, next to Brother Thibault's beloved clock.

"Thank you, Olg. Will you be seeing her again? Can you thank her for sending it back to . . . I mean, giving it to me? It has a great deal of significance for me." She looked at Thibault with an actual twinkle in her eye.

"Yes, Katelyn. I will tell her."

"Now, tell me, Olg. How is my beloved mount Midnight doing? Has he adjusted from carrying my heavy bulk to your svelte figure?"

Brother Thibault burst out laughing. "Katelyn," he said. "You actually said something funny. It warms my heart."

"Olg, tell us everything that's happened to you and Jehanne since I left Chinon," Katelyn demanded, and so for the next hour, Brother Thibault and Katelyn were regaled with tales of Jehanne's exploits, ending with the extraordinary account of the coronation of King Charles VII in Reims.

"Jehanne was there, front and center," Olg explained. "Right there next to the king when he was anointed with the holy oil. The ceremony was unbelievable. It lasted for five hours. There were hundreds of people, and they not only cheered the new king, but they cheered La Pucelle, as well. She is a national heroine."

Thibault smiled and felt warm inside. It was an entire hour when Katelyn thought of someone besides Nicolas. It was an entire hour when it was confirmed to Katelyn just how successful she had been in her mission. It was an entire hour when she was reminded that her sacrifices had served a purpose. Katelyn and Nicolas had changed the destiny of France.

"I am so proud of Jehanne," Katelyn said, and she actually smiled. "I'm just so proud."

"As you should be," Brother Thibault interjected. "Olg, you may not be aware of just how much Katelyn helped Jehanne become the leader she has become."

"Oh, Thibault," Katelyn protested. "She had it all in her. I just helped her find the way to get it out."

"I do know," Olg said. "Jehanne made it very clear to me. She told me that if it had not been for you, she would never have had the courage or confidence to make all of this happen, in spite of her voices. You were her inspiration, Katelyn. She wanted me to tell you that."

"Will you tell her how pleased I am, Olg? Tell her just how very proud I am of her."

"Of course I will, and I know it will delight her. But, you know, her work is not yet done. This war is not over. There is still much to do. This is just the beginning."

"Yeah, I know. Jehanne still has a lot to do," replied Katelyn with that far-away look in her eyes. This was not a good turn in the conversation. The last thing Katelyn needed right now was to think about Jehanne's destiny. Thibault tried to change the subject.

"Now, Olg, let me get that stew for you. You must be very tired after your long journey, and of course, we would love to have you spend the night."

"I will eat some of your stew and visit Nicolas," Olg said, "but then I must be on my way. I left Midnight at a stable on the mainland, and the groom was very explicit about when the tide will be coming back in. Besides, I must rejoin Jehanne as quickly as possible."

"Thank you for being loyal to her, Olg. With me gone, she needs someone she can count on. Unfortunately, even the people she believes she can trust will prove to be . . ."

"Enough of this negative talk, Katelyn. Let the man eat in peace so he can be about his business."

Later, after all of the goodbyes were spoken and the parting tears had been shed, Katelyn returned once again to Nicolas's side. It was then that Thibault made an important decision. He had been thinking about it for some time. In fact, he had spoken to Katelyn about it, but she had refused to listen. This was not going to be easy, and Katelyn would be furious, but it was something that had to be done. He knew he had to do it because it was not simply his idea alone. No, this was what the Archangel wanted. He knew he had been prompted to do this by Michael himself.

He began his preparations. First, he took the sword, the sword he had made with his own hands. The sword of the Maiden, which had been used to change the course of history. He brought it briefly to his lips, savoring the coldness of the metal on this hot day. He placed it on the table, and then he took down the clock from the mantel, the only earthly possession of any value he owned.

The sword and the clock. Yes, they were perfect for Katelyn. The first, a symbol of her courage and obedience in carrying out her mission, and the second, a symbol of hope, which she seemed to have lost. He thought about writing her a message, but he felt it might diminish the power of the symbols. No, Katelyn would understand.

After he had carefully wrapped the two cherished objects, he wished that the tears Katelyn shed so easily and prolifically could come to relieve the grief he felt so acutely. But the tears would not come, and his grief threatened to break his heart wide open.

Chapter 61

WHEN I OPEN MY EYES, I AM TOTALLY and utterly confused. For the life of me, I can't figure out where I am. I look around. Notre-Dame-Sous Terre. I am in Notre-Dame-Sous-Terre.

But the worst of it is, it isn't 1429. The dim electric light allows me to figure that one out. What on earth?

Then, the irony of it all hits me like a pile of bricks. This is exactly what happened to me during the siege of Mont Saint Michel. Nicolas sent me home unconscious, dying of an infection. I didn't have a chance to say goodbye to him. Now, I have apparently left him behind, and he didn't have the chance to say goodbye to me. Well, actually, I didn't get to say goodbye either, and unlike him, I didn't have the chance to leave him a message or write him a letter.

But how on earth did I get here? The last thing I remember is sitting with Nicolas after we had said goodbye to Olg. Yes, that's right. Then in the evening, Brother Thibault brought me some warm broth and sat there with me, insisting I drink it all down. That was it. He had put something in that broth. I don't know if they have any kind of herbs or medicine that make people sleep in the fifteenth century, but I do know that Thibault is a master with food and herbs. He must have concocted something to make me sleep, and then he carried me to the chapel and sent me home.

Brother Thibault had been trying to convince me for weeks to go home, to go back to my time. He assured me he would take care of Nicolas and that Nicolas would come back to get me when he had recovered. But how could I leave? How could I desert Nicolas when he was in a comatose state? How could I abandon him when he needed me the most? How could I allow him to wake up without me there by his side? I couldn't. And so Brother Thibault made the decision for me.

I am furious. Livid. My hand is still on my enseigne in the keyhole, and without even a second thought, I turn it. I am going back. Back to Nicolas, and yes, back to Brother Thibault. I'm not going to let him get away with this.

Nothing happens, and so I turn it again. I turn and turn and turn, and then I cry. This isn't possible! I plead with Michael and with God to let me go back. But the heavens are closed, just as Nicolas had found them during the four years he waited to be reunited with me.

When I finally lift my hand and remove my enseigne, I become aware of my heavy backpack on my lap, and my smaller backpack slipped over my shoulder. Thibault even sent me home with my belongings. And more. My scabbard and Jehanne's sword are strapped around the large backpack. I cry some more when I realize that Brother Thibault has sent me back with the sword. As mad as I am at him, I still think he's pretty amazing. That was so kind of him to do. It was a concrete reminder of all I had accomplished. It was a reminder of the success of my mission, and besides, it's pretty darn cool. *I* have the Maiden's sword, the sword which mysteriously disappeared six centuries earlier. Of course, I can never tell anyone what it is, but *I* know, and God knows. I didn't do any of this for the praise of the world.

There's also something bulky inside my backpack, and I unzip it to find a fairly large object wrapped in burlap and twine. I'll have to check it out when I get back to my room because now I know that I've got to get back to the Du Guesclin Hotel.

I unzip the pocket where I'd left my room key. I hope it's still there, because if not, I've got some explaining to do to my dad and Adèle, especially about how I managed to acquire this real-life sword after all the town shops have closed. It's going to be hard enough to act as if I've never been gone. I mean, so much as happened to me in what for me has been months, but which for them has probably been only a matter of moments. And there are probably physical changes as well. At least I'm not coming back with inexplicable life-threatening injuries like last time, but I bet my hair has grown several inches. Thank heavens Dad has never been good at noticing stuff like that, but Adèle might.

Now, I start to feel a little panicked. I actually have no idea what time it is. If it's like the last time I traveled back to the twenty-first century, it should be within a few hours of when I left. I pick up all my gear and head to the door of the chapel. Fortunately, it isn't locked.

By the time I run up the staircase that joins up with the tourist itinerary to exit the abbey through the Knight's Hall, I am reassured when I see from the windows that it's dark outside. There are even a few tourists left. I remember that Nicolas and I had barely made it to the abbey before eight in the evening. The abbey is open late because it's Christmas week, and there's a special sound and light show going on. I can hear the Gregorian chants, and the mood lighting is pretty spectacular, so I know it has to be the week before Christmas. I just hope it's still the twentieth. If so, I might just be able to pull this off. But one thing is for sure, I'm going to try to come back tomorrow and use my time key again.

Amazingly, I get back to my room without any problems. The fact that I can access the staircase to the room from the outer ramparts helps, because I see only a few people as I jog as quickly as

I can with my bulky load. Until I get to the entrance, I even worry if Gothman is still alive and will find me. He fell over the rampart wall when he attacked me and Nicolas, but did he die? I hope so.

I don't dare peek into the hotel dining room because I know Dad and Adèle are in there, eating their dinner. After unlocking and then opening the accordion door to the stairs as quietly as I can, I creep up the steps. Then, I breathe a sigh of relief when I safely get inside my room.

Yes, my suitcase is placed neatly on the luggage rack, just as Nicolas left it over six months ago. That seems so weird. I've been gone nearly seven months.

The first thing I do is stash the sword under my bed. Before we leave Mont Saint Michel, I'm going to have to convince my parents (oh my heavens, I just called Adèle my parent) to believe that I've purchased an honest-to-goodness sword in one of the Mount's tourist shops. Fortunately, I think there actually are a few shops that sell real-looking weapons. Why I would buy such a thing is another question, but I'll explain that I did my term paper in A.P. Medieval History on Joan of Arc's sword. But how I'm going to get it back to the States is another question. Do the airlines let you pack swords in your checked luggage?

I desperately want to open the package Brother Thibault put in my backpack, but I decide I'll wait to open it until I do something I've wanted to do ever since I saw the jobber's mark on Nicolas's enseigne. I remember the symbol clearly, because I forced myself to memorize what it looked like. It was two straight perpendicular lines that looked like a "t" with the top line pushed over to the left. Maybe, just maybe, it will give me some kind of clue to help me make sense of all that I've been through since I first came to Mont Saint Michel last summer. Maybe it will give me some answers about the secret of the mount, or about what lies ahead for Nicolas and me.

Maybe it will tell me to have faith or trust in the Archangel. I don't know, but I need it to give me hope.

I'm pretty sure the symbol is a Hebrew letter like the marks on the other two enseignes. I pull out my computer and connect to the internet. I google "Hebrew Alphabet." Sure enough, Nicolas's mark *is* a Hebrew letter. It's the dalet, which makes the "d" sound. My letter is the mem, and Jean's is the aleph.

ד   מ   א

I use an online Hebrew translator, changing the order of the aleph and dalet, remembering what Mr. Dreyer taught me. When the mem is notated with the squished corner instead of the 'house chimney,' it indicates that it's the final letter in a word. The only order that makes any sense is to place them with Jean's mark first, Nicolas's second, and mine last. Starting from right to left—again as I learned from Herr Dreyer—the word looks like this:

אדם

The word has two translations: *Adam* and/or *man*. What does that possibly mean? I get that man is the same word as Adam in Hebrew, because after all, according to Jewish and Christian belief, Adam was the first man on earth. But what does Adam have to do with the Archangel or Mont Saint Michel or the secret of the Mount or my calling as a Watchman? I have no idea. This discovery doesn't give me any answers or any comfort. It doesn't increase my faith or trust in the Archangel, and it doesn't give me any hope. I'm just as confused, frustrated, and heartbroken as ever.

I close my computer and then turn back to my backpack to see what Brother Thibault has put in there. Gingerly, I pull the object out, untie the twine, and unwrap the burlap. I gasp. It's Brother

Thibault's clock. His prized possession made by his clockmaker friend back at Landévennec Abbey in Brittany. Why would he send his clock with me? A peace offering so I won't be mad at him? A secret message? I'm not sure. I remember telling him that Nicolas and I never had the time to talk about the future of our relationship. There was always a more pressing issue to worry about, and both of us were convinced that we'd have all the time in the world to work things out. But we were wrong.

The clock is exquisite, but it isn't ticking. It's not working. I look at the little hook inside the open metal workings of the clock where Brother Thibault hung the key he used to wind it twice a day. It's not there. He didn't send the key! I'm not even going to be able to use the clock.

But then as I look at the clock more carefully, I suddenly realize why the key isn't there. The clock's hands are set at 9:30. Nine-thirty. The instant my life changed forever. True, I killed Philippe Montrouge at 9:35, but five minutes earlier, my mortal enemy essentially killed the man I love. True, Nicolas isn't dead. He *is* alive. But he isn't alive to me.

Did I tell Brother Thibault what the time was when Nicolas fell? I don't remember, but it doesn't matter. The man is so perceptive. In spite of the fact that he sent me home and that I'm furious at him, I am also overwhelmed by his incredible compassion. He gets it. He gets exactly how I feel. My world stopped at nine-thirty on July 28, 1429, and he sent his most beloved possession to let me know that he understands. It is his way of telling me how very sorry he is. And he didn't send the key because he knows that for me, time will stand still until Nicolas wakes up and we are somehow reunited, in spite of the time that separates us.

I lie down on the bed and weep in huge, shivering sobs. I have been through so much emotion, so much turmoil, so much trauma, I just don't know how to process it all. But the reality that is hardest of all to accept is *not* that I did something I have always dreaded, which is to take someone's life. It's not that I've travelled back in time six hundred years and carried out my duty as a Watchman not to rewrite history, but to reinforce history. It's not that I've influenced a young woman in a way that helped her change the course of an entire nation, and in turn, the course of the entire Western world. None of these realities means anything to me compared to the reality that I've lost the most important relationship of my life.

I am flooded with memories of Nicolas. His earnest brown eyes that attracted me before I even knew who he was. When he first took me back in time, he thought I was a spoiled brat (which I was), and I thought he was a self-righteous critic. The red velvet gown I wore to our sham wedding. Our supposed wedding night when he came to my room and would have kissed me had not Jean le Vieux interrupted. The moment I realized I loved him. Crossing the sands of the Mont Saint Michel Bay holding onto his waist. Hearing his goodbye message on my cell phone after I got back to my time. Opening the Facebook message from 'le Breton.' Seeing him on the ramparts outside the Du Guesclin Hotel. The first time we kissed when he was hiding from my father in the bathtub of this very room. Stitching up the wound on his arm from Gothman's vicious brass knuckles. Sitting by my side as I recovered from the concussion also inflicted by Gothman. Spotting him that day in the forest outside of Chinon, covered in bruises. Sitting by his side and tending to his injuries in Madame Renard's attic room. Our final kiss when he touched my cheek, kissed me softly on the lips, and said, "Go with God, *mon amour*, and be careful."

But these incidents constitute only a handful of minutes in a multitude of minutes that we have *not* shared. It is true. We have had so little time together.

So little time together, and yet an eternity to remember.

Is it true that time heals all wounds? My mother says that to me, but I still hear her crying at night over her failed marriage. Time may dim the wounds for some, but I don't think time will ever heal my wound. Time will never be my friend. Time has separated me repeatedly from my Nicolas, and I don't know how to get back to him.

But then I think about another aspect of Brother Thibault's gesture. True, his clock is a reminder of time stopping for me, but it is also symbolic of something else: a glimmer of hope. Brother Thibault has given me the *gift* of time. A reminder that for me and Nicolas, time is *not* our enemy, after all. We can travel through time, for heaven's sake! In fact, it just may be our greatest ally, for as long as Nicolas continues to breathe, there is hope.

I feel a warmth come over me that envelopes me like a soft fleece blanket. I stop shivering, and an astonishing calmness and peace permeates every cell. It reminds me of that feeling of overwhelming love and peace I felt when I dreamt that Jean le Vieux visited me. I don't see Jean or hear him, but I feel his gentle touch, just like before. It ignites a rush of heat and reassurance that courses through my entire body. With that peace comes another truth. I now know that Brother Thibault sent me back home out of love for me. He couldn't stand watching me waste away from grief. He wants me to live! He wants me to be productive, and he even wants me to thrive. He wants me to go back to high school and graduate. He also wants me to know that he will care for Nicolas in my absence. He wants me to move ahead and hope that at some future point, time will once again start ticking for my broken heart.

Then, hoping to find Nicolas in the timeless world of my dreams, I pull the covers over my head and find solace in deep and healing sleep.

Epilogue

THE SMOKE RISES IN A GENTLE SWIRL, like a prayer rising to heaven. But the time for praying is past, and the heavens cannot answer this prayer. I know, because as hard as this is to accept, this is God's will. And as hard as this is for me to observe, I am honored that the Archangel saw fit to bring me here as a witness of this barbaric injustice.

After leaving Dad and Adèle in the abbey this afternoon, telling them I would meet them for dinner, I made my way back to Notre-Dame-Sous-Terre to make one final attempt to go back to Nicolas. When I felt the now-familiar intensity of the spinning light, my heart sang out in hope. My key had worked! I was being taken back to Nicolas. But it soon became clear that I was no longer on Mont Saint Michel. True, I had been taken back in time, but I had also been taken through space to some unknown church.

After leaving that church clutching my key, now here I stand wrapped in the heavy, floor-length cloak I'd been smart enough to wear over my twenty-first century clothes. It is overkill for the end of May. No matter. I won't be accused of dressing in men's clothing because no one is looking at me. They are all looking at the horrific spectacle that is playing out before this throng of eager voyeurs.

I push my way through the crowd, suffering some jabs in the ribs and nasty insults for trying to get a better view, but I am not going to back down. After all, I am the Maiden Warrior that saved Mont Saint Michel. I am Jehanne's tutor, and as much as I ranted to Nicolas and Brother Thibault about not wanting to face this day, I now feel differently about it. I am here, and I want my friend to know it. I am her to offer her my support, to let her know she is not alone. The tears are pouring down my face, exacerbated by the acrid smoke that fills the air. I can't even begin to imagine the agony she is going through. I pray with all my heart that God will deaden her senses so that she does not feel the flames that are gradually engulfing her body.

Soon, the smoke thickens, and the blue sky is transformed into a sickly, gray haze. I recognize the uniforms of several hundred English soldiers who still hold the city of Rouen. They look on, exuberant about what they consider to be their just fruits of war. I know they've recently inflicted some humiliating defeats on the French in smaller battles, and they think that this is a symbol of their ultimate victory. But they are *so* wrong.

I see a single bird flying towards us from the south, from the French-held territories. Soon, it too is engulfed by the smoke. To me, it's like a sign of divine approval, not for the so-called English victory, but for the unselfish sacrifice made by one of God's anointed servants.

When I reach the front of the crowd, I call out as loudly as I can. "Jehanne, *je suis là*. I am here." I see her turn her head, and she sees me. Our eyes lock for a single second, and she nods to me before the flames grow higher and higher, blocking her face from my view. But she knows I am here. She knows I am a witness. She knows I know the truth about her, and it is enough. I can hardly bear to watch, but I must. Yes, earlier I prayed fervently that I would not have to witness her execution firsthand, but now I am grateful that Michael saw fit to bring me here. I *had* to be here for Jehanne, and for myself.

At some point when my days of mortal probation are over, I will proudly stand as a witness before God against the men who have knowingly perpetrated this atrocity in the name of religion: the English and Burgundian conspirators, and their impious ecclesiastical puppets, Pierre Cauchon in particular. Even though I understand that Jehanne's life had to end this way to galvanize the French determination to fight for ultimate victory against the English, which is still many years away, I will also stand as a witness against Jehanne's allies, those she helped but who turned their back on her and did nothing to fight for her freedom.

But there is also a more personal reason I am grateful to be here. How could I be her true friend and let her go without saying goodbye? It is only fitting for the two maiden warriors to share a final adieu.

As the flames gain in intensity, so does the output of heat, and I watch as the soldiers stretch out their arms and move backwards, attempting to counterbalance the crush of the crowd. The crackling of the fire and the clamor of the masses are not enough to block out Jehanne's final cries, which I recognize are not cries of submission or agony, but rather pleas to God to accept her sacrifice.

Several of the English soldiers—who I had heard just moments before mocking her and calling her vulgar names—are now standing as still as statues, transfixed, as if in a stupor.

Beads of sweat trickle down the face of one particularly heartless-looking combatant. It is as if the worn soles of his boots are fused to the ground, making it impossible for him to escape the aftermath of the unprecedented decision to burn a human being at the stake for one reason, and one reason only: because she had been successful in her bid to turn the tide of this long war.

Cauchon and the others can call it whatever they want: witchcraft, heresy, cross dressing, asserting to hear divine voices, claiming to be God's servant, but the truth is, their accusations against Jehanne are made just to discredit her reputation and undermine her importance to the French people by saying she has violated the laws of God. They don't care if she's a heretic or witch. They just want to have a justification to kill her for religious crimes so they don't generate a martyr for France. Well, they don't know it right now, but they have done just the opposite. As my friend dies an excruciating death before their eyes and mine, they have no idea that they have just created one of the most famous martyrs who has ever lived.

As I watch the pitiless soldier look around at his comrades-in-arms with drops of moisture running down their faces as well, I see his reaction when the reality hits him. His comrades are not sweating from the heat. No, like me, they are weeping.

Katelyn's Historical Commentary

1. Eleanor of Aquitaine really messed things up for both countries when in 1137 she first married her fourth cousin, the King of France, Louis VII, to whom she bore two daughters. But I guess she wasn't that crazy about being Queen of France or about Louis and so she sought an annulment of her marriage. Louis must have been okay with it because she had failed to produce him with a son and heir to the throne. In those days, only the eldest surviving male could claim the throne. I've learned that's called primogeniture.

    Anyway, after Eleanor got rid of Louis, she turned around and married her third cousin, Henry, the Duke of Normandy and Count of Anjou, who ruled more of France than the French king himself. To make matters worse, Henry claimed the English throne two years later to become Henry II of England. So Eleanor was first Queen of France, and then Queen of England. She and Henry had five sons, three of whom became kings of England.

    Henry II and his wife, Eleanor of Aquitaine, are both actually buried in France, in Fontevraud Abbey in the Loire Valley only about 20 kilometers from Chinon, along with their son Richard the Lionheart.

2. Why did the Dauphin Charles have to have his coronation in Notre-Dame de Reims? It all stems back to Clovis, the first ruler to unite all of the Frankish tribes into one kingdom back in the fifth and sixth centuries. I learned that Clovis was originally a pagan, but his Christian wife, Clotilde, twisted his arm, and he finally saw the strategic benefits, if not the spiritual benefits, of giving up his pagan gods. He wanted a way to distinguish himself

from the many other competing powers in Western Europe, and I guess he decided that converting to the Roman Catholic form of Christianity was the ticket.

So on Christmas Day in 496, in a small Catholic church in Reims (the cathedral had not yet been built), Clovis was not only baptized by Bishop Remigius, but he received what is called a 'holy unction' with oil, a rite symbolizing that Clovis was recognized by God as the lawful king of France. Three thousand Frankish pagans followed their king's example that day and were baptized with him. In fact, Clovis' baptism eventually lead to the entire Frankish people converting to Catholicism.

It was quite a coup for the Catholics, and it later resulted in both Remigius and Clovis' wife, Clotilde, becoming saints in the Catholic Church. Remigius was thereafter known as Saint Rémi.

In the ninth century during the reign of another French king, Charles the Bald, someone opened up Saint Rémi's sarcophagus and supposedly found two vials filled with some type of aromatic oil, the likes of which no one had ever before smelled. And from there the legend grew that one of those vials was the *Holy Ampoule* filled with the sacred oil that Saint Rémi had used to consecrate Clovis as King. And, it was said, the oil for the coronation had been brought down from heaven itself by a dove!

I suppose the archbishop of Reims at the time the vials were found saw a great opportunity to increase his influence and the influence of future archbishops of his city by proclaiming that in order to be considered the rightful monarch, all future kings of France had to be consecrated by oil from the Holy Ampoule, and that meant of course, by the archbishop of Reims, who maintained possession of the said magic vial. Is it all true? I don't know, but the legend grew, and the tradition was instituted.

From there on out, any man who had visions of claiming the throne of France had to receive that holy unction in Reims by the archbishop of Reims. After the cathedral was built, at each coronation of a new king of France, the vial was brought with great pomp and circumstance from the Abbey of Saint-Rémi—where it was kept—to the Cathedral of Notre-Dame in Reims. I guess it *was* a pretty big deal for the Dauphin Charles to make it to Reims.

3. The enemies of the Dauphin Charles were *very* successful at putting doubt in his heart about being the legitimate heir to the throne. The Burgundians had spread vicious rumors about Charles' mother, Queen Isabeau of Bavaria, being unfaithful to her husband because of his bouts of madness. They claimed she had an adulterous liaison with the King's very own brother, Louis, the Duke of Orléans, and that the Dauphin was the result of that relationship. If true, that would have made him Charles VI's nephew, not his son. You know, proving one's legitimacy was kind of a problem in 15th-century France because there was no DNA testing, so if someone wanted to place doubt on a man's claim to the throne, just accuse that man's mother of infidelity.

Even though Charles hadn't dared voice his doubts out loud, it seems he truly wondered if he *was* the rightful heir, and in that climate, with the English claiming the right to the throne of France, it was doubly important to be accepted as the legitimate heir.

Now here's where it gets really complicated. The English had a pretty powerful argument as to why the English king should rule France, in addition to their claims of the Dauphin's illegitimacy. First of all, they got Charles VI to disinherit his only surviving son by signing the Treaty of Troyes in 1420. In that treaty, Charles agreed that King Henry V of England and his heirs would inherit the throne of France upon Charles' death. However, for the French, there was a pretty major flaw with that treaty, and it's that Charles was loony bins when he signed it. Yeah, the French king wasn't in his right mind, so why should his subjects accept such a rotten agreement made under duress?

The second argument wasn't bad either. If the Dauphin *was* illegitimate, the English had another strong claim to throw at any other Valois contenders. Here it is in a nutshell. The mad King Charles also gave England another gift after the Treaty of Troyes, and that gift was more concrete. It was his daughter, Catherine of Valois. Yep, the Dauphin's sister married Henry V of England, and in 1421, just a year after the bogus treaty was signed, she gave birth to the English king's heir, Henry VI, who in 1429, was the very young king of England, because Henry V, like Charles VI of France was dead. So, Henry VI, was not only the legitimate heir to the throne of England, but he was also the grandson of Charles VI, a direct heir, and because of that and the Treaty of Troyes, he had a legitimate claim to the throne of France. Is that confusing or what? I'm still confused, and I've been studying this out in my mind for months.

However, the French could still counter Henry VI's claim with the rules of primogeniture. That's when the right of succession is passed on to the oldest living *male*, rather than to any female offspring. If a king had only a female heir, the right of succession passed to his nearest living male relative, so because Henry VI came through the French king's daughter, not his son, if the Dauphin was not accepted as Charles VI's legitimate son, the throne would go to the mad king's nearest male relative, who at that time was the eldest son of Charles' brother Louis, the Duke of Orléans (who was also dead), with whom the Queen was purported to have had her affair. I know, it's just crazy.

But it gets even more complicated. Because the Duke of Orléans' oldest legitimate son was older than the Dauphin, *he* would have been the heir, even if the Dauphin were the Duke's son. Slight problem there, though. Louis's son, then the current Duke of Orléans, was being held captive by the English at the time. They wanted to cover all their bases! So it was a pretty big deal for Joan of Arc to tell the Dauphin that he was indeed his father's son.

That's another reason the Burgundians and Armagnacs hated each other so much, by the way, because it was the Duke of Burgundy who had the elder Louis assassinated in 1407. That's when the Burgundians threw their support in with the English, because they didn't want the Valois line (a.k.a. Charles) and the

Armagnacs to control France. But don't worry, the Dauphin had the Duke of Burgundy assassinated during what was to be a peaceful meeting of reconciliation in 1419. You get the picture? The Burgundians and Armagnacs (who supported the Dauphin) really didn't like each other.

But wait, there's more, at least there's more as far as I'm concerned. Shortly before he died in 1422, the English king, Henry V, named his brother John, the Duke of Bedford, as the regent of France in the name of his son, who was only a few months old when he died. And since Henry VI was just a boy of eight in 1429, his uncle, the Duke of Bedford was still the regent of France. I have a personal vendetta against the Duke of Bedford because he is the one who got the abbot of Mount Saint Michel, the treacherous Robert Jolivet, to betray his abbey, his monks, and his country. The Duke was also the commander of the English troops in Normandy who ordered the siege of Mont Saint Michel, and thus the commander of Richard Collins, a.k.a. Abdon, who held the mount under siege and tried to kill me in my last adventure. So you can see why I'm not a supporter of the so-called current regent of France. I'll take the Dauphin over him any day.

Author's Notes

I knew when I wrote a fictional, time-travel novel in which Joan of Arc played a central role, I would arouse the ire of many world-wide 'Joanaphiles.' Let me assure you that I was in no way motivated by a desire to de-value the nature of the Maiden's spiritual experiences or explain away her motivation. Remember, Katelyn Michaels herself heard divine voices, so this story is in no way an attempt to deny (or confirm) the source of Joan's inspiration. Although I am a firm believer in God and in divine inspiration, I am neither a Catholic nor a Catholic-hater. Furthermore, I am neither French nor English, so I have no agenda in telling this story. However, after studying Joan's story for several decades, I can state that I firmly believe her appearance on history's stage, with the ultimate result of helping the French throw off the English yoke during the Hundred Years' War, had a far-reaching political impact that helped create a strong, independent France, and may have played a role in the later founding of the United States of America.

Furthermore, this novel is not an attempt to trivialize or offer an explanation of how La Pucelle succeeded in convincing the misogynistic leaders of her era to allow the armies of France to follow an un-tried, inexperienced female into battle. Instead, it was my desire to whet the reader's appetite to learn more about this pivotal and remarkable historical figure. It is up to you to consider the mysteries that still surround one of the most iconic females who ever lived. Did she truly hear divine voices? Was she honestly visited by the Archangel Michael? That is yours to consider.

Neither was it my intent to tell the *entire* story of Joan's life and death. I leave that to the historians, because although an important character, Joan is *not* the protagonist of this novel. In fact, except for a flew flashes forward, this novel concerns only Joan's early years and the very first part of her journey to liberate France because Katelyn's impact on the Maiden was for a very limited period of time—just enough to give Joan a boost in confidence and a sense of her strength. There are also several events I omitted from her early period because they did not further my storyline, including a visit to Charles, the Duke of Lorraine, before her final visit with Robert de Baudricourt.

That having been said, while this is a work of fiction, the historical background given about Joan of Arc is based on known historical facts and widely held beliefs, except for her fictional interaction with Katelyn Michaels and, of course, the accounts employing Katelyn's electronic gizmos. The historical information about Joan of Arc in this novel was taken from an extensive collection of written sources, for indeed volumes and volumes have been written about her. However, it must be emphasized that nearly all of the information that exists about Joan's youth comes from her own testimony and from the testimonies given at her trial and later rehabilitation process, by those who knew her as a child and young woman, or by those who came in contact with her during her brief life. Even her precise birthdate is not certain since there are no extant birth records and because original sources about her younger years—before she came upon the national scene—are virtually non-existent.

The prophecies mentioned in the novel, which indeed circulated during Joan's era, have all been taken from recorded sources, except for the fictional prophecy about Joan being assisted by the Maiden Warrior who saved Mont Saint Michel. This prophecy is my own fictional addition. However, it is true that the abbey library at Mont Saint Michel did contain chronicles with recorded prophecies about a maiden who would save France. Many believe that Joan herself was aware of these prophecies, and that because of these prophecies, it was important for her to emphasize the fact that she was a virginal and innocent girl.

The exact date on which Joan left Vaucouleurs is in dispute, as is the date of her arrival in Chinon. Some state that she departed on February 13, 1429 but others claim that the Dauphin's royal messenger, Colet de Vienne, and his Sottish squire, Richard the Archer, did not arrive in Vaucouleurs until February 19, and that the little group's departure was in fact on February 23, 1429. That a crowd gathered to bid Joan's group farewell is well-documented. Some say she arrived in Chinon on March 4, 1429, but as many testified, the journey took eleven days, which would put her entering Chinon on March 6, 1429.

The question as to why the Dauphin sent Colet de Vienne and Richard the Archer to Vaucouleurs has never been fully answered. Did Charles anticipate that Joan was coming to see him, or was this journey planned long before Robert de Baudricourt gave his permission? Or had the messengers arrived for another purpose and were then asked by Baudricourt to return to Chinon with Joan and her group? The make-up of her little army has, on the other hand, been well-documented, although there are many spelling variations of the men's names. Jean de Metz has also been identified as Jean de Novellempont (also spelled Nouillonpont), and Jean de Dieulouard (also spelled Dieuleward) has also been identified as Jean de Honnecourt. Bertrand de Poulangy's name is spelled as Poulengy in some sources and Colet de Vienne's name is also seen spelled as Collet. I know. It's terribly confusing. I chose one version of each name and stuck with it. Richard the Archer's nickname of Olg is my invention, and yes, there's a private story about that!

According to the testimony given by Jean de Metz, the journey to Chinon was without incident, which in itself is remarkable because the route took them almost exclusively through English-held lands. It is also considered remarkable that they made the 340-mile trip in only eleven days, averaging about thirty miles a day over difficult terrain, in wintry weather, and at night. Katelyn's encounter with the English soldier and the attack by the Burgundian soldiers are my additions and are fictional. That the group basically traveled at night and slept during the day and that Joan slept between Jean de Metz and Bertrand de Poulangy is taken from Jean de Metz's testimony at her trial. He stated under oath: "On the way, Bertrand and I slept every night with her—Jeanne being at my side, fully dressed. She inspired me with such respect that for nothing in the world would I have dared to molest her; also, never did I feel towards her—I say it under oath—any carnal desire." That Joan attended mass in only two cities—in Auxerre and three times in Sainte-Catherine-de-Fierbois—

not doing so as often as she would have liked for fear of being recognized, is information that also comes from the testimony of Jean de Metz and from Joan herself.

Information about Joan's sword from Sainte-Catherine-de-Fierbois is based upon her own and others' testimonies, but that it was the sword of Charles Martel is a tradition that has been handed down for generations, and is, of course, impossible to verify. The fact that she made a point to testify how the rust was easily cleaned away from the sword by the prelates of the village leaves the impression that even she felt it had special qualities. There is also a divergence of opinion about whether Joan sent for the sword before or after her arrival in Chinon, and whether it was before or after she stopped to hear mass at the small church in that town. For the purposes of this novel, I have chosen my own timeline. Nothing is known about what ultimately happened to this sword, and when questioned about it during her trial, Joan herself refused to answer, stating that it was not pertinent to the proceedings. It is also true that Robert de Baudricourt gave her a sword upon her departure from Vaucouleurs, and that she acquired yet another sword from a Burgundian soldier, which, it is said, she broke while chasing 'trollops' from the army camp.

That in order to convince Robert de Baudricourt of her divine calling, Joan told him about the outcome of the Battle of Rouvray (more commonly known as the Battle of the Herrings), and that she also confirmed to the Dauphin Charles that he *was* the legitimate son of his father and thus the rightful heir to the throne of France, have both been suggested by several of her chroniclers, so I employed them in this work of fiction. Also, although the original letter Joan wrote to the Dauphin asking permission to enter the city and requesting an audience has been lost, I have used statements she or others made about its contents, as well as actual statements she made in her existing letter addressed to the Duke of Bedford and the King of England. The Dauphin's reply is my invention. Although she had hoped to meet with the Dauphin immediately upon her arrival, Charles did make her wait for at least two days while he and his counselors debated about whether it was in his best interest to grant an audience. While she was waiting, she was questioned by the local clergy.

The accounts of the two battles I mention during the lifting of the siege of Orléans, St. Loup and Les Tourelles, although greatly abridged, are true, except, of course, for Joan's use of modern-day gadgets on her sword during the battle to inspire her fellow soldiers and to frighten her enemies. It is also true that her brothers, Jean and Pierre, joined her on this campaign. The information about her banners and battle standard is also accurate, and it seems that it was during the preparatory period for this battle that Joan exchanged her love of her sword for the love of her standard, which she claimed to love "forty times better than my sword." She further stated, "When I went against my enemy, I carried my banner myself, lest I kill any. I have never killed a man." It seems that at Orléans, she fully realized that her role was not to kill, but to inspire. Of course, it is fictional that Richard the Archer was at the battle with her and that he then took the renowned sword of Charles Martel back to Katelyn. As noted above, we have only Joan's brief statement about the sword in her trial, and it is not clear at what point the sword was either destroyed or lost, although it may have possibly been after the unsuccessful assault against Paris.

The fact that Joan's role was not primarily as a leader on the battlefield is accurate. She was given what is known as "titular command," which was a prevalent practice at the time, giving a symbolic role of leadership to important religious figures or noblemen. Although she took an arrow in the shoulder at the Battle of Orléans, and later in the thigh in her unsuccessful bid to liberate Paris, she never killed an opponent. She did help outline military strategies, but she did not actively participate in most of the battles. Rather, she served more as an inspiration and motivator to the troops. It is well documented that she did all she could to "clean up" the French ranks of non-Christian behavior, including driving out prostitutes (camp followers), punishing those who stole or used foul language, and even chiding those who refused to attend mass or confess their sins. To this day, military strategists debate what her actual role was and how she succeeded in motivating the French troops. However, that her presence on the national scene at that time in history was the turning point for the French forces is irrefutable.

I have included very little about Joan's story after the battle of Orléans, but it is true that after her remarkable campaign to open the way for the Dauphin to get to Reims for his coronation, she was later abandoned and forgotten by many of the men she had inspired. Most importantly, it is true that the Dauphin, the one man whose destiny she forever changed by ensuring that he became King Charles VII, did little to save her from the Anglo-Burgundian trial, presided over by Pierre Cauchon.

Following in Joan's Footsteps

For anyone interested in actually following the path of Joan of Arc in France, I suggest several must-see sites. Joan's original home in Domrémy and the small church next to her home are still standing and can both be visited. There are still vestiges of the walled entrances to the city of Vaucouleurs, including the gate through which she embarked with her small group on the journey to Chinon. There is also a small museum in Vaucouleurs with a plethora of artistic renderings of the Maiden of Lorraine, which is worth the minimal entrance fee.

Although it is not the original church that existed during Joan of Arc's era, a church dedicated to Sainte-Catherine still exists in the tiny town of Sainte-Catherine-de-Fierbois and is open to the public. There you will see the replica of Joan of Arc's sword, which I used as the basis for the description of the sword in this novel. You can also see a replica of Joan's banner, a statue of her, a plaque noting the spot where Joan's sword is purported to have been found in the original church, and other Joan memorabilia.

The chateau fortress of Chinon is one of my favorite locations and appears on the cover of this novel. Although the chateau itself is in ruins, the French government has done a fabulous job of partial restoration, and there is always an interesting and changing exhibit on its grounds that is particularly well-adapted for families with children. Plan on at least an hour or two to visit the chateau ruins and also some time to walk through Chinon's charming narrow streets that sit at the foot of the fortress. Also, be sure to cross the bridge over the Vienne River to fully appreciate the view that appears on the cover.

Although the famous tourelles, or bridge towers, on the bridge crossing the river into Orléans no longer exist, an impressive statue of Joan sits in the town square. You may also visit the half-timbered home of Jacques Boucher, the general treasurer of the Duke of Orleans, with whom Joan lodged from April 29 to May 9, 1429. It now houses a multi-media museum with a film retracing her life. The lifting of the siege of Orléans indeed gave Joan the name of the Maid of Orléans and forever changed the course of her life *and* the destiny of France.

An absolute must-see, for several reasons, is the magnificent cathedral of Reims, where you can not only appreciate firsthand one of the incredible masterpieces of French Gothic architecture, but one of France's most important historical sites, as well. This is where the coronations of countless kings of France, including Charles VII, took place. Don't miss the large copy of Jehanne's signature inside the cathedral, and the impressive statue of her on her mount to the right of the main entrance. Be sure to visit the Palace of Tau, an outstanding museum next to the cathedral, which has a fine display of medieval art and relics, including the *Sainte Ampoule*, or holy flask, the successor of the ancient one containing the oil with which French kings were anointed, which was broken during the French Revolution. A fragment of the original flask is said to be contained in the present Ampoule.

On a more somber note, a stop in Rouen, where Joan's short life ended, is requisite. First visit the Tour Jeanne d'Arc, which is the only remaining portion of the chateau where Joan of Arc was brought to trial in 1431. She was taken to the dungeon of this chateau to stand before the judges who accused her of heresy (principally because she claimed she had heard the voices of heavenly messengers and because she wore men's clothing), and the tower now serves as a museum in her honor. Then, move on to the *Historial Jeanne d'Arc*, which is a brand new specialty museum dedicated to the trials of Joan of Arc housed in a beautiful old palace. You move from room to room for uniquely-staged audio-visual presentations that really bring Joan's story to life. Headphones to listen in English are available at no extra cost. It is well worth the stop. Finally, visit the town square (*Place du Vieux Marché*) where Joan was burned at the stake. It is adjacent to an ultra-modern church dedicated to her memory. The church has beautiful stained-glass windows and interesting architecture, but I can't help but feel that its style is too much of a contrast to Joan's medieval existence.

And of course, as a tourist in Rouen, you wouldn't want to miss the Cathedral of Notre Dame, made famous by Claude Monet's series of paintings, or the famous Clock Tower in Old Towne.

This is certainly not an exclusive list of places connected to Joan of Arc's history. Indeed, churches and town squares throughout France are filled with paintings and statues of the Maid of Lorraine, including the village church at Mont Saint Michel. Her story continues to permeate French culture and fascinate every French school child.

Please visit my website to see photos of these sites as well as a variety of artists' renderings of Joan of Arc at **www.kathleencperrin.com**.

51376168R10322

Made in the USA
Charleston, SC
17 January 2016